Tronco Ink

J. C. JENSEN
Deacon Wright
Beginning of the End
1st ed.

First edition, December 2019

For Ashlee,
my beautiful blue-eyed beauty.
You will always be my inspiration and
strength. Thank you for believing in me
and never giving up hope.

James 5:3

Your gold and silver is
cankered; and the rust of them shall
be a witness against you, and shall eat your flesh
as it were fire. Ye have heaped treasure for the last days.

Blessed are they that do his commandments, that they
may have right to the tree of life, and may enter in
through the gates into the city.

Revelations 22:14

Table of Contents

ONE
New Year

It's a crisp, cool Saturday morning. The breeze blowing through the open window still smells of sulfur from the fireworks that were going off until what must have been five or six this morning. All the noise from partying Friday night into Saturday morning has finally fizzled out. The thousands of people who had filled the strip in order to watch the highly synchronized firework show have all dissipated. Most, I suspect, are still recovering in their hotel rooms after becoming inebriated by their own celebrations.

I'm not quite sure what the New Year brings, but I have an important meeting Monday morning with the boss that promises to usher in some serious excitement—or at least that's what I'm hoping.

My name is Deacon Wright. After six years in the Navy, I decided to move to Las Vegas. In Vegas, structure and the *up-at-the-crack-of-dawn* type mentality is nowhere to be found, and that's exactly what I need. You can only take a highly structured life for so long before you become a robot—a slave to the machine that causes most, if not all, the problems the United States now faces. Take for starters, the countless wars fought on foreign shores that don't seem to bring any real stability to those we are supposed to be helping—including the Americans that are still struggling to get by day-to-day in this economy.

Look at the places we've been over the last twenty years or so —Afghanistan, Mexico, Iraq, Syria, Venezuela, and it looks like my brothers are finally about to head into Iran. To be honest, I thought that one would've come a lot sooner. The President, the political party in charge, none of it really matters. They are all looking out for number one. It's too bad number one isn't the country they took an oath to defend.

Don't get me wrong, I loved the military and everything it taught me. In fact, if I hadn't joined I wouldn't have been able to accomplish what I have up to this point. That's why I joined—I wanted to do something for the country that has given me so much. After serving several tours in Mexico, Afghanistan, and Venezuela it became blatantly clear that the needs of the people in these countries, or ours for that matter, was not what mattered most to those that call the shots. And who knows if they even call the shots.

Sorry you had to hear that. I guess it has been building up for some time now and I had to get it off my chest. I really don't want to talk politics. Let's just leave it at—they're almost all crooked and out for number one.

About a year ago when I moved to Vegas, I knew I wanted to manage one of the big hotels on the strip, but I wasn't quite sure how I was going to get there. The free ride to college, thanks to the 9/11 GI Bill, helped me out for sure. I enrolled at UNLV in the Hospitality Management program and found a job as a valet attendant at the Bellagio. I figured if I'm going to work at a hotel it might as well be one of the best.

Making good money and going to school, I thought things couldn't get any better. Then, after some hard work, and probably a little bit of luck, I moved up and became the valet manager after just seven months—some of the senior guys weren't too happy. With college money coming in like you wouldn't believe, and a hefty check from the Bellagio, let's just say I'm not hurting for anything right now.

6

You might think living in Vegas I spend a lot of time gambling, drinking, and hooking up with the ladies. That isn't really my style. Growing up I remember my dad saying a couple of things. The first was "a woman is like a drug. She will either heal you or kill you." His eyes would then light up with a mischievous glint and he would continue, looking at my mother and then back at me, "I'm still trying to decide if your mom is healing me or killing me!" Without fail, I would roll my eyes, shake my head, and try my best to chuckle. I knew he meant well. There were times, however, when his eyes grew still and his voice became as calm as a wave rolling onto the shore. "Son, there are people and things in this world that will take away your choice to choose. Don't choose to give away that choice. Once you have, it is almost impossible to get back." I can't tell you how many times I heard that growing up. It's forever etched in my brain.

Living in Vegas for a year, combined with my mere twenty five years of life experience, I'm finally beginning to understand what he meant. I've had occasion to see high-roller Texas Hold'em games where over a million dollars were on the line. The drive for power and strategic superiority seemed to drown out rational thinking and consequential choice. I've seen individuals willing to stake an entire corporation on a hand of cards. When the river card turned, the subtle yet significant difference between a straight and a straight flush has driven men mad.

That is nothing in comparison to the countless individuals willing to gamble away their ability to choose for a brief moment of instant gratification. It has been my observation, especially during my years of service in the Navy, that alcohol is another such gamble where choice is sacrificed. It seemed like anytime my team or I got

7

into trouble, exorbitant amounts of alcohol were always involved. Don't get me wrong, it's all about moderation.

As far as the women in my life go, I can still see my mom's stout frame bustling around the kitchen in her favorite American flag apron with an authoritative determination that would intimidate any recruit. After a less than respectable remark on my part about a girl, my mom would turn, her hell-fire hazel eyes finding mine in that way only a mother's eyes can pierce a son's soul, and shake her head. With a wooden spoon raised in some peculiar display of power she would say, pointing it in my direction like a school teacher scolding a stubborn student, "I didn't raise my only boy to talk that way. It's like your father says, we can heal you or kill you." And with that, the teacher would melt away and she would pull me in for a hug. "Deacon, you'll know you've found the one because she'll be your rock. She'll see the light already in you and keep you pointed toward it." A kiss on the cheek and a warm smile would inevitably follow. I quickly determined that I would never involve myself with a woman I couldn't bring home to meet my mom. As much as I feared the wrath she could inflict, the thought of disappointing her haunted me more.

Since moving to Vegas I've only dated one woman. Christen and I would still be together today if she didn't move to Europe to start a master's program—or whatever they call it over there. It's only been a couple weeks and the pain is still pretty close for me. You may be into long distance relationships, but attempting it for six years in the military set me straight.

I live out in Green Valley, just off the Parkway, in some newly constructed modern apartments. They tore down some older ones in the area and built these luxury living quarters. I was staying with a roommate for seven months when I moved here, but once I started doing well for myself I figured it was time for my own space. I've shared one too many cramped quarters in my time. This spacious two-story loft complete with hardwood floors, a floating staircase, and a luxurious European all-glass shower stands in stark contrast to the platoon of fifty men, rucksacks, and rifles crammed into a cattle car that reeks of sweat, straw, and cattle muck. There's just something about having a place to call your own.

Normally I work Saturday and Sunday nights, but to commemorate the New Year the boss gave me this weekend off. I go back to my regular schedule on Tuesday. However, I have to be in, bright and early Monday morning at ten for my big meeting with the boss. Don't laugh—ten is early for me.

If you work on the Strip, then chances are high that most of your friends do as well. Trying to plan anything earlier than noon is almost always out of the question. A few of those friends and I are going out to Red Rock Canyon around two this afternoon to do some rock climbing.

It must be just after one now because the final climatic cords of Michael Bublé's classic chorus from "Home" are reverberating through my room. Instinctively, I want to roll over and hit snooze. I should have gone to bed before the sun came up. My body tells my mind to go back to sleep, but to no avail. I roll out of bed with a glance at my ersatz Banyan tree in the corner. Wrapped like an accordion around her favorite branch sits Jewels, my green tree python. It's nice to have something else in the house with me, even if it is a snake.

As an act of goodwill or maybe it was just to torture me—I still haven't decided—my buddy Scott gave me Jewels. Handing her over Scott warned, "Mind the bloody fangs. She'll bite you if you don't hold her a lot." I was a little lax at first and have the bite marks

9

to prove it. Jewels has some feisty fangs. After eight months together we are finally starting to understand each other. I'll hold her and she won't strike me.

Speaking of snake strikes...though I try to steer clear of politics, I still like to stay informed with what's happening in the world. Having so many good friends in hot spots all around the globe I can't help but keep up on current events.

I flip on the television hanging on the bathroom wall. CNN instantly comes on. Reaching for my toothbrush, the first image I see makes me cringe—my fellow brothers are dropping missiles on the people of Iran. I didn't realize we had already begun. Looks like the irate Iranians are starting the New Year off with a bang. That means my team is probably already on the ground doing what they do best. I continue to brush my teeth, glued to the television now. I watch a live video feed, like all Americans have grown accustomed to doing. A missile strikes its intended target with pin-point accuracy.

It seems like these days war has become a spectator sport in our country. If only those who have never served could know and feel what awaits those that are still wearing the uniform—the sleepless nights in an unknown country, the sound of an incoming missile or mortar—and, most terrifying of all, a lifeless team member. When you see their bloodied body, you know they've moved on. Just one small glimpse into the sacrifice a soldier makes and I would hope our politicians would see things differently. Sorry, I did it again. Sometimes I just can't help myself.

I walk into the kitchen and pull open the blinds. I'm reminded of why I chose this place—the view is unbelievable. I can see almost all of Vegas. The landscape looks so peaceful from my place. It reminds me of flying through some war-torn country. From the air, everything looks peaceful, almost perfect. When you're in the thick of it though, the picture changes entirely.

I don't have a lot of time so it looks like breakfast will be a bowl of cereal and a banana. I turn on the television in the front room and Fox News has a breaking news alert. I laugh to myself every time I see that alert. Everything they report is 'BREAKING' whether it warrants it or not:

BREAKING NEWS!
WORLD HEALTH ORGANIZATION DECLARES EXERCISE BENEFICIAL FOR YOUR HEALTH.

Who would have thought? I guess they all do it though.

I know what you're thinking—*Why is he watching CNN and Fox News? Those two don't go together.* I try to watch several different news programs so I'm not pigeon holed into one way of thinking. Plus, they all have certain anchors I like to listen to for different kinds of news. I feel it makes me more well-rounded to what is going on in the world. I guess AFN got me used to it as well. I mean really think about it, if I only listened to CNN then I would be led to believe the democrats can do no wrong. If I only listened to Fox, then the democrats can do no right. You already know how I feel about this country's politicians though.

I do read every once in a while, but I like to get my news from the tube. The large television in almost every room keeps me current. The way I see it it's simple—the bigger it is, the better it looks. It also makes watching movies with friends a whole lot more enjoyable.

As I look down at my phone, I realize I have to pick up Scott fairly soon. He lives fifteen miles away so I better get going. I grab my shoes and my pack filled with all my gear and head out the door.

My granite grey Jeep is parked in the underground garage. Since my Rubicon takes me everywhere, I decided that it needed some upgrades. I added a lift, bigger tires, and, after a sticky situation with a tricky stretch of red rock, I added a winch in the front. The soft top isn't ideal in the fall, but it beats swapping out a hard top for the few short months when the weather cools down in the winter. Plus, the garage is climate controlled year round—yet another reason why I chose this place.

Scott and I met at the Bellagio. He's the one that introduced me to Christen. Just thinking about her makes me wish she wasn't so ambitious. I just dropped her off at the airport not two weeks ago. We had an awesome nine months together though. After she completes her two years in Spain, I'm sure I'll still be single, but who knows if she will. I have my doubts. I spent a month over there training with the Spanish Legion forces a few years ago. Those guys sure know how to get the ladies. They love the blonde haired, blue-eyed foreign girls more than any. I might not have much of a chance when one of them gets a hold of her.

Enough about Christen, where was I? Oh yeah, Scott. Scott worked at the Bellagio when I was hired on and we hit it off right away. It was hard at first, him being a former British soldier and me a former Navy sailor, but once we decided I was stronger—okay, maybe I arrived at that determination on my own—we've been best friends ever since. He grew up in Northern England, in a little town called Dunbar. He joined the British army while still in secondary school, as he calls it. After eight years in the service he moved to Vegas with Melissa and started working at the Bellagio. Yeah, he followed the girl over.

He also attends UNLV. I can't remember what he said his degree would be. I just know he's pre-law and getting ready to take the LSAT. When he finishes he wants to head back to his island and get his law degree at one of the prestigious schools of England. For Scott, working at the Bellagio is just a job—a way to make some extra money. I, on the other hand, see it as a foot in the door to managing a hotel of my own. As a result, I guess you could say my motivation to excel is a little stronger than his.

I'm a couple minutes late as I pull into his neighborhood. I call him on the phone to tell him to come out, but realize as I round the corner he's already standing on the curb. I hang up the phone knowing I'll be getting an ear full.

As I roll down the window Scott can't help but open his mouth, "That's the bloody Navy for you. Lost on land again."

If you've never been in the military there's something you have to understand—being in different services is like being from different planets. You always think your planet is the best and there's nothing anyone can do or say to change that. When there's a war it's epic as well. Having served with some British SAS, I know they take that thought process to a whole other level. In all honesty, we do too.

"I'm right on time. What are you talking about?" I call back. I can't let him think I'm late.

"I guess when you've spent as much time as you have sucking air from a can you tend to lose a few brain cells mate," Scott quickly shoots back. "What is it you told me your tanks were topped off with again?"

Before I have time to respond Scott answers his own question, "Oh yeah, I remember, nitrous oxide."

"Whatever," I jibe back. "Did the queen issue you that sense of humor or did you pick that one up all on your own?"

We both laugh for a second and then start toward the mountain. Scott is just like me. We both grew up on the coast. He grew up playing *football*—as the rest of world calls it—around Dunbar. I grew up surfing in Southern California on the beaches around San Diego. We are both right at six feet tall, Scott with brown hair, and me with blonde hair and blue eyes. I'd tell you what color his eyes are, but I don't stare longingly at them too often so I'm not sure, but I think they're green.

Blake and Aaron are climbing with us today as well. They're meeting us up at Red Rock. We've been friends with them since sharing a rock up there about four months ago. Aaron and Blake grew up in Vegas. They too served in the military, in the Army. It's funny how the four of us found each other. Even though we are all out now, it's no wonder we gravitated towards this group of friends. That's why we prefer hanging out together. When we are with others we do and say things people find absolutely crazy or they just don't understand. Let me give you a prime example of something I did.

You might think I'm crazy for telling you this, but maybe it will let you in my mind just a little bit—help you understand where I'm coming from. I told this story to a bunch of people who hadn't served or been overseas. In fact, it was at a dinner party with Christen's family.

My team was in a fire fight in Afghanistan. There must have been thirty or so Taliban fighters firing at us. There were RPGs going off, red and white smoke we had thrown for concealment, and automatic gun fire all around. I believe there was even a building on fire, if my memory serves me. Anyway, my platoon couldn't move. They

14

had us pinned down for a good five to ten minutes, or at least that's what it felt like.

Finally, our sniper Johnny yelled out in exasperation, "Throw a grenade at them!" I don't know why I didn't think of it myself. I prepped a grenade and launched it into a group of five or six of them. When the grenade detonated we all stopped firing—stunned. All anyone could see was an arm and an AK flying through the air spraying bullets into the sky. The enemy fighters even stopped for a second or two. We only paused briefly because they started firing on us again. After the firefight was over we couldn't help ourselves and started laughing as we relived the experience.

You need to remember, I was telling this story to a group of people I had just met who hadn't served in the military. They had asked me to tell them the funniest thing that happened while I served overseas. You should've seen the horrified looks on their faces as I told the story. Christen's Aunt Mabel started choking on her dry dinner roll, her mother dropped her fork and chipped the china, and her father snorted suddenly while trying to swallow a sip of water. They thought I was the most backwards, gun-toting hillbilly they'd ever met. It's a good thing Christen had already known me for some time by then because I think her parents pulled her aside before they left and told her she might want to rethink her choice in companionship.

I guess the easiest and simplest way to sum it up is this—if you don't laugh, you'll cry. The psychologist I saw when I was getting out of the military said that laughing is just a coping mechanism. Maybe I am sick, but it was funny and it got me through countless tours.

As we pull into our favorite climbing spot, we notice Blake and Aaron have already arrived and are setting up the ropes and quick

15

draws. They've also already got their shoes and harnesses on and it looks like Aaron is climbing first.

Scott and I grab our things and head down the trail as Aaron starts lead climbing our warm-up climb. We aren't world class climbers by any means, but we aren't slackers either.

"What took you so long?" Blake questions as he keeps his eyes focused on Aaron. He takes his responsibility seriously.

"We're right on time," Scott and I say in unison.

"Whatever," Blake trumpets back, with an obvious tone of indifference.

"You climbing next Blake, or do you want to keep belaying for a real climber?" I say, with as serious a tone as I can muster.

Out of the four of us, Blake is probably the most skilled. The hardest climb the three of us do today will be the one Blake warms up on I'm sure. Blake knows this and doesn't even acknowledge my attempt at humor with a response.

"How long do you guys want to climb?" Aaron asks, as he clicks on another quick draw and loops his rope through the bottom carabineer.

"Well, you couldn't ask for better weather in January, so I say we climb until the sun goes down," I comment, as I slip my harness through each leg.

January in Vegas is kind of a bummer for sunlight. The sun disappears behind the Red Rocks around five or so. However, three hours of climbing should be just about right. Everyone agrees and Aaron continues up the rock face.

"Deacon, I hear you have some big meeting with the boss on Monday," Scott probes, as if he knows something I might not.

16

Since I thought no one else knew, I quickly respond with a little uncertainty, lifting my eyes back to meet his, "How'd you hear about that?"

"You're not the only one with inside info over there. I have been there longer than you remember," Scott says, with a little smirk on his face.

"Yeah like two months more. What else do you know about the meeting?" I ask, somewhat surprised, but also hoping he has more information for me.

If Scott knows about the meeting then how many others have heard about it? I was specifically told not to talk to anyone about it, which, I must admit, always adds an element of excitement.

"Come to think of it, I just heard the boss as he was strolling into the hotel the other day. All I heard him say as he was talking to the assistant security manager, I think his name's…"

"James!" I quickly respond.

"Yeah, that's him," Scott continues, "he said, 'I'm meeting with Deacon on Monday morning and there's nothing that will change that.' Actually, James looked pretty pissed off too."

I really wanted to talk to Scott and the rest of the guys about my meeting, but I was advised not to. I didn't get this far by blowing off the people over me. On the other hand, I like to know what I'm getting myself into and every piece of information I possess could steer me closer to the inevitable future to come.

"So James was pissed, huh? You didn't hear anything else?" I ask, hoping he's gathered a little more information.

"No, he wasn't drunk," Scott laughs, "He was angry. Nothing else mate. I barely heard that as they stepped through the doors."

Well, I guess that helps a little bit. My mind goes into over-drive now. It's a good thing I'm not climbing. I wouldn't be able to concentrate if I were. What could it be? We did just lose our Director of Security a few day ago—Tom Slack was his name. He was the Director of Security for several hotels on the Strip. From what I've heard over the last couple days, one of the valet attendants caught Tom in the parking garages with a woman who frequents the streets on the strip. I can't see it happening, but that's the rumor. One of my guys got fired as well. I haven't talked to the boss yet, so I'm still wondering myself.

What else could it be, I think to myself as Aaron says, "Maybe you're taking over Tom's spot?"

"No way!" I say, still wondering, the thoughts forming in my head.

Maybe the boss is looking to replace Tom already. I quickly throw that thought out. James would be the obvious choice. Besides, I've only been working there for a year. There's no way they'll put me in charge of security after such a short time. No one knows my real background at the hotel. When I filled out my application I was very vague as to what I did in the Navy.

"Maybe they discovered you're really a blimey bird. They're going to feature you in one of those shows you won't take in. You do have a sexy arse," Scott jokes and they all begin to laugh.

"I can see the title already," Blake begins, "COME ABOOOARD!"

"Sooo funny. You guys know me. Can we get serious for a second? You know I hate to go into these things empty handed."

They aren't much help. I don't even think they really knew what Scott said. I've hung around him long enough now to get all his bloody British jokes. The jokes continue for a couple more minutes before we get back to climbing. Scott has his harness on with the rope tied off as he looks at me and says, "I'm going up. Don't bodge this up."

I grab the rope and weave it through my belay device. Since Scott is up next I'm still stuck here on the ground, which at the moment makes sense. I don't think I'd be too focused right now.

Looks like Aaron's reached the top of his fifty-foot climb. He quickly runs the rope through the chains drilled into the rock so I don't have to lead climb my first climb of the day. I do, however, like to lead climb. There's a little more excitement, danger if you will. When you lead climb you hook into points on the wall every five to ten feet or so. If you fall lead climbing and you've already moved past your last point then you're falling double, if not triple, the distance you were above that point. If your belayer is paying attention, only double, hopefully. Blake is focused though. I, on the other hand, have my mind in another place as I feel the rope quickly slipping through my hand.

"BOLLOCKS!" Scott yells out.

In that moment, I am slammed into and pulled five feet up the wall before I really know what happened. Out of instinct I throw my hand behind my back to stop the rope from slipping.

Scott was already about twenty feet up and five feet past his last point when he misjudged a hold. When he started falling I wasn't watching or bracing myself. He only fell a mere ten to fifteen feet.

"You good mate?" Scott questions with some nervous laughter in his voice as he slaps me on the cheek. "I almost bought it there."

He knew what was going on, and if he fell all the way at least I would have broken his fall. I on the other hand was caught in La-La-land thinking about what the New Year had in store for me.

"I'm good, how about you?" I say as I get both feet back on the ground.

Blake can't help himself, "We can go out to Lake Mead if you'd feel more comfortable in the water."

Another Navy joke, how predictable. The funny thing is they never get old. They will always razz me about being in the Navy, and I will always tease them about being in the Army—American or British—different planets. It's just the way it has to be. We all accept it.

"I'm good. This was such an easy climb I didn't think I would have to do anything," I utter, as I look up at Scott who has already begun to climb again.

"You have me this time mate?" Scott inquires with a more serious tone, as he gives me a quick glance to get the reassuring eye contact.

I chuckle lightly before saying, "I had you that time."

After three hours of climbing, our arms and hands are spent. Besides, the sun has set and the temperature is falling fast. No clouds and very little humidity sure make it cold quick here.

During our three hours of climbing the guys decided to grab a bite to eat on the way home before picking up the ladies and heading out for the night. I didn't say anything about going out tonight. I don't want to hear it from all of them at once. Scott alone, on the other hand, I can handle.

I'm kind of the third wheel right now being the only one without a girlfriend. Scott, Blake, and Aaron have all been together with their girlfriends for some time now. It can get a little depressing to go out with them. That's why I prefer doing things with just the guys right now. It keeps me from thinking about Christen and how much I miss her. It's only been two weeks since we ended it at the airport. When she left she wanted to keep up the long distance relationship, but that wasn't going to happen. With that many miles between us someone would most likely get hurt. It wasn't going to be me again. She wasn't happy with me when it ended. Even though it's over I like to think there's still hope.

Scott is dating Melissa. She's a cocktail waitress at the New York, New York and she loves to have fun. They met while she was doing a study abroad in England. She's is just what Scott needs, someone to loosen up that old crusty Brit. Blake has Bobbi. I'm pretty sure they'll be getting married any day now. Aaron and Natalie have been dating the longest. It's almost impossible to separate those two. Even though it's a little depressing, I do love spending time with them once they've got me out. I just wish I had someone with me.

As Scott and I pull up to his place he asks, "So, ten-pin bowling tonight? I don't want you sitting in your flat all night watching some sappy love story getting all depressed on me."

The funny thing is, that's exactly what I was going to do. I like the chick flicks now, what can I say? The action movies just don't do it for me anymore. Once you've seen it first hand, the movies just can't recreate it. Nor do I want to relive it over and over again. Plus, it makes me so mad when some "action hero" does something that's completely impossible. I know it's for entertainment, but it bugs me now.

"I don't want to go hang out with all of you and your girl-friends," I quickly respond.

"So that's why you didn't say anything earlier. You're not going to sit at home and watch the telly all by yourself. Besides, the next Mrs. Wright could be there tonight," he says, emphasizing the first letter of my last name.

"You're so funny!" I shoot back. "Man, I've never heard that line before."

It's eerie how well Scott knows me. It's like we were twins or something. He does have a good point though. I'm not going to find my Mrs. Wright at home with Jewels wrapped around my neck. Maybe some poor pathetic soul will be out with her friends too.

"Okay," I reply, "but I'm driving myself so I can leave when I want to."

"Oh no you're not!" Scott quips back. "You're hanging out the whole night. We're not letting you get away that easy."

"Fine," I manage as he jumps out of the car.

"I'll drop by at nine. We'll grab a bite to eat. Nachos just won't cut it at the bowling alley. Then we'll head over to Green Valley Lanes," Scott says as he continues moving without even giving me a chance to respond.

I guess I can't handle Scott either.

I step on the gas and head out of the complex. To be honest, I was surprised Scott even let me drive in the first place. He just bought a brand new BMW 3 Series and getting him out of his car is just about as hard as getting him away from Melissa. I guess the prospect of red dust damaging her shinny tan leather was enough that he didn't put up a fight.

As I pull into my parking garage I can't help but think how I'd rather stay home and relax. What were those yahoos thinking anyway? We just spent three hours climbing and our forearms are noodles and our hands couldn't hold a bowling ball even if we wanted them to. I know I have to go though. They wouldn't let me live it down if I said I wasn't coming. I could just lock the door and turn out the lights. No, Scott would kick in the door. He wouldn't let me get off that easily.

The elevators are still in the parking garage. I step in, hit the button for the top floor, and finally relax. I can't wait to take a nap. Before the doors close I see a hand reach in. As the elevator doors open, I am pleasantly surprised to see a very attractive woman with dusty brown hair and beautiful brown eyes step into the elevator.

"I don't know how I missed you," I say, admiring her beautiful face, "but I'm sorry I didn't hold the door."

As she steps in, she turns to push the button to her floor. Before turning again she says, "We must live on the same floor."

"You live on top?" I ask, somewhat surprised.

"Yeah, we just moved in the other day," she says with a friendly smile.

We just moved in. I hope it's a roommate. I was so enamored by her beautiful face I hadn't noticed the enormous rock on her left hand. There goes all my hope for this one. Married is most definitely off limits. I couldn't live with myself if I did something to ruin what she has.

"I'm Deacon. What's your name?" I ask as I reach out to shake hers.

She reaches out for mine and says, "I'm Megan. My husband's name is Danay."

"It's nice to meet you Megan. I look forward to meeting Danay as well."

"I think he's out looking for a gym to join otherwise I would introduce you to him now."

"If Danay wants, I can hook him up with a good deal at my gym. Send him over if he doesn't find one."

"Sounds good. We just moved from California. He had the perfect gym there so priority one for him now is finding a new one."

"I'm from California too, San Diego. What part did you move from?"

"Small world," she starts out, "We were living in LA, but things are getting too crazy out there."

"I understand completely. I've been trying to get my mom out of San Diego for a year now, but she won't budge. Say, you look like you're dressed to work out as well. Why not go with Danay?" I say, noticing the spandex pants she wears so well.

"Yeah. I wanted to check out the campus at UNLV so I put on my running shoes. I can't run on a treadmill like Danay. I have to be outside."

"I know what you mean. I like being outside more. I've been attending UNLV for a couple semesters. I love it. Do you plan on going there?"

Just then the elevator dings and the doors open to the fifth floor.

"I've already signed up for classes. I start Monday," Megan replies.

24

"I know you'll enjoy it there."

"It was nice to meet you Deacon," she says as she steps off the elevator and walks to her door.

"It was nice to meet you as well Megan. I hope you enjoy this building as much as I do," I say as I step up to my door.

"We hope so too. Take care," she says with a smile as she steps through the threshold of her place.

Inside my apartment I toss my gear in the closet. As I head into the kitchen for a drink I remember Jewels has been hanging out in the bedroom all day.

I turn into the bedroom to grab her. She's still hanging out just like she always does. I slowly pry her from her branch and wrap her around my neck. She's such a pretty snake with her shamrock green scales, white and yellow specs, and glittering golden eyes. That's why I decided to name her Jewels.

As I open the fridge to survey my choices I can't help but think, where are all my options? Too much time in chow halls has ruined me. I settle for a Glacier Freeze Gatorade and make my way towards the bathroom. Of course the news is on again. I hear it, but I'm not watching. Since hearing that we're already in Iran, I know the reports of American dead will start streaming out. I really don't want to see it or hear it now.

The climb must have taken more out of me than I expected. Plus I barely slept last night. I feel like crashing at this very moment. Scott will be livid if I'm not ready when he shows up, and I know I'm going down fast. After a hot shower I lay down on the couch in the front room and close my eyes. I want so badly to forget what's going on in my life and the world at this present moment. I can barely hear the news as it quickly fades and I slowly slip away.

TWO
Dreaming

I gaze into the midnight sky. Light from the stars seem to pierce the inky blackness of the moonless night. Sunrise Mountain wraps around me and majestically towers behind me. My Jeep is parked at a scenic overlook on the foothills I'm unfamiliar with. I slowly lower my gaze. Framed perfectly in the Jeep's windshield is a panoramic view of Las Vegas. Ordinarily, the lights of the city would be bright and imposing, making the stars virtually impossible to see. Tonight, however, the entire city is black—almost impenetrably so. The city looks so ominous dressed in darkness. Something is wrong here. I sense an anxious alarm and foreboding fear begin to blanket the city.

In contrast to this pervasive panic spreading throughout the city is the peaceful presence of a hand in mine. As I turn to look, I'm instantly in awe by the most breathtaking woman I have ever laid eyes on, sitting right next to me. I can't keep my eyes off this stunningly, beautiful woman, with her blonde hair, the biggest, most beautiful blue eyes, and the most attractive features I've ever seen. I look down at her hand in mine and am struck with how perfectly her hand fits in mine and how comfortable, almost familiar it feels there.

A wave of conflicting thoughts surge in my mind. Unexpectedly, I begin to hear my phone ring, although it sounds unusually far away. I instinctively attempt to reach for it—to silence it—only to discover that no amount of mental exertion will make my body move. In addition to this unexplainable nuisance, the two most perplexing realizations swirl around in my mind—first, who is this beautiful woman and why can't I remember someone so unforgettable? and second, why the complete blackout in the city?

I have to know her name.

The ringing is getting louder and louder.

I begin to ask her name, but before she can answer, my body surrenders to the incessant ringing and I awaken with a jolt—my heart racing and I'm short of breath.

"Noooo! Why is someone calling me right now?" I yell out.

I look over and see Scott's messed up mug on my phone. Why did that bloody-Brit have to wake me up from such an amazing dream? It was so different from every other dream I've ever had—so much more real. She was so tangible and the peace I felt with her hand in mine was almost palpable.

"You were kipping, weren't you?" Scott questions warily as I answer the phone. I couldn't hide the raspy voice.

"Kipping?" I ask in drowsy confusion. I quickly attempt to clear my throat of any remaining evidence of my tired tone which would only incriminate me further. "I don't know what you're talking about."

"Yeah...you know...sawing logs, taking a nap, sleeping."

"I know what kipping is Scott." I retort with a roll of my eyes.

"You were, weren't you? Admit it!"

"Um...maybe…" I say with a guilty yawn.

"I thought you might be," Scott says with a tone that only a judge could replicate as he brings his gavel down with a final ruling. "I'm leaving my house now to pick up Melissa. I'll be over in thirty minutes. You don't have to shower still, do you?"

"No. I just have to put on some clothes and I'll be ready," I say squeezing out another yawn.

"Okay. I'll be there in thirty," Scott says as he hangs up the phone.

I look over at the clock and realize I've been sleeping for three hours. That climbing really did take it out of me. I reach for Jewels around my neck but find she's no longer there. I look around the room to discover where she slithered off to. She has moved over onto the bar under the coffee table. She likes to accordion her body back and forth over any bar. I think the only time she's not in that position is when I'm holding her or I'm about to feed her. She can smell a little mouse a mile away, and boy does she come alive when it's near.

Now don't you animal activist get all bent out of shape. I'm just helping the food chain continue its cycle here.

I rummage in my closet trying to find something to make myself presentable for the night. If Mrs. Wright does decide to show up, I'd better be looking my best. Who was Scott kidding? Who meets their girlfriend or future wife in a bowling alley—really? The chances of finding my future wife tonight are just about as good as the political parties getting together on a deal that actually makes sense.

We're pulling into your complex right now. Scott texts.

I'll be right down, I respond.

Scott and Melissa are already out front when I come through the lobby door. Melissa rolls down her window and says, "Deacon, are you ready to find Mrs. Wright?"

If I didn't see the smirk on her face, it might have meant a little more. I know Scott put her up to it though. Melissa isn't as cynical as the rest of us. Luckily, Scott's British sense of humor hasn't rubbed off on her too much.

I don't respond to her comment, and as I get into the back seat Melissa turns around and says, "Scott put me up to it. How are you doing?"

"Don't worry and not too bad. As soon as you said it I knew who it came from. Since you won't let me beat him up I'll just have to do it while we play tonight. We all know Scott bowls like a little sissy girl," I say, as I grab Scott's ear.

Scott hits the gas and I fly back into my seat.

"Come on now, just because I'm still single doesn't mean you can abuse me," I manage to mutter as I strap on my seatbelt.

"So where are we going to eat?" I ask, wishing the night was already over.

"Since you boys did your thing already today without the girls, I figure the gals should get to pick," Melissa reasons.

"Why is that exactly?" I question, looking forward to hearing the logic that's about to come out of her mouth.

"Well for starters, remember that we were the ones left sitting at home. We really wanted to come climbing with you guys. So, we figure it's the least you could do, don't you think?" Melissa replies without any hesitation.

As I think for a second, I remember making sure the climbing up at Red Rock today was guys only. I guess what Melissa said doesn't sound too unreasonable.

"Okay, that sounds fair enough to me," I say without a trace of deceit in my voice.

"What? You're giving up the ghost that easily?" Scott says with some amazement.

"Yeah, why not?" I say to Scott before turning my attention back to Melissa. "So where did you ladies have in mind?" I really don't care at this point.

"Well, we know you guys would probably prefer Mexican food, but we were thinking," Melissa pauses for dramatic effect before she tells us what she's decided, "Firehouse Subs."

Scott loves Firehouse Subs. I think he could eat there for breakfast, lunch, and dinner, if they only opened for breakfast. It's literally his home away from home. I really don't mind it either.

"Are you sure that's where the ladies want to go or did someone else talk you into it?" I ask Melissa as I stare at Scott. He's got a grin from ear to ear now.

"I had nothing to do with it mate," Scott says, still sporting the smile.

"I figured if we didn't go tonight the people there might think he died. He hasn't been there once today. I've got to keep my boy happy. Plus, Natalie and Bobbi were fine with it as well," Melissa says as she reaches over and squeezes Scott's cheek.

"Are we meeting up with the others there also?" I ask, making sure our plans haven't fallen through. It's not so bad when I'm out with the whole group, but when I'm truly the third wheel it can get a little uncomfortable. I'm sure more for me though.

"We are all going to meet up at 9:30," Scott says. He knows how I feel about being out with just him and Melissa.

"Sounds good to me," I add, "then over to the bowling alley right?"

"Yep. You know how Scott likes to take his time though. Every bite has to have their special sauce on it. Then he chews every bite so slowly. To watch him you'd think he was shagging his sandwich," Melissa says with a little laughter.

"Oh, I know exactly what you mean," I say as I begin to laugh as well.

Scott doesn't say anything in return. All in good fun. He chuckles a little and just keeps driving. The way Scott drives it's better that he stay focused anyway. We've ended up driving on the wrong side of the road one too many times for my liking.

We pull up to Firehouse Subs at 9:20 and it looks like we are the first ones. I would ask Scott if he wants to wait for the others, but I know there's no chance of that happening.

Scott can't wait to eat, so he orders his and Melissa's food. I'm up next. I get the same thing I always do when we come here—smokehouse beef and cheddar brisket—so tasty. We grab some tables and pull them together. Just as they bring out Scott and Melissa's sandwiches, the rest of the group rolls in.

"I should have known you guys would have been here early," Aaron says as he comes through the door.

The women haven't seen each other all day and greet each other with the customary hug. Being the only single one out tonight I think the ladies feel sorry for me and give me hugs as well.

"How are you lovely ladies doing tonight?" I say.

"We are doing well," Bobbi and Natalie say with friendly smiles on their faces.

"Hey," Melissa complains, "how come I didn't get a greeting like that?"

"You know how jealous Scott gets with me being so much better looking than him," I chide. "I didn't want to start him off on the wrong foot tonight. He needs to remain calm and collected. I don't want him hurting anyone with a stray bowling ball."

Melissa laughs and Scott continues to eat. I don't have to worry about him saying anything for once. His sandwich, if he only eats one, will keep him quiet for at least thirty minutes.

Everyone orders their food and sits down. The talking begins. Bobbi and Natalie are discussing work and the drama that goes on behind the scenes on the strip. Melissa, Aaron, and Blake start talking about the climbing we did today—Melissa really wanted to go. I should feel bad about it, but I don't. Bobbi and Natalie like to climb as well, but I think it's something they do more because Blake and Aaron do it. If Melissa came, all the others would have wanted to come. Scott of course isn't talking, he's eating. I'm eating too, but I'm listening to everyone's conversations thinking about the night. What does it have in store for me? We could probably all sit here together for hours just talking about nothing.

Everyone finishes their food except Scott. He still has three or four inches left from his second sandwich. Just about the time we had all finished our sandwiches, Scott got up and ordered another one. At least he didn't order a large this time.

"You guys ready to go?" Blake asks, standing up from the table. I'm glad he asked and not me. We had been here for a little over an hour already and I was getting restless.

"Okay, okay, I'm ready," Scott mumbles like a child with a mouth full of peanut butter. "Let me just fill up my drink and we'll be off," as he stuffs the last bite in his mouth.

As has become customary when he leaves, Scott walks past the counter and says, "We'll see you gents tomorrow. Keep up the good work." He might not make it in everyday, but I think he does keep the place in business. Everyone jumps in their cars and we head over to the bowling alley.

By the time we get there it's just after 11:00 and midnight bowling won't start for another hour. It's not the cosmic bowling you may be thinking of. They do midnight bowling here which is dollar games after midnight on the weekend. We decide to play one game before midnight.

As we begin our first of many games tonight, the bowling alley starts to clear out. Even though we are in Vegas, this part of town isn't known for its up all night activity. Green Valley is more of a family community as opposed to the strip with its non-stop gambling and booze three-hundred sixty-five days a year.

"What can I get you guys to drink?" the cocktail waitress asks.

Scott leans over to get a better look at the waitress's name tag and asks, "Lexi, when does the pub close down?"

Melissa doesn't drink. I know it's strange as a cocktail waitress, but I guess three years of seeing inebriated patrons managed to set her straight. She has agreed to drive Scott home so he doesn't have to worry about his precious BMW. He may be dumb, but he's not stupid. He wants to pace himself. He doesn't drink that often. More of a social drinker I would say.

"We close at 4:00," she says somewhat perplexed by Scott's question. If she only knew him, everything would make a lot more sense.

"All right then," Scott says as he relaxes back in his chair and begins to think.

"While he takes his time, I'll take a Mai Tai please," Bobbi says as she smiles sarcastically at Scott.

"Okay, okay, I'll take a Sidecar," Scott finally spits out.

"You'll have to forgive him," Melissa says noticing the utterly perplexed look Lexi gives Scott at hearing his choice. "It's a British drink with cognac, orange liqueur, and lemon juice."

"I'll see what I can do," Lexi says. "Can I get anyone else a drink or food from the bar?"

I'm not a drinker. Don't get me wrong, there was a time when alcohol had its place. I decided to quit after my last night out with the team. We were celebrating my last few days in the Navy. I was about to start another chapter of my life and figured I finally better start listening to my dad's advice. I also discovered with Christen I could have fun without downing the booze. The rest aren't big drinkers either. They don't keep it in their homes so I guess you would call them social drinkers as well.

Everyone orders their drinks and we keep playing our first game. It's definitely a warm up. Not one of us will break a hundred points I bet. I think the best I ever scored was the high hundreds and that was probably a fluke. I'm usually in the one-twenties or so, one-fifty on a good day. The rest of the group bowls about the same. It's just after midnight and we decide to forget about the first game and play three more. It can't get any worse, we all resolve. The place has really cleared out now which is surprising. The lanes usually aren't this dead after midnight.

As I turn after paying the attendant, I notice a group of ladies coming through the front doors. There are five of them, and I must say they all have that confident stride as they move through the doors to the front counter. Each one has an element of beauty that suits them just right. They are certainly dressed for a night on the town.

The urge to introduce myself surges inside me. I like to think of myself as a confident person, but going in alone with five single ladies is no small task. I'll let them settle in and make my move a little later once I know their significant others aren't joining them tonight. As I walk back down to our lanes, all the guys look at me and then past me at the ladies, wondering what I am doing.

"I've got it under control, don't worry. They've obviously come here to play. I'll let them settle in and then take it from there," I say as I take my seat to set up the matches since we now have two lanes.

Our ladies are all in the bathroom still as Scott chimes in, "I don't know what you are going to do mate. You have five beautiful birds over there. I know you fancy the blondes so you've got two really fine choices."

"With six of us here, five of them there, and you in the middle, I don't think you'll even talk to them," Blake says, "even though they are quite the lookers."

"I think he'll go talk to them, but I bet they've all got boyfriends. Women like that don't tend to be single," Aaron says as he steps up in preparation to throw his first ball.

"Why are they all here alone on a Saturday night then?" I ask, wondering myself.

"I don't know," Aaron says, "but it's not to meet you."

They all begin to laugh now.

"So, that's one with me and two against. I can handle that," I say as I look over at the girls giving me hope for the night.

"I think we are all with you, it's just I don't see your chances as being too high tonight," Aaron says as he glances over at the ladies.

Just then our women come out of the bathroom and notice the five ladies getting ready to bowl a few lanes down from us.

"Busted," I say, seeing the women have noticed their men checking out the women.

"We got back just in time didn't we," Melissa says as she sits down next to Scott and gives him the look only a girlfriend can give her man.

"Come on babe. You know you're the dog's bollocks for me. Yes, those birds may be pretty, but they have nothing on you," Scott says as he grabs Melissa and gives her a long drawn-out kiss.

"We were just talking about Deacon's chances, or lack thereof. I don't see him walking into that fire tonight," Aaron says as he grabs his ball for his second throw.

"Oh, stop being a big girl's blouse and get over there!" Scott exclaims over everyone's chatter.

"Give me some time. The night's young and the girls are just getting started. They have no idea the amount of confidence that's about to greet them," I say as I grab my fifteen pound ball, waiting for Aaron's ball to strike. He picks up a spare.

I step up to the line to throw my first ball. With my feet positioned perfectly I drop the ball to my side. I slowly glide forward and let the ball slide smoothly down the lane. Every pin falling when the ball hits, strike!

"Yep. That's exactly what you're going to do tonight—strike out!" Blake says. They all chuckle. It didn't matter what I did that round, Blake would have said something I'm sure.

"That's so mean," Bobbi says as she steps up and grabs her ball. "You can get any one of them you want," she softly says with her hand on my shoulder.

"What did she say to you?" Blake sputters quickly after seeing our exchange.

I sit down next to Blake, putting my arm around his neck, and lean in close to whisper, "She said, 'I love you and we can go out when I leave Blake. You're a real man anyway.' I think she was talking about our military service." I'm not a good bluffer and I begin to laugh a little bit before I finish.

"In your dreams buddy," Blake retorts, even though he knew I was messing with him from the get go.

There's nothing in this world that could separate those two and Blake knows it. I guess that's why I can mess with him. Of everyone in our group, Blake and Bobbi are the most secure in their relationship.

"She said I could get any one of them I wanted."

"Only time will tell," Blake replies.

"Just because it's been a while since I've had to approach a woman with the intent to make her want to date me doesn't mean I've lost all my game, come on," I say loudly so the whole group can hear.

"I'm seeing a lot of all mouth and no trousers here mate. I want to see some action. By the way, when was the last time you pulled a lady?" Scott questions.

"Give me a sec."

I put my hand to my temple and start to ponder deeply about the women I've dated. It shouldn't be this hard. It's been quite some time since I had to go in cold—at least back to my Navy days. Now that I'm thinking about it, I can't remember any meaningful relationships during the last seven years besides Christen. I didn't have much hope in the first place I guess. With deployments every six month and non-stop training between that, it made it almost impossible to have a real relationship.

"I've got it. There was a girl about a year before I got out of the Navy. I picked her up at a bar. We went out a few times, but nothing serious."

"And no one helped you out?" Scott says with some skepticism.

"Nope, I picked her up myself," I say this time with more confidence.

"And, just to be sure, does this lady have a name?"

Now I really have to think. I should remember every girl I dated, especially the ones within the last couple years. It has been two years, hasn't it.

"Cat got your tongue?" Scott asks as he steps up to grab his ball, preparing to throw it into the gutter.

"Hold on. I don't want you distracted when you throw that ball. Her name was Stacey. Don't ask for a last name, I definitely don't remember that." Scott has gotten better at bowling, but I would still bet against him any day.

"Okay, so that's one girl in two years you've pulled, right?" Scott asks after walking back from his near gutter ball two pin strike.

"Yep," I reply.

I know I'm out of practice, but how hard can it be? I like to think I'm good looking. The women I've dated are as cute as they come, or at least I think so. That's got to say something about me, I assume. What will I do though? Five distinctly attractive ladies in a bowling alley after midnight on a Sunday morning—how hard can it be?

We continue to play and I don't talk much. I'm thinking about what I'm going to say to pick up the blonde I've been checking out. She's wearing a pair of skin tight jeans and a pretty pink shirt.

Thirty minutes have passed since the women started playing and I'm about to make my move. Then, out of the corner of my eye, I catch a glimpse of the front door opening and a woman's slender silhouette walking through the doorway. As she enters, I am instantly in awe. I stand up, eyes locked on the woman who just walked through the front door. Even though I'm speechless, I know I have to speak to her.

THREE

Blue Eyes

"What's wrong with him?" Blake asks, nodding his head in my general direction.

The entire group turns to look at me and then, following the direction of my smitten stupor, turns to look in the direction of the door. You'd have to be here to believe it. I blink my eyes several times just to make sure I'm not dreaming. The woman of my dreams just walked through the front door. No, literally—the woman in my dream —the same woman who sat in my Jeep while we looked out over the darkened city. I don't know how or why this is happening, but I know I must say something to her. I have to speak to her.

This girl's face is tattooed on my brain. I'd ask someone to pinch me, but if I am dreaming again I don't want to wake up this time. Why is this woman walking into the bowling alley at 12:30 in the morning? The blonde hair and the big beautiful blue eyes, I could see her face from a mile away. To see it now is more than mesmerizing. Her face was all I really saw in my dream. As I look at her entire figure I can't help but think how altogether alluring she is in every way. She is wearing skin tight jeans and a plain white t-shirt under a form fitting coat which definitely does her justice. She looks very athletic and most likely in her early twenties. Her hair is pulled into two pretty ponytails on the lower right and left side of her head, making her look even more attractive. I love that style.

She walks with quiet confidence, catching sight of her friends, she glides effortlessly over and joins them. Of course she had to be with them, I sigh. Now I'm faced with the prospect of going in cold while all her friends and all my friends watch me make a fool of myself. Wait—I'm not going to make a fool of myself. Be positive I tell myself.

I'm awakened to reality as I hear Scott speak, "Are you going to go over there and talk to her or what?"

I blink a few more times to make sure I'm still not dreaming and say, "I didn't tell you guys about this earlier and you're probably not going to believe me anyway, but it doesn't matter. I had a dream about that girl today, the one that just walked in. We were sitting up on the foothills of Sunrise Mountain in my Jeep. We didn't talk. I don't know her name. All I know is I'm walking over there to talk to her now."

"You what?" Aaron says as he comes back from throwing his second ball. "You had a dream about someone?"

Scott speaks for me as he notices I'm not answering Aaron's question, "Apparently, Deacon had a dream about that bird in the white shirt and jeans that just joined the group of ladies."

I can't take my eyes off of this beautiful woman. I know I have to speak to her now. As I come back to reality a second time, I notice everyone's staring at her.

"Don't everyone look at my girlfriend at once!"

"Your girlfriend?" Blake asks.

"That's right—my girlfriend. She just doesn't know it yet," I say so everyone has no doubt she will be my girlfriend before the day is over. I have to think positively.

If my mind wasn't racing before, it's definitely at the head of the race now. I feel like I just got a shot of adrenaline. My heart is beating so loudly I'm sure the rest of them can hear it. I can't mess this one up. I must go in strong. But if we are destined to be together I can't screw this up—right?

"You want a wing man?" Scott says, interrupting my thought process.

"No," I quickly respond. I don't say it, but I know I have to go in alone.

I resolve to let fate take me where it will. What other choice do I have?

I'm still standing, looking at my girl as I turn and tell the group, "Wish me luck. Hopefully I don't get burned."

I begin to walk. My mind continues to race. I know my friends said something as I walked away, but I wasn't paying attention. I'll start with a joke. No, that won't work. I quickly brush the thought from my mind. I'd better come up with something fast. All six women are now looking in my direction. I can only see one. The others have all faded from my sight. Her blue eyes are drawing me in, almost as if I have no control.

Before I have a chance to open my mouth, one of the ladies catches my attention, "Can we help you good looking?"

I haven't even begun, but I'm already feeling better about the flames I've stepped into. The thought of telling my girl I had a dream about her keeps jumping into my head, but I keep pushing it out. I'm pretty sure no girl wants to hear I had a dream about them before they even know my name. I finally realize what I have to say and it starts to flow from my mind, into my mouth, and off my tongue.

"I couldn't help but notice you five beautiful ladies over here for the last thirty minutes, and then this heavenly being walked in and I couldn't stop myself anymore. I had to come over and talk to her.

My name's Deacon," as I move around and take a seat next to her, "what's yours?"

They're all blushing. What girl doesn't like to be called beautiful? I'm not out of the fire yet though.

"My name is Taylor," she says as she smiles and looks away for a second.

Making sure not to exclude the rest of the ladies I continue, "It's nice to meet you Taylor. What are your friends' names?" I can barely take my eyes off Taylor as I ask the question.

"I'm Mandy," the beautiful blonde in the pink shirt replies.

"My name's Savanah."

The other ladies continue to answer. All in all there's Mandy, Savanah, Holly, Sam (I'm guessing Samantha), Ann, and Taylor, the woman of my dreams.

"I can't help but ask—what are all you beautiful ladies doing here alone on a Saturday," I catch myself, "I guess Sunday morning without your boyfriends." Time to find out if Taylor is taken.

Mandy speaks first. She was the one that greeted me so pleasantly before I said a word, "They all have boyfriends who thought it would be better to have a poker night, guys only. I'm the only single one," she says as she stares hopefully right into my eyes.

As Mandy speaks that one word I was hoping would be absent from the conversation some desire drains out of me, my stomach sinks. Then I hear the most glorious thing I've heard all day when Savanah speaks up, "Taylor is single too Mandy," giving her the eye.

That's all I needed to hear. My enthusiasm instantly hits the peak. My dream girl is single and now I know what I have to do. I continue to talk with the ladies for ten minutes or so even though I want nothing more than to be alone with Taylor. When the moment presented itself, I got the feeling Taylor wanted to talk without her friends as well. I ask her if she would like to go for a walk or maybe grab some food. She pleasantly says yes and we say our goodbyes.

When I shake Savanah's hand, she holds on tight and says, "I love that girl. You better take care of her. Don't make me find you."

Savanah must be her best friend to tell me that now, without even knowing me.

Trying not to sound too cocky I look back at Savanah and say, "If you knew me, you wouldn't doubt her safety or my intentions one bit." Savanah just gives me a straight-faced look without saying more.

Walking towards the front door, Taylor questions a little perplexed, "Don't you want to say goodbye to your friends?"

"Trust me, they won't let me get away that easily. I just have to give them a hard time," I say playfully.

We walk towards the exit as if to leave. Every eye stares at me before Scott blurts out, "Get your bloody-butt over here." As we get closer I notice all twelve eyes staring at us. Scott speaks first of course, "I've been bowling for you since you left. Don't worry mate, your score couldn't be any better. In fact, you'll see that it has greatly improved."

I look up at the score screen and notice I'm in last place now. Ordinarily, I would care. And ordinarily, I would have a sharp witticism to wield at Scott in defense of my bowling superiority and another to wield at his unmistakably bad bowling. However, all that escapes me at the moment.

"Everyone—this is Taylor," I say with the biggest grin they've ever seen on my face.

The guys all say hello as well as the girls. The women of course have to stand up and give Taylor a hug as they greet her.

As they all hug, the guys stare at me with sizable smiles of disbelief on their faces. They know I've already made it past the biggest hurdle. Now, will I be able to close the deal, so to speak. In my mind, I already have. If I hadn't, she wouldn't have come with me in the first place. The women can't help themselves and they begin to talk to Taylor like they've known her for years. Melissa, Bobbi, and Natalie are really sweet women. It shouldn't strike me as strange that they welcome her right in.

"Now now ladies, you will have plenty of time to talk to Taylor. We are heading out to grab a bite and talk a little more," I say as I reach to grab Taylor's hand.

"Is Deacon always this assertive?" Taylor says with a sweet smile as she turns towards me. Our eyes meet, she has a playful glint in her eyes. I smile. I'm glad to know she likes to play around. I can tell from her tone that she's giving me a hard time already.

Hand in hand we say our goodbyes as we prepare to take off. Ordinarily, holding a girl's hand this short into a date would feel strange, but something feels right about it—I can't explain it. It is almost as if I've held her hand before. I hope she doesn't feel awkward.

As we walk away Aaron calls out, "Don't let him get to know you too well tonight Taylor!"

"Don't worry, if he gets out of line I've got a Glock under my seat to fix the problem," Taylor says as she squeezes my hand and looks back at the group and smiles.

As we walk out the front door it finally hits me, I don't have my car. What am I going to tell Taylor?

"Sooo," I say sheepishly as I look into Taylor's big blue eyes, "I came with my friend Scott and…"

"Sooo," she slowly repeats back mimicking me, "You don't have a car?" Taylor says as she squeezes my hand tighter and smiles. "This is going to be so much fun. Plus I'll have my gun now if you do get out of line."

I must admit, knowing she carries a Glock makes me that much more attracted to her. We continue into the parking lot towards her car. Taylor walks to the passenger side, opens up the door, and says, "You haven't raped or killed anyone, have you?"

Normally I would open her door but this question has me somewhat sidetracked now—it's always so hard to answer the killing question. It's something I definitely don't want to get into just after meeting her. I think for a second before responding. "Not in the last year," I say with the most innocent smile I can muster. I didn't lie.

She, like everyone else, dismisses it as humor and lets me into her car. I know if things progress I'll tell her about the time I've spent in the military. We are certainly not going to have that conversation tonight though. Imagine the scene: *Hi, my name is Deacon. I've killed…I don't know..100s of enemy overseas. Do you want to get some food? And by the way, I've never raped anyone.*

I think it's best we stick to neutral topics. Taylor closes my door and walks around the front of the car. I can't help but watch her every move.

As Taylor opens her door she says, "Buckle up. You're about to go for a ride."

"Thanks for opening my door. Normally I would do that for you," I say as I buckle my belt.

47

"I hope so. Just so you know, I expect the same treatment the next time we get together," Taylor replies.

This night couldn't be going any better. She doesn't really know a thing about me and already she's talking about the next time we get together. I'm at a loss for words as she turns on the car and punches it out of the parking lot.

"What do you want to grab to eat before we head up the mountain?" she says, catching me off guard again.

"Up the mountain?" I say with puzzlement. "You haven't killed anyone, have you?"

Taylor pauses for a few seconds, "Not in the last year," she says as she quickly glances my way and simpers. She starts to laugh and I do as well.

"Since it's so late I was thinking about grabbing some Mexican food and then heading up the mountain," Taylor adds.

"That sounds fine to me," I respond, not mentioning how much I love Mexican food. "Do you know the area? There's a Mexican place right down the street."

"I'm pretty familiar with the area," Taylor replies with another smile.

"I wanted to talk with you more back there with your friends, but figured the conversation would be easier without five women listening in. I didn't want to be rude and exclude them," I explain.

"I wanted to talk to you as well. One of us is hard enough. Six would have been impossible. I think Mandy would have been more jealous of me than she already is if you singled me out more than you already had."

48

"Being with you I had already forgotten about her. She definitely had her eye on me, didn't she?" I say, hoping she doesn't take my candor the wrong way.

"Oh she did. She wanted you so bad she forgot I had even showed up. I came in late because I was out on a blind date with a guy Savanah had set me up with. Now I'm out with you and I'm sure I'll hear about it later," Taylor says as she makes another right. "My date didn't turn out to be a real man."

"I'm sorry to hear that, but I guess that's good news for me, right?" I inquisitively ask.

"I guess we'll have to see. The night's still young," she responds as she glances over at me again.

As we pull up to the drive-thru to place our order Taylor asks, "Do you know what you want?"

"I'll take two chicken soft tacos and a nacho, please."

As she rolls down her window the attendant asks, "Would you like to try our new Bigger Burrito?"

"No thank you," she replies. "We'll take three chicken soft tacos and two regular nachos. Can you throw in a few of each of your sauces please?"

"You can't beat their chicken soft tacos here," I say, noticing she ordered what I had.

"To be honest, I try not to eat fast food, but their chicken soft tacos are to live for," Taylor says as she pulls around to the window.

I hand her my card so she knows I'm paying and say, "I've heard that saying a thousand times except everyone always says to die for."

"I know. I used to say it that way, but then I realized how much I love life. There's so much more to live for as opposed to die for. Who wants to die for anything?" Taylor replies as the attendant hands her our bag of food.

Taylor checks the bag and steps on the gas again. Normally I would start eating in the car, but since she hasn't reached in or asked for a taco I figure she's waiting. I better wait as well.

"So where are we heading?" I ask as she drives north.

Usually I'm in the driver's seat in these situations. I'm the one letting the excitement build, not telling the girl where we are going. This is quite the role reversal for me, especially on a first date. Is it a date? I guess I'll let the night decide that for itself.

"Up on Sunrise Mountain there's this perfect spot to park and look out over the city. There's also a majestic white building up there," Taylor says as she jumps on the 515. "I always feel good just looking at it. I'm not sure what it was built for—the sign appears to have been removed. A few years back I wrote a story and I transformed this building into a royal palace. It felt right even though I am still left wondering why this building was built, what it was used for, and why it is no longer in use. For now, it's enough just to look at," she confesses quietly.

Good grief, her quiet, yet playful innocence is intoxicating, I think to myself. "You write?" is all I can manage to articulate—completely under the influence of her irresistible charm.

"I dabble. I consider myself a recreational writer. Although, I admit I usually write every day. It helps me to keep things in perspective."

"That makes sense," I reply with a tone of admiration too obvious to disguise. "It's like looking out over the city. I love to see all the lights in Vegas. It is so much better than being right down in it. It's so much more peaceful when you're not surrounded by all the chaos."

"I know exactly what you mean. I grew up here and things are always more serene looking from the outside in. I guess that's the way it is with life though," Taylor adds.

I know exactly what she means when she says, 'From the outside.' I've been in one to many rat holes, flying in a helicopter, looking down at the ground thinking how peaceful and pretty everything appeared. I couldn't see all the trash, the fighting, or the dead bodies as we flew overhead. Then I would get down in the thick of it and remember how bad it really was, always wishing to be back in the air.

I don't say anything for a while, which is strange. Normally the silence would be awkward, but just being with Taylor and letting her take me where she will, seems to take away the awkward feelings that would normally come. She doesn't say anything either. She seems content driving with an occasional glance over at me. This also makes me feel good, as if she wants to drive, but she can't keep her eyes off of me. I certainly can't take my eyes off her.

Taylor takes the Charleston Boulevard exit and drives east towards the mountain.

"So you said you grew up here in Vegas?" I ask Taylor as she heads north on Lamb.

"Yeah. I actually grew up in Green Valley, or right outside I guess. Do you know Dustin Avenue?" Taylor asks as she makes a right on Bonanza to head up the mountain.

"Actually, I do. I live on Green Valley Parkway, right where Patrick turns into Green Valley. That's right next to Dustin," I say amazed at what a small world we live in.

I kind of feel like a moron now for asking if she knew the area. Now the pleasant smile as she said yes makes more sense.

"My parents actually still live over there. My dad built the house and I don't think there's anything that could get him out of it. My mom loves it too. The neighbors on that street are the best," Taylor states matter-of-factly.

"I know what you mean. I grew up in San Diego and there's nothing I can do to get my mom out of the house my dad built," I say hoping she doesn't ask about my family.

My dad passed away about a year ago and I want to keep this conversation on the up and up. All those more depressing details will come out later. I guess it's not really depressing. It's just a part of life.

"So Deacon, what do you do in this twenty-four seven town?"

"I'm going to school at UNLV and working as a manager over at the Bellagio. How about you?"

"I'm a student also. I've been going to UNLV for a few semesters now and I work as a waitress at The Cheesecake Factory at the Forum Shops."

I guess I know where I'll be taking my lunch and dinner breaks from now on.

"What are you studying?" I ask, wondering why I haven't seen her on campus in the eight months I've been attending there. I wouldn't forget her even if I hadn't dreamt about her.

"It's funny you should ask that. My dad has been pressuring me lately about my major. I've been doing all my generals deciding

52

whether to major in creative writing or architecture. I love both. I love to write, but I also love to design things. I only have this semester of generals left and then I'll start one of them. I need to make up my mind soon so I can make sure I get into the program I want. There's a lot of competition, especially in the architecture program. What are you studying?" she asks as she glances my way again.

I love it when she looks at me because I get to see those blue eyes over and over again. I know one night won't be enough so I better get what I can.

"I'm actually in my third semester still doing generals like you. I'm going into the Hospitality Management program. I want to own a hotel on the Boulevard or at least run one someday. Right now I'm managing the valet attendants at the Bellagio."

"I bet you get to meet some interesting people at the Bellagio." Taylor pauses a second before continuing. "Actually, I guess we all get to meet some interesting people working on the strip."

"From the filthy rich to the extra extravagant, they all seem to make it to Vegas. I'm not complaining though. They know how to tip and that's number one for me," I say.

"True," Taylor responds. "For the most part, the people are more than generous. I don't complain. They are paying for my college, so keep 'em coming."

I want to tell her about being in the military, but over the last five years or so the attitude of the public has definitely shifted more negatively. Too many wars and too many soldiers doing awful things overseas have turned the people somewhat against the military. Don't get me wrong, there are still strong pockets of people that love the military. Every time I fly back from overseas through Texas people are lined up like you wouldn't believe to greet the troops. It's as if we were rock stars walking down the red carpet or something. I'm pretty sure Taylor is pro-military, but I'll wait a bit to see how things go.

"So when you're not hanging out in bowling alleys early on Sunday mornings, what do you like to do?" I ask.

"Well, since it seems like all I do is work, study, and sleep these days, I haven't done much of anything lately. When I do have free time I like to go running, hiking, pretty much anything outside. I'm inside all the time. Just getting outside is enough for me," Taylor states as she also tells me we are almost there.

This girl is too good to be true. Am I not seeing something? Why is she still single? I know we won't get into those topics tonight, but I can't help but think about them. She's probably thinking the same thing about me. I think if we could just read each other's minds this whole dating thing would be a lot easier. From where I'm sitting, I don't see anything wrong right now. I just hope it stays that way.

"Have you ever been rock climbing?" I ask, thinking she's probably done that as well.

"Of all the outdoor activities to do that's the one I've always wanted to do, but no one has ever taken me, and I don't have the gear to go by myself," Taylor says. "Do you rock climb?"

"I do. In fact my buddies you met at the bowling alley and I all went climbing today up at Red Rock Canyon. If you really want to learn, I'll take you up there some time. You definitely look strong enough. If you really like it, which I'm sure you will, you can come up to Zion's National Park for my birthday in March. We are going to have a lot of fun climbing and hanging out. Don't worry, the gals will be coming too."

"That sounds like a lot of fun, but what are we going to do for my birthday in February?" Taylor asks.

"What day in February? I know I'm not supposed to ask, but I don't believe in those ridiculous rules, how old will you be?"

"I would ask you to guess, but I won't torture you just yet. I'll be twenty three on the eleventh. How about you, how old and what day?"

"I'll be twenty-five on the seventeenth of March. Yes, St. Patrick's Day. That's why we are heading up to Zion. We aren't big partiers. We'd rather be outside than in a bar getting drunk."

"I'm there with you," Taylor adds, "I don't drink anymore. I did for about a year when I was in high school, but I didn't like what I was doing, so I gave it up. I figured I'd be better without it."

"I agree. It took me a little longer to give it up, though. I drank a little in high school too. I've stayed away for just over a year now," I reply.

"Well, here we are. What do you think?" Taylor asks as she shuts off the car.

I'd been looking at Taylor for so long I didn't realize we had arrived. It's hard to pull my eyes away. As I look out the window, it seems familiar—like I've seen it before.

"I've lived in Vegas for a year now, and I've never come up on this side of the city. I've always gone out to the west by the red rocks. It's really pretty up here," I say as I gaze out the window.

I look back at Taylor and then back out the window again. This time it hits me. I saw this view of Vegas in my dream yesterday. I can't believe this is happening right now. I might not be sitting in my Jeep, but I'm sitting here with the girl from my dream looking out at

Vegas exactly as I saw it. The lights are still on, and I hope it stays that way. Who knows what would happen if the city lost all power. The chaos that exists now would explode overnight. If the lights do go off, I will definitely have to tell Taylor about the dream. I'm tempted to anyway. I'm still fighting that urge.

"I don't know if you saw the building as we drove past, I think you had your eyes on me the whole time, but that's it right over there," Taylor says as she points at the building she spoke of earlier.

I turn to look and instantly the building comes into view—most certainly a majestic building. The whole thing appears to be glowing.

"I must admit, it is a majestic structure."

"I don't know what it is, but it seems so out of place in this city. I think that's why I like it. Not out of place in a bad way, by any means. Like I told you, it just feels good to look at it," Taylor says as she turns from staring at the building to look back at me. "Is that weird?" she asks almost childlike.

"No, it's not weird. It has that quality. How come you've never tried to go inside?"

"I tried to go in one time but the gates were locked. They actually looked to have been locked for some time now. I never see anyone there. I only ever come up here at night. I finally decided not to worry. I like the feeling so much that I don't want to ruin the magic," she says so innocently.

"Well, it is a beautiful building and a magnificent view of the city for sure," I say as I look out over the crazy city I call home.

"It's so peaceful up here. You're the first person I've ever brought up here. I always come up here by myself to think or read or just relax," Taylor says as she reaches her hand over to hold mine.

I don't hesitate and hold her hand as well. I feel like I'm back in junior high holding a girl's hand for the first time. The feeling is more than welcome though. I've needed this closeness for some time now. Christen was never too affectionate when it came to the small things. I just didn't imagine it being anything like this.

"What is your favorite color?" Taylor asks, looking away from me out over the city.

"It has been green all my life until I met you," I say as she turns toward me.

"Why is that?" she asks naively, her blue eyes appearing so innocent.

"Well, once I got one look at those beautiful blue eyes of yours I was hooked."

Taylor's cheeks start to turn slightly red and she looks down for a second before she brings her eyes to look back at mine. "Thank you."

As we stare into one another's eyes Taylor slowly starts to lean forward and I instantly know what she's doing. I too slowly lean in for what I hope will be the best moment of the night. As we kiss it's more than I hoped for. It only lasts for a few seconds. It was nothing more than a simple, sweet kiss, but I feel something I've never felt before. I hesitate to use the word magical, but it's the only one that comes to mind. I know she feels it too. Her lips were so soft.

Just then Taylor says, half apologetically, "I usually don't kiss a guy on the first date, but I couldn't help myself."

"Well, if it's worth anything to you, that was the best kiss I think I've ever had," I say as we continue to look into one another's eyes.

"Thank you for not pushing it too far. I realize now that parking up here might have led you on. I know in today's world most people would already be ripping each other's clothes off, but I can't do that. I hope you understand," Taylor says as she turns to look out over the city again.

It's in that moment I realize I must tell her about the dream I had today. I know she's probably expecting some reassurance to the vulnerable place she's just put herself in. I'm sure what I'm about to tell her will suffice though. Plus, she's let me in so much with what she has said I think it only fair I open up as well.

"I have to tell you something I've been fighting back all night."

"Okay," she says not sure what I'm about to drop on her. She can't take her eyes off me now in anticipation.

"Ever since you walked through those doors at the bowling alley I knew we had to talk. If talk was all it was it wouldn't have been enough, but I guess I could have lived with it. After my friends and I finished climbing yesterday around five I went back to my place and fell asleep. While I was sleeping I had a dream about you."

She's definitely hooked now. She hasn't even blinked and her eyes seem to just get bigger and bigger every second as I continue.

"We were sitting in this exact place, with this exact view, except I was driving my Jeep and you were in the passenger seat. I didn't know your name and we didn't say anything to each other. There was one other thing strangely out of the ordinary for me as well. Not one of the lights were on in the city. After I stared into your blue eyes for a time my phone rang and you were gone. I woke up. I wanted to know your name so bad when I woke up, and now I do."

She doesn't say anything for almost a minute as she looks out over the city.

"You don't think I'm crazy or made any of that up do you?" I say hoping I haven't lost her.

As Taylor turns back, her blue eyes somewhat moist and glistening, she says, "I believe you."

She leans in again to show she believes me. This time is just as good as the first. I hope she drugs me every time we kiss. It's more than the lipgloss though. I wish I could explain it.

"I also want you to know I am perfectly fine with not ripping your clothes off. I'm sure there's a super sexy body under there, but my parents brought me up the way they were brought up. There are certain things you don't do before you get married."

Taylor is more than happy now as she leans over again this time to give me a hug. "Thank you," she says, "that means more to me than you know. I would give you another kiss, but I've already gone over my limit of none for the night and I figure I'm going to be giving you another one when I drop you off so you'll have to wait for that one."

"I can live with that," I say as we pull away from each other.

I've been ignoring the text messages all night long, not even wanting to interrupt the time we've been having together, but I realize Scott was my ride and he's probably been wondering about me.

"Sorry to do this, but I think my friend Scott has been texting and calling me like crazy for the last hour, he was my ride. Do you mind if I shoot him a text and let him know I'm still alive and you didn't take me into the mountain and eat me or something?"

Taylor starts to laugh, "No, go ahead. I'll do the same. I forgot I told my friends I'd call or text to let them know I was okay as well. Savanah's my best friend, and I know she's worrying."

I grab my phone out of my pocket as Taylor grabs hers out of her purse. As I turn it on I see the time, it's 2:18. We've been gone for almost two hours and it seems like no time at all. I see I have three missed calls and several texts from Scott. I know I can't call him so I send him a text simply stating, "I'll tell you all about it today at the gym."

I look back up at Taylor who has already sent her text and say, "He worries about me like we were married."

Taylor laughs again and says, "Yeah, Savanah's the same way with me. We've been friends ever since the fourth grade so I know what you mean."

"I feel like Scott and I have been friends that long, but we actually just met each other a year ago when I moved here. He was working at the Bellagio when I got the job there."

"Where did you move from?" Taylor asks.

"I was living in San Diego. I was getting out of the Navy," I say hoping she doesn't pry too much.

"Now I'm even more attracted to you. You didn't get kicked out, did you?"

"No, it was an honorable discharge," I say feeling like an enormous weight has been lifted off my chest. I should have never doubted someone so well adjusted.

"My dad served in the Navy during the first Gulf War before I was born. He talks about the experience often so I know how difficult it can be. I won't ask more. I'll let you determine the time and place," Taylor says as about as sincere as anyone could say anything.

Who is this girl? How did she grow up so centered and well adjusted? Now I know I have to meet her parents.

"Thank you. I'm sure we'll get to that point soon enough," I say knowing I've hit the jackpot with this one. I know I've got to do everything I can to keep her around. This one's more than special.

I've still got my phone in my hand as it vibrates again. I don't look until Taylor says, "You might want to check that one."

At her request, I look down. As I turn it on I see a number I don't recognize. The message says, "Here's my number blue eyes. Don't lose it." I look up at Taylor and see she has the biggest grin on her face.

"Was that you? How did you get my phone number already?" I say completely surprised by her ability to acquire my digits. Calling me blue eyes doesn't hurt either.

"I can't tell you. Let's just say it was meant to be."

I'm at a loss for words again. I want to press the issue, but I leave it alone. I'm sure I'll figure it out soon enough.

"Well, as much as I would love to stay up all night with you and chat I better get you home. I have to be up early this morning to go to church with my parents," Taylor says as she starts the car.

"I would too, but I better get to bed as well. Scott and I have a date at the gym at ten, and he won't let me miss it."

Taylor begins to drive and we continue to talk and get to know each other more on the way home. I tell her my favorite color is blue just in case she didn't get the hint before. I talk about my job and the interview I have Monday morning. Taylor tells me about growing up in Green Valley and about playing soccer and being a cheerleader at Green Valley High School.

As Taylor arrives at Green Valley Parkway and Sunset she asks, "Okay, where from here?"

"Make a left here." I would have told her to turn on Patrick, but I was too busy talking and we missed the turn. Plus, it gives me a few more minutes with her, which can't be bad. "I live just down this way on the right in the Garden Apartments."

"I know right where those are," she says. "They are fairly new aren't they?"

"Yeah. I think they were finished just before I moved in five months ago. The apartment was brand new."

"I see what you did now. We took the long way so you could spend more time with me. Couldn't get enough huh?" Taylor says as she reaches over to grab my hand.

"I'm never going to get enough," I say as she pulls into the complex. "I live in building B, right over there," pointing at my building.

Taylor pulls up to the front entrance and says, "Stay right there."

She then opens her door and gets out. I was hoping she didn't just lean over and give me a kiss. I wanted the whole experience—a kiss and a long extended hug so I could feel her body against mine. Taylor opens my door and reaches her hand in to help me out of the car. As I stand up I notice for the first time how tall she is. She has to be five foot eight or nine. We walk over to the front entrance in the light so I can see her beautiful blue eyes one more time before I close mine for the night. I hope I can go to sleep. I know my mind will be racing again.

Taylor speaks first, "I'm glad I didn't go home after my awful first date, and I can't wait to see you again. I know this might be hard, but remind me to tell you what my mom told me a few years ago. Don't worry, it's an awesome story."

"How long should I wait to remind you?" I ask wondering why she's putting me through this torture. Knowing she has something to tell me makes me want to know right now.

"Give it a couple months. If we are still together, as I suspect we will be, you'll enjoy it. Trust me, it will be worth the wait."

I lean in first this time, reliving the first two kisses all over again. The third is even better because I'm holding her close. We kiss for only a couple seconds again, but I don't let go. I hold her tight. I smell her hair and take it all in. The smell of tropical flowers fills my insides. I love it. I know she's doing the same to me. Every girl I've ever dated has talked about the smell of a man. Supposedly it's one of the things that attracts them to us. I don't know anything about pheromones, but I know whatever she's putting off has me hook, line, and sinker.

We hug for a good thirty seconds without saying anything, just savoring the moment we know is about to end for the night.

"Normally I would drop you off and walk you to your door. I feel so backwards right now."

"I believe you, but it feels so good right now to be in my shoes, like I'm in control," Taylor says as she squeezes my hand and then pulls away. "How about you pick me up tomorrow? You'll feel better then."

"It's a date then. I'll call you tomorrow," I say as Taylor begins the walk back to her car.

Taylor starts walking backwards and says, "It's a date, and I'll be looking forward to that call."

"Have a good night blue eyes," I say as Taylor walks around to get into her car.

She opens her door, puts one foot in, and before sitting down says, "I've already had a great night—you too blue eyes."

With the dome light still on in her car I get one last glimpse of those blue eyes as the light slowly fades. She then waves and pulls out of the parking lot.

What a night! I couldn't have imagined a better evening. Just then I realize in all the fun and excitement I forgot to ask her last name. It's been a couple minutes now, but I find myself still standing in the entryway. I quickly pull out my phone and send her a text telling her my last name, and apologizing for not asking hers. I was really off my game.

As I wait for a response I put her name into my phone saving hers in my favorites. I even change the vibration of her phone call to a heartbeat.

As I continue to look down at my phone I remember she's driving and probably won't respond until she gets home. I don't know where she lives in Green Valley so it could be some time. I begin to walk into the building and over to the elevator when my phone beats. I look down and it's a text from Taylor, "I was thinking the same thing. Taylor Sanders. It was nice to meet you, Deacon Wright. Sweet dreams!"

I quickly respond back, "It was nice to meet you too Taylor. Sweet dreams blue eyes!"

FOUR
Monday Morning

I don't remember anything after laying down last night. It was the best sleep I've had in a long time. I spent all afternoon and most of the night with Taylor. We talked a lot about our plans and what we've done in our lives. Nothing bad has come up yet, so I'm sure we are both holding back, waiting for the right moment. Everyone puts on the best show they can at first—otherwise, I don't think there would be many second dates.

As much as I'd like to keep thinking about Taylor, and the time we've spent together, I have a meeting in a couple hours. I have to get focused. The boss's secretary sent me a text yesterday confirming the meeting was still on for today at ten. I hope whatever is in store for me today only keeps this high going. I haven't felt this good in some time now. Let's see, what do I still have to do—eat, shower, shave, and get dressed. I have to be at least fifteen minutes early to the meeting, which means I have to leave in just over an hour.

Taylor has been a great distraction for me over the last thirty-six hours. Without her, I'm sure my head would have been racing all weekend with what was coming this morning. Now that it's finally here, I can't stop my mind from going a million miles a minute. The only thing I even know about this meeting is what Scott told me on Saturday while we were climbing. To be honest, I don't think it helped at all.

The funny thing is I can't prepare or practice anything. I have no idea what's to come and my nerves are driving me crazy. I've gone into situations where my life was on the line and I didn't feel this nervous. I trained and practiced and then trained and practiced more for those situations. All I have now is my life and whatever that brings. I guess all I can hope for this time is that whatever I've done to this point is enough. Be myself.

I flip on the television in hopes that it will distract my mind. The news of US servicemen killed in action is already coming out of Iran. Not exactly what I want to hear, but at least it does give my mind something else to focus on.

We've only been in that country a little over a week and already the death toll has risen to forty-seven. How many dead Americans is it going to take this time before our fearless leaders pull us out of the country? I know those that serve will continue to do their job, but to what point, what end? I wonder how unpopular it will have to be before the politicians put our people first. Our forces have been drastically cut over the last ten years which means deployment after deployment for those still serving. Nothing like the thought of war to get my mind off the task at hand.

After eating and showering, I decide to wear a suit to the meeting since I can't get more dressed up than that—not knowing, I figure I'd better look my best. I pull into the employee parking lot thirty minutes before the meeting. I decide to wait in the car until it's twenty minutes to ten. I don't want to look too anxious. If I show up too early I'll look desperate. The music helps to keep me relaxed.

Walking into the building I see a couple guys that work under me. One of them sees me all dressed up and says, "You're looking pretty fancy. What do you have going on?"

Since I'm literally walking into the meeting I say, "I've got a meeting with the boss in twenty minutes." What can it hurt at this point?

They keep walking and wish me luck. I get the feeling they hadn't heard anything about the meeting. Why all the secrecy? I'm pretty sure I haven't done anything wrong. I'm hoping this is only going to elevate me here, not evict me from the premises.

The elevator ride to the top seems agonizingly long. My mind runs through scenario after scenario until the moment the elevator doors open. As they open, I step out into Dean's lobby poised and focused. I hear soft classical piano music playing in the background. Jennifer, Dean's executive secretary, smiles pleasantly as she greets me and asks me to take a seat.

Jennifer looks the part of an executive secretary. She is wearing a beautifully colored skirt and a light-brown blouse. The elegant stilettos I see through the glass desk certainly must give her legs a workout, but do also give her an air of sophistication. Her long brown hair pulled back into a single ponytail says she means business. She also has piercing brown eyes which go perfectly with the light shirt she is wearing. From what the guys have told me, Dean had heard great things about her in the concierge department. Then one day he finally met her and I think the next day she moved up. When the boss needs a secretary, he gets whomever he wants. I've seen her a few times around the premises with Tom as well.

As I settle into a large leather chair, I survey my surroundings. The lobby is both elaborate and elegant. I pick up a copy of *Car & Driver* magazine and start flipping through its pages.

Jennifer's personal cell phone starts vibrating on the glass tabletop. When she answers the call, there is a peculiar absence of the friendly greeting I was expecting to hear. My interest is piqued.

"I can't talk now," she whispers discreetly, shifting her eyes suspiciously in my direction.

I keep my head down, appearing to be completely absorbed in the magazine.

"No, it starts in fifteen. What do you mean you can't find the book?" she whispers even more quietly. "I'll take care of him. You just focus on keeping your head down."

Jennifer quietly sets the phone face-down on her desk and busies herself with her computer before striking up a casual conversation.

"So, Deacon, what did you do for the new year?" Jennifer asks.

I glance up from the magazine article I was pretending to read, "Not a whole lot. A few of my friends and I hung out. Nothing too big. How was yours? Did Dean give you some time off?"

Jennifer glances up from her computer and responds, "Yeah, I had four days off. It was nice. A couple of my girlfriends and I hung out on the strip with the rest of the lunatics. Nothing too crazy." We both laugh. Not crazy and New Year's on the strip don't mix.

Once again, I start flipping pages in my magazine. Since I still have fifteen minutes before the meeting starts, I debate whether or not to ask Jennifer about the meeting—to see if she's heard anything. I do want to ask, but at the same time, I don't. What if she says something to Dean? After ten minutes I finally decide—what could it hurt?—the meeting is about to start.

"If you don't mind me asking, what's this meeting about?" I say to Jennifer as I toss the magazine back down on the glass coffee table.

"I'm sure I couldn't tell you. Dean has me set appointments and take care of just about everything else you can think of, but he never tells me what's going on in there. Sorry, I wish I knew more," she says so professionally rehearsed.

"That's okay. I'm about to find out in a few minutes anyway. Maybe my nerves will finally stop."

"I don't think you have anything to be nervous about," Jennifer says. "When I have heard Dean mention your name it has been nothing but positive. I know that doesn't say a lot, but I wouldn't worry at all."

"Thanks. That does make me feel a little better."

What she says calms me a bit. The nerves are still there though. The question then becomes—what does Dean say about me when she's not around? I continue to wonder as I wait, trying not to overthink the situation. I look up at the clock and see it's 10:00 on the dot. Just then I hear Dean call over the intercom to have Jennifer send me in.

Jennifer looks over at me and says, "Looks like you can go in now."

"Wish me luck."

"Good luck," she says flashing her beautifully wide smile that could put just about anyone into a good mood.

If that doesn't cheer me up I don't know what will. I step up to the door and suddenly feel like I'm about to go before the promotion board in the military. I almost knock when I realize I'm in the civilian world and Dean has already told me to come in. Just relax…there's no one behind the door that wants to kill me, I hope.

I've never been in Dean's office, but I imagined it to be overly large and well-furnished. Every time I see him he's so well-dressed. He absolutely looks the part of a general manager. As the door sways open, my suspicions are confirmed. The office is the size of my entire apartment—a large siting area, the biggest desk I've ever seen, and a view to live for. As I walk in Dean stands up, walks over, and shakes my hand with a firm grip.

After a few seconds of silence Dean says, "I bet you are wondering why I had Jennifer set up this meeting."

"Yes. In fact, ever since Jennifer called me I haven't been able to stop thinking about it."

"Before I dive into the details, I have one simple question to ask you. I want to see if I've made the right choice."

No pressure—right.

"Are you ready?" Dean says with his piercing green eyes penetrating into my soul.

"As ready as I'm going to be sir." What choice has he made?

"Let us take a seat before we begin."

We walk over and have a seat in the lounge area. The brown Italian leather feels cool to the touch. This makes me feel a little more at ease—not so formal. Now, if I were sitting in a chair in front of Dean's massive desk it would feel more like an interrogation—like the ones we did too often when we caught a low level guy we knew had critical information.

After we settle in with a little more small talk Dean begins, "What is the number one threat we face in the hotel/casino world?"

Threat?!—my mind goes into overdrive. I know in the valet world we are always worried about our customers' items being taken from their cars or damaging their rides. In the casino, they're worried about people cheating the system. In housekeeping, they worry about finding a dead body in a room. Those all seem menial when you look

71

at the totality of the hotel/casino business. Could it be competition? What about the economy? All these things race through my mind as I search for the right answer. Then it comes to me. I remember getting a brief just before I got out of Navy—

"Drug cartels and terrorist," I respond confidently.

Over the last several years, the threat of terrorism as well as drug cartels moving more heavily onto US soil has been a major issue for America. With the military being downsized like it has over the last ten years, it's no wonder we face further threats from the cartels and terrorist. They are almost one and the same these days. The nearly monthly attacks in major cities across the US has sent law enforcement officials all over the country on a ride they weren't expecting. Political correctness has really damaged our ability to weed out those that seek to destroy our society.

Dean has a smile on his face as he says, "I anticipated you would say terrorism only, but I'm glad you mentioned both." I feel much better now.

"Do you know what this is?" Dean says holding up a piece of paper.

I lean in to get a closer look and realize it's my application I filled out almost a year ago. Now I'm worried he believes I lied on my application. Remember, I didn't lie. I might not have been completely forthcoming with all that I did in the Navy, but I didn't lie.

"It appears to be my application sir."

What's Dean going to do now? Should I have told them everything I did while in the Navy?

"I want you to just listen," Dean says, waiting for my response.

"Okay," I say shifting slightly in my seat.

"It has come to my attention that you are more than what you have led us to believe. More than what you put on this piece of paper. I have known now for five months, ever since I approved your management position in valet services. Before I ask you another question I want you to understand something. In this world, much like the world you come from, we have to make sure everyone we work with is looking out for all those around them and is not in it for themselves. Anytime we put someone in a management position, no matter what level it is, we put them through a vetting process. Did you know we did this to you when we moved you to your current position?"

The world I come from? My position seems so low, it didn't even cross my mind that they would spend any time checking references or background on me. "I didn't know anything was happening," I say wondering now what he knows.

"We did. We found out some very interesting details that were left off your application. You have served in Afghanistan, Syria, and Venezuela. You have received several silver stars, as well as the Navy Cross. Basically, you have excelled at just about everything you have ever done. I have my theory as to why you left all that information off your application, but instead of hearing my opinion, I would like to hear it from you first."

Dean doesn't say a word as he waits for me to start. I know I have to tell him everything. He probably knows it already anyway. I start way back. Probably further than he expected, but since he wants to know I figure he better understand the whole picture.

"I grew up in a home that was filled with patriotism like you wouldn't believe. I can still remember every Fourth of July and the strong feelings my parents instilled in me for the freedom we enjoy." I pause briefly, "Is that too far back?" I ask not sure he really wants that much detail. He doesn't say a word—just nods to let me know I can continue.

"I remember one event in particular. I think I was twelve or thirteen and my mother was in charge of a Fourth of July program in our church. As the finale to the show, hundreds of balloons were to drop from the ceiling as the fake fireworks went off on stage. The show was inside a smaller auditorium. I didn't tell my mom this, but my friends and I thought it would be a great idea to pop the balloons as they came down to create a more festive feel to the finale, maybe a little mischief too. The effect it added was so amazing that my mom started to cry—she was so overtaken. I still remember her thanking us for the small role we played.

"Anyway, I know that story seems insignificantly small, but it was experiences like that which made me decide to join the Navy. My grandfather also served in the Navy during World War II and I knew I wanted to follow in his footsteps. I joined the Navy, went through basic training, and then off to Naval Special Warfare Prep School. After completing Prep School, I went to Basic Underwater Demolition, SEAL school."

"You can call it BUDS," Dean interjects. "I might look old, but I think you will be surprised to hear where I come from. Continue," he says with a slight grin appearing across his face.

Wondering what Dean has done in his life I continue, "I went to BUDS for six months and completed the training with no problem. Then it was off to parachute training which was a break for sure. Finally, I attended SEAL qualification training. I assume you found out I was a SEAL during my time in the Navy, and now you're wondering why I didn't put that down on my application."

"That is exactly what I have been wondering. I have been waiting precisely five months to hear your explanation," Dean says with a slightly more serious look on his face as he shift his legs.

"By saying this it will seem somewhat of a contradiction, but I hope you'll understand." I pause for a second, contemplating how I will phrase what I'm about to say. "I'm not the kind of person that likes people to know everything about me. I'm happy just knowing my family and fellow brothers-in-arms know what I've accomplished in my life. I guess the one word that comes to mind is humble. I know by saying that some would say I'm not humble, but I think it still holds true."

"I would say you are more than humble. You even left out an important part of your BUDS training," Dean says. "You were Honor Man after Hell Week."

I am completely dumbfounded.

"Sir, I can't help but ask how you know I was Honor Man."

There are guys on the teams that don't even know I was Honor Man. I knew it would just be something they would razz me about so I never mentioned it. Not even my friends know about that one.

"I thought I would get you with that one," Dean says before continuing. "Believe it or not, Jennifer is a resourceful person. When she found out you were a SEAL I stopped her investigation. She would not have been able to find out any more anyway. Just so you know as well, I told her not to tell anyone about you past."

"I understand exactly why you don't want people to know you were a SEAL. I was a SEAL almost twenty years ago. That title brings a sense that you are indestructible. While that might be true in most cases, it also puts a target on your back in the world we live in.

75

So, I understand why you left it off, and I do not hold it against you in any way. In fact, that is why you are here today, but we will get into that in a minute."

Things are starting to make a lot more sense now.

"I was not enlisted like you were. I was an officer. I saw a side of the SEALs you may have never seen since you were only in for six years. Having served with Naval Special Warfare Command, I have many friends that I can reach out to for information—even information you would not believe. That is how I found out all about your record and what you have done. I must say I am very impressed by all you accomplished in such a short time. Which brings me to the next question I have for you—why did you get out after six years? Why not make it a career?"

"I loved serving in the military. I loved everything it taught me and everyone I was able to serve with."

"But," Dean interjects seeing it coming.

"But—I was always serving, always gone. If I would have been married during that time I would have maybe seen my wife and kids for six months to a year with all the training and deployments I did. I hope this doesn't sound selfish, but I wanted some me time. Time to find a wife and settle down. War fighting should be a young man's game anyway."

"I understand completely," Dean says. "In today's war fighting world it is almost impossible to raise a family. I don't think you are selfish in the least either. Six years of service in the most elite unit in the United States military is more than ninety-nine point nine percent of people in this country will do, so don't feel selfish at all. I'm glad people like you serve and get out. We need soldiers like you in the civilian world as well. Which brings me to why you are here in this meeting. What do you know about Tom and the reason he no longer works here?"

"To be honest, I've only heard one thing. Some of the valet attendants said he was caught with a prostitute in the parking garage, but I don't believe it for a second. A man of his position wouldn't chance hooking up in the parking garage. Tom is a smart guy."

"No one knows this here except me, and I am about to tell you. Before I do, I want to know what your plans are here. I know you are going to school at UNLV, but what do you really want to do with your life?"

I think for a second before responding. At this point, I can't imagine telling Dean anything other than the absolute truth. He seems to know everything about me already anyway. Since he currently holds the job I want, telling him anything but the truth seems just plain foolish.

"Actually, I want to do exactly what you are doing. I'm going to school for a Hospitality Management degree so I have a better understanding of hotel operations."

"That would appear to be the conventional way up the ladder wouldn't it. I'm here to offer you a quicker, more direct route—if you're smart enough to jump on it—which I'm sure you will be."

"I think I would have to be a fool if I didn't say yes sir without even knowing what you're offering," I quickly respond, hardly able to contain the excitement growing inside me.

"Yes, you would be a fool. Tom, as well as one valet attendant, were let go because they were working with the cartels that have moved into Vegas from Southern California. Are you familiar with any of the cartels or what they are doing in our area?"

77

I fought against some of these cartels in Mexico not too long ago. I have a pretty good idea of how they operate. I know power and money were numero uno for them. Essentially, they were into anything that brought exorbitant amounts of money, which in turn brought unyielding power.

"Anything beyond drugs, power, money, and assassinations I'm not sure. There was talk that some of the cartels were working with the Middle Eastern extremists. They were trying to bring heavy weapons and possibly nuclear bombs into the country. Last I heard, Pakistan lost some of its nuclear arsenal. You didn't hear that from me though."

A short laugh escapes Dean's lips before he says, "I had actually heard that already from one of my Navy contacts, but I am glad you brought it up. It is the reality of the world in which we live in these days. People do not see them, but we have chemical and nuclear detectors in addition to the metal detectors we have all over our hotels for that very reason. I trust the military, but unfortunately it is run by a bunch of bureaucrats now. In today's world anything is possible."

"I feel the same way. That was one of the reasons I got out of the military," I say feeling comfortable I can tell Dean anything.

"Well, I won't keep you guessing any longer. I want to make you Director of Security. Before you say yes or no, hear me out. I understand it isn't general manager, but think about this—security plays a vital role in every aspect of hotel operations. Whether it is food coming into the hotel or who is getting into our guests' rooms. You will have a part to play in every aspect of the operation. Every general manager will be coming to you to make changes or run ideas past you. If you want to see how a hotel operates, I can't think of a better job for you to take on.

I also want you to continue with your schooling. I know the GI Bill pays for your schooling. I'm not concerned about that. What I will tell you though is keep going. After you set up your schedule each semester, let both James and me know when you will be gone so we stay on top of things. You are not getting this job because of your schooling, but I also don't want you to miss out on that part of your life. What you learn here you can use at school, and I expect you will learn some things there that can improve our operation here. Does that sound fair?"

Unable to contain my excitement any longer, I blurt out, "Yes!"

"Are you familiar with Napoleon Hill?"

"No, I haven't heard that name before."

"It does not surprise me. College professors today teach knowledge, but they do not teach you what to do with it. You have probably heard people say that knowledge is power, but they do not understand an important aspect of knowledge. Napoleon Hill said, 'Knowledge is only potential power. It becomes power only when, and if, it is organized into definite plans of action, and directed to a definite end.' He said that almost one hundred years ago, and it still holds true today. I want you to take that knowledge, and put it into practice here. One other thing I forgot to mention— you do realize Tom was Director of Security over several hotels?"

"If I'm not mistaken he ran The City Center as well, correct?"

"Yes, you will run the security for The City Center as well as the Bellagio. When we finally were able to buy out The Jockey Club we decided it best to merge all our security assets. This way we could keep up with concerns on our little block of the Strip. Every hotel has its own general manager, so you will have to be a team player to make

79

it work. I've already spoken with the other general managers about hiring you and they are all on board."

We continue to talk, less about business and more about the good old days. Dean was no slacker himself, having served in Iraq, Bosnia, Kosovo, and a few other places most Americans wouldn't even know we had troops.

Dean also mentions one other item while we are talking, which takes me completely by surprise. Due to heightened security over the last couple years, they bought one suite in Veer Towers in City Center for the Director of Security. That way they could always have that person close in case of an emergency. I guess Tom fought it and never moved in. It might not be the penthouse suite, but there is no way I'm turning it down.

"Oh, one other thing," Dean starts as we stand up to say our goodbyes. "I bet you'd like to know how much you'll be making?"

I had totally forgot about my salary. "That would be nice to know," I casually say as if pay doesn't even matter.

"I know what you made in the military and I know what you make now, so if you want to sit down for this I totally understand."

"I think I'll be good." How high could it be anyways.

"Okay. We are going to start you out at two hundred fifty. As I continue to hear positive things from the the other managers and daily operations continue we can talk about more."

"Two hundred fifty thousand?" The words leave my mouth in complete disbelief.

"I told you you might want to sit down," Dean says seeing me completely taken back.

"I don't know what to say Dean. Um—Thank you," is all I manage to get out.

As we shake hands before departing Dean says, "Trust me. You'll earn every dollar. I know this is much larger than serving on a team, but I also know the knowledge you learned there is much more than any civilian school can teach you out here. I know you can do this."

I thank Dean for his confidence before stumbling out the door in complete amazement to the amount I will make. Jennifer is waiting outside to see my reaction as I come through the door.

"You must not have been fired because that usually only takes a few minutes," she jokes.

"I not only didn't get fired I got a huge promotion!" I reply enthusiastically.

As I'm about to tell her I'm the new Director of Security, Dean gets on the intercom and says, "Jennifer, could you put a packet together for our new Director of Security? He starts next Monday and there is a lot he will need to get spun up on. Also, give him the keys to his new place."

"Director of Security," Jennifer slowly says after Dean finishes. "I knew you didn't have anything to worry about. Since Tom was let go I actually thought he was going to hire you for the job."

"Thanks again for your confidence."

"I'll get that packet put together and email it to you in about an hour. Does that sound good?"

"Sounds good to me. Have a great day!"

"You too, frogman," Jennifer says as I head out the door. I look back and see nothing but a wide smile flash across her face.

As soon as I leave the lobby, I pull out my phone to send Taylor and Scott a text. To my pleasant surprise, Taylor has already sent me a text this morning, *I hope your meeting is everything you want it to be and more. GOOD LUCK!*

It was everything I could have hoped for and more, for sure. I quickly respond to her text, completely forgetting to tell Scott the good news, *Thanks! He made me Director of Security.*

Within five-seconds I see Taylor has read my message and is writing back.

CONGRATULATIONS! Taylor responds. *I'm at home if you want to come pick me up?*

She needn't say more. I quickly text back, *I'll be there in twenty minutes. I have another surprise we can see together.*

FIVE
Zion

The last two and a half months have breezed by except for the assassination of the president. Who would have ever thought in our modern day that would happen. Not only was the president killed but so was the vice-president and the speaker of the house. If I was a conspiracy theorist I would say something is a foot.

In my life though it couldn't have been any better. The suite reserved for me in Veer Towers blows my mind every time I walk through the doors. Right after my meeting with Dean I picked up Taylor and we went directly over to check out the place. I think she almost fainted as we walked in. She said, 'I know where I'm coming to hang out from now on!' She even has her own room and key now. She can get in whenever she wants.

Jewels loves the place too. I bought a bigger Banyan tree and put her in the entry way. It's best to keep her over the tile. When she decides to make a mess it's simple to clean up that way. Plus, with her in the entryway, everyone gets to see her as they come and go. I don't forget about her this way as well. All my close friends have spent some time gazing at her, wondering why I have a snake as a pet. I'm sure a few of them think I'm crazy. I just say it's Scott's fault.

The view is to live for, as I've come accustomed to saying now. My friends can't help but stare out the floor to ceiling glass that lines the northeast wall. The contemporary feel of the building, as well as every detail of the tower, is a picture of beauty formed with steel and glass. Whenever I come home, the feeling of how blessed I am overtakes me. From the marble floors to the twelve-foot high ceilings. I haven't even mentioned the pool on the roof, the private lounge on the top floor, or the valet parking available twenty-four seven. It's more than I could have ever dreamed. Then there's the pay which still dumbfounds me every time a deposit hits my bank account.

As far as my relationship with Taylor goes, I couldn't be happier. We've opened up a little more about our lives now that we've known each other for almost three months. Everything Taylor told me that first night makes perfect sense now. When she was a senior in high school she got a little too drunk one night at a party and some jocks tried to take advantage of her. It was from that moment on she made up her mind to remain in complete control of her mind and body.

Those despicable human beings had torn all her clothing from her body and were within inches of raping her. Thank goodness someone came into the room and put a stop to it. I tried once to get the names of the jocks, but she wouldn't tell me. Knowing more of my training now, I think she was afraid I would make them disappear.

I can't imagine the emotional strain it has put her through. I will say that she seems a stronger person for it though. What doesn't kill you only makes you stronger. My BUDS instructors would tell us that all the time. Funny thing is—I really thought they were trying to kill us.

Even though I haven't dropped every minute detail on her, she understands the vast majority of what I've done and where I've been as a SEAL. Too much too soon would be more than she could handle I fear. War is an ugly disease that no one need ever see or hear about. Unfortunately, it's infecting the world with its death and destruction like never before.

The job has been a little rough at times. James showed his obvious frustration at first, but after some assertion on my part, things fell into place. Scott wanted a little more action when I moved over as well. I brought him in at the Bellagio. Dean had no issues once he learned of his background with British SAS. I also had a meeting with all the general managers. Dean wanted me to introduce myself and give an evaluation on where I currently saw things and where I wanted them to go. Each one of them was glad I was on board, and expressed their willingness to do whatever it takes to keep their guests safe.

Taylor and I are heading to Zion National Park for my birthday. I persuaded Dean to let me take a few days off. Technically, all the general managers are my boss, but I deal mostly with Dean. The rest of our friends will be heading up tomorrow, so today will be some alone time for Taylor and I.

We left the city early this morning. It's only eight now. We're about an hour north of Vegas, just past Mesquite, when I realize the two-month time period has passed. Taylor probably thought I had forgotten. It's time to remind her of the story she promised to tell me on our first date.

"Do you remember that first date we had? You told me to remind you about a story you wanted to tell me."

I can see she's trying to sleep, but thinking of it just now has my interest piqued. Taylor crashed at my place last night. We stayed up pretty late hanging out at the pool, just talking.

"I know you heard me blue eyes," I say, as I see her rustle a little under her pillow.

"I was hoping you had forgotten about that," Taylor mutters under her pillow. "I don't know why I told you that in the first place. I guess I wasn't thinking straight."

"Well you did, so let's hear it. You said it would be worth the wait, and I forgot about it until now. With everything that has happened over the last couple months, I'm surprised I remembered it at all."

Taylor tilts her chair up and leans over and gives me a kiss. I love every one of them.

"I did say I would share it with you. Let me think for a second. I want to tell you, but I also want to do it the right way."

"Sounds fair. Let me turn off the music so you're not distracted," I say in anticipation.

"A little over three years ago I was struggling with what had happened at the party as well as just being dumped by my boyfriend. My mom sat me down one night and had a very long chat with me. At the end of the talk she told me she felt impressed to share some thoughts she had been having over the last year. She said she felt I would continue to work, date, go to school, and generally enjoy my life, but I wouldn't find the right one until…you don't know how hard it is to tell you this."

"I can imagine. You don't know how hard it was to tell you I was in the Navy. I didn't want to mess up a good thing that first night. Then I told you about that dream I had. I thought for sure you would think I was crazy."

"I didn't think you were crazy. You'll see in a few seconds why."

"I can't wait to hear."

"My mom then proceeded to tell me how she felt like I would continue to date a few more years until I would go on a date with a guy that would absolutely repulse me. She then said after this horrible date I would want to go home, but if I wanted to find someone that would truly treat me as she always hoped and knew that I deserved, I couldn't go home." She pauses briefly to inhale and then lets out a short sigh. "The guy I went out with before I came to the bowling alley absolutely repulsed me. I never told you about him did I?"

"No. You can tell me about him later so I can take care of him. I want to hear the rest of your story," I say eagerly.

"Remind me another day," Taylor says smiling at my comment before continuing. "My mom wasn't sure how I would meet you or how it would work out. It seemed kind of strange that I would have to stay out after already going on a date. But anyway, after my date I did feel like going home, but I knew my friends were at the bowling alley…I really don't want to tell you this."

"Trust me, you have nothing to be afraid of."

"Ok, fine, I'll just tell you," Taylor says fidgeting with her phone with nervous trepidation, and quickening her speech. "She said I would find my soul mate if I stayed out and didn't get discouraged. I had completely forgotten what she shared with me until you told me your dream that night. I don't know if you noticed, but I got kind of emotional that night."

I keep my eyes on the road and lean over to give Taylor a kiss. I wish I wasn't driving now because this moment deserves so much more. I don't say anything for a time, letting the moment speak for itself.

"I saw your eyes were wet that night, but I wasn't quite sure what it was for. I appreciate your story. It was worth waiting for. I didn't tell you this that night either, but in my dream I felt like I was sitting next to someone special. I don't really know how to explain it. It was a dream I've never had before, and I'm sure I'll never have again. I thought you were too good to be true."

"I don't know about that. I was thinking it was the other way around. I don't know if you believe in this stuff. I was somewhat of a skeptic when my mom told me the story, but after meeting you and now looking back at the last two and a half months...I'm a believer."

"Oh, I'm a believer. Something I can't explain has brought me through more difficult times and deadly situations than I can count on all my fingers and toes. I don't know what it is, but I know it's on my side."

"Speaking of my mom, I've tried to get you over to their house several times, but things haven't worked out. My dad seems to be gone every time you have a free second and I want you to meet them together. They are definitely a package deal. Maybe after this trip he'll make it a point to be home. He knows I spend every free second I have with you. They know everything about you."

"When the time comes, I hope I don't disappoint."

"That's impossible! I think you'll really like them."

Arriving in Saint George, we decide to gas up even though we are only thirty minutes from Zion. I don't remember getting gas in Saint George before, but as I look at the prices I'm shocked. Super unleaded is going for eight bucks a gallon. Just yesterday when I drove past a gas station the prices were still in the mid five-dollar range. It can't be that much more expensive an hour and a half up the road. What's going on here?

"Can you believe how expensive the gas is up here?" I ask Taylor.

Taylor looks out the window and instantly her mouth falls open. "What! They have to be out of their minds up here. Don't fill up. I'm sure it's cheaper down the road."

I know gas is expensive on the outside of town, but more than three dollars a gallon seems insane.

"I'll just fill up, we're here already. We only have half a tank so it shouldn't be too bad."

I fill up and then we make it over to the grocery store to pick up supplies for the trip. Everything seems reasonably priced here so I rationalize the owner of that gas station must have been out of his mind.

We jump back on the interstate and continue north until we reach the exit that leads us into Zion. A days head start should be good for Taylor. I've only taken her climbing a few times so the extra day to work on technique should help her out tremendously before the rest of the group joins us tomorrow. As we get closer and closer to Zion the rocks get bigger and bigger, and their color becomes even more vibrant than those we are accustomed to in Vegas. I'm at a loss to describe the beauty contained here. All the trees that line the road add the feeling as if we were driving through a shady tunnel, not so claustrophobic though. Taylor can get a little shaky in tight spaces.

I brought some bouldering pads so we can spend most of the morning climbing a variety of things without having to throw on a harness or worry about ropes or quick draws. Zion has a couple of really nice bouldering rocks in the park. We are headed to a house-sized rock just inside the south entrance to the park. It's too early to check in to our hotel so we figured we'd get an early start in the park.

I haven't taken Taylor bouldering yet so as I mention it to her she asks, "What's bouldering again?"

"It's an easy way to work on technique and build forearm, finger, and hand strength. You'll climb around on a rock not usually more than ten feet off the ground working on anything and everything you can. It's nice because you can just throw your chalk bag on your waist and put your shoes on."

"No ropes or anything?"

"No ropes. When you're climbing I'll have the bouldering pad under you just in case you fall. I've fallen on it from fifteen or twenty feet and it was like hitting my bed at night. Trust me—you're in good hands. I won't let anything happen to that pretty face."

Taylor simpers as I mention her looks. She's so out of this world. I don't think she really knows to what extent. And I'm not just talking about what's on the outside. The whole package makes her more than marriage material. Normally I wouldn't be having thoughts of marriage so soon, but I can't help it. I think about it all the time. Right from day one the whole thing has been a dream. I've already bought the ring. If things go as planned, I'll pop the question this weekend.

As we pull up to the gate at Zion, the canyons come into full view.

"This has got to be one of the most spectacular places on earth," Taylor says as she stares out the window in amazement.

"I told you you would love it. I still can't believe you've never come up here with your family. It's so close."

"I know. What was my dad thinking? I guess if he had been home more it might have happened."

90

"What did you say your dad did again?"

"He's a hydraulic engineer. He works for InMotion on their international projects. That's why he's always off to the Middle East or South America or some other country most people haven't heard about."

"I remember you telling me that now. At least he gets to see a lot of the world."

"He does. I think he's been on every continent several times over the last twenty-one years with the company. I know it's been hard for my mom, but I also know it's made her stronger."

"Let's plan a date with the two of them when we get back. We can go over to their house or out to eat, they can decide," I suggest, truly hoping I hit it off with them.

"I'll set it up as soon as we get back," Taylor says as we pull into the parking lot.

Just west of the main entrance I see the gigantic rock we will spend most of the morning on. It's probably not more than twenty feet high with a variety of difficulty levels for Taylor to work on—from easy to inverted.

"I know we are climbing this morning, but what do you have planned for the rest of the day?" Taylor asks as we step out of the car.

"I was thinking of climbing for three or four hours before we check into the hotel, shower up, and then head back into town. I don't want us to be too tired before the climbs tomorrow."

"I think we'll have to go all the way back to Saint George. It didn't look like there was much to do in those last few towns we passed through."

Taylor is right. There were a couple of fast food restaurants, but I didn't see much of anything at all for entertainment. There was a theater, but it looked pretty dinky.

"We'll head back in to Hurricane first and check it out, but I bet you're right. There wasn't much there."

I get on the rock first. I figure I'll show Taylor why bouldering can be so beneficial and then set her loose. I climb around on the rock for ten minutes before Taylor says she wants to give it a try. When she does hop on she takes off. She looks like a natural. I could watch her all day from this angle.

"See if you can climb all the way around the rock without touching the ground."

"I can do that," Taylor says with confidence.

She continues to climb as I carry the pad at my side. She hasn't gone more than five feet off the ground yet. I think she's building up her confidence first. I know she's not afraid of heights, but at the same time she doesn't want to fall. The rock is about a couple hundred feet around so if she makes it she'll certainly show good stamina.

I continue to watch as Taylor arrives at the hardest section of the rock. A couple feet ahead the rock inverts at a seventy-degree angle making her use more upper body strength than normal. The inverted section spans twenty feet. I don't say anything, but I move in closer with the pad. If she does fall at least it will be soft. If she makes it through this area I will be thoroughly impressed. I know she's tough, but even I have had rough times in this section.

"Have you done this before?" Taylor asks as she looks ahead.

"Yeah—I won't tell you it's easy. I've fallen through this part several times."

"So, that's why you moved closer with that pad?"

"Make it through this part and you'll be ready for anything I throw at you tomorrow. I'll even buy you lunch today."

Taylor begins to laugh before saying, "You would buy me lunch anyway. I don't think you've let me pay for a thing since we met."

"Are you complaining?" I say in a playful manner.

"Not at all. It's more than I could ask for and I thank you for it. Even the tips you give me at work are more than generous."

I went to The Cheesecake Factory before, but now I love to go. Taylor all dressed in white looks like my own personal angel. It's a nice break to my day also. Every time she brings the bill she tells me not to tip her. What can I say, I feel like I'm investing in the future.

"I think with your tips alone I can pay for my next semester's tuition."

I work five to six days a week and I make it in everyday she's there. She was already working the swing shift when I met her due to school so it worked out perfectly.

"Do you have that pad ready? I don't know how much longer my hands will hold on," Taylor says with uncertainty audible in her voice.

"I'm right under you. You're good."

As Taylor started traversing the inverted section, she started to climb higher and now sits about ten feet off the ground.

"You can make it. You've already made it further than I did the first time I tried this section," I say hoping to help build her confidence before she doubts herself more.

Just then her hands slip. Using both hands to hold onto the rock, she wasn't able to chalk up. They must have gotten too sweaty causing her to slip off. I'm right there as Taylor falls on the pad. As I reach down to help her up, she pulls me onto the mat with her.

"Give me a big kiss," Taylor says as I land on top of her.

I tell her what an outstanding job she did for her first time bouldering.

"I think I could have made it if my hands weren't so sweaty."

"I think you could have too. You look like a natural up there. The view was outstanding."

"Thanks," she says with her innocent smile. "Let me see you climb through that section. Watching you will probably give me some tips. For starters, how do you reach one hand into your bag when you need both on the wall?"

"I'll show you. Sometimes you have to get creative. It all comes with time though. You'll be there before you know it," I tell Taylor as I pull her to her feet.

I get on the rock in the same place she did so she can see another way to traverse the area. Taylor is a quick learner so I don't say much as I climb. I know she's watching intently and will pick up the subtleties that make climbing easier. Strength is important, but technique is even more important.

"You're right—the view is great from down here," Taylor says as I continue to climb.

After I traverse the inverted section Taylor wants to try again. She tries a couple more times before finally making it on her fourth attempt.

"I knew you could do it."

"I thought I had it on number three. At least I made it though."

"I knew you wouldn't give up until you did. Now you can practice just climbing up that section."

We climb until noon before heading to the hotel. We were worried about not being able to check in early, but the receptionist was more than accommodating. Taylor hops in the shower first while I lie on the bed and watch the news.

Things have been getting pretty crazy in the world since getting my new job. The stock market hit thirty thousand for the first time in history a month ago. The economists have been saying it's only a matter of time before the bubble pops. The feds have been pumping so much money into the market over the last few years, even I have taken notice.

Normally I don't follow financial matters, but with Europe falling into financial crisis and the Middle East following suit, I can't help but wonder when it will hit here. On CNN they're talking about oil commodities and how the price of oil has gone through the roof due to every ally we have in the Middle East and South America shutting off our supply lines. Not to mention the uncertainty of the United States with the designated survivor still siting in the presidents place.

Now the outrageous gas prices in Saint George make a little more sense. I didn't see a station before we left Vegas, but I bet we'll be in for a rude awakening when we get home. On FOX, they're reporting on the war in Iran and how many allies in the region have thrown in support for Iran since we started the invasion. Our leaders might have bitten off more than they could chew with this one. It isn't good for the military either. It will only make their job that much more difficult.

"It's your turn Deacon," Taylor says as she steps out of the bathroom wrapped in nothing but a white towel.

I wanted so much to jump in the shower with her. What can I say—I'm a sailor, not a saint. With the feelings of love growing stronger by the day and the thought of marriage popping into my head all the time, it's getting harder and harder to restrain myself. If I were to make a move I don't know what she would do. I can't tell you how hard it's been. Especially with her crashing at my place all the time now.

I've talked to my mom quite a few times about the situation and each time she's made me stronger. Each time she's said, 'Just think how much more special it will be when it happens on your wedding night. I know you are strong. You can do it. Also, try not to put yourself in those tough spots.' I tell myself that every time she's over late, and inevitably she ends up staying. It's a good thing Taylor's a rock because I probably would have faltered two months ago. Every time things get a little too heavy, she stops and changes the subject. I don't know how she does it. Her will power is off the charts.

"Sounds good, you've got to see what's going on right now," I say, barely able to turn my attention back to the television. "Remember that eight dollar a gallon gas this morning? I think it's here to stay."

"Why is that?" Taylor asks, wondering what I've just seen.

I tell her about Iran and our oil prices going through the roof. I can see the price hitting ten dollars a gallon before the week is over.

Taylor knows I could sit and watch the news for hours. She indulges me most of the time because she knows I have a vested interest in the lives of those serving overseas. She does as well, but it's not quite the same—it's much more personal for me.

"Get in there Deacon," Taylor says as she caresses my shirtless back. "I've got to get dressed and you know you can't be out here when I drop this towel."

"Okay, okay. You know you're making this harder and harder looking like that," I say as I give her a slight slap on the butt. "Be thinking about where you want to eat though."

"Will do," she says with her mischievous smile.

When I get in the shower I can't help but think how great my life is now—even though it seems the world is falling apart faster each day. I have an outstanding job, great friends, and the most wonderful woman in the whole world.

As I start to wash my face I hear Taylor open the door. Then with the most fearful tone I've heard to date she says, "Deacon—something dreadful is happening on the strip."

SIX

Chaos

Chills are running up and down my spine, and it's certainly not being caused by the water running over me.

"What's going on?" I say, concerned by the fear I hear in her voice.

"I would try to explain it to you, but you need to see it for yourself."

Now I'm really anxious. What could possible be happening on the strip? It's the middle of the day. The trip is just getting started. Everyone's coming up tomorrow.

"Let me rinse off real quick and I'll be right out."

Taylor closes the door and I quickly wash the soap from my body. Turning off the water, I can hear Taylor talking to someone in the other room. About to ask Taylor who called, she opens the door again and hands me the phone.

"It's Scott," Taylor says with the same frightened look I saw just seconds ago.

Wrapping my towel around my waist and grabbing the phone I say, "What's going on?"

"There's panic in the streets here. I don't know what's happening, but you better get back here quick."

"Is anything happening in the hotels yet?"

"I'm in the Bellagio right now, and it hasn't spilled over here yet. I haven't been able to get anyone else on the radio so I'm not sure what City Center is looking like."

"Okay. Do me a favor. Call James and see what he needs you to do. I'm throwing some clothes on right now. Taylor and I will be back in town in an hour and a half, two at the tops. I'll call Dean and then call you back."

Taylor just stands there—as if paralyzed—while I talk to Scott. I watch her intently. It is clear that she is unsettled. She furrows her eyebrows. For a second, I catch her eyes. They are a deep blue—filled with agitation, foreboding, and an undeniable longing. They look like the sky just before a storm.

"Taylor?" I ask quizzically, "are you okay?"

Even though she is in the same room with me she feels so far away. I reach out and softly trace my fingertips down her arm and into her hand. I gently pull her in one step closer. She looks up at me. Our eyes meet.

"Deacon, I…I'm…"

I watch her eyes lower and follow a droplet of water run down my chest.

She steps closer. I can smell her. I close my eyes and drink in the sweet smell of honeysuckle and jasmine. I feel her exhaling softly near my neck. I hear an almost inaudible gasp as I wrap my hands around the small of her back and pull her into me.

"I love you Taylor," I whisper in her ear.

I feel her surrender her fears to the protective strength of my arms.

She looks up at me, her blue eyes penetrating deeper and deeper into my soul. It feels as though she sees me in a way that no one else has.

"I love you too Deacon."

A nuclear bomb could have gone off in the next room and neither one of us would have known.

"Just promise me Deacon," Taylor begins, pulling away slightly to look in my eyes. I see tears glistening in hers. "Never mind Deacon," Taylor finishes, shaking her head slightly in an attempt to fight off the emotion that is surging. She turns quietly and walks out of the bathroom.

As I step out, I see Taylor fixated on the television—she's never been so drawn to the television.

"Scott said there's chaos in the streets and he can hear gun fire out in front of the Bellagio. What did you see?" I ask.

Taylor doesn't respond or even turn to look at me. She's focused and unwavering as she stares in disbelief at the television. Walking over to get a better view I instantly see what has her tongue-tied. The major news networks are reporting the stock market has lost more than seventy-five percent of its value and it's plummeting still by the second. I thought they had stopgaps in place to prevent that. In between reports of the stock market crash, the national news keeps cutting to major cities across the country that have fallen into complete chaos as looters and gangs ransack businesses and shoot people openly in the streets.

"Pack your stuff! You're right—we have to get back there now."

Just then my phone rings again. It's Scott.

100

"What's up?"

"I can't reach James and there are mobs of people going into the Paris hotel right now. It's only a matter of time before they make their way up here. I haven't been able to get anyone on the radio. What do you want me to do?" Scott says in a tone I've never heard come out of his mouth.

Hearing Scott's apprehension and knowing his background truly has me worried now. "Put all the buildings on lockdown. No one in or out. Go to the safe and give everyone you trust a rifle with the standard load. Once you have the Bellagio secure go to City Center and do the same over there. Find Matt. He can get you into the safe. We have hundreds of rifles in there. Can you handle all that?"

"I can manage," Scott says with a firmer voice. Confidence comes with carrying a rifle over just a handgun hidden on your side.

"One other thing—you know our rules of engagement are different here than where we've been. Not being there, I trust your judgement. Remember—your life and the life of those that work for us come first. Don't forget the guests as well."

"I've got it. Just hurry back here."

"I'm moving as fast as I can. See you in a bit and stay safe."

Taylor still watches the news, not able to pry herself from the destruction and senseless loss of life occurring all across the country. About to grab Taylor and bring her back to reality, the news cuts to a helicopter shot over Las Vegas Boulevard. A crowd of one to two hundred people are moving south down the boulevard just in front of Treasure Island. I can't see it due to the distance they're flying, but I'm sure they're carrying weapons. They're about a mile away from the Bellagio. I'll never make it back before they get there. Let's hope they get held up by the other hotels en route.

"Taylor," I say as I step right in front of her, blocking her view of the television. "We have to get our stuff together and get back there now."

"I don't want you to go back there," she manages to spit out. "Let's just stay here. It's peaceful and no one is trying to kill anyone."

As tempting as that sounds, I know I have to go back. I wouldn't be able to live with myself if I left my team and Scott there to fend for themselves. Six years of my life has been spent training and fighting for moments like this. To stay and hide now would be the most shameful thing I could possibly do. How do I get Taylor to understand that though?

"As much as I would love to stay with you right here forever, I have to go back. This whole thing will blow over within twenty-four hours once the police get involved."

"This isn't a local problem," Taylor begins. "This madness is consuming the country. Do you remember reading about the L.A. riots in school? Those lasted for days. This mess makes those look like child's play, and these are playing out all across the country. Who knows—maybe across the globe."

"I understand, but I wouldn't be able to live with myself if I stayed here. What if Scott got killed? What if Bobbi or Melissa or Savanah or any one of our friends on the strip got killed and we could have been there to help them? I know you didn't know me as a SEAL, but trust me when I say this, I can handle this with your support." I don't like to bring up my SEAL days, but I hope it garners some strength in her to trust me now more than ever.

Taylor doesn't say anything for a long minute as she continues to watch the news. On the east coast where organized crime is more prevalent, the situation looks more serious. There are massive fires in Philadelphia and New York. The destruction looks far worse than what I saw in Vegas. I don't want to rush Taylor, but we need to get going now.

"Okay, let's go. I'm not leaving your side once we get back," Taylor says with decidedly more conviction as she starts throwing her things back in her suitcase.

"Okay," I agree. I don't tell her this, but I know I have to get her up to my place so I'm not worrying about her. Once we get back into Vegas I hope she'll see that the safest place for her is tucked away in Veer Tower, suite 2312.

I quickly get dressed and throw all my things in the suitcase. Taylor has finished packing as well. As we rush out to the parking lot I'm struck with a surreal feeling I've never experienced before. I look around the park and everything is so peaceful, so serene. In comparison to what we just witnessed on television. The grass is green and vibrant, the rich red rock cliffs pierce the brilliant blue sky like spires, and the soft breeze blowing through the trees stirs the soul. I get the feeling Zion won't erupt into chaos like the rest of the country—like it's different here. I didn't know how to describe it earlier, but now, as I look at the beauty, it feels like what heaven would be like if there is such a place. When this chaos clears, Taylor and I will have to come back here and finish what we started. Maybe we will even get married here.

"I'm glad we already filled up. Now we can jump on the interstate and head straight back," I say as Taylor and I jump in the Jeep.

Taylor doesn't respond. She still looks worried. I have to get her mind off what she just saw play out on television. She's a strong woman. I know she can handle this.

"When this all clears up we'll have to come back up here with your parents. They'll be…"

"I have to call my parents!" Taylor interrupts as she fumbles through her purse in search of her phone.

I messed that one up. Now she's going to be worrying about both them and me. I hope she gets them on the phone otherwise her concern will double if not triple on the way home. I better call my mom too. I didn't see any footage from San Diego, but I'm sure it's bad there as well.

Taylor calls her dad first, unfortunately he doesn't answer. Then she calls her mom a little more frantic—luckily she answers the phone. Taylor learns her dad is at the store and her mom is home alone. She had been watching the news and was worried about Taylor. Nothing has happened in her neighborhood yet. Taylor tells her mom to lock all the doors and get dad home as fast as possible. When she hangs up the phone she seems a little bit more relaxed knowing her parents are safe.

I was able to get a hold of my mom as well. She lives in a more affluent neighborhood right on the beach, like Taylor's parents, except for the beach. Everything appeared calm there. She didn't seem frightened at all. I hope it stays that way. I won't be able to make it to San Diego for quite some time if she does get in trouble. I let her know Taylor and I are headed back to Vegas. She had seen the madness there and worried I was right in the middle of it.

'Son, This is the beginning of the end. I love you and be safe.' Those were her last words to me before we hung up. My mom has been a religious person her whole life. We went to so many different churches when I was growing up, I hardly know what denomination she belongs to. I know she believes Jesus is her Savior, but apart from that I couldn't tell you.

As for me, I've seen too much in this world to have much of a belief in anything anymore. Even though I try not to let it occupy my thoughts, I understand her reference to the beginning of the end comment.

Even though my mom knows all about my past and my training, she is still my mom and will most assuredly worry about me. Her motherly instincts have kicked into overdrive when such obvious danger finds its way into the picture. During my time in the Navy she didn't want to hear my war stories. She said she would only worry more if she knew what I was doing. When I got out she asked to hear one story. I related one not so dangerous story, and that was enough, she didn't want to hear any more.

After getting Taylor's emotions somewhat in check, I remember I need to call Dean. I call several times, trying his cell phone as well as his office line, but to no avail. Jennifer is always at her desk— I'll give her a call. I call her desk phone and every time it rings and rings until the machine picks up. I try her cell phone next and nothing. Not able to reach either one of them I give Scott a call back. Scott doesn't answer his phone either.

"Can you keep trying Scott's phone? He isn't answering," I ask, handing my phone to Taylor.

Sensing the apprehension in my voice, she gently responds, "I'm sure he is fine. I'll keep trying though." She reassuringly rests her hand on my arm as I drive south. It is such a simple gesture, but I draw such strength from her warm touch.

Taylor also tries to call Savanah. She works in The Forum Shops at Cesar's Palace with Taylor. She doesn't get a hold of her. I can only imagine what a mob of miscreants would do running rampant through those shops. I hope Savanah got out safe. She came climbing with us the few times we were able to get up to Red Rock Canyon. I've come to enjoy spending time with her as well.

"Do you think Savanah is safe?" Taylor asks, unable to hide the concern in her voice.

"Our friends are resourceful. They are strong. I'm sure they're all okay."

After hearing the fear in Scott's voice and seeing the news, I know they're in serious trouble. I don't want Taylor to know how bad it really is though. She has to stay collected if I want to keep her safe. A disheveled daisy never pleased anyone—it always withers and dies. I can't let that happen.

As we approached Mesquite, the freeway remained fairly empty. Mesquite is relatively small so it's no wonder everything looked under control as we passed through. We are now almost to the Indian reservation—a half an hour outside of Vegas. Taylor still hasn't been able to reach any of our friends on the strip. Dean and Jennifer are still not picking up their phones. I don't tell Taylor, but I don't have a good feeling about what we're going to find when we get back there. As we pass through the Valley of Fire, Scott calls.

"Are you almost here?" Scott asks with more fervor than the last time we spoke.

"We just passed Moapa. What's going on? Have you talked to Dean or any of our friends? We've been trying to call everyone, but no one's answering."

"It's not good here. At least I have the Bellagio secure. Melissa made it over here as well as Bobbi, but I haven't heard from anyone else. I haven't had time to do anything. I haven't even made it up to Dean's office. There was a gun fight at one of the west entrances to the hotel, but I think we have it all locked up now. I don't think Matt and I will be able to make it over to City Center. There are hordes of people outside trying to get in right now."

"Okay—stay put. If you can, go up and check on Dean and Jennifer. As soon as we get back we'll secure what we can of the hotels at City Center. Have you been able to see the news? Am I going to be able to get into Vegas?"

"Last I saw, the interstate was clear. You won't be here for another twenty minutes though—anything is possible between now and then."

"I just hope it's clear when we get there. Stay safe and call me back if anything changes."

"Will do. Be safe out there. It's complete pandemonium in the streets here. I wouldn't come down the Boulevard if I were you."

"We won't. We'll find another way in."

I know Taylor will worry, but knowing Melissa and Bobbi made it to the Bellagio gives me hope that Savanah made it out safe as well.

"Since Scott has the Bellagio locked down, we are going to City Center. We have to make sure those hotels are safe. After that's done I'll drop you off at our place and head over and talk to Dean."

"Do you think I'll be safe there? What if the mobs have already made it inside?"

"Those two towers are fortresses. I've spent lots of time with the security at all the hotels, but probably a little more at Veer Towers. People live there year round, so the general manager and I put a few extra security precautions in place. The security is top notch. They have their own arsenal there as well. That reminds me—jump in the back—under the seat there is a long lock box. The code is seven, three, two, five. Inside you'll find a rifle and two handguns. Grab all three."

Taylor goes right to work without even questioning my instructions. She might be stressed, but she's not stupid. She knows the advantage a rifle can be in the hands of someone who wants to protect life—someone who will only take life when there's absolutely no other option.

"Do you want all the magazines out?" Taylor asks.

"Yes. Just set everything up on the seat back there."

"What are these little white cylinder things?" Taylor asks.

"Those are flash bangs. It's all the noise of a grenade with none of the punch. It's amazing the things you can get when you run security for such a large corporation. I thought I'd never have to use them. That might just change in about fifteen minutes."

"Hold on babe!" I yell out as cars come barreling north in the southbound lane.

At exit fifty-eight, just outside of Vegas, traffic was traveling north in the southbound lane as I came around the bend. Taylor couldn't grab anything fast enough and as I swerved she hit her head on the back bar.

"You alright babe? I don't know why there are cars driving in our lane. Hurry and jump back in your seat. I'll feel safer once you're buckled up."

"I'll be okay. It's going to leave a bump though," Taylor says as she climbs back into her seat holding her head.

I reach over to feel her head, "I'm so sorry. I should have been more careful babe. We'll get some ice on it as soon as we can."

"Look at all these cars heading out of Vegas," Taylor says still holding her head. "I hope we can make it in."

"We'll be fine. Look at us. We're the only ones dumb enough to drive into Vegas while all these bright people are bailing out." Taylor laughs a bit at the thought.

After dodging a few cars, the entire city comes into view. The dark, black, billowing smoke dotting the city doesn't look too enticing. Up ahead on the interstate there appears to be a group of people creating a road block with cars on the northbound lanes. The southbound lanes still appear to be open. The traffic heading north makes more sense now. I hope we don't get into anything on the outskirts of town.

Just north of the Las Vegas Speedway, a gang of troublemakers appears to be moving hundreds of cars onto the road so no one can get out of the city. We barely make it through the southbound lanes as one of the lookouts begins firing at us. I grab Taylor's head, pushing it down, as one bullet breaks through the back window on the driver's side and out the front passenger's side window—just barely missing Taylor's head. The glass spiders where the bullet exited the car just next to where Taylor's head would have been.

"That was close. Are you alright?" I ask Taylor, completely aware now of what we are facing.

"I'm fine."

"Have you ever been shot at?" I ask Taylor in preparation of getting her mind wrapped around the notion that she must listen to every single word I say.

"Never," she said, her voice cracking.

"Ok. I need you to listen very closely. We are going to be shot at more before the day is over. If you want to stay alive, like I want you to, you must listen to every word I say without fail. I might seem harsh at times and even mean, but know that everything I do from here on out is for your safety."

"I'll listen." Taylor pauses as her eyes begin to well up again, "I love you."

Those three words mean more to me than she can imagine. The situation seems so surreal I'm at a loss. If my determination to keep her alive wasn't permeating my every thought before, it certainly is now.

"I love you too babe, but listen carefully. Everything I tell you is to keep you and me alive. I don't want you thinking for a second we are not going to make it through this. You need to get those negative thoughts out of your head. Don't let them creep in."

"Okay," Taylor says fighting back the emotion.

"I do love you Taylor. Probably more than words can explain."

Taylor leans over and gives me a kiss on the cheek as she whispers in my ear, "I love you too."

She doesn't realize it, but focusing her mind on the future will help her get through the present. I, on the other hand, must focus on

110

the here and now. We've already been shot at and we're not even downtown yet. I can only imagine how bad it will be.

"We're going to stay on the freeway. At Harmon Avenue we're going to park and enter into City Center through the Vdara. My guys should have that placed locked down tight already. From there, we'll hit Aria and the Mandarin. Once I know those three places are secure we'll go over to Veer Towers. With you inside my place and fully armed I'll make my way over to the Bellagio to check on Scott and the rest of my team. Can you handle all that?"

"Yeah. I should be good at that point. How long do you think you'll leave me there by myself?"

"I should be back in less than an hour. Last time I talked to Scott, he had the Bellagio locked down. I should be able to get in and out. I just need to talk to Dean—see what he wants to do."

Taylor is so focused she doesn't hear her phone ringing. "Someone's calling you," I say pointing to her phone.

Taylor flips her phone over to see her mother calling. She answers the phone and pleasantly hears that her dad has made it home and they're safe. Taylor tells her mother she's back in the city and about to go into City Center. Her mother doesn't like that idea, but hopes she's in good hands with me. Then Taylor hands me her phone and says, "My mom wants to talk to you."

As I put the phone to my ear, I know what she's going to say before she utters the words. Before she has a chance to speak I say, "Mrs. Sanders, your daughter is in good hands."

"Call me Nancy, please. She's my only child. Please keep her safe."

"I know I've only been with Taylor for nearly three months, but I love her more than life itself. I'll keep her safe."

"Thank you," Nancy says as she hangs up the phone.

"Remember how you said there's nothing worth dying for? I think I've found something."

"I love you too, but remember you said we don't need to talk about those things. We are both making it through this," Taylor says with her beautiful smile and bright blue eyes.

When we arrive at Harmon Avenue there are only a few cars moving on the interstate. We pull over under the overpass and get out of the car. I quickly grab one of the handguns and hand it to Taylor.

"I've never seen you shoot, but I assume you know how since you carry one with you. I need you to cover our six. Can you handle that?"

"I've shot quite a bit," Taylor says. "I can hold my own when it comes to hitting a target."

"That's good because you may just need to hit a target before the day is over." I know she's never shot at something shooting back, but keeping her confident right now is paramount.

I grab the assault rifle and handgun off the back seat and load every pocket I can with magazines. I give Taylor a magazine and have her load the handgun to see that she knows how to work it. She performs the load and rack flawlessly, like she'd executed it a million times.

"Impressive," I utter. "How many magazines do you want?"

"I can put one in each pocket, so give me two more, please."

"Where is this renewed vigor coming from?" I say, not able to understand the strength she now exhibits.

"You said we'll make it through this. I'm confident. I've also been shooting guns ever since I can remember. My dad wanted to make sure I would always be safe if he wasn't there to protect me."

"You ready?"

"Let's do it," Taylor says holding her right index finger on the slide of the gun. Dad taught her well.

"Do you see the employee entrance to the parking garage just on the other side of the fence? Once we get inside I'll feel a little better. From there we'll be able to go all the way into the hotel."

"Okay."

We run across the interstate, and I jump the fence first. Taylor hands over my rifle and her handgun before leaping the fence like an Olympic athlete. I tell Taylor to stay behind the bushes as I make sure there's no one guarding the rear entrance. Everything looks clear as we start our run across Frank Sinatra Drive.

"Stay right on my back!"

Suuup.

A gunshot sails past from the south under the overpass. As I hear the bullets fly past, without thinking I turn, acquire the target, and put one round through their head. I have no idea who they were or why they were shooting, but I know they just tried to kill one of us.

As I turn to tell Taylor that we have to keep moving my heart hits the pavement—Taylor is laying facedown on the ground motionless behind me.

SEVEN
Flash Back

"Good afternoon Miss Jones," I cheerfully greet Dean's secretary as I open her door.

"Deacon, please call me Jennifer," she replies with a subtle roll of her eyes at my stubborn professionalism. She turns and gracefully slides out of the car.

"I see you got a new car. How are you enjoying it?"

Jennifer stands tall next to her brand new diamond white Mercedes C-Series sedan in her four inch, open-toed stilettos, highly tailored charcoal grey pencil skirt, and fitted white button-down dress shirt. A satisfied gleam dances in her eyes as she gazes over at it.

"It's amazing! Tom kept nagging me about it. He said it was time to put my old Honda Accord out of its misery."

"It is definitely a beautiful car. This isn't the AMG S model is it?"

"No. I did take the AMG for a test drive though. I know it sounds crazy, but I loved feeling the acceleration pull me back into the seat. It was exhilarating." She pauses and laughs playfully. "It was almost intoxicating," she sighs.

"I can imagine."

"Anyway, I loved it. Tom can be pretty persuasive. He claimed it was time that I finally spoiled myself a little. I was tempted, but I just couldn't bring myself to do it. It seemed too extravagant—even if it could go 0-60 in 3.9 seconds. I'm happy with my C-350. I'm completely sold on it. So much so that I've refused to let anyone drive it.

You should consider yourself lucky Deacon. I'm even going to let you park it. Take care of her. I don't want a smudge on her—much less a scratch."

"Don't worry another second. She's in good hands."

Jennifer shoots me a threatening glare as she reluctantly drops the keys into my open palm.

"There's nothing to worry about Jennifer. Enjoy your day. I'll have your keys brought up as soon as she's parked," I reassure her as I slide behind the wheel. I have to hand it to her, she did pick out a very nice car—conservative yet capable.

Inside my pocket, my phone vibrates. I pull it out and see I received a text from Christen. Her text seems unusually cryptic. She wants to meet me in the lobby of the Bellagio in thirty minutes. I look at the time and quickly text back:

Sure hon, sounds good. See you shortly.

Inside the Bellagio, below the beautifully blown glass I see Christen sitting in the most comfortable lobby chair waiting for me. She never shows up like this. What could it possibly be?

"Hey Deacon," she says as I step up to greet her with a kiss and a hug.

"What's going on hon? I wasn't expecting to see you this early. Everything alright?" I say, still a little unsure of myself.

"Um…I was going to do this tonight after you got off, but I can't wait any longer."

"You can tell me anything Christen. You know that," I say, this time with a little trepidation.

"I know this is probably the worst possible time, being the Christmas season and all, but I wanted you to know…that I'm moving to Spain for a couple years," she says somewhat sheepishly.

"You're what?" I say completely taken back.

"I didn't tell you because I didn't want you to worry, but I applied for a master's program in Spain about four months ago, and I start in January. I just got the acceptance letter today. I have to leave before Christmas so I can get my place and everything settled in."

"When are you leaving?" I say, the frustration evident in my tone.

"I leave next Friday babe. I'm so sorry. You don't have to wait for me, but I really hope we can do the long distance thing. You can come visit me and I'll come back here to see you."

Realizing my tone isn't going to be professional in the least, I take a second to breathe before simple saying, "We'll talk tonight. I'll pick you up at eight. Don't worry. I'll get off. I'll pick you up at eight and we'll figure this whole thing out."

"Okay. I do love you Deacon," Christen says as she puts her hands out for a hug.

"I know you do Christen. I love you too, but…" I pause, feeling my emotions getting the best of me. "We'll talk tonight, okay?"

We hug briefly and then I give her a quick kiss before telling her goodbye. She returns the gesture and then quickly makes her way out.

What is that woman doing to me? Just when things were getting good she has to go and do something stupid like this. Maybe she doesn't…I don't finish the thought. I don't want to even think it.

116

EIGHT

City Center

"Taylor!" I cry out.

As I reach down to grab her, she lifts her head to look up at me.

"Taylor!" I gasp. "Are you okay? Did you get hit?" I quickly ask as I look over her body for any signs of blood.

"I don't think so. When you stopped so suddenly, I tripped over your leg, and then I heard you shoot so I stayed down. You did say to stay right on you."

"Please don't do that to me again! My heart stopped beating when I turned around and saw you on the ground. I thought you'd been hit."

"I'm good. Let's keep moving" she says as I pull her to her feet.

We head into the parking garage, making our way quietly, but quickly, as we approach the rear entrances to the Vdara.

"If my guys did as they've been trained, the door should be locked. Luckily for us, my access card will still get us in."

Taylor and I approach one of the rear entrances and cautiously peer inside. There doesn't appear to be anyone guarding the door. Trying the door, I find it locked which gives me a sigh of relief. I hope the rest of the doors were locked in time as well. Pulling out my access card I place it to the magnetic strip hoping to get the green light. The door clicks.

"I've never been so happy to see a green light in my life," Taylor says as I open the door.

With a quick nod, I keep all my attention on what we're about to find inside the hotel. Since the parking garage is for employees only, I didn't expect to see much in the way of patrons back here. We make our way down the hallway leading out into the lobby and I'm not hearing much of anything. As I walk past the few offices found on this corridor, I peek through the windows to find the lights on with no one inside. We keep moving down the corridor when suddenly the lobby door comes flying open. I raise my rifle in preparation to shoot when I notice Brett staring down the barrel of my rifle pointed squarely five feet from his face.

"Don't shoot!" Brett screams out.

I quickly lower my rifle to my side so he can see that it's me. Brett has been the security manager at the Vdara for a few years. He has been on board with everything I've done since I started at the beginning of the year. At six feet three inches, he's a pretty intimidating guy.

"I was just heading back here to check the rear entrance and call you," Brett exclaims with his heart still racing. A gun in your face will do that to you.

"We just got back from Zion. This is the first hotel we've made it to. How are things here?"

I now notice Brett's automatic rifle slung across his back. I'm glad to see he's carrying, but at the same time it also worries me.

"For the most part, it's been pretty quiet up here. There have been a few stragglers from the mobs who have made it up to our roundabout. They thought it would be funny to fire a few rounds through the lobby windows. I've got guys manning all the entrances and all the guests are back in their rooms or at least those that were here or made it back here," Brett says, proud of his accomplishments.

He should be proud. With what I've heard from Scott and what I've seen for myself, albeit very little to this point, Brett has done an outstanding job.

"How are your wife and kids? Have you been able to get a hold of them?" I ask wanting to make sure his head is in the game.

"Nicole calls me every fifteen minutes to check in. I think they are far enough away in Summerlin that there shouldn't be any issues. I know she's worried about me though."

"I understand completely. As soon as I've spoken with all the security managers for each hotel, we'll work out a plan to get guests out of here and then start rotating security out to check on families. Have you heard anything from Veer, Aria, or the Mandarin?" I ask with a glimmer of hope.

"I talked to Patrick twenty minutes ago. He said Veer is locked up. I finally reached Rob as well. The Aria had a few issues when the madness started, but Rob's got it locked up now. As for Mandarin and Crystals, we haven't been able to contact anyone."

I had totally forgotten about Crystals. The high-end shopping mall right on the Boulevard has probably been lost. The thought of my guys fending off hundreds if not thousands of looters has me worried. It makes perfect sense though. Why would anyone come up here when there are millions of dollars in diamonds and merchandise for the taking right out on the Strip? The Mandarin and Aria are our only hotels with gambling so only one out of two falling apart isn't too bad.

We head out to the lobby to find it almost completely abandoned. One receptionist stands behind the desk answering phone calls from residents. As she looks up, I see the fear clearly painted on her face. Two bullet holes in the ornately painted wall behind her head probably explain the expression. There are three others in the lobby carrying rifles. Security standing their post—I couldn't ask for anything more.

Looking around I ask Brett to run down security for me. Brett speaks of several guys who took off when the chaos started. It was only three, so I feel good about that. He also points out the three guarding the main door. He has a man posted at all major entrances and exits to the building. Brett also talks about the staff—how room service is doing everything they can to accommodate those stuck in their rooms.

"It sounds like you have this place running as well as you can under the circumstances."

Just then I notice a man and a woman running up to the front entrance in complete panic. I don't say a word as Brett's guys spring into action. The couple doesn't appear to be carrying any weapons and immediately are let in. Brett's team searches the male first and then the female. One guy keeps a rifle at low ready while the other does the searching.

The other one, still looking out to make sure no one is approaching, appears ready to go to war. They ask the couple if they're staying here, and of course the answers comes back yes. After searching the two, they're escorted over to the receptionist's desk and checked against our guest list. They are clear. It makes me feel good inside to see my team perform so well. It reminds me of my team days —how we all did our job flawlessly.

"What are you doing for people who don't have a room?" I ask Brett.

"We are checking them in for the night. The city might be falling apart, but that doesn't mean we still can't make some money. A few have asked to just hang out in the lobby, but I don't want anyone loitering in the lobby. If they're here, they have to be in a room."

"Well—looks like there's nothing for me to do here. You have this place wrapped up tight. Can you get me a radio?"

Brett heads back into the security office as Taylor walks over to talk to the receptionist. Taylor noticed that she was almost in tears and wanted to talk with her, reassure her.

"How are you holding up?" Taylor tenderly asks as she walks around the counter and puts her arms around her.

Marie doesn't say a word at first except to let out an uncontrollable sob as Taylor embraces her. I've spoken with her before. She's one of the newer hires to Vdara. This was her first job out of high school. I put on a new hire orientation each month and she came up to me after the meeting. She hadn't worked all through high school due to sports and academics. She's a bright girl, but probably lacks real world experience. This must be more than she can handle right now. Taylor will reassure her.

As Taylor begins to talk with her the phone rings. "I've got it Marie. Talk to Taylor and take a few seconds for yourself."

I see it's room 415 calling as I reach for the phone, "Front desk—how may we help you?"

"How long are you going to keep us here?" an irate women yells through the phone.

"Can you hold for just one second please?"

Brett steps back into the lobby and I ask him what he's been telling people who want to leave. He says he's told them it would be better to hang out until things cool down a bit, but hasn't forced anyone to stay in the hotel. Most have seen the wisdom of those words and have been content.

I pick up the phone again. "Ma'am—you have a couple options. Since you sound determined to leave, you may leave if you choose. A member of my security team will escort you to your car to ensure you get out safely. Option two, and the one I would strongly suggest, involves you relaxing in your room, ordering some room service, and turning on the television to watch a movie."

"I have to get out of here. I've been watching the news and the strip has turned into a war zone. It's only a matter of time before they make it in here," room 415 exclaims.

"I assure you ma'am, we will keep you safe inside. Once you leave I have no control over what happens, and as you said, it is a war zone out there. But, if you are determined to leave, you can head down now and we'll get you out safely."

"I'm coming down now," room 415 says as she slams the phone to the receiver.

As I hang up the phone, Marie and Taylor look at me. "Room 415 would like to check out," I say to Marie.

"Can you grab 415's keys and have one of your guys escort her to her car? Take her out the back—directly into the parking garage."

Brett agrees as he hands me a radio. We also agree to do a radio check every thirty minutes to make sure everything remains secure here.

Taylor is still talking with Marie which gives me time to call Rob on the radio. I want someone waiting to open the door as we approach so we're not outside any longer than we have to be. With Taylor at my side still, I don't want to take any chances. Rob answers right away. He's relieved to hear I'll be there in five minutes. Aria stands a mere block away through the roundabout. It should take us less than a minute to run across.

Trying to remain sensitive to Marie, I step over closer to listen to their conversation. "You're strong. A weak person would have run, but you stayed. That's more than the others who took off. Your family is safe and you couldn't be any safer than you are right here. I know you can do this," Taylor says as she hugs Marie one more time and looks at me.

I quietly mouth the words, "We have to go."

Taylor reassures her again that everything will be okay and we make our way over to the front entrance. I let Rob know we're headed over as Brett's team opens the doors.

As I step through the front door, I turn to my team and say, "Keep 'em safe, and keep up the good work." I couldn't ask for better people here.

With Taylor at my side, we head out the front doors. As I glance past the colorful canoes that form the abstract art in front of the Vdara, I get a quick glimpse of Las Vegas Boulevard. There were people and cars heading south in what can only be described as pure pandemonium. I keep running, but can't help think they are heading straight for Crystals. I have to get there quick. Taylor can't be with me, and I better bring some help.

One hundred feet from the entrance I see Rob waiting with the doors open. Fifty feet from the doors I hear tires screeching around

123

the roundabout directly behind us. I glance back quickly to see a large, black, unmarked SUV. Rob screams for us to hurry up. Just as we approach the doors, I hear gun shots. The windows in front of us shatter, showering us in glass. Lifting my head, I see Rob raise his rifle as he starts firing round after round.

"Get down Taylor," I yell as Taylor makes it through the open door. She doesn't say a word as she hits the floor.

As I turn with rifle raised, ready to put every last round I have into the SUV, I see they've made the full circle and they're heading east down to the Boulevard. The limo tint on every window makes it impossible to see who or how many were in there.

"It's almost as if they knew you were heading across there," Rob says and we both move inside the hotel.

"Yeah it does," I say keenly aware. That probably won't be the end of that.

As soon as I step through the door, I notice things are not quite as calm here as they were at Vdara.

"What's the situation here?" I ask Rob as we start to walk into the casino. I'm amazed to still see people playing cards and sitting at slots.

"We've tried to get people out of the common areas and back to their rooms, but they just won't listen. We've tried to be as accommodating as possible, but we can't make them all happy."

"Our employees come first. So here's what we're going to do —" I say, hoping Rob won't feel like I'm stepping on his toes. "Start closing up tables and getting all the money under lock and key. Do it as subtly as possible. We don't want the guest to get any ideas. Start pushing people to slot machines. I don't care what you make up—just get our employees out of the common areas. Escort them to their cars or put them in a room if they don't feel comfortable enough leaving right now. Close down all the restaurants and snack shops also. Button them up after the gambling is closed down. Once you have most of the people cleared out and everything closed down, you can think about opening some things back up if it's not too chaotic."

Rob listens intently as I explain what he needs to do. "Can you handle all that?" I ask.

"We can handle it," Rob replies.

"Have you been able to talk to Sammy over at Mandarin?" hoping he knows what's going on over there.

"I haven't had time to do anything—let alone talk to Sammy," Rob spits out a little frustrated.

"It's okay. I'm not mad at you. Everyone here looks safe and that is what is most important right now. Remember, stay calm and collected and let your guys know exactly what they have to do and everything will work out. You have the best team working for you here."

Rob goes to work. Taylor and I continue to walk through the casino. I wish I could blend in right now, but the rifle and handguns we're carrying make it somewhat impossible. I need to get over to the Mandarin and then to Veer Tower. I watch as tables, one by one, close up and people go to their rooms or leave the hotel. Not many leave though. Rob has an army at the entrance keeping people out.

It's not quite like clockwork here, but at least the guest are moving now. We watch for twenty minutes before I call Rob on the radio and let him know we are going to the Mandarin. While waiting, I tried Scott several times, but he didn't answer. Dean and Jennifer still aren't picking up either. There are several high-end stores inside the Bellagio, and I must say, I'm still concerned about the mob I saw coming down the Boulevard. I have to trust in Scott and the rest of my guys though. What choice do I have at this point?

Still unable to get anyone on the radio at Mandarin, I take a couple of Rob's guys with me as we head out the main entrance of Aria. Now we are right in the middle of City Center and for some reason it's too peaceful here. The waterfall sounds so calming as we quickly move along the sidewalk. The Mandarin, just like the Aria, sits only a block away. We reach the entrance in less than a minute. Now that I have two more men with rifles, I let them take point while I pick up the rear. Taylor, of course, sits tucked in the middle. She has been such a trooper through this. Shot at two times in less than an hour and still moving forward, unaware of what awaits her.

Arriving at the doors, we find them locked. We quickly move down to a door I can slide my access card on and enter through it. I expect it will be quiet as we move into the pseudo lobby. There is no one here—which doesn't surprise me since the main lobby is on the twenty-third floor.

"Go check the security office. See if you can find Sammy," I say to Brad and Steve.

Pointing out the simple but elegant beauty in the entrance to distract Taylor, I signal to the others the bullet holes and blood on the ground. We put the main security office at this entrance just in case we needed someone down on the ground. Sammy's office sits upstairs, but he spends a bit of time down here with his guys. We didn't want someone on twenty-three to have to take the elevator in an emergency.

As they move out, I take a brief second myself to enjoy the simple beauty here while wondering what we'll find upstairs.

Brad returns alone with an unpleasant look on his face—almost as if he'd seen a ghost.

"What's wrong?" I quickly whisper, hoping Taylor didn't see the look on Brad's face.

"You need to come back here. You might want to leave her here," Brad whispers, motioning to Taylor.

I have Taylor take a seat. Brad then continues, "Sammy's dead back there. He's not the only one either."

Brad heads back to be with Steve as I talk to Taylor. "They've found some dead bodies back there so I need you to do something for me. There's a secret room behind that door. You'll be completely safe inside until I get back. I don't want you to worry or be scared at all. I'll be back before you know it."

The door is locked as I reach over to open it. I slide my card and to our complete shock a male receptionist sits inside already. He is in even more shock as he sees me come through the door with my rifle.

"Please don't kill me!" he manages to mutter with his head buried between his legs.

"I'm not going to kill you Danny. I need you to keep my girl safe. This is Taylor."

Danny looks up and sees that it's me. His panic-stricken face is immediately replaced with a look of relief. Danny then begins to stutter and stammer as he relates what he saw. I manage to glean a little information from his almost incoherent rambling.

Apparently, five guys got off the elevator in the main lobby on twenty-three and started shooting. Danny managed to get into the stairwell without being noticed. He then heard more gun fire and people screaming. He left the hotel, but realized it wasn't safe out there either so he came back in and locked himself in.

"Calm down Danny. You're safe now. How long ago did the five men come in?"

"I don't know. Maybe an hour ago," he manages again between sobs.

"Why didn't you call 9-1-1?" I ask.

"I have tried. It has been busy every time."

"Listen Danny, I need you to keep Taylor safe while I take care of some things here. Can you handle that?" I ask, knowing he won't be able to.

"Are we going to stay locked in here?" Danny asks.

"Yes, stay right there. I have to talk to Taylor for a second first, okay?"

"Okay," Danny says, still curled up on the ground.

I pull Taylor back out of the office so Danny can't hear our conversation. "You're going to take care of him, okay? Don't give him a gun and keep the door locked. Before I unlock the door I'll knock a tune so you know it's me. If you don't hear the tune and you're certain someone is trying to break in open fire."

"You should knock 'Twinkle, Twinkle, Little Star.' No one would possibly do that before entering."

"Okay, I'll knock Twinkle just for you. Talk to him. Keep his mind off what just happened. I'll be right back."

"Be safe," Taylor says as she heads into the office after giving me a kiss.

I close the door behind her and move out quietly to the security office. As I head down the hall I can see where someone has dragged a bleeding body. The guests in here must be terrified. Entering the security office I see Sammy lying on the floor with several holes in his chest and one in his head. Brad and Steve have checked the remainder of the area and it's all secure. There are two more employees who suffered a fate similar to Sammy's. My heart sinks as I think of their families. No time for that now though.

"I saw some movement in the ballroom hallway from the camera. I also saw one man with a rifle walking the area up there," Steve says after letting me take in the scene.

"Since none of us have suppressors on our rifles we are going to have to take him out without firing a round. Did you see a way to sneak up on him?" I ask.

"Not really. The walkways are all rather large here. We might have to just shoot him and hope for the best," Steve suggests.

"Okay. I'm going to take point with Steve in the middle and Brad I want you to pick up the rear. Make sure no one surprises us. Let's move out."

We quickly jump on the elevator and ride to twenty-three. Getting off the elevator we slowly move through the lobby and then down the hall with Steve warning me of the man's exact location. Several bodies lay lifeless in the lobby as we quickly move through. No time for the dead now when there are certainly people still living. I come to the last corner. Just before I walk out on the unsuspecting degenerate, I hug the wall and peek around the corner. What is this man doing in my hotel? He's walking away from me as I check the corner.

Looking back at Steve I say, "I know what we need to do. Steve—I want you to run across this hall keeping straight for twenty-five feet. Once you've hit twenty-five feet hit the floor. If this works like I'm thinking, that man will come chasing after you without even looking back this way. Once he heads down your hall I'll put one round in him."

"What about me?" Steve says, perplexed at my plan.

"That's why you better run fast and hit the floor even faster. I would wrestle him to the ground and tie him up, but if more come after you we could be in real trouble and we don't have time for that now. Can you handle that?" I would prefer not to kill these men but time and serious constraints in man power are limiting my options.

"Sounds easy enough. You're a good shot, right?"

"You won't be disappointed," the words come out like I've said them a million times. "Brad, just keep watching my six."

"I'm all over it," Brad says with adrenaline coursing through his veins.

Steve heads across the hall as loud as he can. I don't peek out, but I can hear the man running this direction. As he turns the corner after Steve I fire one round through his head. From twenty feet it couldn't have been easier. Just then I hear doors open up in the direction of the ballroom. I hear one set of foot prints coming my direction. The plan again formulates in my mind as if it were second nature. I step out to see there's just one coming and instantly he sees me.

I look back at Brad as I start to run in the same direction and say, "You've got this one."

Shots go sailing past as I run twenty feet telling Steve to be prepared as well. I figure between the two of them I should be safe. I slide to the ground and turn on my back with my rifle pointing at the man that will definitely come racing around the corner. There's one thing I've always found with criminals—they're so predictable. As the man rounds the corner in a dead sprint I hear one gun shot from across the hall. Brad hits him dead in the back and the man hits the ground right next to his pathetic friend.

I lay on the ground for another fifteen seconds listening for more feet running in our direction. When I hear nothing I get Steve up to watch my six as I scan the hallway from where our two just came from. There's no movement. I motion for Brad to come over and take Steve's spot. As Brad walks by I tell him, "Good shot."

"That's two out of the possible five that came in. I'm sure the leader and two others are in there with our people. Grab that first guy's hat and jacket for me. We are going to go down there. I'll draw the other three out. I'll put on his jacket and hat and open the door to have them come out for a second. When they do you both have to be ready to shoot number two and number three. Brad, you take three and Steve, you take two. I'll keep walking away from you guys. When I hear your first shot, I'll turn and take out the first guy. Sounds easy enough, right?"

"Um—sure," Steve spits out as Brad remains silent.

We quickly, but quietly, move down the hall making sure there's no one else out watching. Once Brad and Steve are in position I open the door slowly, my head turned down. I quickly mutter, "Get out here quick," in the only voice I can manage. I let the door close and quickly move down the hall.

I hear the door open and a voice behind me says, "What's going on?" as they continue to follow me down the hall. I don't say a word as I hear one shot. As I turn, with my rifle ready to shoot, the man following me down the hall falls to the ground.

"What happened?" I quickly ask.

"He was the only one that came out so I shot him," Steve says.

"That was easy enough. That means there could be two more in there though," I say keeping my eye on the door.

We sit for a good minute listening outside the ballroom door for any sign that someone could still be in there. Without hearing a noise, I prep my two guys to go in like a SEAL team hitting a house full of tangos. I will go in first and to the left, the second man in and to the right, and then the third man straight in. I figure that will cover the massive area we'll have to oversee as we enter the ballroom. I also explain that I will toss a flash bang into the room—as soon as it goes off we will make our move.

"Remember, the bad guys probably have guns. If you don't see a gun, don't shoot," I say hoping to avoid any unintentional loss of life.

I slowly open the door to toss the flash bang ten feet into the room. I know the fuse runs about three seconds so I begin to count in my head, one-thousand-one, one-thousand-two, one-thousand-three.

MOOB

The blast goes off.

NINE

Taylor

Still slumped, fetal position-style in the corner of the office, Danny's body shudders in submission to the uncontrollable sobs he has finally managed to subdue. He slowly pulls himself up to a standing position—pausing half way in between to take a deep breath. He seems to be giving himself a silent pep talk to convince himself that— yes, he can stand up—and yes, he can cope with the situation.

"So Taylor, how long have you been dating Deacon?" Danny questions, feigning a calm demeanor.

He couldn't fool anyone, especially not me. The sickly green pallor painted across his face coupled with his over-eagerness to appear nonchalant with small talk only made me suspect even more that he was about to go into shock.

"Three months or so. Here Danny," I say, putting my arm around him and trying to redirect the conversation a little, "let's sit down for a while. There's no use being uncomfortable while we wait for Deacon to come back."

Down he went, without a word of complaint. From the drop of sweat I see slowly making its way down Danny's forehead, it is obvious that he's losing the battle over his anxiety.

I smile. "How long have you been working here at the Mandarin?" I inquire.

"Just over a…just over a year," Danny stutters. He pauses briefly to wipe his forehead with the back of his clammy palm and straighten his slouch ever so slightly before continuing, "My brother-in-law works on the maintenance team. He was the one who swung the job for me. He said it would be a breeze—you know—not a lot of stress, but with a decent paycheck."

"Sure, I get that," I respond. "I'm a waitress at The Cheesecake Factory. Not exactly a stress-free job, but the pay check is nice. There are days I would just love to have a less stressful job. So—are you working full-time? Going to school or what?"

"My mother thinks I should go back to school. She says, 'If you're going to be successful in life, an Associates degree in General Education is not going to get you there,'" Danny spouts off in his best motherly nagging imitation.

I can't help but chuckle quietly to myself.

Before I have a chance to vocalize the empowering pep talk that was at the tip of my tongue, Danny continues, "I had met this really great girl, and things were getting serious. She was beautiful, intelligent, and unbelievably kind. She was perfect. The problem was— my mom said she wasn't good enough. She didn't come from a rich, influential family. Apparently, it didn't matter that we were in love—it didn't matter that she was my whole world—it didn't matter that she gave purpose to everything I did or ever wanted."

"I know how you feel Danny. I know exactly how you feel."

"You've been thwarted in love too, huh?" he sighs, dejected.

"Uh, not exactly," I pause for a minute, hesitant.

"Deacon?"

I nod slowly. "Don't get me wrong," I respond quickly, "Deacon and I are far from being 'thwarted in love' like you described. It's just…," I trail off. I am baffled why I am even contemplating discussing this at all—not to mention with a perfect stranger.

"It's just what?" Danny prods.

"It's just—hmm—there are things about Deacon that I absolutely love. It's like you said, he has become my whole world, my everything. I love how attentive he is. I love how driven he is to achieve his dreams and to accomplish his goals. I love how he embodies everything I've only ever dared to write in my heart. And his laugh —hearing him laugh absolutely electrifies me."

Once again, I pause. I pause as the memory of Deacon's laughter echoes in my mind and causes me to smile uncontrollably, simply at the thought of him.

"But there are things that I'm worried about with him—about us. I don't know, I'm probably concerned over absolutely nothing and it will all work itself out with time."

"What do you mean? What are you concerned about?"

"Well, it's hard to explain. Like I said, there are so many things that I love about him. It's almost as if he is too good to be true. Like this is all a dream—a dream that I will wake up from and he will be gone. I don't know that I would ever truly recover should things not work out between Deacon and me for whatever reason."

"That's how I felt about my girl too. In fact, I still don't know that I've completely recovered after losing her."

"And then there is his military background," I ramble off, unable to stop the momentum of the conversation I somehow got pulled into, all in the name of 'distraction.' "I worry that all his training has taken away some of his natural, spontaneous emotion. Sometimes, it feels as if he is forcing a reaction—especially if something tragic or difficult is going on. He knows people are sad and hurting, but occasionally he comes off seeming mechanical—almost beyond feeling—

because for so many years he was required to suppress his emotions, to not let his emotions jeopardize the mission. Does that make sense? It's almost like he isn't quite sure how to react in certain emotionally-charged situations and so, when he does, his actions seem too calculated or pre-planned—almost awkward.

One day he told me this story about one of his missions. To save you from all the bloody details, it involved saving these women and children from a life of rape and heaven knows what else. He had to kill a man with his bare hands. I was speechless. I honestly didn't know how to respond. On one hand, I was impressed. Hearing how he survived what surely could have been his last moments on earth, but I was also frightened to know the man I love was capable of such an act. In one sense it made me feel safe and protected, which is important to me. You have no idea how important that is to me. When I was younger, I was in a similar situation and hearing this story showed me how much he values women and reassured me that he would defend me and protect me should the need arise. And, clearly it has—hence our current protected imprisonment," I conclude with a grin and a wave of my hand to indicate our surroundings.

"That's intense," Danny responds with a look of brotherly admiration. "Deacon has done an amazing job as head of security from what I've seen and heard. Plus, based on what you've said, man, I'm just glad we're on the same side. I wouldn't want to go up against him —ever."

"I agree. Which brings up another point. I've worried about this too, although not as much because I haven't seen much evidence to support it. But, what happens when Deacon and I don't agree on something? Is he going to go into military mode and fight his way through? Am I going to be the next victim of his interrogation training? I understand all the psychological training was required. I get that. Knowing Deacon, I'm sure he excelled at it. He excels at anything he puts his mind to. I just don't want to worry that he is using all his psychological training on me. I want to feel that he will always be genuine with me. I want him to feel safe with me—safe enough to let his raw emotions show—safe enough to let me see his weaknesses, his vulnerabilities, his shortcomings—safe enough to be himself. And frankly, I guess I need the same thing. I'm getting close, but I'm not there yet. Doubts and insecurities sweep through me like a wildfire. The doubt burns hot, but only temporarily, and then it seems to go out almost as quickly as it started.

"What have you got to be worried about?"

"It's ridiculous, I know, but I wonder why a guy as amazing and accomplished as Deacon is choosing to be with me. I've never been an integral asset to our nation's security. I'm a waitress—a waitress who grew up in a home where my dad was barely around and I spent my winters curled up in a window seat in our library when it was too cold to be in the pool."

"I wouldn't worry about that at all. You're smart—if you don't mind me saying, very beautiful, and it's obvious he loves you. You've got nothing to worry about."

"Thank you Danny. You're too kind. There's one last thing I worry about."

"What's that?" Danny quickly asks, not sure if I'm going to say.

"He only just broke up with his ex two weeks before we met. I don't want this to be a rebound relationship."

"I wouldn't…" Danny begins, as Twinkle, Twinkle, Little Star begins to be knocked out on the door.

TEN
Almost There

Brad, Steve, and I fly through the door as big and mean as we possibly can—not sure what we'll find on the other side. I dig my corner left and find it completely empty. Steve does the same on the right and finds his corner vacant. When Brad comes through the door we are all facing into the room to find a crazy scene of employees and patrons cowering behind tables in absolute horror. Not one person carrying a gun.

Seeing nothing but friendly and frightened faces, I turn to look at Steve and Brad and say, "That was a big build up for nothing."

"Yeah it was," they both say in unison as we turn our attention to what we've stumbled upon.

"Brad—watch the door while we see what's going on. Whistle if you hear or see anyone coming."

Brad opens the door and peeks left and right before stepping out so he can see everything.

"Leave the one door open and don't go chasing anyone down."

"I'm not that stupid," Brad says as he chuckles to himself.

As I survey the crowd there are lots a familiar faces, but I can't pick out any security.

"Do we have any security team in here?" I ask, hoping we have at least a couple. We can leave them to protect this group and can continue on.

"Yes," I hear a voice call out. "There are six of us here."

I couldn't see who called out, but it sounded like one of my guys. They all jump up and come forward while Steve begins to talk to the rest of the group. All together there are six guys—Jacob, Jamison, Colten, Mark, Jackson, and Shane.

"I assume you guys don't have any weapons. Fortunately, there are three dead bodies out in the hall who would love to hand over their rifles. Check them completely—knives, wallets, handguns, everything. Keep all the weapons to divide amongst yourselves—just bring me their wallets. I want to know who we're dealing with. Who has the most knowledge about what's going on here?"

Jacob speaks up, "I do. Sammy probably would, but we haven't heard from him since this whole thing started."

"Okay Jacob, you'll stay with me while Steve and Brad go with your guys to get the bodies. You got that Steve? Get the bodies and everything back here. If there's anyone else left in the hotel we don't want them immediately tipped off."

"I got it. Let's go guys," Steve says to the group.

"Have Brad keep an eye on our door still. He can watch your six."

"Will do," Steve responds.

The five guys and Steve move down the hall as Jacob begins to relate what he knows. Jacob tells me there are two more guys inside the hotel with Mandy and Sammy. Mandy has access to the vault and Sammy does as well. I inform Jacob that we found Sammy dead in the security office with a couple others, but we hadn't seen Mandy. Jacob gets somewhat upset after hearing the news, but continues to fill me in. He states that the men let them know they were only there for money and didn't want to hurt anyone if they didn't have to. He says Mandy and the two other men have been gone for twenty minutes or so.

As Jacob finishes his story, his five men make it back to the room with the weapons and bodies. I have them place large tablecloths over the bodies so the guests and employees don't have to see them. I wish it wasn't this way, but dead bodies don't even bother me now. The smell can kind of turn my stomach, but let's be honest—who wants to be that close anyway?

Seeing my men are armed, I know where we have to go next—into the basement where the vault, as well as a maze of offices will be found. If they hear us coming, it will be almost impossible to sneak up on them.

"Deacon? Is that you?" I hear from a familiar voice in the crowd.

As I turn to look I see Savanah with black mascara running down her face—she has obviously been crying.

She starts running over to me as I ask, "How did you end up here?"

She doesn't hear my questions, and as she embraces me she asks, "Where's Taylor? Please tell me she's okay?"

"She's fine, she's fine. She's actually right here with us," I say, knowing that will cheer her up.

"Where?" she asks, barely able to contain her excitement as her head starts swiveling around the room with a huge smile on her face.

"I left her in the front security office with Danny. I didn't dare bring her up here until I knew it was safe," I say wiping the mascara from her cheeks.

"Can you take me to her, please?"

"How about I bring her to you? She'll be so excited to see you. She's been worried about you ever since we saw the news up in Zion. You didn't tell me how you got here though. Were you working when things fell apart?" I ask, still confused how she made it clear down here from Cesar's Palace.

"I was having lunch with a girlfriend at the Monte Carlo and when I started walking back the streets descended into chaos. I came running up in here to get out of it and have been stuck here ever since. How bad is it out there?" Savanah asks, unsure of the danger waiting outside.

"Let's just say, it's not good. I have to take care of one more thing here and then I'll get you and Taylor back to my place. You'll be safe there."

With everyone gathering around me now, I need to calm their fears and let them know what's going on.

"Listen up everyone. There are still at least two guys roaming the hotel that would love to shoot each and every one of us. I know you've been in here for some time now, but I need you to stay a little longer."

"I need to leave right now," a male voice calls out from the crowd. Two or three more join in.

"Trust me—I want to get you out of here, but you won't be good to anyone dead in the hall or on the street. I'm going to leave three guys here with guns to keep you safe until we get Mandy back and take care of the other two men roaming my hotel. It should be less than twenty minutes. Can you wait twenty minutes?"

They all agree. The prospect of getting shot today doesn't sound pleasing to any of them and they resolve to wait it out in the ballroom.

"Steve and Brad—since you don't work this hotel I'm going to have you stay here to keep this group safe. Jacob, pick one more guy to stay with them and then we'll move out."

"Jamison, stay here with Steve and Brad?" Jacob commands.

"Yeah. I'll stay and keep them safe," Jamison says holding his handgun.

"That means the rest of you are with me. We have to make one quick stop before we hit the basement. Taylor and Danny are still alone and I want to bring them back here with the rest of the group."

No one questions my call and the six of us head out. Moving in a diamond shape with two on point, two in the rear and two covering our three and nine, we move down the hall. Not hearing any noise in this main hall, and pretty confident that Mandy and the miscreants are in the basement, we jump on the express elevator and head down.

Knocking out Twinkle, Twinkle, Little Star, I open the door. Taylor looks up and smiles at me, her eyes sparkling with hopeful confidence.

"Deacon!" she exclaims, jumping up and throwing her arms around me.

"Hey beautiful," I whisper in her ear and then look deep in her eyes. "You okay?"

"Yeah, sure. Danny and I had a nice talk. We'll have to talk about it later, okay?"

"Okay."

Danny seems much more relaxed now. Leave anyone in a room with Taylor for five minutes and they'll feel better. She has that way with people. She has decided to be an architect, but her real calling is in counseling. She always has the nicest things to say and she loves to talk to people. She loves making people feel better. Right now it's perfect—keep her mind focused on helping and she won't think about all the craziness of the current situation.

"I have a surprise for you Taylor. Come with me. You too Danny," I say stepping through the door.

"What is it?" Taylor asks, wondering how I could possibly have a surprise for her at a time like this.

"Taylor—you have nothing to worry about," Danny says, as we head for the elevator.

"Thank you Danny. It was very nice talking with you. I hope you feel better," Taylor says.

When I give Taylor the furrowed brow look she whispers, "We'll talk later."

"Okay."

I leave the gang there to guard the entrance and jump back on the elevator to drop Taylor and Danny off. I'm sure the reprobates are still in the basement, so I tell them to keep an eye out and wait for my return.

Arriving at the ballroom door in no time, I let Danny go in and hold Taylor back. "Before you go in, remember, you have to be quiet," I say, knowing that if I don't remind her she'll let out a squeal that anyone in the hotel would hear, even if they are in the basement.

"I will be," she says still unsure what I have for her.

Taylor opens the door and walks through. I follow right behind just waiting to see their eyes connect. As soon as Savanah sees Taylor the waterworks begin again. Taylor briefly glances my way as she runs to embrace her best friend. As they hug, Taylor beaming at me, I mouth I love you and let the door close.

I quickly move down the hall and jump on the elevator to head back down to link up with my make-shift team.

I know all the hotels, but since I've got men who work it every day I let Jacob and Shane take point. I pick up our three o'clock and the rest of the team falls in place. When we get to the stairs, Jacob tell us all to move very methodically. Metal stairs and twelve feet moving makes for a lot of noise. Jacob also informs us if they're still here they will definitely have to come back this way.

We make our way through the door leading into the administrative level and down the maze of halls and offices to where the money is kept. There is an elevator behind all the money cages leading down here, but Jacob assures us Mandy would have led them this way. We slowly move down the hall making our way into the cubicle farm. Still unsure what we'll find, we pause in place for fifteen seconds to listen for any movement or sound. When we don't hear a pin drop, Jacob moves us forward.

The vault lies just beyond the cubicle farm—down the hall and to the right. After slowly making our way through we pause again, listening. Jacob says he can hear two men talking in Spanish down the hall. He suggests that we lay and wait here until they come walking past and then ambush them. An ambush does sound like a great idea, but I also can't help but think of Mandy. Once she's of no use to them they'll dispose of her quickly—who knows, she could be dead already.

"We have to keep moving," I whisper. "Even if there's only a slight chance Mandy is still alive, we have to do everything we can."

"There's not a lot of cover once we round that corner," Jacob sounds off with concern.

"I understand. I'm sure we won't get both of them, but we are going to do the same thing we did to draw out the three upstairs. The last will stay put if Mandy is still alive—he'll hide behind her until one of us shoots him in the head. Who wants to be the guinea pig?" I ask, unsure who would be best suited for the job. I should know all of my people's strengths and weaknesses, but with over one thousand guys under me, I don't have them all down yet.

"Colten—since you're just carrying a handgun, I'll have you go," Jacob decides.

Without giving Colten a chance to respond, I start explaining exactly what I want him to do. In order for this mini operation to work, I tell him he has to walk down the hall like he has no idea there are people in the safe. When he rounds the corner and sees the safe open, he needs to call out as if he was surprised to find the safe open and people inside. When the criminals see he's alone, the leader will send the last follower after him. Colten will then run around the corner into the cubicle farm to take cover. When the man runs past, we'll take him down without firing a shot, or at least that's the plan. I don't like to kill people if I don't have to and we've got numbers now.

"You have to let him see you when he rounds the corner though. He has to believe you are running for your life. You can do this," I say, questioning to myself if he really will be able to handle the task.

"I can handle it," Colten whispers.

"One other thing—you have to tuck that gun into your pants. I don't want them seeing you with a weapon. It could tip them off."

Colten doesn't say a word as he contemplates what I just asked of him. It takes a few seconds to sink in, but he finally sees the logic and begins to tuck the gun in his pants under his belt. I would take it from him, but that would be too much. If I were him, I wouldn't let anyone take a gun from me at a time like this.

We all take our positions in the cubicle farm—ready to attack as Colten starts down the first hall. Being the smallest two, Jackson and Shane have a gag and telephone cord prepared for our unsuspecting delinquent. If we don't have to shoot him, we've decided it's best to gag and tie him up before he yells anything back to his buddy. Jacob will keep an eye on the hall just in case the other one comes running. From my position, I can see without being seen when they round the corner. I'm the biggest, so I will be tackling the man as he comes past.

We can't see Colten, but we definitely hear him as he rounds the corner and finds the vault open. He's playing the part perfectly.

"What's going on back here!" he calls out in surprise.

As the two criminals come into view, Colten calls out again, "You two can't be back here!"

Then my heart sinks as I hear gun shots impacting the wall at the end of the hall. About to jump up, I hear running feet coming down the hall. Then I see Colten round the corner running with a smile on his face I wasn't expecting.

As Colten sprints past our position he exclaims, "Mandy is still alive!"

As he passes, we listen for the sound of another set of feet running our way. It only takes a second and we hear one of the men coming. As he rounds the corner, I see a small, dark-haired Hispanic man with a rifle—I can take him. He doesn't know what's about to hit him. As he passes my position, I pounce on him like a lion on his unsuspecting prey. I hit him from the side—catching him completely off guard. He didn't stand a chance against my two-hundred pounds.

We crash into a cubicle wall, crushing it as we fall to the ground sending computers and equipment all over the area. As soon as we hit the ground, the rest of the group jumps on top of us. I hope Jacob doesn't get too excited and forgets he has to watch for our lone survivor. The last thing we need now is for the last man to come down the hall and shoot us all in the back. Shane quickly shoves the shirt we found in his mouth as I attempt to grab the man's arms before he has a chance to shoot anyone.

Grabbing his left hand, I hear his gun explode. Instantly, Mark's face turns white as he reaches for his side. When I see the blood, I get a burst of adrenaline and quickly grab both arms as Jamison grabs the gun and points it in the man's face. He tries to fight, but quickly realizes he's way over his head on this one.

We quickly hog-tie him, making sure the t-shirt stays securely in his mouth. As much as I'd love to talk to him, I know he won't give up anything. I don't want him giving us away either.

With the area clear, all my attention turns to Mark. Laying on the ground somewhat pale, Mark gags, "Am I going to die?"

"You're not going to die," I say still unsure where he got shot and how bad his injuries are.

As I lift his shirt, I see the blood coming out the side of his stomach. Understanding the hole is usually more extensive where the bullet exits, I quickly roll him on his side to see the exit wound. It's bigger than the front, but not too bad. Knowing Mark will be okay, I quickly take the jacket off my back and put pressure on the exit wound while telling Colten to grab something for the entry wound.

"It was a clean shot," I tell Mark. "Right in and right out. As soon as we get some quick clot on it you'll be better than ever."

"Are you sure?" Mark asks, still not grasping just how insignificant his injuries are.

It's a good thing Taylor saw the first aid kit when she was getting out the guns. As I pour the clotting agent on Mark's entry wound, he gasps in pain. With the blood stopped in front I pull the jacket away in the back and place the clotting pad in its place. Confident Mark will be alright, my focus moves back to Mandy. I also see Jacob has done his job faithfully, keeping an eye down the hall.

With Mark finally content we hear a man calling out, "Pete— ¿Todo está bien?"

Realizing now we are going to have a hostage situation, I call out, "Yes—he's still alive. If you want to live, I insist you walk out here with your hands up!"

With the silence so thick you could cut it with a knife, we slowly walk down the hall to the t-intersection leading to the vault. As I peek around the corner, I see the man standing in the safe behind Mandy with a gun held to her head—did I call it or what.

"You don't want to do that!" I say, as tears fall from Mandy's terrified face.

"Why not?" the last man exclaims defiantly.

"Let me make it very simple for you to comprehend," I say, as I step into the hall so he can see me. "There are six of us and one of you. Three of your guys are dead already. The other one is hog-tied—probably wishing he was dead—and if you shoot that innocent girl we'll put so many holes in you the rats will think you're Swiss cheese. Is that what you want?"

He doesn't say a word, but he starts to tremble. He continues to think as one by one the remainder of my guys step out into the hall with me. Jamison drags our hog close to keep an eye on him.

After several minutes of silence he finally realizes the predicament he finds himself in. "How do I know you didn't kill my guy already? I heard a gun go off," he says.

"Pull our prisoner out here," I say to Jamison without taking my eyes off Mandy's captor.

Jamison grabs our hog and drags him into the hall. Still not sure what to do, he doesn't say a word. I know he doesn't want to give up, but he also doesn't want to die. The criminal dilemma has fully sunk in now.

"Oh—okay. What are you going to do with me if I give up?" he manages to get out.

"We aren't going to do anything with you. We'll let the courts decide that," I call out. "We don't have all day, though. As I'm sure you're aware, there's a war outside and I have to get back to it. What's it going to be?"

After a moment of contemplation, he lowers the gun from Mandy's head and pushes her forward. The relief in Mandy's face sets in immediately as she begins to run down the hall finally escaping her captor.

"I knew you'd see the light." I say with Mandy only a few steps away from us. "I hope you get everything you have coming to you,"

As Mandy embraces me, our last man standing surges with stupidity as he begins to raise his weapon to fire. Holding Mandy and unable to shoot quickly, I'm surprised when a shot rings out in my left ear and then my right. Our last man standing gets hit directly in the chest and then the head, almost simultaneously. As he falls to the ground I glance left and right to see Jacob and Colten—they both have smoke steaming from their barrels and my ears are ringing.

"I don't think he's getting up from those two," I say, still holding Mandy. "Well done guys. Someone go check him to make sure he's dead, and then we'll head back upstairs."

Colten runs down the hall to check. "We didn't make him Swiss cheese, but we started," he yells back.

I hold Mandy as she can't help but cry. I tell her she's alright over and over, but it doesn't help much. We quickly secure the vault and grab our prisoner and move back up stairs. Still wanting to make sure everything has been secured, I send two-man teams around the building to make sure everything has been locked up tight.

Arriving back at the ball room, I see Savanah and Taylor talking as I expected. When I open the door with Mandy in tow the room starts to clap and cheer. I always get embarrassed at moments like these. I raise my hands and lower them, to let them know it isn't necessary, but they continue anyway. My face starts to turn slightly red. It's much easier when no one knows what you've done in some far-flung country on the other side of the world.

Taylor sees my embarrassment and comes over to me. "I love you babe. I'm glad you're safe." She knows why I do what I do, and it definitely isn't for the praise.

"You two ready to get back to my place?" I ask, as Savanah walks over.

Savanah responds first, "Yes, can we please get out of here?" Taylor nods in agreement.

Feeling we have the hotel under control, I pull Jacob over and let him know what he needs to do. I explain how he needs to let the rest of the guests and residents in the hotel know it's safe inside now. It would be best if they stayed in their suites though. Those that don't have a room can be given rooms if they'd like. If there are people who want to leave and their cars are in the parking garage he will need to have two men escort them out. The number one thing he needs to get back up and running is room service. Jacob agrees and prepares his men for the tasks ahead. I also inform him he'll have Steve and Brad since the Aria has plenty of security and things are already running smoothly over there.

With the situation looking better, I call Rob on the radio to make sure things are still flowing as I had hoped. Rob answers quickly, "We are locked up and looking good over here." Just what I wanted to hear.

There were more employees in the ballroom than patrons. I watch as Taylor and Savanah go to work making the guests feel as comfortable as possible. Jacob puts two men at the front entrance to keep the concierge safe and protect the rest of the employees and guests. The rest of his security team roams the hotel keeping an eye on the other doors in and out of the hotel. After watching for ten minutes, I'm pleased with the progress and I tell Jacob to keep up the good work. I also have him get a radio so we can stay in contact.

Next, I call Brett on the radio to make sure the employees and guests are still safe at the Vdara. "We are doing well here," Brett replies. "Where are you?"

"We are at the Mandarin. There was a little hiccup here, but it's over now. We are about to move over to Veer Tower. Keep up the good work."

"Will do," Brett responds.

Ready to take off, I say my goodbyes to Jacob as Steve and Brad check the outside. I also call over to Patrick to ensure that he has the west tower open. With Patrick ready to receive us, we move out the front door making sure the women know to stay right on me without tripping over me if I have to stop quickly. Brad and Steve follow us across the valet lot and up the stairs. This little stint is further than the last ones and I want lots of firepower just in case. With a sidewalk, three lanes, a wall, three more lanes, and another sidewalk to the tower I don't want to take any chances.

Halfway across the street I get a sinking feeling in my stomach again as I hear the sound of screeching tires. Looking up, the same black SUV from earlier comes racing down the street directly at us.

ELEVEN
Crystals

"Shoot up the car," I yell to my team while telling the women to keep running for cover at the Towers. Instinctively, I begin to put every round in my magazine through the front windshield. Once Brad and Steve see what I'm doing they join in as round after round impact the passenger side. Impossible to see into the dark vehicle, I continue to shoot at the driver's seat as the car continues straight towards me.

With the vehicle getting closer by the second, my flight or fight instinct kicks in—get out of here. I then hear rounds coming from Veer Tower. I glance over just long enough to see the women are safe and Patrick has made his way to the street. He is putting every round from his rifle into the driver's side window.

Just then, one of our rounds finds its target. The large black SUV swerves hard right—impacting the barrier and sending the driver through the front windshield twenty feet onto the pavement.

Still not sure why these low-lifes are trying to kill me, I glance again to make sure Taylor and Savanah are safe before moving up to the vehicle.

"Steve! Get up here and cover the passenger side! Brad and Patrick, keep your eyes open!" I yell out as I approach the vehicle with caution. I walk past the driver laying on the pavement making sure he won't be moving again. As I approach the vehicle, I see another man in the passenger seat slumped over. Making sure Steve has him covered I approach the driver's side throwing the rear door open. With no one in the back seat and finding the cargo area empty my attention turns completely to the man in the front seat.

Pulling the front passenger door open, my eyes stare in disbelief as the man sitting before me comes into full view. Steve speaks first, as he can see I'm tongue-tied at the moment.

"It's James!" Steve exclaims.

Why is my number two man sitting in this car with a company rifle in his lap? I know it's the same vehicle from before when Taylor and I were leaving the Vdara. How did he know the exact moment we would be leaving both hotels? All these questions and more race through my mind as I hear him make a gurgling sound and then see him move ever so slightly.

With more anger than I've ever felt in my life, I pull his almost lifeless body out of the car and slam it on the ground. His body thuds to the ground as his head snaps back crashing into the pavement.

"What are you doing?" I yell in James' face as I pull the rifle from his dying fingers.

As James attempts to speak, I see his throat has filled with blood. He does nothing but cough and choke on his own fluid. Wanting to keep him alive, I look over his body to find several wounds in his chest and in his side. He won't make it more than a minute before he suffocates. I'm sure his lungs are filling with blood as the anger still builds inside me.

"Why are you trying to kill me?" I yell again.

James doesn't say a word. As he feels his life slipping away, a smile appears on his face as he looks dead in my eyes and fades into the next world.

Thoughts continue to race through my mind as I contemplate the predicament I'm now faced with—who else on my team is working for someone else? Is Tom behind this? Does Jennifer have a part to play? Is Patrick working for the cartels? As that question enters my mind, I quickly jump up to see Patrick is still watching the street with his rifle at the ready. I can see Taylor and Savanah—they look safe. I then glance over to Steve to see he is watching the street as well. Brad is doing the same. If any of them were trying to kill me, they would have done it already—right?

That thought renews my confidence in them. What about Patrick though. I haven't seen him until now. He did just put several rounds into the vehicle, or at least that's what it appeared like.

I look past the vehicle in the direction Patrick was shooting to find bullet holes in Mandarin's facade. Did he deliberately shoot past to make me think he was shooting the car? The ideas continue to run through my head as I tell Steve and Brad to get back in the Mandarin and lock it up. I then quickly run across the street, hopping over the median and making my way into Veer Tower.

No one shot at us leaving the Aria. Brett is the one factor between leaving the Vdara and Mandarin that makes any sense. He can't be the one running the show though. It has to be someone on the outside.

Sensing the confusion in my expression, I'm awakened to reality as Taylor grabs my hand and asks if I'm alright. I quickly respond that I'm fine—not wanting Patrick to think anything out of the ordinary.

"You have your key to the room still?" I quickly ask, hoping she hasn't sensed the uncertainty in my voice.

She's only known me for a little more than two months, but she can see the concern on my face. "Are you sure you're okay babe?"

156

With my breathing more under control, I answer her again, "I'm fine babe. Can you and Savanah head up to the room? I'll be up in a sec once I know all is well here."

With concern still painted across her face, she agrees. She gives me another hug and tells me she loves me. I do the same and then send her on her way. Not wanting to take my eyes off her, I reluctantly turn my attention to Patrick—is he friend or foe? With an army inside Veer Tower able to occupy North Korea, I ask Patrick if we can talk in his office. I don't want anyone hearing what I'm about to ask. Plus I need him to feel more comfortable so he will let his guard down a bit. If he's lying to me I should be able to pick it up.

Patrick agrees and lets his men know we'll be in his office. We don't say anything as we walk down the hall into the office. I hope it's just me, but the tension seems to be building. As we step into the office, he takes a seat behind his desk and motions for me to have a seat.

"It's pretty crazy out there," Patrick states with amazement in his tone.

"It is," I respond. "How have things been over here?" I ask, testing the waters. I need a baseline before I ask any telling questions.

"We've been pretty quiet here. As soon as we heard the commotion outside we quickly put our plan into action."

"How many men do you have on right now and where do you have them stationed?"

"You saw the army in the lobby, but we also have five men in each parking garage letting residents into the building."

"Has anyone tried to leave?" I ask, watching his eyes, his chest, his hands—anything that might change when posed with the questions I'm still formulating in my mind.

"Only one," he quickly resounds calmly. "I tried to talk them into staying, but they said they had to get out of town before things got worse."

Patrick's hand movements, eye contact, breathing, and just about everything I can watch has remained fairly consistent as I continue to ask general questions. We talk in a casual manner for five minutes until the line of questioning I need to ask comes to mind.

"Do you think you hit the driver in that black car outside?" I ask.

"I'm pretty sure I did. I think I put just about every round through his window. Did he have any holes in the left side of his head as you walked past?" Patrick says with the same calm he exhibited over the last five minutes.

"It was hard to tell with his head hitting the pavement at that speed. It was difficult to tell he even had a head."

"Since he swerved right, and seeing almost all my rounds impact his window, I bet I hit him," Patrick says with confidence.

I hadn't thought about the car swerving. Patrick's confidence and calm have me feeling much better. I just have one more question for him, maybe more of a statement. I want to see his expression when I drop the news on him.

"I don't know who the driver was, but James was riding shotgun. He shot at us leaving the Vdara less than an hour ago," I say with the surprise still evident.

"What?" Patrick blurts out. "Your security manager James?" he asks in complete disbelief.

"The same. Are you working for the cartels or anyone else that would seek to do me or anyone else in this organization harm?"

Patrick looks dumbfounded as I ask the question. "Absolutely not," the reply comes back. He looks completely sincere in his answer and my fears cease. "If James is dead, as I presume he is, then I work directly for you and only you," Patrick adds.

"You don't know how good it sounds to hear you say that. I didn't believe you were working for anyone else, but I had to ask the question. Unfortunately, I believe James and Tom have infiltrated our security team and there may be more that are working for him."

"Do you have any idea who?" Patrick asks, still unable to comprehend the situation.

"I'm pretty sure of one. I'll let you know because I'm positive he can't be trusted. Both times we were shot at Brett was aware of our location and where we were going next. I think he's working for Tom, which I have under good authority works for the Zetas drug cartel."

"I would ask you if you are joking, but I can clearly see you're not. What do you want me to do?" Patrick asks, starting to grasp the situation we find ourselves in.

"Keep doing exactly what you're doing. Watch your men a little closer maybe. I'm going to run up to my room and make sure Taylor and Savanah know what to do, and then I'll be back down. I'll need to borrow part of your army to head down to Crystals and then over to Bellagio."

"If you go out with guns, you'll definitely get shot at. Why don't you do what we've been doing? Carry a concealed handgun just in case you need protection, but go out there like every other thug running the streets—blend in."

Patrick's logic makes perfect sense. I'd been trying to grasp how we could possibly go into Crystals without starting a war. I don't want to put innocent people in jeopardy if we don't have to.

"That's a good idea. Do you think you could talk five of your biggest men into coming with me?" I ask Patrick, grateful for his insight.

"It shouldn't be a problem. I know just who to send. They'll love knocking some heads together down there. They've been itching to see some action anyways," Patrick replies with excitement.

I thank Patrick for his leadership and jump on the elevator. When I get in my place I quickly find Taylor making Savanah some food in the kitchen. Savanah has propped her feet up on the counter looking much more comfortable than I found her not more than thirty minutes ago.

"You women doing well?" I ask as I walk into the kitchen.

"We're good," Taylor responds.

"I'll grab the rifles and handguns out of the safe so you're ready should something happen before I get back."

"You're still going to Bellagio?" Taylor responds, the fear etched in her tone.

"You know I have to. I have to do everything I can," I respond as I hold Taylor in my arms.

I give her a quick kiss and then go to work making them feel as safe as possible. I move a couch to the front entry so they can wedge it against the door and wall once I leave. I pull out some flash bangs and every rifle and magazine and place them on the counter.

"You two can manage for an hour or two until I get back, right?"

"We'll manage," Savanah responds.

"Here you go," Taylor says, holding up a sandwich. "You're going to die of starvation if you don't eat something."

"What would I do without you?" I say, as Savanah sighs at my affection.

"I don't know," Taylor replies as she leans in to show me how much she cares.

I gratefully take the sandwich and walk over to the window. From this floor I have a perfect view of the strip. Eating my sandwich I can't help but wonder how long the chaos I see will continue. The abandoned police car on fire in front of the market place doesn't look too promising.

Taylor brings me back to reality as she grabs my hand at the window. "It's going to start getting dark soon."

I hadn't even noticed the hour. I give her hand a squeeze and head to the front door. Taylor follows me, still holding my hand, not wanting to miss one second of her time with me. When I try to pull my hand away she clutches even tighter, hoping that if she just holds on I won't have to leave.

"Move the couch in front as soon as I leave okay?" I say, gently brushing a loose strand of hair behind her ear.

"Okay," she says with desperation in her eyes.

"I love you babe."

"I love you too," Taylor says with tears building almost to the point of falling from her big blue eyes.

"Don't cry. I'll be back before you know it. I'll call you every thirty minutes or so to let you know I'm okay."

"You better."

I step out the door and listen as Taylor locks the door and slides the couch in place—that's my girl.

I head down to the lobby to find Patrick. To my pleasant surprise, he has my team assembled. All are seasoned security officers and most make me look small in comparison to their bulk.

"I'm glad to see you're all out of your uniforms. Does everyone have a handgun concealed where they can get it quickly if backed into a corner?"

Everyone nods in affirmation. I then ask if they comprehend completely what I'm asking of them. Again, without saying a word, they nod.

If we want to make this look believable we'll have to go down to the Boulevard and enter in through the main doors. I run down the plan one more time so they hear it from my mouth. I don't want there to be any confusion once we get inside.

No one says a word as they listen intently. I run down the importance of staying in two-man teams, only acting to save people, and most importantly, only pull out your handgun when a life is in jeopardy. The looks on their faces as I explain that last fact brings a somber tone to the group.

"I know what I'm asking won't be easy, but if we stay in two-man teams going from store to store, we should be good. If you can clear out a store and lock the gate, do it. If the task looks too daunting, find every employee left in the store and get them to the security office on the main floor. Once we've secured every store or saved every person, we'll get them out of there. If we're lucky we'll get the place locked up."

Patrick wishes us good luck as we move out the same entrance I just came in. Moving in two-man teams at one minute intervals we move down City Center Place to Las Vegas Boulevard. Less than one-hundred feet north of City Center Place and the Boulevard, I enter the main doors to Crystals.

Until the moment I step through the doors, I hadn't truly imagined how good or bad it might be inside these high-end shops. At first glance, I see lots of shops have their steel gates already closed with the lights off inside. This gives me great hope for the remainder of the stores throughout the two-story complex.

I team up with Mike—a six foot three inch brute who would scare anyone just to look at him. Walking through the doors, he sees the same thing I do. There are three men holding a female employee from one of the restaurants on the ground. We both survey the ground as we begin running to assist.

Mike gets there first and hits two of the men so hard in the head one of them lies unconscious on the ground and the other one appears dazed, but starts to fight back. Only a second behind Mike, I grab the third, putting him in a choke hold that's sure to turn his lights off in five seconds. Struggling for air, he claws at my face forcing me to turn on top of him slamming his head hard into the ground. Never letting up pressure around his neck, he didn't stand a chance. I release his lifeless body and check his pulse—he's still breathing.

I then look at Mike who has beaten his man to an almost bloody pulp.

"I think he's good!" I tell Mike, as I attend to the female. "Are you alright?" I ask, helping her pull her clothes back on.

"Yes," she says between sobs.

"You're safe now. Mike, check these three for weapons and then hog tie them all together." Every team brought zip ties and rope for the flunkies we were certain to encounter.

Looking back at the damsel no longer in such dire distress I say, "You'll be safe now. What's your name?"

"Misty," she quickly responds.

"Stay with us until we can get you into the security office."

She nods in agreement as I pull her to her feet. Mike finishes tying up the threesome and we start looking for our next target. The Gucci store just inside the doors looks mostly cleared out, but there are a few stragglers still causing havoc within. Mike and I make our way over as Misty follows closely behind.

There are five or six unwanted people inside and I can't see any employees. Mike and I quickly assess the situation and then go to work. Mike takes to the degenerates as Misty and I head toward the back. We find all four employees cowering in the office with the door locked.

I quickly knock—not knowing if they'll let me in. Who knows what degree of panic has set in here? I've tried to make these shops my second priority since they sit directly under Veer. As I look through the small window into the office, I notice one of the female employees has recognized me. She quickly opens the door to let us in.

"Did all the employees make it in here safely?" I quickly ask, letting Misty through the door first.

"Yeah, we're all here. We couldn't get the gates shut. Seth tried, but you can see the bruises that earned him," the manager replies.

"I'm going to leave Misty here with you until Mike and I clear out the store. Once that's done, we'll close the gate and then have you let us out. Can you do that?"

Not asking anything of them but to wait until everything is secure, they all nod in agreement.

I quickly get back out to the front to see Mike has beaten three people so bad they are fleeing out of the store with a couple items. Mike didn't want to beat the two females in the store. I think he's waiting for me to help grab them. I quickly make it over to see two women scared out of their minds. I don't ask, and Mike doesn't say a word, as he flies at the larger of the two. I quickly grab the other, forcing her to drop everything she's trying to take from the store. We pick them both up and kindly, but firmly, escort them out.

"I didn't want to hurt you in the store, but if you come back in here I will make you look like those other three," Mike says, as he tosses his girl to the ground.

With Mike standing guard in front of the store, they don't dare make their way back in. I reach over and turn the key to have the gate come down as Mike walks inside confident no one will try coming in now. With the gate shut, I run to the back room to have the manager come back out. Still in the back room, I hear Mike yell we need to hurry—another employee is in trouble. The manager quickly opens the gate just enough to let us roll under.

Mike points out our next destination. Another female employee was trying to get out when two more thugs came in and grabbed her. I have to get someone down here or this will be a never ending problem. Still inside the store, I call Patrick on the radio to send four men down here fully armed to guard the front door. Patrick answers quickly and says they'll be down in less than two.

165

Mike and I quickly move to the problem, grabbing both men. Towering over both of them it isn't much of a fight. They quickly get smart and run right out the doors they came through. I quickly grab the employee and move her to the Gucci store. The manager was watching and already had the gate slightly open for her to slide underneath.

Turning to see our next target, Mike has already started moving to another store in the same predicament. Mike is like a kid in a candy shop as we clear store after store. We continue clearing stores for thirty minutes until all the stores are locked up tight and every employee and patron we can find has safely found security behind a large metal gate.

The one thing I hadn't expected as we entered Crystals seems completely clear now—no one was carrying guns. They were just looking to loot and figured they would take advantage while they could. We also find several security locked in the office, not sure what to do. They didn't want to shoot people without guns, but they also knew five guards against rioting zombies wouldn't turn out very well. We also found that a few of our security team had secured a few stores and were locked inside not daring to breach the chaos by themselves.

With the stores and building secure, I pull all the security together to give them a quick brief before starting the next leg of this adventure.

"You've done an outstanding job—unfortunately, it's not over yet. I need all of you back in the security office to get your rifle before manning a position. I haven't seen anyone coming in so we should still have four guys at the main entrance on the Boulevard. I need all the other exits covered."

I continue to talk—telling each man where they need to go once they're armed. I also explain that those who were left tied in the middle of the mall can stay there until the situation calms down. Gag them if they make too much noise. They all smile as I explain prisoner treatment. I'm sure a few would like to get revenge seeing the bruises and black eyes they endured doing their jobs.

"I couldn't ask for a better crew," I say, sending them on their way. I keep my five brutes with me as the rest disperse to the office. "I can see a few of you took some licks here so I'm going to give you a choice—you can stay here or head back up to the tower. It's your choice. I just have one favor to ask—I need one person to come with me over to the Bellagio. That's my last stop before I can rest a little easier."

"I'm going with you," Mike says. "I haven't had enough of this yet. Since we've already worked together for the last forty minutes it only seems fitting."

"Sounds good to me. What about the rest of you?" I ask.

"We're heading back up to the tower. They have plenty of people here to keep this place safe," Bob says. The rest all say the same and I thank them for what they've done.

"Let the guys out front know they can head back up once the Crystals' team has relieved them."

"We will," a couple say, relieved their fight is over for now.

Finally with a chance to think, I realize the thirty minute timeframe has passed and I remember to call Taylor. She answers the phone quickly to let me know she's on the other line with her mom. Her mom and dad are still safe and her mom was relieved to hear Taylor is safe and back at my place. I tell her I love her and let her know the shops are torn apart, but at least the employees are safe and the mall sits secure for the moment. I let her know I'll have Mike with me as we take off for Bellagio which also makes her feel a little better. Knowing I have to get going, I tell her to keep talking with her mom, and I'll call her again in thirty minutes or so.

"You ready to go?" Mike asks eating some food from one of the little food shops.

"Ready as I'm going to be."

We make our way to the north entrance to find a guard already manning his post. As we look outside, the darkness is setting in which will certainly bring more madness to this ever worsening situation. We've taken care of James and his driver, but are there any others out there working for Tom? I guess only time will tell as we prepare. The images from the television hit me now. I sure hope we don't run into the crowd I saw earlier. That would cause a most serious setback that I don't have time to deal with now.

TWELVE
Bellagio

Making our way through the north entrance, I realize we are still basically unarmed. A handgun works great in a jam, but moving over this large distance without a rifle worries me. Mike must have been thinking the same thing because he asked if we should have grabbed a rifle from Crystals before we left. I tell him we don't have a lot of time, and we keep moving.

"I thought you were crazy when you took over Tom's position," Mike quietly says as we make our way down the road, much too dark for my liking now. "Putting rifles in every security office under your control seemed insane, but boy am I glad you did. I just wish I had one now."

I don't respond to Mike as we continue moving. When we come out the north entrance I remember the Cosmopolitan hotel that sits on the northeast corner of City Center property. Why they didn't want to join us when we bought out the Jockey Club I still can't figure out. I hope things look tranquil inside as we make our way past because I don't have time for another fiasco like the one we encountered inside the Mandarin.

Still trying to play the part of just another tourist, we round the corner at Harmon and the Boulevard to see multitudes of people moving in and out of the hotel. Not wanting to start anything, I tell Mike we are just going to move past regardless of what's happening inside. He agrees to the idea and we continue on. As we stroll past the shops that line the entrance, I see looters have already taken what they can and there's not much left. Display cases are toppled, leaving shattered

169

glass all over the floor. Clothes racks are turned every which way but up with no clothing left to be taken. Cash registers have been pried open with I'm sure, not a nickel left to be had. At the entrance to the Cosmopolitan, I glance inside. It looks like the Aria did when I first arrived. Chaos is everywhere, but we have to keep our focus on the goal—make it to Bellagio in one piece without further distractions.

Moving a little quicker as we pass the final building, the Bellagio comes into full view. The great entrance located right on the Boulevard looks like the safest route. Rioters fill the streets in front of the fountains. The complete lack of police presence down here after several hours since things went downhill seems a little odd, but I guess understandable. I wouldn't come in here with a badge and gun if you paid me a million dollars.

The escalators aren't moving as we approach the stairs and quickly move to the top. As we crest the peak of the stairs, the long corridor lined with coliseum-type columns looks like an Italian tragedy waiting to happen. The path leading to the front entrance is still quite a distance, as we both look at each other and start moving.

Moving side by side, I take the right while Mike watches the left. The Italian music playing as we make our way past each column gives me an eerie feeling. I'm not fighting to the death right now, but I can't help but feel like a gladiator moving to some epic battle in Rome. We continue to move when out of nowhere two young women in their early twenties jump out from behind a bush.

"Please don't hurt us!" the first one yells, seeing the handguns.

Mike answers them first, "We're not going to hurt you."

"We are trying to get into the Bellagio to make sure our people are okay," I quickly say in follow-up. "Are you two okay?"

The second female answers this time, "We will be a lot better if we can come with you," she says with hope in her eyes.

I look them over and it quickly becomes apparent they are not carrying any weapons. The short shorts, tank tops, and high heels they're carrying couldn't hide a cap gun. They also aren't carrying purses so I assume those were either left behind or taken from them during the mayhem that has ensued on the streets. The looks on their faces leads me to believe they haven't had the most enjoyable time over the last hour or so.

"We'll take you with us on two conditions," I quickly utter. "First, you have to be quiet. We don't want anyone to hear us coming. Second, you have to watch our backs as we approach the hotel—unless you want to be out front?"

The first one quickly speaks up at the suggestion, "You've got to be crazy!"

Mike and I both chuckle to ourselves.

The more composed one then says, "We'll stay behind if you don't mind."

"I thought you would," Mike responds. We start to move out and the women fall into place.

Without another interruption, we quickly arrive at the front entrance to find it locked up tight. Several guards are standing watch inside. Glancing through the severely damaged windows, I see Scott's team. They recognize me instantly and quickly open the door to let us in.

One of my good friends from my time as a valet is standing guard. I instantly feel better. Joe and I have worked together ever since I started here and I know he would do anything for me.

After making it inside and getting the front doors locked up again, I lightly say, "Looks like you guys had a war here."

Joe is the first to reply. "Yeah. If you would have been here you would have had a blast."

We all laugh lightly, while still appreciating the gravity of the situation.

"Is Scott here? What about Matt?" I quickly ask. Joe tells me of the trouble they've had here with looters trying to break in from every entrance they can. He thinks they have it locked up now, but it was quite rough for a while. Joe tells me he hasn't seen Matt, and Scott just barely took off to make his rounds of the entrances and exits. This place covers acres of ground and making sure the guys are still in position stands paramount. There is no one in the casino. Scott has done his job here. The amount of training we've been put through would prepare anyone for just about everything and this scenario is no different.

Seeing the radio on Joe's waist, I ask him to call Scott back up here. Scott responds to Joe quickly saying he'll be here in a minute. Remembering the two females in tow, I ask Joe if they have someone who could get the two lovely ladies a key so they can go relax in a room. Joe, not wanting to miss the opportunity to meet a single lady, jumps into action as he introduces himself. He then escorts the ladies to the front desk while telling us to wait here for Scott. I knew Scott would have this place running smoothly.

As I survey the entrance, I can't help but notice the beautiful blown glass still hanging from the ceiling in the foyer. Every time I come through these front doors I am blown away by the elegance here. The blues and reds and greens are tantalizing together. The kaleidoscope of colors is so mesmerizing I don't notice Scott walk right up behind me.

"You lost mate?" Scott asks jokingly as he sees he has caught me off guard. "What took you so long?"

"That's the million dollar question isn't it," I reply, reluctantly pulling my gaze from the million dollar ceiling. "How much time do you have?" I say, as more of a statement than a question. "I'll tell you the story once I've talked to Dean. Have you been able to talk to him yet?" I ask, hoping to hear that he has.

"I haven't had time to eat let alone make it up to Dean's office. I thought I finally had this place locked down and was about to grab a bite when Joe told me to get back up here. I thought we were about to have another incident. Then I walked around the corner and saw you standing here. I can't tell you how relieved I am now. I did my time mate. I didn't sign up for World War III when you brought me over."

"You whining Mr. SAS?"

"You know what I mean. This is ridiculous."

"I know. It will settle down in no time. Melissa and Bobbi are here with you right? Why didn't you have Melissa or one of the guys grab you something?" I ask.

Scott hadn't thought about Melissa for a while with all the running around. He grabs his phone to call her as he says, "Even if someone had brought me something, I wouldn't have been able to eat it with all the running around I've done. Give me a second. I need to call her, now that you mention it."

I quickly tell Scott I'm going to go talk to Dean and I let Mike know he can grab some food and then report to Scott for an assignment. I tuck my handgun into my waistband and start moving to Dean's office.

On my way to Dean's office I call Taylor.

"Oh Deacon, I can't tell you how nice it is to hear your voice. Are you okay? How's Scott and Melissa? Is everything okay?" Taylor shotguns me with these and many more questions.

Although I don't admit it to Taylor, hearing her voice soothes me and fills me with peace and confidence.

"Everything is going as well as can be expected. I made it to the Bellagio and Scott, Melissa, and Bobbi are all safe. How are you and Savanah holding up?"

"We are doing fine. I'm glad they are okay. It looks like a war-zone on the Strip. Every time I look out the window it looks like the chaos is spreading further and further. I called my parents and thankfully they are still safe. I heard on the news that due to the stock market crash the federal government is contemplating another quantitative easing—the largest in history."

"That's been the government's plan for decades. Throw more money at the problem instead of coming up with solid solutions to fix the fiscal fiasco we've been in. I don't know if any amount of money will fix what's happening now."

"You're probably right."

"Taylor, I just want you to know how much I love you and how much I appreciate how positive and optimistic you've been to-day—even though we've been through a pretty crazy adventure."

"I love you too Deacon. I could get through just about anything as long as I have you by my side."

174

We continue to talk as I ride the elevator to the top floor. I tell her to get as much food as possible from room service just in case this lasts longer than anyone could imagine. The elevator bell rings announcing my arrival. As the elevator door opens, I understand why Dean put his office up here. Even the view from the elevator is amazing. As I step off the elevator into the lobby, fear sweeps over me. Jennifer is not at her desk and things are in disarray. I calmly and quietly tell Taylor I have to go.

"Something's wrong isn't it Deacon?" Taylor asks with apprehension. "I understand if you don't answer. Be safe. I love you."

I shove my phone into my pocket while at the same time I retrieve the handgun from my waist.

Without making a sound, I scan the room and listen for any signs of movement. The room is completely still. I can't hear Jennifer's manicured fingernails tapping against the keyboard—I can't hear the office chair wheels rolling into place behind the desk or the click of Jennifer's stilettos approaching—I can't hear the buzz from the intercom or the sound of the classical piano music Jennifer always has playing softly in the background. The room is completely still. I quickly make my way around the lobby—checking every nook and cranny for any signs of life.

I see the door that I've passed through time and time again to talk to Dean and suddenly it looks as big as it did the first time I met him here. I quickly move over to the door and listen for anything that would suggest danger. The bullet holes splintering the door suggest automatic gunfire which doesn't settle my nerves. Apparently the door was locked leading to Dean's office because the doorknob has been obliterated.

Once again, the silence is deafening. I quickly open the door and make my way in. My fears are instantly confirmed. Paper is strewn all over the room. Drawers are pulled out. The office has clearly been ransacked with the intent to find something—something that someone believed was in Dean's possession. Continuing to scan the room, I see legs on the ground poking out from behind Dean's desk. The five hundred dollar leather shoes on the feet instantly tell me who it is lying there.

I maneuver around the massive office. I quickly move over to Dean's lifeless body to find several bullet holes in his chest and one in his head. Having been around more than my share of dead bodies, it becomes apparent that whoever did this wanted to make sure Dean stopped breathing for good. The hole through his forehead was done at close range in the exact spot he now lays, lifeless.

My relationship with Dean over the last two months had grown so much that as I look now at his body an anger wells up inside me that makes me audibly cry out in pain. I have seen dead bodies before and even had good friends die right in my arms, but something about seeing this giant of a man lying dead in his office in the civilian world gets me. I guess when you're at war you prepare yourself to lose good friends, so to speak. You don't want to, but you realize the realities of war.

What if Jennifer did this? The thought strikes me like a dagger to the back. It can't be. My mind races as I attempt to throw the thought from my mind. I can't help but think of all the times I've seen Tom and Jennifer together. They had to be dating. The longing looks and loving embraces could only mean one thing.

Lost in a mix of hate, grief, and a fair amount of betrayal and suspicion, I am brought back to reality as I unexpectedly hear a noise behind me. In one fluid motion, I quickly turn and point my gun—finger at the ready and not a single reason why I should hesitate at all to pull the trigger. A door concealed as a bookshelf begins to open slowly and someone emerges from a room I didn't even know existed. To my surprise, Jennifer slowly comes out with her hands in the air. Her eyes look ice-cold and her face completely expressionless.

"Jennifer?" I acknowledge.

"Deacon, I'm so glad it's you."

I start lowering my weapon when I notice there is blood on her clothes. I instantaneously rethink my initial decision to lower my weapon and train the weapon once again on my target.

A new look enters her eyes. "Deacon, it's me—Jennifer."

I don't flinch.

"Lower your weapon Deacon," Jennifer begins slowly. "I know this looks bad, but it's not what you think."

"You'd better start explaining."

"Dean and I were here in the office meeting as we always do every day before I go home. Today seemed less formal based on everything that has been going on, but Dean is always so insistent that we plan and coordinate appointments every afternoon at 4:30," Jennifer begins. She looks over at Dean's body and then quickly averts her eyes uncomfortably before continuing. "We heard the elevator arrive on the floor and instantly gunfire erupted. Dean quickly grabbed me by the arm, opened the hidden door into the safe, and told me not to come out no matter what. Almost as soon as the hidden door clicked shut, I heard the shooters make it through the locked door and into the office."

I could tell that Jennifer was fighting to maintain composure. Her face, although still remarkably expressionless, was growing more and more pale.

I figure a little air would help her, so we walk out of Dean's office and into the lobby near her desk.

"I heard yelling," Jennifer continues, still ashen. "Someone kept threatening Dean for a disc. 'Hand over the disc Dean,' I heard someone say over and over again. Dean must have made it back to his desk and had grabbed the handgun he had concealed there because the man told Dean to drop the gun and tell him where the disc was. You know Dean, he is a stubborn man, a stubborn man with morals..." Jennifer's voice breaks for the first time since the interrogation started. "He was a stubborn man," she corrects herself.

Jennifer clears her throat before continuing, "Then Dean said, 'If there is such a disc, as you claim, I certainly wouldn't give it to you. There will be ice skating in hell before I turn anything over to you.' I heard Dean take a shot or two and then an automatic weapon fired. The gunfire stopped and the room was silent."

Jennifer reaches and places her hand on the corner of her desk to steady herself, either for dramatic effect or necessity.

"Then there were footsteps and I heard one final shot. "

"Jennifer, did you fire that final shot?" I ask, point blank.

"No! How could you even ask that?" Jennifer retorts, the color returning to her face.

"How do you explain the blood on your dress?"

Jennifer looks down in surprised bewilderment.

"What blood?" she says, her voice trailing off as she sees the blood. Her eyes filling with tears.

178

"That's Dean's blood, isn't it Jennifer. You and your boyfriend Tom have been planning this for months, haven't you?"

"Deacon, no…," Jennifer stutters.

"Dean told me about the disc, months ago, in fact. He said he suspected there was a mole in his organization. How could you Jennifer? How could you?"

"You know about the disc?"

"You and Tom didn't anticipate that did you? Well, I know more…"

Jennifer interrupts me.

"Listen Deacon, I can explain the blood. Whoever was here went through the office. I heard them rifle through the desk and knock books off of the shelves. I assume they were looking for the disc. I don't think they found it, though. I heard one of them curse angrily and then I heard them leave. I stayed in the safe room for five or ten minutes before venturing out. I came out and saw Dean. I knew it was impossible, but I just had to see if he was still alive. I must have gotten blood on my dress when I was trying to check his pulse. Before I could do much of anything I heard the elevator arrive on the floor again and I ran back into the safe room."

Both of us jump when we hear the ding of the elevator. I point my gun toward the elevator.

"Scott, you almost gave me a heart attack," I quickly spout off.

"Why are you pointing that bloody thing at me? What in the world happened here?" Scott asks, peering around the disheveled lobby.

"We are still trying to figure that out."

I pull Scott aside.

"I need backup. I need eyes on Jennifer. Things don't add up with her." I glance over at Jennifer who has sat down at her desk and is staring blankly.

Scott radios down to Mike who comes up to guard Jennifer and the lobby.

I don't want Scott to feel responsible. It's probably good he never made it up here. If Tom was here with automatic weapons and several guys he probably would have been caught off guard like I was and who knows what would have happened.

"What is going on mate?" Scott asks as I close the door to Dean's office.

"Jennifer claims Dean was killed by someone looking for a disc. He or they then spent almost an hour looking through the office for this disc," I answer in reply.

Scott doesn't say anything as he finally sees Dean's legs lying on the floor behind his desk. He slowly walks over to the desk without saying a word. Knowing what Scott has seen through his life I know he can handle the terrible scene he is now gazing upon.

In complete amazement Scott looks back at me and says, "How long ago did she say this happened?"

"Jennifer said she was locked in the hidden safe for almost an hour while someone, most likely Tom, murdered Dean and then ransacked the room."

Trying to put the puzzle pieces together Scott says, "That's about the time we had gun fire at one of the rear entrances. By the time we had numbers to secure the area we couldn't find anything more than a little blood. I had the men search the entire area. There was no one and nothing more than a few spent casings. We couldn't find Don anywhere and figured he couldn't handle the assignment and split. We didn't have any other issues inside after that and figured nothing of it."

"If it was Tom coming in at that time only an army would have stopped him. He knows this building better than any of us. He would have got in one way or another. Don't beat yourself up over it. You and I are going to find Tom and if society hasn't put itself back together we'll take care of things ourselves. I don't care if it takes years. What he did to Dean must be returned in kind."

Scott doesn't say a word. He didn't know Dean as well as I did, but one elite soldier to another recognizes the loss.

"Why didn't you cover his body?" Scott asks.

"I didn't have the time. As soon as I discovered his body Jennifer popped out. I don't trust her Scott. Her involvement in this whole thing worries me. Let's grab something to put over him though, we owe it to him."

We quickly grab a blanket out of the closet and cover Dean's body. Knowing it wouldn't do any good to call for a mortuary, I resolve to leave his body there until things calm down. Remembering the disc Jennifer told me about, I move into the safe to look for it. The safe isn't enormous like the rest of the office so it shouldn't be too difficult to find. Dean has some old rifles in the safe that probably would fire if I needed them to, but sitting on the shelf above them lays the perfect SCAR 17 decked out like it was when I was back on the teams. Looking at Scott I say, "I think I've found my new rifle. I'm pretty sure Dean won't mind. He'd want another SEAL to have this anyway."

"That's just like you pups, every little toy you can attach to your rifle you do. What ever happened to being a good marksmen and relying on that?" Scott chides back.

"Oh, I'm a good marksmen. The toys just make the acquisition quicker."

We continue to look through the safe as Scott pauses and says in amazement, "What kind of night vision are these? Don't tell me these work?"

Seeing the box in his hand I have an idea what he's talking about. We only started fielding those during my last year on the teams, "NVCs," I say, hoping they are in deed. "I guess it shouldn't surprise me that Dean has those. Have you not heard of those?" I ask in surprise.

"I don't know if you realize this, but you guys get everything before we do mate. You would think my government would want the best for us, but that just isn't the case. The US Government throws millions, if not billions of more dollars at Naval Special Warfare than the British Parliament would dream of giving us. You are the favorite sons in specops while we are the red-headed step children across the pond."

"I know you know NVGs, but those are NVCs, night vision contacts."

"Those don't really work do they?" Scott asks in complete disbelief.

"They not only work, they perform better. The natural blinking of your eyes charges something in them and you can see just as well if not better than your natural eyes. Not to mention they don't weigh anything and you have unrestricted vision and complete depth of perception without anything getting in the way. Are there some in there?" I ask hoping there are at least a couple pairs.

Scott opens the case and to my amazement all five pairs are there just like we fielded on the teams.

"I've got to try these out," Scott says, still unsure just how great they will let him see in the dark.

"You'll get your chance. You're coming back to my place once we find this disc aren't you? I want you to know everything I know so if something happens to either one of us the other one can continue on and even take care of Taylor and Melissa."

"Yep, we're coming back. I don't think Melissa will want to go anywhere with the chaos happening in the streets."

"I'm sure you'll figure out a way to get her to come with us. We'll take all the back roads I should have taken on my way over here if I could have bypassed all my resorts. We'll also have Mike if you think you have enough security over here without him."

"We should be good," Scott replies.

We continue to look through the safe room and eventually find the disc in a folder inside a separate safe in the wall. It's a good thing the safe wasn't locked. The cd doesn't have any writing on it, but we found it in a red and white folder labeled Top Secret. It doesn't look like the typical military top secret file though. Dean had quite a bit of gear in his safe room. All and all we were able to get the NVCs, the disc, the rifle, some binoculars, and a backpack filled with some MREs and ammunition for the rifle. Dean was definitely ready for hard times. Normally I would feel bad about taking a dead man's gear, but I know he would want me to be prepared.

As we move out to the lobby I see Jennifer has most of her things back up on the desk. She seems anxious and is absentmindedly organizing her desk while talking quietly to Mike. Their whispered conversation ends abruptly when Scott and I walk into the room. Mike's eyes shift away from my gaze and he withdraws back to the doorway.

Jennifer looks at me expectantly. "Did you find it?" she asks with a little too much anticipation.

My face remains completely expressionless as I look at her, an awkward silence enshrouds the room.

Scott clears his throat and glances over at me.

"What are we going to do now?" Jennifer asks, breaking the silence, and glancing down at her blood splattered skirt.

"You have two options...," I start. "...you could go home, which I wouldn't suggest at this time, or you can hang out here in one of the rooms until things are safe enough to make it home. That is what I would suggest. Relax, take a hot bath, and watch a movie until you fall asleep."

"I'll just go to Dean's place in the penthouse."

"I'll have one of my men come check on you shortly," I respond curtly.

I know I'm not done with that one. Scott calls Joe on the radio to meet me in the lobby while Scott runs to get Melissa and Bobbi. I quickly move out to the lobby while Mike runs to get some food from one of the shops.

Meeting Joe in the lobby I quickly explain that he's the boss here and I go over the importance of keeping the employees and patrons safe. "Try to give your guys a break so they don't get burned

184

out. Hopefully this whole thing gets better tomorrow, but I think it's best you keep everyone here tonight."

"What if people want to leave? What do you want me to do?" Joe asks, unsure if he can handle this assignment.

"If they are a patron, encourage them to stay, but we can't make them. If they are employees, promise them more money if nothing else works. You'll be getting a raise too with this new position so keep up the good work."

I also make Joe aware of the insider threat from James and all the current security members. When I tell Joe of Tom and what happened in Dean's office I can see he is saddened, but he's trying to remain tough. I know he'll do an outstanding job here. After talking with Joe I move to the southwest exit to find Scott, Melissa, Bobbi, and Mike all ready to move out.

With our plan in place, Joe's security unlocks the doors and then locks them as we head into the darkness. Outside, moving past the perfectly manicured gardens and crystal clear pools, everything appears so magnificent in this part of the resort. Scott looks over at me with an enormous grin on his face. Without him even saying a word I can tell he is in awe of the NVCs.

We continue to move up and down, in and through the labyrinth of stairs and bushes when I hear one gunshot ring out from behind me. The pain instantly envelopes my body as the lights start to fade just before I hear one more shot.

THIRTEEN
Heaven

With my last thoughts focused on the two shots I heard before everything went dark, it seems somewhat strange to find myself traveling through space in what I can only explain as a ball of light. The light is brighter than anything I have ever seen, but at the same time my eyes are having no problem gazing upon it. What's going on?

And then, within a split second, I find myself in the most heavenly field my eyes have ever beheld.

"Am I dead?" I say out loud. I look around to see the most beautiful green grass, stunning flowers, and majestic trees that have ever been created. The feeling of peace here baffles my mind. Is this the world I've known my entire life? Tranquility and serenity fill my entire being. Trying to take the whole scene in, I barely notice a man in the distance moving towards me. As I squint my eyes to get a closer look, I realize he's still more than a quarter of a mile away, but I can see him perfectly as if he were standing right next to me.

Starting at his feet, I notice he is not wearing any shoes and his skin appears to be slightly glowing like the soft glow of thousands of fire flies lighting up the night sky. Next, I notice his long white robe that seems to defy all description and also appears to be lightly glowing. Until now I didn't think earthly objects could be made so white as to radiate light. The long robe covers him from his ankles to his neck and hands. His hands glow just as his feet. As my gaze turns to his face, my mouth falls open and a joy unspeakable enters my body, completely consuming my entire being.

If I hadn't seen pictures of my dad in his late twenties I might not have recognized him, but seeing him now coming towards me makes the joy and pain so bitter-sweet. I'm either dead or dreaming. I don't know how Scott will explain to Taylor or my mom what has happened to me. This very moment is undeniable—wherever I am and however I got here my dad has come to greet me. The sensations are so real.

As he approaches we embrace each other in a hug unlike any I have ever felt or experienced on earth. As we touch, I can feel his thoughts, and know better than I ever have before that he loves me completely. As we embrace and begin to talk I realize he has not opened his mouth.

Sensing my uncertainty he says, "We do not have to open our mouths to communicate here son. We still can, but it is much more efficient to talk from spirit to spirit so as to convey everything, not just words. Our thoughts and emotions can be understood without question."

Not sure where to begin as we step back from each other I ask, "Where am I?" with my mouth, still not sure of my capabilities here.

"We are in paradise son. Your angel mother taught you of Christ, do you not remember what Christ said as he hung on the cross?" my dad asks, desiring the knowledge to come to me.

Then the words come to my mind as if I've always known them, "To day shalt thou be with me in paradise." There was something different about the words this time. It was as if I heard Jesus speaking them directly to my mind—for they had so much more meaning than earthly man can comprehend.

Without saying a word my dad nods in agreement—hearing my thoughts and feeling joy in what I have discovered. I continue to think without opening my mouth.

"Why am I here Dad?" I ask without opening my mouth.

"This is a place for us to rest from our labors. What we do here now is just as important as what you do on earth."

I look at him quizzically.

Dad smiles, "Let me explain it to you in a way I know you'll understand. Before I do, I want you to know something—your body is in good hands. Your grandfather and grandmother are with Scott and Melissa ensuring they continue to work on your body. To them, it might appear to be dead, but Llewellyn and Sylva are helping them and encouraging them to keep fighting for you."

"Why are they doing that?" I ask, not sure why that's important if I'm already dead.

"You have been given a rare opportunity son. Not many people have this blessing. Where do you think Lazarus was for four days while his body lay in the tomb?"

"Here," I say without any doubt.

"Remember, with God all things are possible. You have the choice to remain here to continue the work or go back to earth and continue working to bring about righteous purposes. I have been given permission to show you what will happen if you choose to go back. You must know you will be a witness to events and experiences that have not been seen since God placed Adam and Eve in the Garden, but have been foretold by righteous men since the days of Adam. At times they will be so horrible you will wonder why they are happening, but remember they all have a purpose. God's ways are not man's ways."

As my dad begins telling me what will come it's as if a vision was opened to my understanding and I could see the events in which he was describing.

I see fighting that started because of the economic collapse. I see major cities, the whole world over descend into utter chaos. Men and women everywhere shooting and looting in order to get gain. This war appeared to turn state against state and city against city in the United States. It was so bad I was surprised to see anyone living as the natural disasters became more destructive than ever before. Great earthquakes appear to swallow whole cities, and if the earthquakes didn't do the job, a fire would start and consume everything in its path. The west coast was hit so hard that the seas swept the inhabitants and their cities into the ocean causing what appeared to be small islands all up and down the west coast.

In the Midwest an earthquake split the continent in half from the Great Lakes to the Gulf of Mexico running down the Mississippi River. The earthquakes are so devastating in this region that the water from the lakes and gulf rush in to fill the gigantic chasm that separates the country. The river must have been more than several miles wide as I gazed upon it.

Upon seeing this widespread destruction a thought formed in my mind, "Why?" to which my father immediately answered.

"In order for God to remind the inhabitants of the world He must shake them at times as He has done since the flood. If the destruction didn't occur, the fighting would continue until the whole world was consumed. Remember son, God is the same yesterday, today, and forever. If you choose to go back I will tell you one last thing, but you must know what is in store before you make that decision."

He then continued to unfold the great destruction that will most certainly befall the United States and the world. I see the east coast almost completely burn to the ground. New York, as well as many other big cities burn to the ground.

Sensing my apprehension to the overwhelming evil I've witnessed, my father shows me the righteous who separated and saved before the complete chaos ensued. I see the oceans heaving themselves beyond their bounds and covering almost half the country.

Next he shows me a sickness so devastating and so far reaching I could scarcely behold the death and pain it caused across the globe. As I continued to watch I see much of the same destruction and disease befall the world. Then an army almost as innumerable as the sands of the sea came to the United States' shores from the east and the west to conquer the country. I could not see who was fighting, but I saw in the west the army reach the Rocky Mountains and then it was repelled by the power of God. Another force, just as numerous as the west coast force came to the east coast, but again I could not see who the army was as if it was being purposely withheld from me.

As my father continued to unfold the destruction, the next thing I see is a great cold come upon the land which lasted for what seemed like an entire year. Many more people were killed unable to find shelter. I then was able to see pockets of light all across the country, but mostly centered in the Midwest. I was not given permission to see closely, but was made aware they were those who had chosen to follow God and were spared from most of the destruction.

A light so bright began to form in the Midwest, but again I was not given permission to behold the people or what they were doing. As my father continued I saw another army, just as innumerable, if not more, as the ones that came to attack the United States marching towards what appeared to be Jerusalem. They crushed everything in their path until they reached a point just outside the city walls. It was there that I saw two more lights like the one in the Midwest brighter than anything earthly possible. The lights stood bright in the city, repelling the advancing army.

Again the thought formed in my head to know what or who the light was which was protecting the city, but once again I was told I could not know. Then, to my utter amazement, I saw the lights go out and the army began to celebrate for several days until the lights shown bright once more and ascended into heaven. It was at that time the inhabitants of Jerusalem began to flee the city when another light even brighter than the two before came down and caused an earthquake so grand most of the army was destroyed.

From that point on, the people in Jerusalem began to shine as if they had received the same light that I had seen ascend into heaven. The city began to grow just like the area in the Midwest. Sometime during this whole process of wars and earthquakes something else happened which seems impossible for the human mind to understand—the continents came back together forming one giant land mass which I was made to understand was the original form it was created in the beginning.

When the vision closed to my mind my dad said, "I have not shown you the order these events will take place nor what part you will play because it must be by faith that you accomplish the work you have been called to do if you so choose it. You will lose loved ones, but know you will be protected and I will be there to guide you as you continue to do everything in your power to do what is right."

Seeing perfectly what will happen on the earth doesn't make my decision easy, but as I grasp hold of the love I feel for Taylor the choice becomes easy, "I WILL GO BACK!" penetrates every fiber of my being.

"It will not be easy. Your body will have to recover, and you will have to trust those around you for a time, but remember I will be there for you to guide and direct you if you but listen to the promptings that will come."

As I look out at the beauty that surrounds me I tell my dad how amazing it is here and how wonderful it must be to live here. He nods and says, "It's time for you to go back to your body. Remember, God's ways are not man's ways, but I know He has His reasons. You will probably not remember everything you've seen when you go back to your body, but there is purpose in everything. Since you have chosen to go back there's one more piece of very important information I have been allowed to impart to you."

"Will I remember this part since it is so important?" I ask, not sure what to think about what my father has just conveyed.

"You will remember. When your spirit returns back to your body write down what I'm about to tell you as well as what you've seen as soon as you can. You will not have much energy, but with effort, I know you will be able to do it. You will come into contact with a family fleeing the chaos in Las Vegas. When you do, you must not only help them get out, but you must listen to the message they have. I will show you who they are so when you do find them you will know without a doubt this family is the one you will save physically, but they will save our family in a much more far reaching way."

In that moment another vision opened to my mind. A beautiful family with a dark haired male and a light haired female with two girls in their early teenage years penetrates my understanding like I'd known them my entire life. Their faces, like Taylor's beautiful smile or blue eyes, were etched into my mind so clearly I can never forget them.

"You cannot tell anyone of these things until you have fled the city with this family. At that time, and you will know when the time is right, you will be able to share your knowledge of the destruction that is befalling the world. The family will know more about this destruction and bring back to your memory what you have seen. Your friends who have listened to your wise council will then be able to move forward with an understanding that will get all of you through the hardships that will most certainly befall the United States and the world."

"I can do it Dad," I say, with as much emotion and strength as I can manage to convey with thoughts.

"I know you can and that is why you have been chosen and prepared. You have received all the earthly training possible to carry yourself and others through the trouble that has begun. This family will give you the strength you need to get through the spiritual darkness that is also coming. If you listen and do as they ask, you will feel the same feelings you are feeling now in paradise. The same feelings of peace you feel here, you can also feel on earth even through all that mayhem."

I don't say or think a word as I look out over the landscape that defies all description. Way off in the distance I see enormous creatures grazing on colorful trees over a hundred feet high. As I take in the creatures I can't help but think, "dinosaurs?"

"Yes," my dad instantly answers back. "They are God's creatures too."

The creatures and colors here don't exist on the earth. They defy anything possible on any earthly sphere. How can I explain what I've seen and heard when earthly words cannot describe the beauty and peace that's found here?

Breaking my thought process, my dad's words enter my mind, "It is time for you to make your way back. Follow me."

We begin to walk to another area I had not yet seen. As we make our way, I see many people going about their business as if they were on earth—talking, laughing, eating, and doing many of the things we do on earth. We don't stop to talk to any and my father doesn't say a word about them. As we move closer to a group of people I notice a large, translucent, what can only be described as a curtain, jetting up into the sky. It becomes apparent that many people are there waiting.

"Why are they all here?" I ask my dad, not sure why he has brought me here.

"They are waiting for their loved ones. They are here to greet them and introduce them to their new world or their new birth as we like to call it. The term death as you use on earth and all the pain it causes is not something we discuss here. Death truly becomes a new birth for those that have lived upstanding lives. They were not perfect, but they strived to live the best they knew how. Death for those that have been evil on earth is something much different, and they do not come here. I would reveal more of their state, but I have not be given permission to show you the prison they find themselves in."

Refocusing my attention on the curtain, I look at one group in particular. They are so happy as they talk and wait for their loved one. Just then a man comes through the curtain as if it wasn't even there. His spouse greets him with a hug that seems to be a reunion that would suggest it has been a long time since they had seen each other. Even from this distance their love radiates through my body. I can feel the bond that began on earth not only did not diminish, but it has grown stronger over time. Their feeling of love makes the love I feel for Taylor pale in comparison, and I determine in that instant to reach that same level of love with her.

Feeling my thoughts, my dad says, "That's right son. You too can have that love with Taylor as you listen to and follow the guidance of the family I have shown you."

"I hope to have a love that strong Dad."

"You will. I know you can complete the task that has been given to you for your family. It's time for you to head back now. One last thing—when you see your mom tell her I love her and I'll be waiting for her."

Just then my dad moves forward to embrace me before I go. He doesn't speak a word as we hold each other and I feel his love envelope me even stronger than the first time. I too let him know how much I love him and look forward to the day when we will be together again. He also helps me to remember everything I was just shown and makes it very clear that it will hurt when I go back, but he will be with me to help me get through and guide me to do the things I need to.

I step away and move over to the curtain. Looking back at my father, I tell him one more time how much I love him and then step through the curtain not sure what will happen to me.

As I step through I am again enveloped in a white light that moves me back to my body. It appears to be the same sphere I traveled through to get here except this time I can feel it pulling me towards my body.

As I get close I can see my body and my grandparents there working to influence Scott, Patrick, and Bobbi to do all they can to bring me back from the dead. My body has been moved from where I got shot to the bottom floor of my tower and they are working on me in the lobby. I see Scott working feverishly to breathe life back into me. My body is not bleeding, but I'm still not breathing. Scott then positions himself to give me chest compressions, and Bobbi moves in to start giving me breaths.

When Scott starts the compressions this time I feel the pain as my body pulls my spirit back. Everything is now dark. I feel the pain in my chest from Scott crushing my heart. I then feel air enter my mouth and fill my lungs knowing Bobbi is breathing life back into me. In that moment I open my eyes slightly to see Bobbi about to give me another breath. As I see her face I can tell she's been crying. I then lift my hand to let Scott know I'm there. I don't know how much more pounding my heart can take.

FOURTEEN
Pain

"I'm here. I'm here," I manage to whisper. Scott sits back and Bobbi comes closer to hug me.

"Don't you ever do that to us again," Bobbi manages sternly, wetting my shirt and holding me like she never has before.

"I won't," I softly say with the undeniable truth I have just witnessed. It all seems like a dream now as my earthly surroundings come into view. Was it a dream? The pain shooting through my body and the rudimentary almost mundane way my surroundings appear to me tell me I had to be dreaming.

"I know I'm not supposed to say this mate," Scott starts, pulling me from my pain and confusion, "but I thought you popped your cog. When Mike shot you point blank and you began falling, I thought you were a goner."

Mike shot me? I don't know who to trust. After everything we went through, why would he shoot me. He had plenty of opportunities before then.

And then it hits me.

Jennifer—I think incredulously to myself, the thought sinking like concrete in the bottom of my stomach. She must have suspected I found the disc. At a minimum, she believed I knew about the disc. I was a liability and needed to be eliminated. She must have tipped off Mike back in Dean's office. Or maybe since she thought I had the disc, Tom told Jennifer to get it. They were looking a little suspicious when Scott and I came out of Dean's office.

Scott continues, "I shot Mike without thinking and then Melissa, Bobbi, and I carried your lifeless body back to the tower."

"I can only feel the pain in my chest and ribs right now. Where did he get me?" I ask, not exactly sure what happened.

"From what I can tell it was a clean shot through and through. I don't know why you stopped breathing, but that probably then stopped your heart. Are you having a hard time breathing now?" Scott asks with a puzzled look on his face.

Now that Scott mentions it, I do feel like I really have to fight hard to get my breath. I look down and can see that I was bleeding from my right side. "I think my right lung has partially collapsed," I quickly say as I gasp for air and my heart starts to race.

Scott quickly grabs the medical kit again. He grabs a needle and lifts my shirt again to find a spot just between my broken ribs to stick me. "I've done this quite a few times, but usually the person I stuck was already passed out from lack of oxygen. To the living it always brought immediate relief, but I can't tell you if it will hurt," Scott says, ready to plunge the needle into my lung.

"Go ahead," I gasp. "It's getting harder to breathe by the second."

Scott pushes the needle through and almost as if a balloon was being blown up I can feel my right lung expanding. "Compared to the pain I feel in my chest that puncture wound was nothing," I say to Scott with the faintest of smile on my face. "I need something to write with and write on. Bobbi, can you get me something please?"

Bobbi jumps up to find something when Scott interjects, "Let's get you upstairs first before you start writing a novel mate. I'm sure Taylor lost her bloody mind when Melissa got upstairs. I sent her

198

up there when we got back because she was having a hard time and I'm sure she hasn't brought any comfort to Taylor. Do you think you can walk?"

"Let me give it a try."

Garnering as much strength as I can, I start to sit up and the pain hits me like a piano dropped on my chest. Having been trained to fight through the pain I sit there for a minute trying to muster enough strength to stand. After a minute Scott asks Patrick if there are any wheelchairs in the building.

"Take it easy. You don't have to conquer Mount Everest right now. Patrick stepped out to get a wheelchair. I'll wheel you upstairs to your bed where you can rest," Scott says.

Patrick comes back with the wheelchair and through more pain than I thought imaginable I manage to make it into the chair. Scott starts rolling me down the hall as he thanks Patrick for all his help. On the way up Scott and Bobbi don't say much. I think they are just happy to feel safe for a change without having to hold a weapon or fear for their life or mine.

When the doors open I see Taylor and Melissa waiting to get on. When Melissa sees me breathing the tears that had slowed start free-flowing again. At least they are tears of joy. I then look to Taylor who was already crying, but the peace of seeing me alive brings a sigh of relief as her tears also start streaming from her beautiful blue eyes. Scott wheels me off the elevator as Taylor comes close to kiss me.

"You'll have plenty of time for snogging later," Scott chirps. "We really need to get him lying down. He's in a lot of pain right now even though he's trying to be a tough guy for you Taylor. He has a needle sticking out of his chest to treat a collapsed lung and two crudely patched holes. He's probably still bleeding somewhat, if I had to guess."

At hearing the news of my condition, Taylor jumps up and takes over. She relieves Scott of his responsibility and wheels me into my room.

"Do you need any help getting onto the bed?" Taylor asks as she comes around to kneel in front of me.

I know Taylor wants to help, and I can still remember what my dad said about it being hard for a while so I might as well rest as much as I can to get my strength back. "If you could help me on my left side to roll into bed that would be great."

"I just thought you might want to clean up some before you get into bed. Let me wheel you into the bathroom, and I'll clean you up and make sure you're not bleeding. We'll put some better bandages on instead of these makeshift ones Scott has here," Taylor says as she starts to push me into the bathroom.

As she rolls me in I notice that my shirt and pants have blood all over them. "How about you just roll me into the shower to rinse me off. You can clean me up best there before patching me up proper-ly."

"That sounds like a good idea," Taylor responds. "That way I can get a good look at your body," Taylor pauses for a second, "strict-ly medical purposes only of course," she concludes with a wink.

I'm glad to hear she's already lightened up a bit. I only smile as she looks at me. Not wanting to forget the amazing experience I had while Scott and Bobbi were saving my life I say, "I don't want to forget some things. Will you get me a pen and paper to write a few things down when we're done here? Before I pass out there are some things I have to remember."

Wondering why I would need to write anything down at a time like this Taylor asks, "What's going on?"

"Remember when you told me you had something to tell me, but I had to wait a few months?"

Anticipating what I'm about to say, Taylor spits out a yes that tells me she doesn't want to wait, but knows what I'm about to say.

"Your story was worth the wait, and this one will be so worth the wait too. I think it will save both our lives. I don't mean to discount your story in the least, but what I have to write and what I will tell you will help us find something I think we've both wanted our whole lives. I want to tell you now, but I have to wait. Trust me—it will be worth it."

Taylor kneels down to kiss my cheek and says, "I can wait. I love you."

"I love you too babe."

Taylor slowly removes my shirt and pants to see the crudely placed bandage Scott managed to put on me. All things considered, he did a pretty good job. Quick clot sure does miracles. Whoever invented that stuff has literally saved thousands of lives.

I know Scott wasn't alone in his efforts. Melissa and Bobbi helped, and the guidance grandpa and grandma gave probably brought me back from the brink. I will have to thank them next time I see them. Taylor continues to work as my mind wanders back to my time with my dad. The memory and message sits so strongly upon my soul I'm certain I couldn't have been dreaming. The embrace, the emotion, the pure knowledge I felt in paradise seems undeniable.

Lost in my thoughts, Taylor puts her hand under my chin to get my attention. "You all right? I was looking right at you and talking to you. You weren't answering me."

Her gentle hand on my chin snaps me back to reality. "I'm good honey. I was just thinking of some things."

"Well, I've got you all cleaned up. Here is a pair of underwear for you to change into. I'll leave you for a second. Are you hungry?"

"Actually, now that you mention it, I could use something before I lie down. Thanks."

Taylor gives me a quick kiss before heading out of the bathroom. I slowly change, not wanting to move very fast for fear of hurting myself even more. My chest still hurts as I realize Scott probably broke some of my ribs while giving me chest compressions. I'm definitely going to need them wrapped if I want to feel the least bit comfortable in bed. I slowly roll myself out of the bathroom to see Scott coming into my room.

"Taylor told me to come check on you. You feeling a little better now?"

"Clean yes, but in lots of pain. I think you broke some ribs."

"Yes I did," Scott says. "I could hear a few of them crack when I was saving your life. You want me to get you some ice or anything for it?"

"Actually—out in the kitchen cupboards there are some pain pills and a wrap. Could you grab me two pills and help me wrap my chest?"

"Sure thing. You want me to wheel you out there or do you prefer to wait in here?"

"I'll go out there. Could you just grab me a shirt from my closet? I couldn't reach any so I didn't even bother. Also, since you have the most medical knowledge here, what do we do with this needle sticking out of my chest?"

"Do you feel like you're doing better?" Scott asks.

"I feel much better."

"I know you didn't notice, but you don't have a needle there anymore. I put a one-way valve on there so your chest cavity can let all the air out. That bullet must have punctured your lung which then filled up your chest causing that pressure you felt right before I stuck the needle in you. It probably caused your blackout too, but it alls seems a little strange to me still."

I look down at the puncture site paying more attention to the small device sticking out of my chest. "I've had that little thing in my first aid kit for some time now and I never quite knew what it was for."

"Most people don't," Scott responds. "Since a tension pneumothorax has been one of the major killers of soldiers in the past they are pretty standard in every military grade first aid kit now. I'm surprised you haven't been trained to use them."

"I'm pretty sure I have. I just never actually had to do it on anyone, and it must be one of those skills that I lost. I'm sure glad you knew how to do it though."

"Can I be honest with you?" Scott asks looking behind him to make sure we are the only two in the room.

"You know you can," I respond.

"I've cared for lots of nearly dead or dying soldiers and civilians in my time." Scott pauses as he puts his hand to his mouth not

203

sure of his next words. "When I saw you fall I thought you were dead. After taking care of Mike, I knelt down at your side. As I was about to resign you for dead, I heard a voice speak to my mind very clearly. Now, don't think I'm crazy, but it said, 'Deacon will be ok. You can save him. We will help.' The words were so clear and so full of feeling I asked Melissa and Bobbi if they heard them. They of course didn't, and it didn't matter. I heard them Deacon."

"First off, you're not crazy, 'cause if you're crazy then I am too. I'm going to tell you the same thing I told Taylor. There will come a time when I will tell you what happened, but that time is not now. I know you were inspired to do what you did to save me and for that I will be forever grateful. I know Taylor will be also."

"That's exactly what I was going to tell you mate. I've struggled through saving someone's life before, but I've never been guided so clearly. It was if someone was sitting right next to me telling me what to do and when to do it. The voice was so clear and left an impression so unforgettable that if I heard it again I would know it in an instant."

"There's so much I want to tell you, but I can't now. In due time I will explain it all to you. All this talking is really causing some pain. Can we get me wrapped up and in bed?" I ask Scott, hoping I haven't offended him by not telling him everything.

At hearing my request Scott sees my dilemma and understands. He grabs me a shirt and slowly wheels me out to the kitchen. I now realize Scott will be receptive to my message and I feel grateful I was not the only one to experience something not from this world. When the time comes I know he'll listen.

Savanah, Melissa, and Bobbi are all sitting at the stools watching the news in the kitchen. Taylor continues to make me some food

204

as Scott wheels me in. All four turn to look at me as I make my grand entrance. When Melissa sees me she jumps up to give me a hug and tells me how ecstatic she is I'm alive. I tell her thank you and have Taylor grab some pain meds and long bandages for Scott to wrap me.

As Scott begins to wrap my chest Taylor finishes my sandwich and sets it down at the table.

"When you're finished hurting him, wheel him over to the table Scott," Taylor politely asks.

"Will do."

Scott wheels me over and I slowly eat—trying not to move a muscle or tendon. As I continue to eat, I see the madness in city after city and country after country, as the financial crisis turns into complete madness across the globe. What little I've been dealing with thus far in Vegas pales in comparison to the complete breakdown of society that's happening all across the planet. Police in every major city had to pull out, if they could, because they were being killed like little blue canaries. Having seen what is to come, I'm not surprised with what is playing out on the television.

As we all look on in complete silence Taylor says, "How long do you think this is going to last Deacon?"

I want to tell her everything will be alright and there's nothing to worry about, but the destruction that awaits makes what we are seeing look like a Sunday picnic. "To be completely honest, I don't think society will ever be the same. Hollywood has been showing us zombie movies for some time now, but these zombies are even worse. Not only do they want to kill everything in sight, they want physical things, and will continue to kill to get them. At least with a zombie you know he just wants to eat you. With these zombies they want to kill, steal, murder, rape, hurt, and anything else they need to do to satisfy their lustful hunger. It will only get worse I fear."

At those words, Taylor comes over to take me to my room. As she wheels me out, I thank everyone for saving my life and let them know they are more than welcome to stay as long as they like. I also ask Scott to come to my room to help Taylor get me into bed.

They slowly help me into bed and I ask Taylor for a pen and notepad again. When she leaves the room I ask Scott to make his way through the hotel to get as much food as he possibly can. Scott tells me he had already planned to start scrounging for everything he could.

"Take care of Taylor for me, ok?"

"You know I will. Get some rest. When you wake up this whole thing will have blown over," Scott says, trying to help me relax.

"I wish it would brother. I wish it would."

Taylor sets a pen and a notepad at my side and asks me if I need anything else. "I think that will be good for now." As she leans over to get one more kiss, I caress her soft face and whisper, "Have I told you how much I love you today?"

Taylor pauses for a second before saying, "I love you too Deacon. Get some rest." She then gives me a long kiss and heads out the door.

Lying in bed the z-monster kicks in. I pick up the pen and pad to begin writing as sleep slowly takes over. As I begin to write, my mind reflects back to how this day began. Now that it's ending I realize it couldn't have gone more wrong and more right if I had planned it on paper.

"You still awake?" Scott asks softly, not wanting to interrupt my much needed rest.

"Barely," I manage to mutter without opening my eyes.

"I almost forgot about your contacts. I'm going to take them out and put them and the disc in your nightstand. I don't want you to feel any more pain than you already feel. By the way, they were fantastic."

I open my eyes to see Scott ready to pinch them out. He holds my eyes open with one hand and gently removes the night vision contacts. I hadn't noticed them with everything else that has occurred since we left the Bellagio.

"You need anything mate?" He asks as he closes the drawer.

"I'm good. I think I just need some rest."

"Okay. Get some rest. When you wake..." I don't hear him finish.

FIFTEEN

Taylor

Deacon's breathing remains deep and rhythmic. His defined, masculine jawline has been brushed by a five o'clock shadow—times three over. Not long enough to be soft, but thick enough to be rugged and show how much time has passed since his last shave. He's been in and out of consciousness for almost a week now.

"Deacon," I whisper quietly, taking my hand off his and running my fingers affectionately through his hair. "It's time to wake up. I know your body doesn't want you to, but you've got to keep fighting. I just need you to. I need you, Deacon." The words trail off and get swallowed up in the silence.

I pull myself out of the dining room chair I had brought in so I could sit next to Deacon's bed, grab my journal and black pen from the nightstand, and climb into bed next to him. I slide up against the crisp, white padded backboard of Deacon's platform bed. I pull my right knee up, level with my chest—my bare foot resting on the smooth birch wood surrounding the entire perimeter of the mattress. I prop my journal on my knee and let its ink-filled pages fall open. I look at the date—January 2. Instinctively, my left hand drops down to rest affectionately on Deacon's shoulder as I begin reading:

My whole world changed today with the rising of the sun. You know how they say the night is at its darkest point just before dawn? The moment right before the sun's first ray breaks above the horizon? That is the point that I felt I've been at lately. Worried about school. Worried about choosing a major. Oddly, worried about my dad. This sounds strange, but I'm worried he is in some kind of trouble. He's been distant lately. Overbearing regarding my choice in majors, but distant about everything else. There have been times when I have been over at the house visiting and I see him in the library, with his reading glasses on, absolutely pouring over a well-worn leather book, either making notes or repeatedly flipping back and forth between pages. As soon as he sees me or I walk in, he hides it away underneath another book. Something just doesn't feel right.

Plus, on top of it all, my date with Austin ended up being a huge mistake—no, that's an understatement—it was a mistake of gargantuan proportions! "On paper", so to speak, everything seemed great about him. He was one of the few guys who seemingly had some direction in his life: a promising career, his own townhouse (roommate free), and a car (which turned out to be a truck). Oh, how fleeting the promise of stability can be.

Savanah had set us up. (I know...I know...a blind date...that should have been my first clue that disaster was imminent.) She had such nice things to say about him. She was convinced that our personalities would "click" instantaneously. I suppose there was a portion of me that really wanted her prediction to be true, having had my share of frustrated relationships. She had shown me a picture of him. He was handsome enough. However, it was the way she described his personality that convinced me to take the chance. Savanah should go into marketing. Either her definition of "honorable" or even "acceptable" is extremely low or she could convince you a lemon was an exotic passion fruit. Regardless of the misconception, she and I will be having a conversation or two about this. I've already blocked his number.

Based on the description I received, I was expecting...I don't know exactly...I was expecting something different than the lifted, blacked-out Ford truck that came screaming up and over the curb, rudely squeezing out a minivan in order to get to the last available parking spot. I was standing, as we had previously agreed, near the entrance to the restaurant. When I realized that he was my date—the one I was allegedly supposed to connect with instantaneously—I was shocked. I felt I should give him the benefit of the doubt. Perhaps he was nervous and didn't realize how fast he was going. Or, perhaps the huge cloud of smoke his turbo diesel emitted as he roared over the curb impaired his vision sufficiently that somehow he missed seeing the humble, filled-to-capacity mini van with the "wash me!" message written in advanced toddler on the back. I suppose that could be true. But during dinner, when his snaky hand found its way on my knee, and then, without a single hesitation, from my knee up to my thigh, I knew I needed to take matters into my own hands.

I turned, smiled sharply, put my hand softly on his, and then skillfully pulled back his thumb across the backside of his hand—almost to the breaking point. Austin yelped in pain instantly.

I quickly stood up, eyes blazing, and said, 'That is a liberty you have not been awarded—nor ever will be—in your lifetime or mine' and then I picked up my drink and tossed the contents forcefully in his face.

'Thank you for dinner,' I said curtly and then turned and walked out of the restaurant.

I was outraged. What is wrong with people? Why do some men think that kind of behavior is acceptable? Or that they are somehow immediately entitled to physical pleasantries simply because they find themselves with a person they find attractive? Without even a passing thought of how the other person may be feeling? We had just met. I *didn't know him. Which makes what happened next all the more surprising.*

Following my disastrous date, I needed a moment to settle my nerves. So, I took a quick drive just to clear my mind. I knew Savanah and the others had planned a girls' night out bowling. I'll be honest. I did not feel like going. I felt like going home and soaking in a hot, lavender-scented bubble bath or popping some popcorn and binge-watching a new detective show. I did not feel like bowling. But, as hard as I tried to rationalize it, I knew I had to go.

The persistent nagging stayed with me until I glanced up and saw him walking over in my general direction. I was venting to Savanah about my date when he approached. I think I stopped breathing for what felt like forever. When I exhaled, the persistent nagging feeling left my body; when I began breathing again, the whole world had changed and I felt different...I felt...curiously peaceful.

One thing led to another and before I knew it, he had taken my hand in his and we left the bowling ally. All my friends and his were staring at us in shock. I'll admit, it was unexpected and certainly not the most rational thing to do. I knew his first name and I managed to get his phone number without him knowing, but that's it. He could have been a serial killer for all I knew. This was so unlike me. Even for that horrible blind date, I had done my research.

So here I was, walking out of the bowling ally, holding the hand of a man I barely knew, and I felt peaceful. I can't explain it. Nor can I explain how it is that I became so enamored by him and so instantaneously comfortable being with him that I kissed him. I kissed him, not once but three times! Wasn't I just on a rampage about how much I despise it when the opposite sex simply assumes that they are entitled physical pleasantries because the other person is attractive?

211

Wasn't I just the one who nearly broke a man's thumb because he dared touch my thigh on the first date, after we had had such a rocky start no less? Yes, yes, that was me. That was all me. I would be lying if I said he wasn't attractive. He is. Very attractive in fact. It is more than that though. It was the way he put me at ease. It was the way he made me feel both protected and empowered all at the same time. It was the way I felt as though we had known each other forever. It was the way he made me want to fight for him.

I pause my reading to look up at Deacon. He is still laying quietly, his chest rising and falling peacefully. The line of my journal repeating over and over in my mind, *"Fight for him. Fight for him. Fight for him."*

"Okay Deacon, off I go again to battle. You are worth fighting for—no matter how many battles I have to fight."

As if by fate, I see Scott walking past the doorway. This is my opportunity. "Hey, Scott!" I quietly call to get his attention. I quickly and quietly run on my tiptoes over towards the doorway.

"Scott, we need to talk about Deacon. I'm worried about him —really worried. He's been in and out of consciousness for almost a week now. How much longer can we really hold out—hoping that he will pull himself out of it or waiting for things to calm down out there?" I inquire.

"Taylor," Scott begins with a worried sigh, "I really didn't want to have to tell you this." His marked lack of eye contact with me tells me he is worried and trying to shield me from what he is about to say. When he finally does look at me, his gaze is conditioned and his voice is flat, as if he can somehow hide the fear that is evident there.

"Taylor," he begins again, looking like a man who has just walked in front of a firing squad, "I think Deacon has an infection from the gunshot wound and the rudimentary way we had to put him back together. Who knows what got in there? The fact that he can't talk to us anymore—or at least in any coherent way—worries me."

"I know. It bothers me too. For the record Scott, I am so grateful you were able to get him put together at all—considering the conditions. Deacon keeps getting worse, though. We need to do something. I know it is bad out there. If there was another option I'm sure we would have thought of it by now. There isn't another option. Deacon needs medicine Scott, and I need you to go out and find it for him. This is Deacon we are talking about—the man who would do absolutely anything for you, for me, or for anyone else lucky enough to know him."

Unexpectedly, my phone starts ringing. Cell phone service have been hit and miss ever since this fiasco started, so I'm surprised to hear the phone ring at all. As the phone continues to ring, I glance down and see that it is my mother calling. The emotional tension that I had thus far controlled so well begins to surge.

"Scott, I gotta take this. You know how mothers are. I'll come talk to you shortly," I explain, as I slide my thumb across the face of my phone and answer the call. I walk down the hall to the spare room I have claimed as my own. I close the door behind me as I enter the room.

"Hello sweetie. How are you holding up?" I hear my angel mother ask.

That's all it took. That simple question unstopped the dam of emotion I've been holding back for a week.

As I cry, my thoughts go back to Deacon. Is he dreaming? Is he fighting to live? How long will this last before I see those eyes and that smile that bring me to life? Before I feel the warmth of his em-

213

brace or the touch of his lips? I finally find the man I want to spend the rest of my life with and now I must wait, but wait for what? That's what worries me.

I look around the room and everything I see reminds me of him. I see a place that I have come to call my own. It's like my home away from home. Since Deacon was always working late and I typically would get off work just after midnight, I started coming here to crash while I waited for Deacon to get off work. I could have gone straight to my place, but I wanted to see him. I wanted to hear how his day went. I wanted to hear that contagious laugh of his. Typically, I would write as I was waiting for him to get home. Sometimes, however, exhaustion would get the best of me and I would end up falling asleep. He started checking on me before falling asleep himself. I loved it when he would come in and give me a kiss on the cheek. Then, like the amazing gentleman he is, he would tell me that he loves me and march himself off to his room. I never thought I could love someone so much in such a short amount of time.

I sob for a good thirty seconds, as my heart longs for Deacon, before my mom attempts to comfort me.

"Oh honey, everything is going to be okay. Things will work out. Tell me what's going on Taylor."

Receiving a small amount of relief, I begin, "Deacon has been basically unconscious for almost a week now. Scott thinks he has an infection. I was in the process of asking Scott to brave the mayhem and try to find Deacon some medicine and the other medical supplies that he so desperately needs when you called. I'm so worried mom."

Another wave of emotion sweeps over me. I let out a sob before continuing, "What if Scott can't find what Deacon needs? What if the infection has already gone untreated for too long? What if...," my voice trails off, as if the words are cutting off my air supply, "...what if he doesn't make it?" I blurt out, as if I was finally able to break the grip the words had on me.

No one speaks for a minute, the weight of the situation hanging heavy.

"Taylor, do you love him?" she asks quietly.

"You know I do mom."

"Yes, I've heard you tell me that you do. Remember how you told me you knew Deacon was the one you would marry, the one I told you that you would meet after a long day?"

"Of course I do mom. How could I forget? Date after date and relationship after relationship you reminded me of the impression you had. For years I was convinced that recognizing my future spouse would be easy based on your impression. But when it comes right down to it, that isn't the reason why I love Deacon and why I want to marry him. That isn't the reason at all." Suddenly, everything is so clear and focused. "I love Deacon. I love him for so many small and significant reasons. I love him with my whole heart and soul and I am willing to do anything and be everything for him. I love him more than life itself."

I have thought those words for some time now, but I never really internalized them until now. My mom's dream could easily apply to every man I ever dated—Deacon, however, is unlike every man I ever dated. Simply put, I would do anything for him. People are worth living for. Then it hits me like the sun lighting a dark sky on this, my darkest night ever—I would do anything and be everything for him, even die for him.

"I am so happy for you sweetie. I want you to know how proud I am of you and the choices you are making. I'm sure you're anxious to get things worked out with Scott, but I want to tell you a story first." She doesn't give me time to speak before launching into a story I have never heard.

"When your dad and I were first married he was away on an assignment. This particular time, he didn't come home when he said he would. I got a call on the phone from one of his coworkers. The man stated your dad had been injured and he might not make it many more days. To be brief, I flew to Philadelphia where he lie in a coma on the verge of death. I won't tell you what happened to him except to say he was shot in the chest. Obviously, you know he did not die and that brings me to the point of this story. I never gave up hope. I would lie by his bed, sit next to him, and wait day after day until he woke for short periods of time. Just long enough for him to tell me he loved me and eat before falling back asleep."

"Thank you Mom. That means more to me than you know." The thought of my dad getting shot sends questions racing through my mind. I will have to get to the bottom of that for sure. Deacon is my first priority right now though.

"One last thing," my mom speaks with all the love she possess before letting me go. "Talk to him. Pray for him. Lay by him. Let him know you're there. Your dad said at times, though he couldn't talk or see me, he knew I was there and it gave him the will to come back from where he was."

"Of course I will mom. Thank you so much. Take care and be safe. I love you so much."

"I love you too sweetie."

216

The moment I hang up the phone, the room seems a little brighter. The hope swelling inside me makes my entire body shiver with excitement. As I walk past Deacon's room I glance inside again. I stop at Deacon's door to see him still sleeping. The rise and fall of the fuzzy blue blanket resting on his chest gives me comfort. I pause for just a moment to think about the future. I don't know what the future holds for us, and it's been eating me up inside. Any future Deacon and I may have together seems so close—almost within reach—yet still so far away. However, I feel optimistically hopeful. Hopeful that things will work out even with all the uncertainty—or perhaps in spite of it. The renewed faith propels me forward.

As I walk into the kitchen I hear Scott talking to someone at the Bellagio. It sounds like people are still trying to shoot their way into the hotel.

"Scott—I need to talk to you." I mouth to him silently. He nods his head in agreement. He talks for only a minute or so longer.

"What's up?" he asks, without an ounce of worry in his voice as he opens the fridge.

"I have a favor to ask." He just nods for me to continue. I continue, trying not to arise any suspicion in the others sitting in the living room. "I know Melissa will have to be on board, but I have to ask. Will you go out and find medicine for Deacon? I have a bad feeling the infection will kill him without the proper drugs to fight it."

Scott doesn't speak, I know he's pondering everything that my request entails. Then he makes eye contact with Melissa and waves her over. "I can't do this without her." I nod, knowing she would have to be involved. I'm not sure I'm ready to ask this of her yet.

Melissa comes into the kitchen not sure what to expect. The expression on her face is one of *what am I getting myself into.* "What's going on Scott?"

Her question is so simple, yet in the context of the current circumstances becomes something entirely different. I'm asking her boyfriend to risk his life for mine. It's not the conversation I thought I would ever be having.

Scott talks first which brings a little relief so I can slow my heart. It felt like it was going to burst out of my chest. "Deacon has a major infection in his body. If left untreated I fear," he pauses not wanting to say the words as he glances at me before looking back to Melissa, "I fear he won't make it."

The uncertainty had been building for the last week. With Deacon not waking and no one daring to utter the words, the fear kept building and building. The room that once felt so big, now almost feels like a prison. Now that the silence has been broken I feel we can move on. I look at Melissa for the first time. She's still looking at Scott—unsure what to say. I'm afraid she will say that absolutely under no circumstances will she let him leave this place. The death and destruction that waits out there would keep even the most courageous woman from allowing her closest confidant into that world.

"When would you go?" Melissa asks, still not making eye contact with me.

"The sooner I go, the sooner we can get him back to the land of the living. He really needs something in his body to fight what's going on."

"I'm no doctor but he needs a catheter," Melissa adds.

I hadn't thought about that. In the week he's been out, I only changed the bed once, and he hasn't been getting up to go to the bathroom either.

"So are we all in agreement then?" Scott interjects.

"I don't like it," Melissa responds, "but I don't see any other options."

"You're not mad at me are you Melissa?" I ask as her head slowly turns my way.

When her glistening green eyes meet mine I can see the love in her expression. She walks towards me without saying a word and embraces me like we've been best friends forever. After a minute she finally speaks, "I would be asking the same thing of Deacon if the roles were reversed. So who am I to deny what you want most, and what Deacon needs most?"

With her utter selflessness I can't restrain the emotion built up in me. The sobs come flying out as the tears flow down my shirt onto Melissa's bright pink blouse. Normally I would divert my tears, but it's my pink shirt she's wearing, so what does it matter. I couldn't ask for a better group of friends to be stuck up here with. My sobs also bring the others out of their television-induced comas.

"What's going on?" Savanah asks as if she's missed something a best friend should be involved in.

I can't say a word as the emotion still flows.

"I'm going out to find some medicine for Deacon," Scott relates.

"I'm okay Savanah. The tears are tears of joy and maybe a few tears of the unknown."

Savanah comes in and the three of us embrace for quite some time. No one says a word as I cry. Savanah and I have been friends for some time now and my emotion, or lack of controlling it, finally gets to her as the tears gentle roll down her rosy red cheeks. She has been a trooper through this whole thing. All my friends have. With Deacon out I don't know what I would have done without her here.

As we embrace I attempt to tell her what I've been bottling up, but between my incoherent sobs Savanah says, "It's okay Taylor. I understand, and I'm here for you. You don't have to say a word." I hold on tight not wanting to let go as I get control of my emotions. I want to believe everything will work out, but the unknown still has my mind swimming.

It's just after midnight when I finish talking to Savanah. I told her everything I had been bottling up. She does her best to keep my mind at ease, but my mind can't help but think of what I've asked Scott to do. He has been preparing for the last hour. He went down to talk to Patrick at Melissa's request. She might be okay with him going out into the unknown, but she isn't stupid either. She wants him to get at least one more man to go with him.

When he comes back with one of Patrick's men, they discuss the pros and cons of having a rifle. They decide the quickest and most discreet way in and out of where they'll be going is to just carry concealed handguns. It seems a little crazy to me, but I resolve to let Scott's many years of experience dictate my silence.

As Scott prepares to leave I see the concern and worry painted on Melissa's face. The way she clings to him makes me wish I didn't have to ask this of him or her. With backpack on, Melissa gives Scott a kiss that stretches on and on.

"You come back to me," Melissa says, barely able to hold back the tears.

I've got everyone in here crying now. As Scott opens the door I say, "Scott—hold on." As he turns to look at me I walk over and give him a hug and tell him thank you. I want to say more, but I need him to stay focused.

When the door shuts I slowly walk to Melissa and embrace her. She is stronger than me or at least she knows how to keep her emotions under control better. I used to be a vault like Melissa, but experience has taught me personally that I must let it out. "He'll be back before you know it," I say hoping to give her strength.

"I sure hope so," Melissa adds with as much confidence as she can manage.

Time barely seems to tick by as we sit in the living room without saying a word. The silence is so thick we'd get stuck if we tried to move. It's been one hour when Melissa's phone rings. As soon as she sees the screen her eyes light up with excitement. That smile only comes for one person right now.

"Are you okay?" Melissa asks in anticipation. We all sit apprehensively as Melissa's excitement fades to uncertainty. "Why are you whispering?" she asks. We don't say a word not wanting Melissa to miss anything. "Don't try to be a hero. Just wait and when it clears, come back." Not wanting to interrupt, but wanting to know if he's got medicine to save Deacon's life I sit and wait. The suspense is going to kill me. "I love you," she says as she turns the phone down.

"Is he okay?" I ask first, not wanting to discount his life and get right to the question that wants to explode out of my chest.

"Yeah. They're safe. There was a mob that formed in their path back so they hunkered down. There's no way around I guess. Not the kind of group they'd fit into I guess. While they were hiding they heard a man talking about fighting the government and not letting things ever get back to normal. He makes it sound like there are hundreds in their path."

Barely able to wait for her last word I ask, "Were they able to get medicine?"

"Sorry. I should have told you that first. They got some antibiotics from a pharmacy that had been ransacked. I guess antibiotics aren't in high demand for the people roaming the streets. He would have been back sooner and missed the mob, but he said he kept looking for pain killers or something to feed Deacon with, but the pain meds were cleaned out and all he could find was a needle set to start an IV, but no bag."

"How long before they'll be back?"

"He isn't sure. They're still hiding, hoping the mob clears out. I guess they almost ran right into them, so they had to dive behind a wall before they were seen."

"Did he say how far away they are?" The questions keep coming to my mind. For Melissa's sake, this is the last one I'll ask. I don't want her to worry more than I'm sure she already is and will continue to until Scott walks through the doors of his own volition.

"He said they are about twenty minutes away on Harmon and Paradise when they had to duck down."

We all sit back a little relieved, but knowing they are not totally out of the woods yet. If I thought the clock was running slowly before it must be going backwards now.

222

After one hour of silence I couldn't take it anymore. I jump up and ask everyone if they want something to eat. It's a good thing Deacon was prepared and had three months of food stored in his place. Scott has made one run for fresh eggs and almond milk through the hotels. He brought back so much we should be good for quite some time. If this chaos continues for more than a month we are going to be stuck eating noodles and rice. It's just after two, so I figure I'll make waffles. Who doesn't likes waffles at two in the morning?

Normally everyone would be passed out by now, but the suspense courses through our bodies like a drug keeping everyone alert and ready for the door to open at any moment. I know Melissa worries and wants to call him, but knowing the trouble he could be in if his phone rings or vibrates she doesn't. She just sits patiently watching the news, trying to keep her mind off what Scott is going through.

When the first golden waffle comes off the griddle I call Melissa over to start eating. As she sits I can see the worry in her light green eyes. "I never noticed how pretty your eyes are Melissa," I say, hoping to help her relax.

"Thank you, and thank you for the food."

We talk, not about today or what's going on in the world right now, but about our childhood. She grew up in Vegas too. We both went to Green Valley High School at the same time, but obviously didn't know each other. With a graduating class of two thousand plus, it isn't surprising. Over the last few months we have gotten to know each another better. We have a lot in common. It's crazy the things that keep you from extending your circle of friends in high school. Once you leave that world—and trust me, it is a completely different world—you realize the things that moved you day to day just don't matter anymore. We both agree life after high school is much better as we talk and I continue to make waffles. Bobbi throws in the occasional comment. She's having her own trouble. Blake's phone goes right to voicemail so her ship is still out to sea so to speak.

Lost in our conversation and the most delicious waffles I've ever eaten, Melissa almost falls off her chair when she feels a hand on her shoulder. I saw Scott come around the corner with that mischievous look I've grown accustomed to seeing. One finger to his mouth as he moved to embrace Melissa said it all. He squeezes her like he hadn't seen her in days. The worry and heartache she'd been feeling flies away like a seagull sailing out to sea.

Not sure what just happened and still in shock Melissa says, "You okay? Everything went well?"

"Everything went well," as he tosses a bottle of antibiotics my way.

I look around and notice I've got like six waffles waiting to be eaten. "Are you hungry?" I ask Scott.

"Starved."

I move in close to give him a hug and tell him how much I appreciate what he's done. "Now eat up."

Scott sits down next to Melissa as I make my way through the living room. "Hey," I call out to Savanah who had fallen asleep on the couch, "there are some waffles on the counter. You better hurry though, before Scott eats them all."

As I walk into Deacon's room I see he's still breathing. As I sit down I grab his hand hoping I will get a response. To my complete amazement, I hear him speak in a whisper, "Windsor." I look hoping to see something in his blue eyes before speaking. He's eyes are closed as his body moves ever so slightly.

"Are you there Deacon? Can you hear me?"

Again he says, "Windsor."

He must be having a dream.

"Babe—are you there? Wake up," I say with my cheek against his. The stubble growing roughs up my cheek as I rub against his hoping for any signs of life. I lay against his body for a several minutes before I hear his voice again.

"Hello," is all he says. I quickly sit up to get a better look at his eyes to see them glossed over like they might be open, but he has no idea what's going on.

"I have some pills for you to take. Open your mouth."

He's response is simple, "Okay." I grab one pill and push it through his barely open mouth.

"Here's some water to take them down." He takes a sip and from what I can tell as I open his lips the pills are gone.

"How are you feeling Deacon?" He's gone again, I finally accept after five minutes of trying to get him to respond. I sure hope these pills help.

We do the same thing for days without any real responses except to take the pills down. To be honest, I'm surprised he's even taking them.

After five days of feeding him pills three times a day I notice his hands are starting to get red and the site of the wounds looks worse and worse. I convince Scott to go back out for IV medicine and nutrients to feed him. He can't last if we don't get more fluid going into him.

When Scott leaves this time the plan will take him to Sunrise Children's Hospital to get everything he needs. It's almost four miles away which on any given day would take five minutes. Unsure of what he may encounter he decides to go under the cover of darkness again. Knowing he must get everything, he lets Melissa know he could be gone much longer this time.

We wait for hours. He left at 11:00 P.M. and now the sun breaks over Sunrise Mountain—lighting the city I find hard to call home at this moment.

"He's been gone for seven hours," Melissa says, not sure what else to do or say.

Not really sure what to say myself, Savanah reassures her, "He'll be alright Melissa. He wants to make sure he's got everything he'll need. If Deacon has the kind of infection Scott mentioned before he left, you both know how important it is he gets the right stuff."

"It's been long enough though, hasn't it?" Melissa questions with the worry evident in her strained voice. We barely slept at all last night. Every time we would doze off for a second, one of us would wake up thinking we heard Scott coming through the door.

"It has been some time, but be patient. He will make it back before you know it."

"That's easy for you to say Savanah. You don't have a boyfriend out there risking his life."

"Okay," I interject, "everyone relax." The tension had been building all night. "Everyone will be okay. We're tired. We're hungry. We've been cooped up in here for a couple of weeks almost. How about I make some breakfast? I bet before I'm done Scott will come walking through the door."

With those words everyone stops talking. As I walk into the kitchen, Savanah follows me in to ask if she can help. Melissa has got to get her mind off of where it's been all night, wondering where Scott landed and if he's okay. I don't blame her for being a little unhinged. The not knowing takes a toll on you. I know it has for me. Lost in my thoughts and trying to throw some breakfast together I don't hear Savanah talking to me. She finally has to come tap me on the shoulder to get my attention. "Are you okay Taylor?" she asks wondering why I've ignored her for the last fifteen seconds.

"I'm fine. There's a lot going on and the last thing I want to see is my closest friends in this world fighting."

Savanah has always been level-headed with everyone she's interacted with and her composure doesn't surprise me this time. Melissa is going through something neither Savanah nor I can imagine, though I have a glimpse into how she feels.

"I wasn't trying to cause any problems Taylor. You know that, right?" she asks with genuine concern.

"I know. I know you understand Melissa's state of mind as well. Maybe just go sit down with her while I make breakfast. She doesn't know you as well as I do. I know you'll win her over."

Savanah doesn't say a word as she looks me in the eyes before embracing me. Savanah is more than any friend could ask for. She has always been there for me. As she moves away, giving me one last look only a true friend could give, I notice how beautiful she is standing there. I've always thought she put me to shame, by the way her strawberry blonde hair falls across her face and her emerald green eyes contrast her light complexion. I can't help but think she needs a man like Deacon. She too, like me, has been through a lot.

I continue to make breakfast as I listen to Savanah and Melissa's conversation. They talk softly not wanting to wake Bobbi. She, of all of us, has the most to worry about. It's been two weeks and she hasn't heard a word from Blake. I can't even imagine the grief she holds in. I know Blake was on the cusp of asking Bobbi to marry him. Now she sleeps mostly to get away from the pain I'm sure. We've talked a few times and she does have hope, but I think the sleep brings relief. Relief from the pain she has growing inside. Relief from the unknown that eats away at all of us right now. When it comes right down to it, Melissa has got it made. Scott will be back any minute and all her fears will cease. If only Bobbi and I could find that relief right now.

As I turn to let them know it's time to eat, I see them hugging. I'm glad they're feeling better and getting along. I know it wasn't really a blow-up, but it certainly had all the makings of one, definitely something none of us needs right now.

We all sit at the table ready to eat. "I didn't do much, but at least we have something," I say as I look at the meal. I'm trying to conserve the eggs and bacon for when Deacon wakes up. The smell of a fresh fried eggs however, cooked in a little bacon grease sure would hit the spot right now. Maybe it would bring Deacon back to life as the smell of bacon wafted through his bedroom door.

"Cereal and a bagel sounds great!" Savanah says, showing me how much she loves me.

"Thank you Taylor," Melissa adds, "I really do appreciate how your optimism has held us together here."

"You don't have to thank me," I say, not wanting any of the credit. "We are all in this together and it has been each one of us that has got us this far. As long as we keep moving forward we'll be better off for having lived through it. I just know we can't revert to the savage, almost animalistic beings, that roam the streets."

228

We all sit without saying much more. Each one of us lost in our own thoughts. Bobbi joins us after five minutes. She doesn't say much. She slept pretty much the whole night, but the dark spots under her eyes tell a different story.

Oh, how I wish I could comfort her. Not hearing from Blake and not knowing what happened tears at her, it is evident in her eyes. The smile that first greeted me the night I met Deacon's friends no longer graces her full lips.

As we finish breakfast and clean up the table and then the kitchen, I can see the disappointment on Melissa's face. The way the right side of her lips slightly droops down tells me she really believed he would have been back by now.

We all move to the couch and Bobbi flips on the television. The news seems so depressing right now. I don't know how they can watch or how the anchors are still reporting the news.

After thirty minutes of the same death and destruction we've become accustomed to seeing now, I realize I hadn't checked on Deacon yet. "I'm going to go lay by Deacon. Let me know if you hear anything from Scott," I say to Melissa walking from the living room.

Walking down the hall, the front door startles me as it slowly opens. Scott wasn't expecting me to be right there and the way he quickly throws his head back I can tell I startled him as well.

"Don't say anything," he whispers, as he puts his pointer finger to his mouth yet again. "I got everything Deacon needs plus more just in case," Scott adds.

I don't say a word as the feeling of gratitude beyond belief wells up inside me. He sees the emotion building and places his hand on my shoulder.

"You're welcome Taylor. I'll be in to set him all up in a second."

Scott then slowly walks down the hall into the living room to surprise Melissa. As he rounds the corner into the living room Melissa hears something and turns. I've never seen Melissa move that fast or break into tears as quickly as she does. When she grabs a hold of Scott you can see the love she has for him, the emotion in the air is almost palpable.

As I walk down the hall I can't help but long for that embrace. Climbing into bed with Deacon so I can feel his warmth I notice how hot he's become. He said something about his whole body hurting a few days ago, but we couldn't get much more out of him. When Scott peeled back his eye lids they were completely blood shot. As I check now the red still remains. Struggling with my emotions, I grab hold of every ounce of hope inside me. Things will work out. Scott has everything Deacon could possibly need. I settle in—curling up to him—and start to sing him a song, *Twinkle, Twinkle, Little Star*—with my own variation.

SIXTEEN
Weeks or Months

The pain is excruciating. How long have I been asleep? The light beaming through my windows keeps my eyes shut. My head burns like I've been walking in the desert for days on end. What is happening to my body? I thought dying and coming back would be the extent of the awful pain I would experience. Then it hits me. 'It won't be easy,' I remember my dad saying. Every muscle in my body seems to be in pain.

With confusion fully set in, Taylor walks through the door. I am finding it very difficult to even open my eyes as I imagine some-one pounding on my head like a big bass drum.

"What's going on?" I ask Taylor. "I feel like I'm burning up and my head feels like it's going to explode."

Taylor comes over and gently puts her palm on my head. "You are really hot babe." How does the rest of your body feel?"

Through my now noticeable daze, I guide my thoughts to evaluate my condition. The slight rash on my palms and the pangs throughout my body don't make the process easy. I don't say a word as Taylor notices my palms and sees the sweat coming down my face. "I'm going to go get Scott," Taylor says, sensing my uneasiness as I remain silent, not completely sure what I should say.

As I lay in bed waiting, I notice Taylor has the television on. I try to focus on what the anchor communicates, but between my blink-ing to focus and the difficult time I'm having reasoning, I resolve to keep my eyes closed. Mustering the mental strength to focus was hurting my head more than I could bear. What is happening to me? My head burns with a fever I've never felt before. The nausea makes my head spin as if it's a morning after with my team, which is a feeling I don't wish upon anyone. If that wasn't enough, the muscle aches and abdominal pain are beyond description.

I attempt to grasp all these symptoms through the almost unbearable pain as Scott says, "How you doing buddy?" I didn't even realize he was standing there.

I open my eyes for a second. Just long enough to get a glimpse of Scott and Taylor standing next to me. I guess I wouldn't fair too well in a fight right now. Unable to concentrate right now I manage to answer, "I don't know."

"You've got to give me more than that Deacon. I need to know what we need to do for you."

Next I hear Taylor suggest, "He said he was burning up. Should I get a cold rag to put on his head?" Scott tells her to grab one as he touches my forehead.

"What hurts Deacon?" Scott asks with a much firmer voice. I think I manage to relate all the pain coursing through my body but I'm not certain. I feel like I'm going to pass out.

The next thing I know I'm able to open my eyes without a problem—though I still hurt throughout my body. It's dark now with just the glow of the television lighting the room. I look left to see my door closed and then right towards my bathroom. To my complete surprise, I see my dad sitting next to me.

"What are you doing here?" I ask my dad with complete astonishment. I can't be dead otherwise I wouldn't feel all this pain.

"You're not dead," my dad says sensing my thoughts. "You're just in a lot of pain and will be for some time. Remember what I told you?"

Having him say the words brings his prior counsel back to my memory. I really don't want to talk and now realizing even here he can hear my thoughts I just think them to keep the pain at bay. "Yes. How long will this last?"

"I can't tell you son. This experience is a trial for your well-being. You've been through many trials and experiences, both physical and mental. This one will be much like those. I'm here to assure you if you don't give up you will make it. I have to go now. I will come see you one more time before you get out of this bed. Then you will not see me again. I will be with you when I can, to guide and strengthen you."

I wake, unable to open my eyes, not sure how long I've been out. Was my dad here or was I just dreaming? How long have I been laying in this bed? These thoughts and many others race through my head as I recognize the pain shooting through my entire body. I vaguely recall Scott, or maybe it was Taylor forcing pills down my throat, unfortunately, they don't seem to be helping because the pain seems stronger than before.

"Are you awake?" I hear a voice whisper at my bedside.

Not sure who has come to see me in this awful situation and not understanding their voice I simple say, "Yes," I think.

"Are you feeling any better?" they ask. I feel a cool hand gently make contact with my forehead.

I must not have responded or maybe I thought I did and really didn't. I'm not sure what I am doing anymore.

"I don't think it's helping," I hear a female voice exclaim. It must be Taylor, but it's hard to tell.

"I'm pretty sure he has toxic shock syndrome," a male voice states. Was that Scott?

"What is that?" the female questions, obviously concerned.

"It's a serious staph infection. I'm going to have to go find a different antibiotic for him. We'll have to give it to him intravenously," the male voice relates.

Not sure if I'm dreaming, sleeping, or somewhere in-between, I continue to listen to what I believe is their conversation. They continue to talk softly. What I have seems to be a serious infection probably caused from the gunshot wound I received in my lower abdomen. That would probably explain why my stomach hurts so bad.

It has to be Taylor and Scott talking, though their voices sound so different. I resolve it must be my inability to comprehend. Taylor asks Scott what she can do. Scott doesn't say much except 'keep your eye on him.' He relates how it's still relatively dangerous out there and how normal services such as police, fire, and emergency services pretty much don't exist right now.

Taylor must have asked Scott what he's going to do because I hear Scott say, "I have to go back out there and find the right medicine." Has he already ventured into that chaos once?

I must have passed out again from the pain because when I come to there's an IV bag hanging next to my bed. Still barely able to keep my eyes open I follow the line coming from the bag. It dips below my bed and then flows back onto the bed directly into my arm. I can't feel the needle penetrating my arm. When did he put the needle in? I don't remember eating much either as I notice my body feels extraordinarily weak.

The pain is still unbearable, but the dazed feeling I've felt seems to be dissipating somewhat.

"Society has completely broken down," I hear someone say. I look around the room to notice a news anchor on NBC reporting the news. I then see video streams from all over the globe of the complete chaos that has caused normal society to come to a stand still. I hear talk of martial law being implemented in the United States, but from the pictures and videos I see it doesn't seem to be taking hold or making a difference at this point.

"Is he going to make it?" I hear Taylor say through sobs. I feel her cool hand holding mine.

I don't open my eyes. Knowing she's there with me gives me hope.

"He'll make it," I hear Scott respond. "He's not out of the woods yet. As long as we keep an eye on the infection site and change out his bandages every day I think he'll make it now. Keep talking to him even though you don't think he's listening. Don't give up on him."

The next words I hear are music to my ears, "I will never give up on him." Taylor's love will keep me alive if nothing else. I know her faith surpasses anything I'm capable of at this time. I know my friends are pulling for me. I know my dad has said I can make it through this. All that is left for me now is to believe I can make it. Without saying a word I reaffirm in my mind that I am strong. I can beat this sickness. I can do anything.

My mind fades again.

To my complete surprise I'm awakened to Taylor lying in my bed singing a song. I instantly recognize how much better I feel when I wake. It takes everything I have to keep my eyes closed so she continues to serenade me with her sweet voice:

Twinkle, twinkle, little star,

How I wonder where you are.

In this world so dark and dire,

How I need you and admire.

Twinkle, twinkle, little star,

How I wonder where you are!

When the blazing sun is gone,

When there's nothing to shine on,

Then you'll show your little light,

Twinkle, twinkle, through the night.

Twinkle, twinkle, little star,

How I wonder where you are!

In this room we're up so high,

In your arms, I will sigh,

In this blue, dark world I find,

Longing to hear, just your mind.

Twinkle, twinkle, little star,

How I wonder where you are.

Twinkle, twinkle, little star,

How I wonder where you are.

"I've never heard that version before," I say, as I open my eyes. I can see the tears well up instantly at the sound of my voice.

She finally manages to sob the words, "I love you so much Deacon."

"I love you too Taylor. Thanks for not giving up on me."

"I could never give up on you babe," Taylor says still sobbing.

"How long have I been here?" I ask, thinking it's been a week or two at the most.

"You've been in and out of consciousness for almost three weeks now," Taylor relates not quite sure how I'll take it. "I've sung you that song so many times wishing you would come back to me."

"It's been that long?" I ask in complete amazement. I've been laying here for nearly three weeks without realizing it. I try to get up, but with the pain still evident in my abdomen it's pretty clear I'm not going anywhere.

As I start to sit up Taylor says, "Oh no you don't! Scott says you need your rest or you'll make things worse. I don't know where you were and I can only imagine how much pain you were going through. Scott at one point took me to the kitchen and told me you might not make it. I told him that wasn't an option. I've been here by your side ever since."

"How have you been babe?" I ask, hoping she's still my bright, blue-eyed beauty I remember.

"I won't lie Deacon. It was rough for a while. The not knowing for certain was the hardest, but I tried to stay strong and have faith that you would make it. I've never been one to pray regularly, but when you make it through this I think I'll be converted," Taylor reveals with her blue eyes locked on mine.

I cannot fathom the pain and sorrow she has felt as she's witnessed me comatose day after day at death's door. I don't know how she did it.

"I'm feeling really tired still. As much as I'd love to stay awake and talk to you, I think I'm going to fall asleep again. Keeping my eyes open this long isn't helping either. Is that okay?" I ask hoping she won't take my lack of energy as anything but that.

"That's fine Deacon. Are you hungry?" Taylor asks just ecstatic I've been able to talk to her as long as I have.

"No. I don't know if I'll be awake long enough to eat it anyway."

"Ok," Taylor says as she leans in to give me a kiss. "Get some rest and know I'll be right here next to you when you wake."

I see her as she says those last words and then close my eyes wishing I could keep them open. How much longer do I have to be in this bed?

I find myself walking down Las Vegas Boulevard without a pain to speak of. Odd thing though, the streets are completely empty. The street glows from the lights that line every square inch, but the lack of noise and people feels quite refreshing. Why am I seeing this? As I pose that thought in my head I hear my dad's voice resonate through mine.

"This city, and more importantly, this street, has beauty all around. What man has built here truly deserves praise from an architectural stand point. This place most assuredly sits as an oasis in a vast desert."

Not sure what has happened and why he is talking to me about the strip I ask, "What is going on Dad? Did I die again? I was feeling so much better."

"You're not dead. You are dreaming. Believe it or not we use dreams to communicate with people on earth. As for the strip, I wanted to just talk with you in a familiar place. I know how much beauty you find here and thought the same, just better without the people and noise."

Just talk? Why does my dad want to talk? These thoughts and many others run through my mind. Forgetting again that my dad can understand and perceive my thoughts, he answers:

"I'm here for two reasons son. First, when you wake from this dream, the time will have come for you to get out of bed. You will be sore and your body will be weak. However difficult and painful it may seem, it is important that you begin to strengthen your body. You'll need to use it very soon. Second, do you remember the family I told you about?"

I nod.

Automatically, I recall their faces. It feels like I have known this family my whole life and they have somehow always been a part of me.

"Before you meet the family I told you about Deacon, you will have to help Taylor's family," he instructs, his stormy blue eyes staring intently into mine as if trying to judge my reaction.

"Help Taylor's family? What happened to them?" I think to myself, recoiling in surprise just slightly.

"You will know in due time," my dad relates, perceiving my thoughts again. "I cannot tell you more except that you have been chosen to help save our family and hers. Everything you've done throughout your entire life has prepared you for what lies at the door. Never give up, and don't be afraid to ask for guidance when all seems lost. Remember, I will be there to guide you."

"How am I to ask for guidance Dad?" I ask, not sure what exactly he expects me to do.

"I know I wasn't the best example as you grew up, so think of your mom. Though she still searches, she has faith that one day she will find the answers she seeks from God. She seeks God every day through prayer. She doesn't know it, but I have been there many times to whisper in her ear the answers she seeks. You may find this hard to believe, but God uses family members that have passed on to convey messages, protect, serve, and guide—if you are but willing to come to Him for that guidance."

Those ideas enter my mind like a thousand truths, filling my soul with an understanding I've never felt before. Though I know I'm dreaming, my whole body tingles and feels warm. Not warm as it did before as I lay at death's door, but warm like the sun that strikes your skin as the first rays come crashing over the mountain in the morning on a cool winter day. The feeling seems so surreal as we walk in the light down the Las Vegas Boulevard.

"That feeling that has enveloped your body is the light of God son," my dad says helping me to understand where all light comes from.

I don't say much or think much as we continue to walk down the street. He relates over again the things that must shortly come to pass so they are engrained in my mind. As we walk there are no burned out cars, no bullet holes or broken glass. The beauty here without all the distractions truly takes your breath away.

240

We stop in front of the Bellagio. I begin to stare across the pond completely forgetting that my dad stands at my side. How I wish the fountains would come to life and play the song my dad gave me when I was born. 'Feeling Good' by Michael Bublé has always helped me to remember him. Whenever I've had a hard time since he passed it has cheered me up. As these thoughts pass through my mind, the fountains begin to rise and the beginning notes to my song begin playing. I glance toward my dad to give him a smile, but find him absent. His voice rings through the music, "I love you son."

I don't say a word as I watch the beauty of the fountain. The way the water twirls and moves mesmerizes the living. The way it comes to life in my dream is magical. Not only does it play a version of my song I've never heard before, it also has colors and a power I know the fountain has never been able to produce.

"I love you too Dad," I say as the lyrics fade and the fountains go back to sleep.

The song finishes and I find myself back in my bed feeling better than I have since getting shot. Taylor also lays across my upper chest. She appears to be sleeping.

"You sleeping babe?" I ask hoping she's not really asleep. Taylor turns her head and looks into my eyes with the most breathtaking smile. Before she has time to say a word I grab her and pull her closer. "I love you so much Taylor."

"I love you too Deacon. You had me worried for way too long. How are you feeling?"

"I feel a hundred times better now. How are you doing?"

"I'm doing great now," she says with that same smile that greeted me. "You want to try and sit up?"

I know I need to get up, but this moment feels so perfect right here, right now. I need to move though. I know my body will be weak from the three weeks of laying here. I have to get back into shape. Although, I'm not sure what has happened since I've been out. I can only imagine the house cleaning I will have to do.

Taylor sits up next to me, prepared to help me into place. "Let me try first babe. If I need help, I will ask." It's not that I don't want her help. It's just I have to see how weak I've become so I know what I need to do. I try to use just my stomach muscles to sit up at first like I've done a million times. The pain doesn't let me do what I've always done. I now roll towards Taylor and with my right hand push myself up. Only a pinch of pain as I sit up next to Taylor. How has my body healed so fast?

"I knew you could do it," Taylor says as she moves in to embrace me. She smells like lavender. I can only imagine how I must smell to her after laying here so long without a bath.

"Do you want to try to stand up and walk around?" she asks, not sure how far I want to take this little adventure.

"Yes. I need to get moving. Heaven only knows what awaits me out there and I need to get back into the swing of things."

"Things have been bad the whole time you've been unconscious Deacon. The Army has moved in. The acting president declared martial law and for the most part the violence has stopped. They can't be everywhere though," Taylor says with apprehension in her voice. "We've also already taken out the IV and removed the catheter."

The thought of having a catheter in my body doesn't seem too bad. The thought of Scott putting it in, however, seems a little off. I don't say anything as I slide myself to the edge of the bed and swing my legs over. Taylor stands at my side ready to help if I need it. I put one foot on the ground and then the other.

I can do this. I feel a strength in my legs I wasn't expecting as I stand. Taylor keeps one hand on my arm just in case my legs give out. Once she sees I can stand with no problem she takes my hand and without saying a word starts walking towards the door. I think she wants to show me off to whomever remains. We move slowly, but surely to my bedroom door. Turning the corner into the living room I see Scott, Melissa, Savanah, and Bobbi all watching the news.

As we round the corner Taylor exclaims as happy as can be, "Look who decided to join us!" They all turn.

"You finally decided to join the land of the living!" Scott exclaims.

Melissa, Bobbi, and Savanah all congratulate me and tell me how happy they are to see me on my feet. We chat for a few minutes about the state I was in. They've all been hanging out here since making it back, not daring to venture outside. I guess martial law was called for a week after the collapse started, but the army wasn't able to get here and settle things down until a week ago.

Bobbi still hasn't been able to contact Blake since this whole mess started either. The worry she wears on her face makes her reality obvious. I try to reassure her—he's a resourceful guy and he's probably out there helping others—probably looking for her too. I guess the phone lines have been hit and miss and she's never been able to get a hold of him, which doesn't give me hope either.

I walk to the window to look down at the Boulevard. By the shadows I see it must be just after noon. Where did Taylor go? I look around and see she has moved into the kitchen. She's making me some food. Not that a woman's place is in the kitchen, but that woman couldn't be more perfect for me. I feel like I haven't eaten for weeks. She knows what I need before I even think it.

"Are you hungry Deacon?" she asks, glancing over her shoulder.

"I'm starving babe. I love you."

"I love you too," Taylor whispers, as she turns her head to kiss me. "Boy have I missed this. I've kissed you so many times over the last few weeks. I only got a few responses though so this feels wonderful."

Taylor puts a sandwich and chips together and sets them on the counter as she walks around and sits down next to me. I don't want to look away from those blue eyes, but I have to eat. We don't say much as I begin. She just stares—amazed to have me back. I hear the chatter behind me. The news anchor speaks of the continued chaos, but it's just background noise now. We don't say a word until I take my last bite.

"You want me to make you something else?" she asks.

"I'd better not overdo it. Thanks again." I'm sure my stomach has shrunk some. I don't need to give my mid-section any more reason to make me feel sick right now. I lean in to kiss her softly. How I've missed those tender sweet lips against mine. She holds my rough checks as she returns the kiss.

"Not to take away from this moment. I've been waiting weeks for this. I love the beard. You look like my rugged mountain man but —do you think we could shave it off?" Taylor asks so sweet I know I can't deny her. I hadn't thought or really realized I had a beard until I felt her smooth hands run through it.

"For you babe, I'd do anything."

She smiles and slides in for one last mountain man kiss.

I walk down the hall into my room. The lack of mobility has weakened me for sure. Whatever I had ravaging through my body didn't help either. I'll talk to Scott about that when I'm done in here. I turn on the light in the bathroom and for the first time get a look at my reflection. I haven't seen my beard this long before, but something about it now sends a chill through my body.

Maybe it's because this beard represents my past. The same past that has come back to haunt me here in Las Vegas. I was so hoping to put it behind me. Unfortunately, the beard will go and the killing will continue—if what my dad has shown me comes true. I want to push those images from my head—the destruction, the chaos, the disease. I want to turn them into just another bad dream like I had so often in the service. But the reality and images are too real. The words still ring in my head like he was relating them to me now.

I feel a pain in my side and realize I probably have a scar from where I was shot. I lift my shirt over my head to reveal the damage done. Having had many friends shot, the scars don't surprise me. The small scar in back pales in comparison to the one in the front. I can only imagine Scott without all the necessary supplies—trying to put me back together.

Six years in the service in the most dangerous places in the world and not one bullet through my body. Just over one year in Vegas and look what they've done to me. I know it will fade in time. Just another unforgettable memory of this time. Not sure it will be one I want to remember, but a memory none the less.

Lost in my thought, I hear Taylor speak as she gently touches my shoulder. "You with me Deacon?"

"I'm good babe. I was just thinking about my past." I wish we could stay here forever. I would never have to see Taylor in trouble. I would never have to raise my weapon to take someone's life again. We would be happy. I know it will not be though. We must prepare and continue to live the life we've been dealt.

"Would you like some help shaving?" she asks. She already knew where the shaver was and had begun pulling it out.

I don't say a word and nod as she plugs it in. I haven't had someone take care of me this way since I was a kid. The thought of my mother comes racing into my mind. I wonder if she's okay. Did her neighborhood escape the looters and violence? I don't voice the concern, wanting only to focus instead on the beautiful blue eyes that stare into mine and the soft hands that so delicately shave my beard. The hair falls to the ground. It's as if the memory of my former life fades with each pass. As she sets the shaver down, I turn to look in the mirror. I see the stubble of a two day rock climbing trip and realize those days are most likely over as well.

"I can finish the job now, if you'd like." Taylor asks again as she pulls out the shaving cream and razor. I lean in to kiss her again, but she pulls back at first contact. "You know I love you babe," she says in the kindest voice I've ever heard, "but the short stubble is worse than the long beard. It really hurts."

A quick chuckle escapes my lips. I've never had a girlfriend that liked to kiss me with stubble. Just to feel it with my hands lets me know it can't feel good against cheeks as soft as Taylor's. "I understand completely. I'm enjoying this treatment too much so if you'd like you can continue." She leans in this time to kiss me before she applies the cream.

The silence brings comfort. The cool cream against my face calms me. The noise of the blades sliding up my neck so slowly cutting my hair is mesmerizing as I look into her eyes. What else will we have to go through? What does tomorrow bring? A thousand different questions pass through my mind as she continues to cut.

"You've done this before," I say not sure how she knows to go so slow or to cut from the top down and then the bottom up to get the closest shave possible.

"When I was growing up I would watch my dad shave all the time. He would often have a beard like yours and I always found it fascinating and frightening at the same time. He would transform from this man I knew was my father to a man I didn't recognize and who almost seemed like he was hiding something, something that made me afraid. When I got a little older, and watching wasn't the same, I asked him one time if I could shave his face. Of course he said yes and from that point on it became a tradition for me to shave his face when he returned from a long trip. It was a very special bonding time between him and I."

"How does it feel to shave my face?" I ask, hoping it's a different kind of experience.

"Well," she pauses before continuing. "My dad always had clothes on." I almost forgot I'm sitting here basically naked. "He was also my dad, who I do love, but obviously never had the feelings I have for you."

That's a good thing for sure.

"If I had to rate the two, I would say shaving my dad was a daddy-daughter bonding time—a good chance for us to catch up. Shaving your face while you're half naked and still looking as good as ever makes me want to break my own rule and rip all my clothes off." How tempting is that? I know she wouldn't do it even though she's thinking it. It's good to know she's human.

As she wipes the last bit of shaving cream from my face with the hot rag, she doesn't wait for me to stand. She pulls me to my feet so she can get a better hold of me and holds me as if we hadn't seen each other in a year. She also kisses me and gently caresses my now baby smooth face.

We kiss for who knows how long until I hear Scott clear his throat behind us. "I see you've only got your knickers on in here. You weren't thinking of taking advantage of that precious lass, were you?" The tone in his voice so obvious. He can barely contain the laugh. Even at a time like this he has to play games.

Before I have a chance to jibe back, Taylor speaks up. "He's not taking advantage. I am," she says slapping my butt. She smiles at Scott and then back at me. Oh how I love my girl.

"Well then, if you're about done at first base with him, just know that he doesn't know what second even looks like. I have some news I know he'll want to hear, but you can finish up at first and then send him back to the dugout. Just make sure he puts some trousers on before coming out."

I don't have a chance to say a word before he slips out the door and back to the living room. I try not to think of what he could possibly want to share at this moment I was enjoying so much. Taylor pulls me in close again rubbing her soft hands across my naked back and then over my chest. She gives me one more kiss before telling me she doesn't want me to get too excited and sends me out the door as she pulls my shirt back over my body and throws me a pair of shorts.

We walk into the front room—not sure what Scott has to share. I hear the radio and Scott talking to someone on the other end.

"Are you sure?" Scott asks. The man on the other end says yes. What could it be that has Scott looking like his best friend died again?

"What is it?" I ask, the fear evident in my tone.

"It's Jennifer. She's gone without a trace, and the penthouse has been tossed."

I attempt to call her cell phone, but it goes right to voicemail without a ring.

SEVENTEEN
Unexpected

Why would Jennifer take off? Without saying a word, I walk down the hall back to my room. The cold grey colored marble on my feet feels soothing. I move as quickly as I can without hurting myself any further. I must admit though, I do feel pretty good. I open the nightstand hoping the disc still lies where Scott left it.

Every wish within me drives my desire to find something on that disc that will lead me to Tom. I want to believe Jennifer is a friend, but they're so many unanswered questions with her. I have to stop the infection that has spread through my department. James was one of Tom's lackeys, I'm sure of it. I know there has to be more dubious characters on my detail.

I walk back to the living room and slide the disc into the computer. I open up the finder and click on the disc. How does Tom even know about this disc? Dean must have told him before he got wise to what he was doing. The little wheel spins for a second and then my suspicions are confirmed. The material is password protected.

"What could it be mate?" Scott asks. I didn't realize he was looking over my shoulder.

"I don't have the slightest idea."

I know I can trust everyone in this room, but the explanation and the thought of verbalizing it right now doesn't sound too appealing. "I've got to find out what's going on, and then I'll fill you guys in. We'll have to do this together." I know they want to help, but my mind seems foggy. I'm having a hard time focusing on what I need to do. There are so many unanswered questions. I need to call Dean's intel contact in the Navy. If anyone can help me figure some things out it's got to be him.

After a month on the job while talking to Dean he gave me his contact's name and number. He told me I should never have to use it, but thought it would be better I had it just in case. Only one problem remains though, I have no idea where my phone ended up. I hadn't even thought about my phone for the last three weeks.

"Do you know where my phone is Taylor?" I feel like a child as I ask the question. Growing up I would misplace my things every now and again. Luckily my mom was always there to steer me in the right direction. I don't know how she knew every time. It must be a mom thing. Maybe it's just a woman thing—more detail-oriented you know.

Taylor doesn't say a word. She sees I've taken a seat at the computer staring at the pop up asking for the password. I glance her way and she gives me a smile that says, 'I would do anything for you even if you didn't just almost die.' I watch her walk down the hall. The white summer sun dress she's wearing keeps my attention. The thought of marriage pops into my head again, completely taking my mind off the events that have transpired. Taylor disappears into my room. I turn back to the screen—lost for words or ideas. It has to be a SEAL thing, but what in particular? The only thing that comes to mind is the year the SEALs were formed under President Kennedy, 1962. It can't be that easy though. I vaguely remember Dean saying something about a disc before I left for Zion, but he certainly didn't tell me the password. Something about good guys and bad guys, but I can't remember anything else.

I begin to type in the one, then nine when Taylor sets my phone in front of me. Before I can tell her thank you she smiles again and says, "You're welcome."

"Thank you babe. What would I do without you?"

"I don't know, but let's not think about that."

I turn back and type a six and then two. Taylor puts her hands on my shoulders as she stand behind me. I look up. The anticipation in her eyes fascinates me.

"Here goes nothing."

It can't be that easy. I hit the enter key and the screen goes black. What have I done? Then, to my complete surprise the screen comes alive. Red numbers flash across the screen. It must be an animation because they make no sense to me. Hopefully it's not deleting the disc.

"You did it," Taylor says as if she had no doubt I would figure it out.

"Yeah, but what did I do?"

'Knowledge is power' as Dean shared with me, but with this new found knowledge comes action or it's all for nothing. I want Taylor to know everything, but at the same time I don't. Sometimes the less people know in these circumstances the better off they can be. If she were ever taken from me I wouldn't want her to know anything so if they wanted to torture her she would honestly be able to say she doesn't know a thing.

Torture can make the most courageous man cry like a baby. Survival training from my team days, or two-two-five and two-two-six as we called it, taught me a thing or two about torture. The biggest, baddest, brother could be reduced to tears if the right form of torture was found to do so. They always find the right method too. They don't stop until they do. I'd rather not go down that road though. Too many bad memories.

As the animation finishes I see three red folders with file names in all capital letters—FRIENDLIES, CARTELS, and NUCLEAR. The rush of sitting in on a top secret brief before heading out on a mission hits me. The adrenaline courses through my veins. I already know my target, but will I find his name or at least a lead for my mission? I click on CARTELS first, wanting, no hoping, to find Thomas Slack among the degenerates. As the folder opens I see several more folders: PLAYERS, SAFE HOUSES—I'll certainly be checking those out—and BANKS. I click on PLAYERS first. I scan the list of members. As the files appear in alphabetical order, I scroll down to see it, SLACK, THOMAS, in all capital letters.

In his folder there's a treasure trove of information—known associates, homes, hang-outs, and tons of other information that gives me the kind of start I was praying I would find. After about an hour of writing and scratching my head at the information I've found, I go back to the main folders wondering what else I might find. I click into the NUCLEAR folder not quite sure I want to know this information. Contained inside I find PLAYERS, FRIENDLIES, and CARTELS. As I searched Thomas' file it was filled with references to obtaining nuclear materials for the cartels who had lots of Middle-Eastern connections. It should surprise me, but knowing what I know, it doesn't. Money will make some people do just about anything, even destroy their own country. Just look at the leaders we elect.

I peruse the PLAYERS folder finding many references to attacks that would send most Americans running for the hills. After reading this they wouldn't think twice about living in a city with a sizable population like Las Vegas. Dean's words flash into my mind, 'Make no mistake, they would die to set a dirty bomb off here.' When he said it I believed him, but now his words seem so real, so prophetic.

After getting my fill of bad news, I click back and go into the FRIENDLIES folder. It would be nice to know some guys that are playing for the right team. I glance through the files by name clicking on a couple as I make my way down the list. In ANKERMAN, ERIC I see his resume—which includes tours in Special Forces in his day as well as where he works now undercover for the FBI. I click into a couple more and find the same information. It seems these silent soldiers have literally saved the lives of millions of people across this globe and most people will never even know.

I continue to look through the list of individuals, jumping in and out of individual folders when I see a name I think I recognize. As I near the bottom of the list I see a folder assigned to a SANDERS, DENNIS. The thought quickly enters my mind, Taylor's dad. I try to push it out as fast as it came in. He's an engineer with a big firm. It can't be him.

Taylor no longer looks over my shoulder. I've been studying the files for more than an hour. She is sitting on the couch writing, probably able to relax for the first time since I was shot. "I can't remember you ever telling me your mom and dad's names Taylor?" I ask, wanting to clear the doubt resting squarely on my chest.

"Dennis and Nancy Sanders," she quickly quips back without a care in the world. I think an elephant just landed on my chest. I click on the file still hoping this Dennis Sanders is not related to my Taylor. Every folder, just about, has had a picture and I'm hoping I can dismiss this one without calling Taylor over. As I click in, I see a tall man with brown hair and big blue eyes that have faded with age. They may have faded, but it's not what I wanted to see. I study his features. The photo appears to be recent and it's hard to tell if it's Taylor's father. The facial features are similar though. The smaller nose that's just a little pointed tells me I've got to have Taylor look at this picture. How will I do it though?

I look through the file for thirty minutes learning everything I can about him while thinking about what I'm going to tell Taylor. If this Sanders is Taylor's father he's certainly seen his fair share of action. After thinking for another five minutes I resolve to just bring her over and show her the picture and see what she says. "Hey Taylor, can you come over here for a second?"

She jumps up without giving my request a second thought. I've hidden the image on another screen so she doesn't instantly see it. "Do you need something?"

"I do babe. I need to show you something."

"Okay." I flip to the page with the photo and turn to look up at Taylor. As she squints her eyes, her mouth falls open. I know it's her father. She's wondering why I have a picture of her father on my screen.

"How did you get that?" she asks as confused as I've ever heard.

"Is that your father?" I ask, wanting no doubts about it.

"Yes," the answer comes back with more confusion than before. "Did you find that picture on your disc?" I was hoping she wouldn't ask that question.

"I did." I can't lie to her. I then begin to tell her all about her father—how he served in the Navy as a nuclear technician, how he was recruited to work for the CIA, and how he has been doing so for twenty plus years now. She doesn't say a word as she stares in disbelief.

"The gunshot to the chest my mother told me about, coupled with the long trips and long beards makes a lot more sense now."

"Your father got shot in the chest?" I ask.

"Yeah. While you were out my mom called and she told me he almost died just like you before I was born." The lights have certainly come on now. Everything that has happened her whole life with her father and family falls into place and has much more meaning. "At least I know I'm not crazy now."

"No—you certainly are not."

"Only one question remains—why didn't they tell me? I could have handled it." As much as she thinks she could have handled it, I know her father did it for her safety.

"I'm going to give them a call right now," Taylor adds a little testy.

"I wouldn't do that right now. Don't you think this conversation would be accomplished best if you sat down with them?" Taylor doesn't say anything as she mulls over the idea. "Plus, I could meet them both for the first time. Should make for an interesting conversation. He might be able to help me out as well."

Again Taylor ponders what I've proposed before saying with a big smile, "That's an excellent idea. When can we head over there?"

"Since things have calmed down I'm sure we can drive over there in my Jeep. Call your mom and let her know we'll come over tomorrow afternoon. Just tell her that I want to meet them so they don't suspect anything."

"That's a good idea." Taylor is beaming from ear to ear. This new understanding has made her ecstatic. I think she feels like she's got one up on them. She'll learn quickly that it was for her safety, but I don't want to interrupt this euphoric feeling.

Taylor grabs her phone and dials her mother with excitement. When her mom answers, it takes everything within her to remain calm. "How are you doing Mom?"

They talk for a few seconds before Taylor tells her that I'm alive and I'd like to come over tomorrow afternoon and meet them before I start off on my next adventure. After hanging up, Taylor informs me that they'll be expecting us for an early dinner around four.

With the time set, I have lots to do before we move out tomorrow. I still have to call Dean's Navy contact. I also need to make sure things are still running smoothly through the hotels, barring the hiccup we have with Jennifer. The security detail didn't see anyone come or go so Jennifer is somewhat of a wild card now. I also have to recruit Scott to be my right hand man, which shouldn't be hard as long as I can get Melissa on board.

I think if Melissa can see the outside world first hand tomorrow it will certainly help my case. We can't stay in this place for the rest of our lives. A quick visit and dinner with the future in-laws then back to the tower—what could possibly go wrong with that?

When I look down on the strip I see cars moving intermittently. That's a good sign for tomorrow's adventure. Though things may seem calm, we'll still go fully loaded. The only thing I'll have to worry about are road blocks and vehicle searches by the military. We can't go unarmed, so the checks we'll just have to chance.

"I'm going to head down to the parking garage to check on the Jeep," I say to the group that has resumed watching the news.

"The Jeep isn't down there babe," Taylor reminds me. With everything that happened I totally forgot we never made it back here in the Jeep.

"Well—I guess we'll be taking a predawn stroll."

Melissa looks my way with the realization that I only meant Scott and I. Then she turns back to Scott still sitting on the couch. She doesn't say a word. She just slowly shakes her head back and forth as if no one else would notice. I can't see her eyes, but you can bet they are pouting with fear.

"It will be okay Melissa," he says. "We'll be gone before you wake and back before you even know we left." Again the silence kicks in. She knows I shouldn't go alone, but she also knows how much she has risked already.

"Don't worry Melissa. Tomorrow afternoon we are all headed to Taylor's house for dinner. Then you'll see how much things have calmed down out there."

They're calm now. Unfortunately, I'm afraid it's just the calm before the real storm strikes. Of course I don't tell her this.

It's just after ten now and the streets are lit but empty. The military isn't messing around with the curfew they put in place. The JLTVs look pretty mean as they roll up and down the strip. The low profile, hardened chassis and sides, plus the bullet proof glass clearly says—don't mess with me. If everything else it said wasn't enough, the turret rotating back and forth with a 50 caliber machine gun would deter even the dumbest criminal. Those bullets will rip an arm or leg right off. The military finally moved away from the soft-shell, canvas-covered HUMVEES that killed thousands of soldiers back in 2002 when the United States invaded Iraq and Afghanistan. What politician thought that would be okay for the troops?

Still standing by the window, Taylor comes over and puts her arms around me. I love the warmth her touch brings. Her bright smile in this dark world does just what I need. I need to remain focused. I need to know there's someone and something worth living for. Someone that's worth fighting for. We don't say a word as she holds me and we both stare out the window. The unknown can drive you crazy, but we have a purpose. We have a goal. Unfortunately, I only know a fraction of it.

As I stare out the window with Taylor beside me, my mind wanders back to what my dad showed me. My dad taught me a ton, and although so much has happened and the memory has faded a bit, I can't forget what I saw and how I felt. Something won't let me. Every time I think about it the memory comes flashing back. It's almost like a bad nightmare I relive every day. Unfortunately, this nightmare will come true. I just hope to make it through with my friends and family.

We stand there for a long time before Taylor brings me back to the here and now, "I'm going to bed Deacon. You should too. You need your rest."

"I will babe. I need to run down and talk to Patrick real quick. I want to take a couple more guys to get my Jeep, just in case, you know."

"Thank you," she smiles back as she holds me. "That will make Melissa much happier too."

"Let me tuck you into bed before I head down."

"Don't mind if you do," Taylor quips back, as we move down the hall to the bedroom. The sleeping arrangements have been interesting I guess. While I was out, Scott and Melissa had Taylor's room, Bobbi and Savanah slept on the couch, and Taylor mostly slept by my side—although I didn't know she was there most of the time.

Now that I'm alive again, Scott and Melissa get to share the front room. Taylor, Savanah, and Bobbi share her room. I guess since I need the most rest of anyone, I get my bed to myself. There was a smart-alecky comment from Scott about Taylor and me sleeping in the same room somewhere in that discussion, but we didn't pay it much mind.

When we get to the room, Bobbi is lying on the bed fast asleep. "We need to help her find closure. I can only imagine the heartache she feels not knowing what happened to Blake," Taylor says, knowing more about drowning in sorrow that any of us.

"How about we go by Blake's place tomorrow on the way to your parents. She's welcome to come too, if she likes."

"That's a good idea. I'll ask her tonight if she wakes up or before we leave in the morning."

Taylor leans in for one last kiss before she jumps in bed. "Don't think me too forward Deacon, but I want to marry you more than anything, so don't you go and do anything to jeopardize that." The words fill my body with a warmth I can scarcely comprehend.

"Trust me—I won't. I love you Taylor, and would love to marry you," I say, as I pull the sheets up and tuck her in.

"I love you too Deacon," she says as her fingers smoothly slide across my face. I walk to the door and give her one last look. In the dark, the light from the hallway makes her eyes sparkle like the precious blue diamond she has become in my life. One day we will get married. When we do, it will be the most exquisite moment of my existence.

Scott and Melissa are still watching television. I let Melissa know we'll be taking some extra men when we leave in the morning.

"I'm headed down to recruit those men from Patrick. We don't have too far to go, but a little extra muscle and machine power won't hurt."

"Sounds good," Scott shoots back without turning his head. He's still watching the news. They are showing video footage from Europe. I think it's Spain. From the looks of it, we are in much better shape than they are.

Walking out my front door and into the elevator, I think of my mother. She's all alone in San Diego. The fighting there looks out of control still. After mulling over the idea of calling her, I know I have to. I don't want the distraction either way. If she is safe, I'll feel better. If she's not, I'll know to head that way as soon as possible. If she doesn't answer, I'll assume the best and keep trying to get a hold of her. I dial her number and after three rings she answers. "I've been so worried about you," she blurts out before I have time to talk.

"I've been worried about you to mom. How are you doing? Are you okay or at least safe for now?

"I am. Things have been relatively calm here. The neighborhood has really pulled together and they've been checking in on me every day."

"I'm glad to hear that mom. I'm doing well. It was rough there for a bit, but Taylor and I are doing great." I don't want to worry her so I leave out the details of the past few weeks and what proceeded it.

"What are your plans?"

"I have to take care of some things here over the next couple of weeks and then I want to come get you mom. I don't feel safe with you being there all by yourself."

"I'm fine. They are taking good care of me. I have plenty of food and water, so don't you worry about me."

I know I won't win this one. "Okay. If you need anything or feel like things are getting worse, don't hesitate for a second to call me mom."

"I won't son. I love you. Take care of that sweet girl and yourself."

"I will mom. I love you too. Take care and I'll talk to you later."

As I slide the phone into my pocket, the doors open to the lobby. No unusual noise and the team stands ready. "Where's Patrick?" I ask, not to any one in particular.

"He's back in his office," Seth quickly answers back.

"Thanks. How have things been in the hotels? I've been down and out over the last few weeks. I'm hoping to get caught up."

"Things have been stellar here, but around town it was crazy for two weeks. Not sure about the other hotels. I bet Patrick knows though."

"Thanks Seth."

I head down the hall to Patrick's office to find him talking to someone. When I walk through the door his mouth drops open.

"Can you hold one sec?" he says as he places his hand over the receiver. "You're alive!" he exclaims. "I didn't think you were going to make it there for a while. Every time Scott came down, the prognosis scared me. I guess that last trip he made did it."

"Yeah, it did. It was rough going for a while there, but I'm feeling a hundred times better now. How are things operating around the hotels?" I ask hoping he's kept in touch with the security managers.

"Give me one sec. My wife is still holding. I'll let her know that I'll call her right back."

"No. Don't let me take you away. Go ahead—I can wait."

"No, it's fine. She's just complaining about the kids. Everything's good."

When he hangs up he tells me all he knows about Jennifer, which isn't that much, and the unrest that kept everyone busy for a solid week. Overall, things are running smoothly in the hotel—which is good news. I really don't have a lot of free time to put things back together here if I'm going figure out what happened to Jennifer and take care of Tom. He also fills me in on the road blocks and generally clear roads he's found coming to and from work.

"It's a good thing you set us up the way you did before this whole debacle started. We could have lost a lot more men had you not done what you did."

"Plan for the worst. Hope for the best. I'm glad things are running smoothly—which brings me to the real reason I'm here now. I need to borrow a couple sharpshooters tomorrow morning at four. I need to go get my Jeep—if it's still there."

"If you want to get more rest, I could send some guys out to get it so you don't have to go," he offers. The thought is so tempting. If I knew who I could and couldn't trust I would do it in a heartbeat.

"I need to get out. I've been stuck in a bed for too long. I need to feel the wind in my face and see what my body can handle. So, if you could just have two guys ready in the lobby at four sharp, Scott and I will be down."

"You want them carrying rifles, handguns, or what?" That's a good question. We will be taking mostly back alleys and will be relatively unseen from most people so long guns shouldn't stand out too much should they?

"Loaded to the nines—rifles, guns, and grenades. If there is a problem, I don't want there to be any doubt who's going to win." If only they were real grenades, we would definitely be in business.

We chat for a few more minutes before I head back up to my room. Patrick wanted me to know everything. I wanted the information, but with how tired I am right now I don't know if I retained much of it anyway. He's a good guy. If he's playing for the other team, he sure knows how to hide it.

EIGHTEEN
Jeepers

My alarm goes off at 3:45. When I walk out of the room five minutes later, Scott waits with an orange in his hand. "I managed to scrounge up some of these the last time I went out," he says as he hands me one.

"Thanks."

"I figure we need something to run on."

"Yeah, we do. Thanks for looking out for me Scott," I say as we slowly close the door to my place and lock it.

"You're not going all soft on me now are you?" Scott asks.

"You know what I mean. I couldn't do anything. I would have died, I'm sure. If you hadn't been here…so thanks," I say as we wait for the elevator.

"You're welcome."

"What—no other snide remark. No jab?"

"No." He pauses for a few seconds, "It's too early for that."

We ride the elevator down as Scott tells me about what to expect out there. He's the expert now as far as I'm concerned. He tells me all about what he saw and heard, but confesses he hasn't been out since the military cracked down so it could be a whole different ball game now.

"Let's hope for that."

When we step off the elevator into the lobby the two men Patrick chose are waiting. They are looking out the windows so I'm not sure who they are yet. I look down at my watch to see it's only 3:55.

"How long have you chaps been waiting?" Scott asks as we stroll up alongside them.

"A few minutes."

"Did Patrick tell you what we're doing?" I ask, making sure we're all on the same page.

"Yeah. Should be pretty easy now."

"That's what we're hoping for. Let's go."

We slide out the south entrance onto City Center Place. Normally we would still find people walking the streets or driving in and out of this area, but it's eerily quiet as we make our way west. At the round-about, the lack of noise from the falling water just doesn't seem right. I always enjoyed strolling through this area with Taylor or while making my rounds. Taylor and I would sit for hours and watch the water cascade down, creating just the right amount of noise for great ambiance.

"Come on," Scott whispers as we move into the Aria. The guards were already aware we were coming and had the doors open for us.

"How have things been here?" I ask Brian as we move into the Aria.

"Pretty quiet. Actually—it's been too quiet lately."

"Let's hope that's a good thing and not a sign of trouble brewing," Scott states matter-of-factly.

"Keep up the good work," I say as we continue west through the casino.

When we reach the west entrance I see the boarded up glass where James first attempted to kill Taylor and me. As I move closer, the memories of that day are worn way too close to home. The gunshot and subsequent fighting for my life for weeks will take some time to fade from my memory. I just hope this little outing is a simple stroll in the park.

The security crew from Aria open a door as the four of us file through towards the Vdara. This side of the hotel never has too much action. There are taxis and limos and what not, but for the most part it's quiet over here all the time. The sound of vehicles racing north on Interstate 15 makes more noise than anything usually. We continue up and over Harmon Avenue towards the entrance of Vdara, everyone watching their area as we move through the open doors of Vdara.

Walking through the front door a realization hits my chest like a ton of bricks. Brett better not be here. That's all I need now—someone working for Tom to tell him I'm out and about.

"How have things been here?" I ask Robert. He doesn't say much except things have been quiet. "Is Brett here?" I ask, really hoping he's not.

"Nope. He doesn't come in until ten these days."

"Okay. It's best if no one knows we were here—not even Brett," I say hoping my subtlety doesn't stoke any suspicion. We move down the hall to make our way through the parking garage. I peek through the west window into the garage to see no movement or lights.

"Let's just go. There's no one up at this time," Scott says with a little impatience as he pushes the door open and heads into the garage.

"Fine, fine."

The garage, cloaked in darkness, seems unfamiliar. Normally this place is lit up like a Christmas tree, but the darkness seems somewhat ominous as we move past car after car with broken windows.

As we approach the west exit to Frank Sinatra Drive, the memory of Taylor lying motionless on the ground enters my mind causing the hairs to stand up on the back of my neck. I don't know what I'd be doing right now if she had been killed that day. She certainly my reason for living.

"The Jeep is just over the fence and across the freeway," I say as we all stop just inside the garage.

"I don't think we all need to go," Scott says. "You two mind this side of the freeway north and south on Frank Sinatra. Once we get into the Jeep, you two head back to the tower. There's no reason for all four of us to get stopped by the cops or military armed the way we are."

"Good idea," I say looking first at Scott and then making sure my two guys are okay with the plan.

We move across the street as they take their positions.

"You need help over old man?" Scott asks in jest.

"I may be a little sore, but if I can't make it over this fence on my own strength, shot me now."

Scott leaps over the fence like he's done it a million times. As I climb up to the top I'm feeling good so I throw my feet over and leap to the ground.

"I shouldn't have done that," I say, grabbing my stomach. Nothing feels broken, just still bruised for sure.

268

"You good?"

"Yeah, I'm fine," I muster, not wanting Scott to think I'm weak. "Let's get across the freeway and into the Jeep so we can get home."

The lights on the freeway are absent as we move through the dark. The faint outline of my Jeep sits across the highway exactly where I left it. I'm glad, in my haste, I didn't leave the keys in the car or any weapons. I open the door and jump into the driver's seat as Scott takes his seat.

"Oh man, I forgot the keys. Did you grab them?"

"Are you having a laugh?!" Scott exclaims with an obvious tone of disgust.

"You want to go back? You can move faster than I can."

"Brilliant, just brilliant!" Scott says incredulously. "You seriously can't be that daft."

I don't say anything for about thirty seconds when Scott opens the door and says, "I can't believe you. Are you sure you were a SEAL?"

Scott swings the door open with frustrated disdain and steps out of the car with a look I don't normally see on his face.

"You're the best," I say innocently.

As Scott slams the door shut I reach in my pocket, grab the key, and put it in the ignition. I turn it over and instantly the engine comes alive. Scott shoots me a look and quickly opens the door. "I knew you weren't that big of an eejit. I was seriously rethinking our friendship."

"I can't believe I actually got you."

"I figured in your less than emblematic state you had a lapse of common sense. I'm glad to see your typical self still shines through."

"Emblematic. Wow. Someone's been reading the dictionary. Are you sure you used that correctly?"

"No—but it sounded good didn't it?"

"It did. I'm not even sure if you used it right. Let's go."

I flip on the lights and look across the freeway to see my guys heading back into the parking garage. They should make it back with no issue. I sure hope we can too.

NINETEEN
Prep Time

The trip back was uneventful. By the time we pulled up to the parking garage my two guys were already waiting and ready to let us in. Normally my key fob would work, but I'm assuming they still have everything turned off to ensure everyone going in and out of the Towers is legitimately supposed to be there.

We park in the lifeless garage and head back to the room to find it completely quiet. Without saying a word, Scott jumps back into bed with Melissa. I quietly open Taylor's bedroom door—Taylor, Savanah, and Bobbi are still fast asleep. It's a good thing I put a king size bed in here. I slowly walk over to Taylor's side and lean over and give her a kiss on the cheek. She doesn't move and I quietly slide out the barely open door, closing it behind me.

Normally I would be tempted to jump in bed with her, but with Savanah and Bobbi lying next to her it makes it easy for me to refrain. It's good though—I need to get more intel before we head out today. I still haven't called Dean's contact, nor have I seen all there is to see on that disc.

The computer is still on with the screen saver sliding slowly across the face. I sit down and slide my hand across the pad. The computer comes back to life in an instant. I perused the enemy list pretty extensively last time. Now I need to know those I can trust should I find myself in a precarious predicament. The list of friendlies seems just as extensive as the list of foes. I didn't read in detail all of Mr. Sanders' file so I resolve to read it first. Knowing is half the battle—and we will definitely be in some battles before this whole thing blows over.

Mr. Sanders' file is massive. By the time I've read every file in each folder the sun is just about to crest and it's been about an hour. His folder was so interesting I didn't notice my stomach turning, telling me to put something in it. I haven't had a chance to check the fridge since coming back from death's door. I sure hope it's not completely empty.

Walking into the kitchen, I hear a door open. As I peak around the corner I see Bobbi heading my way. I continue into the kitchen and she follows me about five seconds later.

"I didn't realize anyone was up," Bobbi says, taken back by my presence. She must not have seen me peek around the corner.

"Yeah," I answer back. "Scott and I have already been out this morning to get my Jeep. How are you doing?" I ask, hoping that she's feeling a little better.

She doesn't say anything. I can see she's thinking about where she's found herself over the past few weeks. Not knowing what has happened to Blake slowly eats at her as day after day passes without any word.

"I'll tell you what Bobbi, we are going out today to Taylor's parents' house in Green Valley. If you would like to come, we have an extra seat. We can go by Blake's place on the way and see what we find."

She still doesn't say a word—lost in thought at the prospect of knowing. We sit silent for a couple of minutes. Her tightly closed eyes and the wrinkled lines on her forehead say so much. Leaving her lost in thought, I pull open the fridge to find it still well-stocked. Scott must have raided every kitchen he could in every hotel.

"I would love to come," she starts, "but…," she trails off without finishing.

"It's okay. I get it completely. How about we go by there on our way, and if you'd like, I'll give you a call once we find something out. Or, if you'd prefer—and I think this would be better—we'll fill you in once we get back from her parents' place so you're not alone when you get the news—good or bad," I add.

Again she doesn't say a word as her emotions get the best of her. With tears welling up in her eyes, she walks over and embraces me. She holds me for some time and I can't help but think how awkward this would look if Taylor or Savanah—or anyone of them for that matter—woke up now and found us here. Six or so in the morning with everyone asleep and Bobbi and I embracing for what must be a whole minute or more in the kitchen. I didn't want to be the one to let her go, not sure how much contact she needed in her moment of emotional crisis. Her body shudders as she sobs trying not to make too much noise.

"Thank you Deacon," Bobbi finally sputters out as she releases me, having wet my entire left shoulder.

"You're welcome Bobbi."

I want to say that she'll be okay. I want her to know that everything will be alright. Those reassurances seem so shallow knowing what I know. If Blake is alive he'll find her. If he's not, he'll probably be better off. I can't tell her that though. We'll just hope for the best and let come what may.

We each busy ourselves throwing together food without talking. I decide on my tried and true turkey sandwich. Bobbi settled for a can of peaches.

Light is slowly streaming through the half open blinds bringing me back to the day and all that it could entail. What does this new adventure hold? I really hope we find answers for Bobbi. One way or another, I hope she can find closure today. I must admit though, the idea of talking to Taylor's dad today and hopefully getting even more intel gives me hope for finding Jennifer. Don't get me wrong—I hope we find Blake alive, but he was and continues to be a one of the elite. If he hasn't found us yet, knowing where we would be held up since this whole thing started, I don't have a lot of faith left that he's alive. Only time will truly tell though.

As Bobbi and I sit at the counter, lost in our own thoughts, I feel the gentle caress of a cold hand slide up my back. I turn to see my bright blue-eyes staring back at me.

"Good morning you two," Taylor says with a smile. "Glad to see you made it back," she says, looking me in the eye.

"Morning," Bobbi says.

"Good morning to you sunshine," I say as I lean over for a kiss. "We didn't see a thing moving this morning when we got the Jeep. I don't think we'll have any problems today going by Blake's place. Then we'll head over to your parents."

"Oh. He's already told you we are going by Blake's?" Taylor asks.

Knowing the fragile state Bobbi is in this morning, I answer for her, "Yeah, she's been up for about ten minutes. We've already covered it. She'll wait here for news."

Bobbi doesn't look up from her can of peaches as I shake my head back and forth to let Taylor know not to pursue the topic. She gets my hint and mouths the word, "Okay."

Changing the topic Taylor exclaims, "That's what you two are having for breakfast?" in more of a how could you tone than a question.

"What did you have in mind babe?" I quickly chide back, as if my turkey sandwich are somehow inferior to whatever she's got in mind.

"Well, since you're almost done with that sandwich, I better take it so you still have an appetite," she says as she scoops up my plate and heads towards the fridge. "Bobbi, would you like me to make you something else?"

"Thank you," Bobbi says before continuing, "but I think I'll finish these and then go lay back down." She doesn't say more and I know Taylor wants to talk to her.

"Well, I guess you can surprise me with breakfast. I'm going to go jump in the shower so I'm ready for the day," I say as I nod my head towards Bobbi.

She knows exactly what I'm doing and mouths the words "Thank you" so as to not tip off Bobbi who is most certainly lost in her own mind. If anyone can get something out of Bobbi I know Taylor will. Hopefully she can help her feel a little better today so no matter what comes, she'll be fine.

I close the door behind me and head into the bathroom, hoping the hot water will take some of my cares away. There's nothing like a hot shower to put your mind at ease and relax the body.

I turn the water on and start to undress. As I remove my shirt, I see the bruising again on my lower torso. Standing in front of the mirror, I turn and slowly remove the bandages Scott has affixed. The crooked exit wound on my stomach makes me curious to see the entrance wound again. Having seen bodies in just about every condition imaginable, the wound doesn't surprise me. The entrance hole looks to be the size of a dime or so. The exit wound however presents quite a bit bigger. I can only imagine what the shot did to my insides. It really doesn't look that bad—all things considered. The after affects sure did take a toll on me though. I'm actually surprised how good I feel—short of jumping over fences.

I continue to undress and then open the shower door. The hot water streams onto the dark gray cold tile floor. It's crazy the things I've taken for granted my whole life. Hot water has always just been there when I needed it, and though I've taken my share of cold showers, the two most definitely do not compare. I can see the steam billowing up. I step in and close the door behind me. The hot water pours over my tired body, bringing instant relief to my cares. I don't reach for the soap or shampoo. Instead, I just stand, one hand against the tile wall. The water cascades across my beaten body covering me from head to toe. All thoughts cease in that second as I clear my mind and relax completely.

"Deacon!" a voice calls out.

I don't bother to open my eyes to see who's calling. "What?" I mutter back.

"You've been in here for thirty minutes mate. It's time for some bangers. Oh, and on a side note—do some sit-ups or crunches or something before you come out here. All that lying in bed hasn't been good for your mid-section."

I turn to see Scott's heel carrying him through the bathroom door. Only Scott would come in here far enough to see me naked and make a comment like that. I must have really been out if thirty minutes have passed. I quickly wash my raged frame and rinse off.

Turning off the shower and wrapping the towel around me, I hear a knock at the bathroom door. "Who is it?"

"It's me babe. Are you dressed?"

"I'm covered," I call back.

"That's good enough for me," Taylor says as she pushes open the door. "Mostly naked I see."

"Was I really in here that long?" I ask.

"Thirty minutes at least. Bobbi and I talked for a good fifteen and then I whipped up some banana pancakes and sausage for everyone. I think the smell woke Scott up. Then I was going to come in here and get you, but Scott couldn't resist doing it himself."

Taylor steps closer to give me a big kiss before she tells me to get dressed and then heads back out to the kitchen. I quickly dry off and throw on my clothes for the day.

Walking out into the hall and towards the kitchen I can smell why Scott might have come as well. The banana pancakes smell divine. Where Scott even got bananas throws me for a loop. Without even bothering to ask, I sit down and pour syrup all over my pancakes. Scott has already devoured several I'm sure, and waits eagerly for more.

"It's a good thing you were so quick, 'cause I was about to eat your bangers," Scott says eyeing my sausages. I don't say anything. I'm too hungry and my mouth enjoys the first bite too much to respond.

Taylor must have convinced Bobbi to eat because she seems to be enjoying her pancakes and sausages as well. Melissa sits next to Scott, but she still looks half asleep as she lazily eats. Then there's Savanah. Wait, where is Savanah?

"Where's Savanah babe?" I ask, almost forgetting she was even here.

"She didn't want to get up. I'll leave her one or two ready to eat when we're all done."

I hope Savanah wants to stay here today. It would make one less person for me to worry about and give Bobbi someone to hang out with.

No one says much except to thank Taylor as we all enjoy the pancakes and sausage she's thrown together. Scott and Melissa finish first and then head back to the couch. Bobbi finally finishes her one pancake and heads back to the room leaving Taylor and I alone.

"Now—wasn't that better than your cold, turkey sandwich?" Taylor asks sarcastically.

"Was there any doubt?" I quip back.

"Nope. There wasn't and you're welcome. I figured we might as well start the day off right."

"How did your talk with Bobbi go?" I ask, hoping she'll be alright with most of us gone today. Savanah and Bobbi really aren't too close. They are more like acquaintances than anything. To be fair to Savanah, it certainly hasn't been for a lack of trying from what Taylor has told me.

"It was good. I think she'll be alright. I'll talk with Savanah before we leave so she knows what's going on. She can be somewhat direct, which works well sometimes, but probably wouldn't be the best in this instance."

"That's good. I was thinking the same thing. Savanah should stay here with Bobbi."

"What time are we planning on leaving today?" Taylor asks to get an idea of the timeline for the day.

"I was thinking around eleven to give us two to three hours to look for Blake. I figured that would be the least we could do for her and Blake. I know it's not a lot of time, but today will tell us if we need to look more, should we find any leads. The condition the streets are in and a variety of other factors will tell me what we can and cannot do. Above all, I just don't want you and Melissa in danger."

"I appreciate that babe." Taylor says as she sits down next to me. "I know Bobbi will as well."

She leans over to kiss me and we continue to eat. I know the future must seem frightening to her. If she knew what I know, she would never let me leave this place. She surely wouldn't go out there either. I used to think the unknown was the most terrifying. Not that I know exactly what awaits us, but I'd almost rather not know. The scenes I've seen unfolding across the globe, and more specifically right in front of me, will not be easy for anyone.

"Deacon," Taylor says, sensing I was lost in my own thoughts. "How about you go get some more rest and I'll clean up the kitchen and then come lay down with you?"

"Sounds good. Thanks again for breakfast."

"You're welcome again," Taylor says with a kiss.

I'm not sure I'll ever know what I did to deserve a woman like that. I go to my room and quickly slide under my covers. I close my eyes as my mind starts to mingle the events of the day.

TWENTY
Bottoms Up

I must have been exhausted, or maybe just not fully recovered, because the next thing I feel sends a soothing chill through my entire body—Taylor's cool hand on my warm back. I can now hear the alarm going off that Taylor must have set. I roll over and embrace her —a moment I never want to end.

"Do we have to get out of bed?" I ask, knowing the answer before it leaves my lips.

"Unfortunately," Taylor says. I can tell she must have fallen asleep as well. That deep sexy voice makes my mind wander. "Don't be getting any ideas now Deacon. We have a lot to do today and that is not one of them." She reads my mind so well, or maybe the slight grin that flashed across my face gave me away. Not that I would have. But it's hard not to think about it at a moment like this.

"It's a good thing you continue to be my rock," I say after planting one on her.

"Someone has to be," she says with a wry smile.

Taylor jumps out of bed, I think to stop my mind from wandering more. I quickly follow her lead and head into the bathroom to brush my teeth. If I'm going to meet my future in-laws, I'd better look presentable, as I look down at my half wrinkled clothes.

"What should I wear today?" I ask Taylor as she brushes her teeth.

Spitting out her toothpaste, Taylor turns with a look of surprise and says, "You've never asked me what you should wear before. Is someone nervous?"

"I wouldn't say nervous. I just want to make a great first impression with your parents."

"Don't worry sweetie. I've told them so much about you—and, if I might add, how much I love you. You could show up naked and they'd probably still let you in and love you."

"So you're saying I should show up in my birthday suit huh? I don't think Melissa and Scott would appreciate that as we are driving down the road," I say with a chuckle.

Taylor lets out a quick laugh. "You know what I mean. They already practically know you and love you as much as I do." She pauses for a minute like she was going to say something she wasn't supposed to. "Pluuuuss…," she continues slowly, "I may have let it slip that you were a SEAL. That pretty much sealed the deal with my dad, no pun intended," she says with a laugh. Knowing his background now it all makes sense.

"That does make me feel a little better, but honestly, what should I wear?"

Taylor walks into the closet and pulls out her favorite pair of jeans and a nice polo. "Put this on. This is the outfit you wore the night I met you. It was hard to keep my eyes off you that night, if you remember."

"Oh, I remember."

As I start to undress, Taylor gives me a kiss and promptly moves out without saying another word. I throw on the outfit along with a pair of my favorite tennis shoes and take one last look in the mirror before walking out to the kitchen.

When I arrive, Melissa and Scott look ready. They're still relaxing on the couch with the news on. Bobbi also sits, although I wouldn't call it relaxed. She's propped against the arm rest, looking quite uncomfortable, the fear evident on her face. Savanah looks like she just barely got out of bed. She sits, slouched at the counter eating cereal, her pancakes already devoured.

"Good morning Savanah," I say.

Barely audible she mumbles back, "Morning."

Turning my attention to the news and anything that could help us out today I say, "Scott, anything crazy going on in the city?"

"Same old, same old," he says. "Blockheads out at night causing mischief and then scattering in the morning like cockroaches when the lights come on. They did say someone has been working on killing the power to the city. The police and military have stepped up patrols around the city's power stations now. It's really a miracle it's still on."

"That would make this adventure a whole new ballgame without light, wouldn't it? Well—hopefully they can keep them at bay. This city would burn to the ground without power."

I turn my attention to Taylor. She quietly talks to Savanah in the kitchen. As I meander over, I can hear her talking about Bobbi's fragile condition and the need for her to stay here to help her or at least make sure she doesn't run off or hurt herself. Savanah doesn't say anything. She just continues to nod her head in agreement to what Taylor says. I continue to listen and look at the clock on the microwave. It's 10:45 and about time to go. With Savanah on board and Bobbi staying here, things are going well this morning.

"Scott, you ready to head on out? We need to make sure we're fully loaded. Do you want to give Melissa a gun?" I ask, not quite sure of Melissa's skill level with a lethal weapon.

"Hey! Why are you asking him? How about you ask me," Melissa calls back, her annoyance evident. I can see Scott just chuckling without even turning to look in my direction.

"Okay, okay. Sorry. I didn't know. Melissa, do you feel comfortable carrying a weapon?"

"You bet I do. I want a rifle and a handgun if you've got them."

When Scott turns and gives me the side to side motion like he doesn't think that's a good idea, Melissa catches a glimpse and slugs him on the arm. "You know I can shoot. Why are you shaking your head? I've been shooting as long as I can remember."

"I know Melissa," Scott says. "I'm just having a laugh. She can shoot. I trust her to carry whatever she wants," Scott says looking at me.

"Then it's settled. We'll all leave out of here like Rambo and hopefully we don't have to use anything."

Taylor, listening intently to our conversation, grabs my hand and says, "I'll just take a handgun with some extra magazines. I haven't done much rifle shooting believe it or not."

That's surprising knowing her father like I do now. "If that's all you want that's fine. Between Scott and I and GI Jane over there we should be good," I whisper, not wanting Melissa to hear.

"Alright then gang, let's head on out. What firepower we don't have up here we'll grab downstairs on the way to the Jeep."

In the lobby, we meet up with Patrick to give him a quick run-down of our plans—feeling that I can fully trust him. He of course asks if I want some more men, but hoping to stay a little more inconspicuous I decline his offer. We only had two rifles up in my room so Patrick opens the vault and the four of us head in to load up.

As Melissa steps through the door her mouth falls open, "Were you preparing for World War III or what?"

"I figured it's better to be prepared and not need it. As you've now seen, it's a good thing we were prepared."

She can't argue with that. She doesn't say anything else as the perfect rifle catches her attention. A simple but effective AR15 with some 30 round magazines.

"Do you guys have any Glock 23s in here?" Taylor asks so innocently.

"Right over there," Patrick points out. Taylor's excitement is evident in her smile as she moves over to collect her weapon of choice.

Normally I wouldn't condone women in battle. Some have called me sexist for that, but in our current situation it's better they are prepared than left helpless should something happen to Scott and me. I'm more in favor of men on the front lines. Unfortunately the front lines have now come to us, which necessitates women doing all they can. Let me get one thing straight though—I have never said women aren't capable of doing it. I've been more in the camp that they shouldn't have to do it. Call me old-fashioned.

With everyone now loaded to the nines, we head down to the parking garage and load up the vehicle. Scott and I each grabbed a few flash bangs just in case. The women even grabbed a couple. Until we walked into the vault I had forgotten we had stocked it with cases of MREs. We grab a case, just on the off chance we get stuck somewhere and we need some food.

With the parking garage open, we slowly roll out and move toward Las Vegas Boulevard. I'm pretty sure we'll be good, but the last thing I need now is some moron taking pop shots at the Jeep and hitting one of the women.

There are only a few cars on the street and even fewer pedestrians moving about. "Do you know where Blake lives?" I ask Scott.

"I do. You do too," Scott quickly quips back. "Why?"

"I'm just wondering what you think will be the easiest, fastest, least-likely-to-run-into-road-blocks-way to get there. You've at least been out here since this started, so I was hoping you would tell me."

"Oh," Scott says seeing my point now. "I obviously haven't been way outside the area. He lives towards Nellis. I think we should head south on the Boulevard. Then west down either Tropicana or Sunset before heading north again. The faster we can get away from the strip the better. I'm betting there's less police and military presence the further away we get. The area around the base could create another problem though."

"I guess we'll figure that one out once we get there."

We turn right on the Boulevard and the adventure begins. Scott and I sit up front just in case we have to react quickly. The women are glued to the windows in back as we move south. The ransacked buildings and shops are everywhere. Burned out cars line the roads, obviously pushed to the side by the military to allow the free flow of traffic—or the lack thereof I guess. As we continue to drive, the things I was shown seem even more probable. With where we've sunk, it's no wonder we'll never get back to where we once were.

Pulling up to Tropicana we see a road block to the east so we keep heading south to Sunset in hopes that the military hasn't completely locked down Las Vegas Boulevard.

"Hey—look at the lion!" Taylor exclaims as we all turn to look. "Why would they do that?" she asks in amazement.

The once majestic lion adorned in gold in front of the MGM has been completely covered in red paint. "Commies," Scott mutters.

No one says a word as we continue south past the Excalibur Hotel. It's amazing to me that the hotels still look unscathed. I'm sure the insides look like a rhino has run rampant through them. Further south on the Boulevard there are fewer shops and major hotels so the damage and abandoned cars have thinned.

Approaching Sunset Boulevard, I can see a road block, but it appears they are only stopping those coming onto the strip. We turn left and start the unknown trek east toward my old place in Green Valley. There's a park and shops this way, but nothing too major so things should be relatively quiet on this side of town.

"He lives in the Amber Ridge Apartments on Stewart and Nellis right?" I ask, hoping I haven't imagined our destination—or at least our starting point for the day.

"Yes, from what I remember. I've only been there a couple of times," Scott says sounding uncertain.

The roads are pretty clear as we continue east. When we pass Annie Oakley Drive, Taylor tells us her parents live just down that street. I do remember her telling me how close we must have lived when I first moved here. The day has finally come. I get to meet her parents. Under different circumstances would be preferred, but I guess since things aren't getting any better, now's as good a time as any.

With the traffic almost completely absent and no road blocks since the strip and Sunset, we make good time and I feel pretty confident getting back. We are now within a block of Blake's place. Driving further north things begin to look worse and worse. We see homes reduced to ashes, more burned out cars, and some shops that definitely won't be opening again. This is not what I want to be driving myself into. Certainly not somewhere I want to be taking Taylor and Melissa. The lack of military and police presence since the strip says it all. I know it's cliché, but the saying "when the cat's away the mice will play" certainly comes to mind.

"You know which number Blake is in right?" I ask Scott as we pull into the complex.

"Yeah. He's in M302. It's on the top."

"Okay. I'll pull up and if things look pretty clear and quiet we'll stay down here while you go up to his place and see what you can find."

"I want to go with him!" Melissa says.

"I'm not touching that one Scott. It's your call."

"Melissa," Scott begins in the most caring tone he can manage, "if things look quiet you can come with me, but please trust me. If I ask you to stay in the car, then please stay in the car."

"Ok," Melissa says smiling back and running her fingers through Scott's hair.

Building M sits at the back of the complex, which I'm guessing plays to our favor. At least it's off the main drag and less likely to get looted. I still think we're on a wild goose chase though.

As we round the corner to the back of the complex, I immediately hit the brakes, not sure what I'm seeing in front of me. There's a group of fifty plus people drinking and having a barbecue in the parking lot in the middle of the day. I guess ordinarily that wouldn't be out of place, but given the current circumstances this world finds itself in, I'm at a loss. The fact that I see guns in the crowd doesn't bode well with me either. They are all laying against vehicles, which settles my nerves a bit.

About to put the car in reverse and slowly back out of there, I notice Blake's roommate in the crowd and the people are waving us in with friendly smiles on their faces.

When I put the car back in drive, Melissa scowls, "Oh no you're not! We're not going in there."

"I see Blake's roommate over there. I don't remember his name, as I only met him the once, but I'm pretty sure we'll be safe. Plus, from my experience, a barbecue and beer equals good times. What do you think Scott?"

He surveys the situation for a few seconds before responding. "We did come here to get word on Blake's whereabouts. His flatmate is the best hope we have to find him. If you girls feel more comfortable staying in the car then you can, but Deacon and I should get out and at least talk to them."

Scott's logic leaves Melissa speechless. She's seen the pain in Bobbi's eyes every day for weeks so I know it makes perfect sense to her. Though she has fears, she knows we are doing the right thing. I pull up to the crowd and back into a parking spot.

As I park the car I add one more word which I know will upset Melissa, but I want these people to know we aren't there to cause trouble, "We have to leave our weapons in the car."

No one says a word. I think the women are in shock. Scott figures it out first and without saying anything leans his rifle against his seat before opening his door. He steps out and quickly closes his door and opens Melissa's. The look on Melissa's face screams I want to kill you Deacon. As she grabs Scott's hand, she reluctantly leaves her rifle leaned against the seat.

Though we look unarmed, I know Scott still carries his handgun concealed on his right side ready to step into action at a moment's notice. I too am carrying, and I know Taylor has her 23 in her purse. Melissa will just have to trust us on this one.

These thoughts pass through my mind as I step out and close my door before opening Taylor's. I take her hand to help her out. "We can do this babe," Taylor says as she grabs my hand.

"I know. I'm just glad you know," I say with a delightful smile showing on my face as her foot hits the pavement.

Taylor and I walk hand in hand toward the crowd, but more specifically toward Blake's roommate. "I met him once, but I can't for the life of me remember his name."

"Don't worry, I've got it," Taylor adds, squeezing my hand and flashing those blue eyes my way.

As we get closer Blake's roommate sees us and calls out, "Deacon! Scott! What brings you guys out this way?"

Scott speaks first as he extends his arm to shake hands, "We are looking for Blake. We were hoping we would find some answers here." I too reach forward to shake his hand, hoping he has answers for us.

"I wish I knew," he calls back. "Ever since the city fell apart I haven't seen him. He left for work that morning and I haven't seen him since."

Hoping there's something more I ask, "He hasn't called or anything huh?"

"No, nothing. Someone did break into the apartment while I was gone one day. They ransacked the place a bit and a bunch of his stuff was taken, but they didn't take any of my things. It made me wonder if someone he knew had come by to get back what was theirs, but he still hasn't turned up. Once a little order was established I went by his work to see if they had seen him, but even they said he had vanished."

"Did they say if he made it into work that day?" Scott asks, reading my thoughts.

"Let me think," he pauses with his forehead furrowed. "Now that you mention it, they did say he was there that day. He got a phone call, probably the same time things went terribly bad, and then said he had to run somewhere real quick. He never went back. That's all I know."

"Have you checked any hospitals or anywhere else?" I ask, hoping to eliminate some of our search area.

"No. Just his work. Sorry. I really wish I knew more. I hope Bobbi's okay. I haven't heard from her either."

Taylor jumps in now giving me a slight grin before speaking, "She's doing okay, but definitely could be better. Sorry, I haven't met you. My name's Taylor. What's yours?"

"My name's Jeff. Nice to meet you." he says as he shakes Taylor's hand. Melissa to shakes his hand and introduces herself.

"Jeff, would you mind if we went up to his room and took a look around? If we could find anything that would help us I know Bobbi would be grateful," I ask, hoping he trusts us enough to take us up to his place. I know the women will feel a little less on edge to get out of this crowd.

"Yeah no problem. Anything for Bobbi. She's a great girl and please tell her I wish I knew more and I'm glad she is alive and has made it through this mess. Let me just let my girl know I'm heading up to the room. In fact—do you guys want a drink or something to eat? This is our first big get together since everything happened. Most of us that live here are ex-military or still in and we were able to scrounge up everything for a decent barbecue."

"The offer is tempting, but we just ate and we have another appointment after this, but thank you," I say, hoping he's not offended.

"No problem. Just give me a sec."

As he heads over to the grill where his lady must be hanging out, we don't say a word as we continue to survey our surroundings. The crowd, filled with guys and girls, appears to not have a care in the world.

Scott breaks the silence, "If I hadn't been outside this little space right here, I wouldn't think anything was wrong in the world. But then I see the weapons all over the place and realize the world is going to heaven in a wheelbarrow."

No one responds to Scott as Jeff waves us toward him. "Let's go guys," he calls out over the crowd.

We walk up the stairs and Jeff shows us into his place and into Blake's room. There isn't much left—clothing hanging in the closet, furniture too big to carry, and little things here and there. I'm not sure what we thought we would find, but I figured it couldn't hurt to look.

"Well guys, let's just look through everything really quickly to see if there's anything that could possibly help."

Melissa quickly questions back, "What are we looking for exactly?"

"I wish I knew."

On hearing our conversation, Jeff interjects, "I did often see him writing in a black journal, but it's gone along with the little lock box he kept in his room."

"When you say often, how many times a week would you see him write in it?" Scott asks.

"I would say two to three times a week at least."

"And you've looked for the book or box specifically and you couldn't find it in here?" I ask, this time realizing that would have probably been our best hope.

"Yeah. He kept the lock box on the shelf in the closet and it's gone. I kind of picked up in here after the person broke in and I didn't see it anywhere."

"Well, thanks for letting us come up and look around. We'd better get going. I don't think we are going to find anything else here that will help us."

"No problem. Like I said, I wish I could be more helpful."

"If you hear anything or learn anything new, could you text me or give me a call?" I ask.

"Yeah, no problem. What's your number?" Jeff asks as he pulls out his cell phone.

I give him my number as we head down the stairs to the Jeep. Everyone thanks him as we shake hands and part ways.

As Jeff walks away, he looks back in our direction and says, "Stay safe out there. There are too many crazy people roaming around now."

"We will," I call back. "You too."

As we pull out of the area Melissa says, "Even though we didn't get what we wanted, that went a lot better than I expected."

"Yeah it did," Taylor says in agreement.

Scott and I both agree and we quickly head toward Taylor's parent's place. With traffic this scarce, we turn onto her parent's street within twenty minutes of leaving Blake's. We head down Dustin Ave past one cul-de-sac to the second where Taylor says they live right on the corner. As we pull up, a sleek white Mercedes peels out, making a right hand turn driving east.

"That's odd," Scott exclaims.

As we pull up to the front of the house, its size sets me back. The house is an English Tudor style home that is easily five thousand square feet. Its craftsmanship is precise and proper, kind and comfortable. I would have never thought Taylor's parents lived here. There is a weeping willow on the corner of the property line. Bright green leaves are appearing on its long wispy branches. Pine trees dot the enormous landscape covering every square inch with a soothing shade.

Pulling up to the front walkway, Taylor's gasp and the tight grip she placed on my shoulder cues me into what she's seeing. I immediately snap out of my amazement to see a man lying on the steps by the front door still bleeding out.

TWENTY ONE
Flash Back

When a Roadster II pulls into the valet station I can't help but notice. This time was no exception. The clean lines and solid black exterior slide in without making a noise.

"I've got this one Pete," I yell out as he starts to make his move.

Walking behind the car I notice the model is a P200D. Not only does he like quiet, he likes speed. As I open the door to let a true connoisseur of quiet perfection step out, none other than Elon Musk looks up to greet me.

"Mr. Musk, it's nice to meet you. What brings you to the Bellagio today, business or pleasure?" I say, still holding the door open.

"A little of both," he replies as he steps from the car. "Business first, and then hopefully a little bit of pleasure. Dean should be expecting me."

Normally Dean informs me when celebrities or someone famous is coming, but this time I'm feeling a little caught off guard. I won't let Mr. Musk know that though.

"You are staying with us for a few days then?" I ask, without skipping a beat.

"I am."

"Pete," I call out. "Can you help Mr. Musk to the V.I.P. front desk and let Dean know at once that Mr. Musk is here."

"Please, call me Elon," he says in his most casual tone.

"No problem Elon. Have you stayed with us before?"

"Actually, I have several times. That's why I keep coming back," he says with a smile.

"Well—we must be doing something right," I say with a playful tone. "Pete here will help you to get checked in, and I'll have your bags brought to your room in no time. Don't worry one bit."

"Thank you. Sorry, what is your name?" he asks, seeing I don't have a name tag like all the others.

"My name is Deacon, I'm the manager here. Anything else we can do for you Elon?"

"No. I think I'm good. Thank you very much, Deacon," he says as he reaches in his pocket before shaking my hand, handing me a crisp hundred dollar bill.

"Thank you Elon. Have a great day and follow Pete right over here. We'll get you all taken care of."

I wasn't expecting to meet Elon Musk today. We get famous people coming through here almost every week, but Elon wasn't one I'd expect to see. He has a meeting with Dean to top it off. I wonder what he has going on. Must be something to do with power.

I slide into the sleek black interior. My body fits like a glove. After the bad news Christen gave me today, this somewhat takes my mind from the obvious pain I will be feeling when she finally leaves for Spain. Why does that girl have to be so stubborn sometimes. To top it all off, Jennifer called me to set up an interview with Dean just after the New Year as well. Talk about stress.

I put the car in drive and punch it out of valet, any thought of Christen completely leaves me as the sheer acceleration pulls me into the driver's seat like I was just launched from Cape Canaveral. The elegance and comfort have me rethinking the Jeep I just purchased.

Pulling into the parking garage, I see Tom and Jennifer talking aside Jennifer's new diamond white Mercedes I had parked earlier that day. The car is so quiet as I pull in behind her spot. They don't even turn to look. Just about to get out of the car, I can see they seem pretty heavy in some serious discussion. I roll down the window and listen with anticipation.

"...do that. He'll know. We need to wait longer before we make our move," Jennifer says, the frustration evident on her rosy cheeks.

"Trust me Jen. He's about to let me go. I know it. He needs to be put out to pasture. The people running this town are tired of dealing with him."

"I'm telling you, it's too early Tom. We need to wait," her cheeks growing more red by the second.

"Fine," Tom spits back. "I'll see you later."

"Alright."

With that exchange they kiss briefly and Jennifer jumps in the car and takes off. Tom heads back into the hotel without noticing I was there.

What in the world just happened there? After Jennifer is gone and Tom has disappeared, I exit the car. Grabbing Elon's bags, I make my way back inside a little uncertain to what I just witnessed.

TWENTY TWO
Dire Circumstances

As I round the corner of my Jeep with my rifle at the ready, I see Scott has already rolled over the body of the lifeless man and has begun to assess him. I quickly move up the half a dozen long steps just past Scott to keep my eyes fixed on the front door that lies wide open with the fire alarm blazing inside.

Taylor, seeing the bloodied face of the man lying on the steps, yells out in desperation, "Deacon, that's not my dad!"

Peeking through the front door I see blood all over the beautiful Persian rug that greets guests in the entry.

"We've got to get inside the house Scott. We have to clear the house and make sure her parents are okay," I say in a flash, knowing Taylor has come apart in the car.

"Okay," Scott fires back. "This one's not going to make it anyway."

Then in a voice of panic and with all pretense of pleasantries gone, Taylor yells, "DEACON, HURRY INSIDE! Make sure my parents are okay." I don't see them, but I know there are tears streaming down her face.

"We're going in now. If someone you don't know comes out this door, I want you to take off as fast as you can until I call you," I yell back, wishing I could hold her in her moment of need.

I turn to see that Scott has already made his way through the front door, abandoning the lifeless man. I quickly catch up. Since he has already surveyed the layout from the entrance, I follow his lead.

Right now I wish I had been here before, so at least I would be familiar with the layout of the house.

The house is a split level. As I enter, the alarm is deafening. At least we'll have some cover for our movement. I see stairs leading down to a lower level as well as stairs leading up. The smoke is clearly visible, curling and twisting in the air directly in front of us. Aside from the obvious smoke, the house smells pleasantly of well-seasoned roast beef, freshly baked bread, and a hint of sweet strawberries.

If someone is here they probably know we are here too, but no need to tip them off any more to our exact location. A slight surprise will most definitely be in our favor.

Scott heads right, just off the entrance, and enters a library as I watch the six. As I enter the room, I see it is surrounded by shelves that reach from floor to ceiling, lined with rows and rows of books. There is a window seat in the large bay window facing the front yard. I can imagine Taylor stretched out there relaxing with a good book or writing. A black leather love seat is nestled in the corner near the fireplace. A simple black end table is immediately to the right of the love seat. On it sits a reading lamp, a pair of reading glasses placed neatly on top, and a framed picture of Taylor. In the picture, Taylor couldn't have been more than ten years old. She appears to be jumping exuberantly out of a second story window in perfect cannonball form into the sparkling swimming pool below.

We quickly move through the library and through the two-way door into the kitchen. There is a small room to the right which Scott clears quickly and lets me know there is a half bath and a door to the garage which appeared empty. There are no signs of blood, although we do find the source of all the smoke. Clearly, dinner preparations were interrupted abruptly. I glance over at the stovetop. There's a sauce pan of red goop, bubbling over like lava. The more the glaze bubbles over, the more the stovetop element burn and smoke. I quickly pull the sauce pan off the burner and turn off the stovetop. Seeing the double ovens each hard at work, and not wanting even more smoke, I turn off each one. The angel food cake cooling on the counter and the diced strawberries explain the red glaze.

The noise here pierces me to my core, but I decide not to fan the detector in hopes that it will continue to cover our tracks. Scott clears the kitchen to the right and I continue to watch our six. The kitchen, library, and just about all I see is of the most exquisite making.

We quickly move through the kitchen and into the dining room. There is a large mahogany table—elegantly set with four pure white china place settings, slender crystal stemware, and complimented with a striking flower arrangement of deep red roses and bright white daises. I guess we forgot to tell them Scott and Melissa were coming. As the dining room was clear of any signs of struggle, we circle back around to the stairs.

Blood, either from the man lying dead on the front porch or possibly someone still in this house, lies both on the stairs going up and the stairs leading down. Scott takes the stairs going up first. I quickly gaze down the steps leading into what appears to be the lowest level. With no clear sign of which way they could be, I follow Scott up the stairs.

Without saying a word, Scott stops before getting to the third level to look back at me. He gives me the signal to watch the steps that lead up to a fourth level. I see at the top of the steps that we have doors leading everywhere. I give him a nod and cover the fourth floor to our twelve and the steps heading to the lowest level, while Scott takes the first door on his right.

No sooner had he gone in then he came back out. It must have been a bathroom or closet. He takes the next door on his right. I move in with my back to the bathroom, watching the stairs down as well as the stairs leading up and the doors to my one, two, and three o'clock. Scott returns after ten seconds to whisper "master—trashed" as he taps me to take lead and continue the search while he watches the unknown.

I quickly start with the door to my three to find it's a closet with a laundry chute to the lowest level. The next door slowly creaks open to reveal a bedroom and a walk-in closet—both with no signs of disturbance. I find the same behind the third door. As I come out, I can see Scott has already moved to the stairs and is watching both up and down. I tap his shoulder and he quickly moves up the stairs. I wait to watch our still unknown. When he reaches the inside of the room he quickly turns to motion me up.

As I enter the room, I see Scott has already moved left to clear behind a chimney that blocks the view to the whole back left half of this massive room. I know he must be thinking the same thing as I am —this house is enormous and we haven't even seen the bottom floor yet. Scott moves past the chimney to the left as I move to the right, keeping my eye on the small door that must lead out over the garage. Every second or so, I glance behind me making sure no one has come up behind us.

I reach the tiny door first and move through to the east, while Scott follows right on my back to the west. It's just an exercise room with a pitched roof and no signs of blood or anything out of the ordinary.

"Let's move down to the bottom floor," I say, moving back through the little door as fast as I can.

"Sounds good. The master was trashed and there was blood on the carpet, but nobody was there."

"Okay. They're either downstairs or in the back of that Mercedes we saw flying out when we were coming in."

We aren't going to search the rooms on the third floor. We can only hope no one has double-backed on us. We move quickly down the stairs to the first floor to find another overly large room that appears to be a family room. The family room is large, but we clear it quickly with only a couch to check behind. We are also seeing more blood down here than we saw upstairs. There's a hallway to the right and a second kitchen. This kitchen is much smaller, and when we came down the stairs we could see no one in it.

We quickly move down the hall, clearing each door as we pass. Scott clears the right and I clear the left as the smoke alarm finally goes off. The first door I come to is another closet where the laundry chute I saw upstairs leads to. Scott clears the next room quickly and prepares to go into the room at the end of the hall. I move through my last door on the left to find the one thing I was hoping I wouldn't. What can only be a bleeding and thoroughly beaten Mr. Sanders lies motionless on the floor at the foot of the bed. Making my way in and after clearing the closet I see what must be Mrs. Sanders. She too has received her share of beatings. There's a gun in Mr. Sanders' lifeless hand which would probably explain the deceased man outside.

"Watch my six," I say quickly as I kneel down beside the both of them.

With a rope still tied around his left hand, I slide it aside and check his pulse. He still has a pulse, but barely. Next I check his breathing. It's faint and fading fast from the looks of his beaten body.

"Mr. Sanders," I call out in hopes that I won't be going out to greet Taylor with the worst news she's ever received. He doesn't answer. The blank stare in his eyes is all too familiar to me. His body is going through the final unalterable end of its life. From the looks of him, and the man out front, he didn't go out without a fight.

His eyes appear to have been hit numerous times. The rope around one wrist speaks volumes. Whoever was here must have been torturing him—trying to get information. I'm positive they didn't succeed. Even with all the bruising I'm positive it's him.

With all my attention on Taylor's dad, the hand of her mom grabbing mine startles me. I quickly turn to look. Her tear-filled eyes look into mine with a hope that I just can't honestly give her.

I'm not one to cry, but these two are my family. I've never met them, but I feel a love for them that brings an emotion to my heart I haven't felt since my own father passed away.

"Help him," Mrs. Sanders gurgles.

Scott, on feeling we have cleared the house, kneels down on Mr. Sanders' right side and goes to work while I attend to Mrs. Sanders.

"Where does it hurt Mrs. Sanders?" I ask, as I focus all my attention on her.

"My name is Nancy," she says softly.

"Okay Nancy. Where does it hurt the most?" I ask again, knowing that if the patient can speak they are usually the best source of information.

Her eyes close as she tries to move. I can see the pain in her body by the expression that flashes across her face. The wince and gritted teeth tell so much.

"I can't move my body," she says as she opens her eyes and looks up at me.

"Okay. We'll get help coming as quickly as we can get them here. I'm Deacon and Taylor is in the car out front. I hesitate to get her, but…" I pause not sure if I should say the words.

My mind races. I realize if the roles were reversed, as hard as it would be, I would want to say something to my father while he still had life in him—however little that might be.

"…but," I continue, "I hesitate to bring her in with your husband barely clinging to life. Even with that being said, I think she would want to be here."

Without saying a word she nods her head in agreement.

As I stand up, Scott taps me on the shoulder and urges, "You better go quickly. He only has minutes if that. I wish I could help him, but he has already lost too much blood and he's barely breathing."

I quickly run up the stairs and out the front door. Taylor and Melissa are parked across the street now facing out of the cul-de-sac for a quick getaway. As I bound down the long front steps Taylor opens the door. When she sees my face she knows it's not good.

"Your mom is alive and y-your dad," I can't say the words. "Your dad's on his way out. You need to hurry. They are both downstairs in the last bedroom on the left. Give me a sec and I'll be right behind you."

Without saying a word and with the tears already free flowing, Taylor takes off. Melissa has also exited the car and stands next to me frozen.

"Will you call for an ambulance?" I ask Melissa as the tears stream down my own face. "I think her mom has a broken back and her dad will be dead before the ambulance arrives."

Melissa too now has tears forming in her eyes as she simply says, "Okay."

Seeing the pain flow down my face, Melissa embraces me. She doesn't say a word knowing words won't help right now.

With Melissa taking care of medical services, I quickly run back into the house hoping for a miracle. Scott did wonders for me. Maybe he can do the same for Dennis. As I come through the bedroom door, I see Scott turning his attention back to Dennis. Taylor's tears wet her mother's face as she looks from her mom to her dad. As I kneel down next to her, I put my arm around her hoping to give what little comfort I can.

"Did you call for an ambulance," Scott asks as he shakes his head in reference to Dennis's unchangeable ending.

"Yes. Melissa's calling right now."

"Mom," Taylor starts out between sobs, "can I do something for you?"

"Taylor," Scott says with a bit of trepidation before her mom has time to respond, "You need to say your goodbyes now. Your dad only has seconds to live." Holding Taylor I feel the shutter shake through her entire body as Scott utters those fateful words.

Her mom lets out an audible gasp as Taylor embraces her dad for the last time in mortality. She holds him for quite some time as the sobs grow and grow.

"Dad, I-I love you," she weeps, holding him in his final moments.

With Taylor's attention completely engulfed in her dying father, Scott and I turn our attention to her mom. Scott speaks first, "I'm pretty sure her back is broken. I've stopped the bleeding from her leg and arm, but we need to get her to the hospital sooner than later."

"Do you think we can move her?" I ask, not sure how we would get her in the car let alone out of the house without causing more damage.

Just then Melissa comes through the bedroom door. "They'll be here in twenty minutes."

"That's not bad," Scott adds.

On seeing the horrific scene that Taylor has been thrust into, Melissa can't contain her emotions. Melissa's complete breakdown in the doorway hits us all hard.

Without skipping a beat Scott jumps up. "I'll take her out and look for a board to put Mrs. Sanders on. She's stable for now."

Scott takes Melissa around the waist and holds her as he moves down the hall out of sight. With just the four of us left, I turn my attention back to the scene unfolding before me.

Taylor presses off the ground to look her dad in the face.

"I love you too Dad. I will." Taylor's words are clear and undeniable. Then almost as if the Hoover Dam had broken free, Taylor falls upon her father and the flood gates open. He must have said something to her and then passed on.

Nancy, on hearing her daughter's distraught state, manages to move her right hand to Taylor's back. Upon feeling her mother's best attempt at being part of the moment, she turns after a few seconds and wails—holding her mother. No words are exchanged. The somber mood calls for silence. The blood that was splattered across Nancy's face has been completely washed away by Taylor's tears. I too can't contain myself as I slide over and embrace both of them. The three of us sit still—lost in the moment.

Scott makes his way back and discretely clears his throat to get my attention. "Deacon," Scott whispers, waving me out to the hall

Leaving Taylor holding her mom, I quietly get up and head out. In the hall is a crudely fashioned stretcher.

"We need to get Taylor and her mom outside into some fresh air. We can take her out the back door on this," Scott says pointing to the stretcher, "and then out to the front yard without worrying about going up or down steps."

"I think that's a good idea," I respond back.

"I'll let you make the call on how to tell them," Scott adds, unsure of what to say.

We both step back into the room. The scene that lays before me is more than anyone should have to bear. Like I had never left, I slide up to Taylor and her mom again to embrace them.

After about a minute I whisper, "The ambulance will be here in five to ten minutes. We have a stretcher here to get you outside into some fresh air."

Nancy nods in agreement after looking at Taylor and then back at me. She knows some air and a little distance will be good for Taylor right now.

At seeing our exchange, Scott sets the crudely fashioned stretcher to Nancy's left side. From the looks of it, he found a piece a plywood and a couple of two by fours and fashioned them together in the perfect makeshift stretcher.

"We need to keep her head straight when we roll her body and slide this under her," Scott instructs. "Taylor. Can you slide this under while Deacon and I move her body?"

Upon hearing Scotts request, Taylor releases her mother and nods her head.

"Alright Deacon, I'll hold her head while you roll her body."

"Mrs. Sanders," Scott begins, turning to look at her, "tell us...."

"Call me Nancy please," she interjects, abruptly interrupting Scott's instructions.

Between muffled sobs, Taylor lets out a little sigh. "Mom," she lovingly scolds, as if to tell everyone that addressing her as Mrs. Sanders is perfectly fine.

"Okay Nancy," Scott corrects himself quickly as he shoots a glance at Taylor with an almost invisible smirk in his eyes, "tell us if anything we do hurts."

"Okay," she responds.

With Scott's lead, we lift her body in unison, and like clock-work, Taylor slides the board under her potentially broken back. We gently roll her back onto the board and slide her slightly over so she lays centered on the make-shift stretcher.

"I know this isn't going to be comfortable, but it will have to do until you're lying comfortably on a hospital bed," Scott adds.

In an attempt to get Taylor engaged I suggest, "Can you please open the doors and gates for us as we take your mom outside?"

"Of course," she manages as she gets to her feet.

Scott and I slowly lift her without any issues and make our way through the door into the hallway before heading through the laundry room and out the back door.

Stepping through the back door I see the beautiful garden that Taylor has mentioned plenty of times. The walkway is lined with deep purple and pure white crocuses—just emerging from the rich, dark ground. I also see the giant pool house and the massive pool that fills the back yard. There is an olive green charcoal grill nestled near the pool house and a wooden picnic table—worn smooth from years of summer barbecues, pool parties, and countless birthday parties.

"Just down this sidewalk and we'll be out front," Scott says leading the way.

No one responds or says a word as reality has fully set in and our minds are muddled with thoughts of what happens next. At war, things are easy so to speak. Don't get me wrong, you feel the loss and it hurts, but necessity dictates that you keep moving or you will die also. The real grieving doesn't usually come until after. You also don't have mother and daughter dealing with emotions they most likely thought they would never have to face. We're probably all in uncharted water as we walk slowly down the sidewalk to the front yard.

Coming through the gate into the front yard I glance to my left and a new emotion takes hold of my mind. I see the deceased unknown laying in his blood and my mind reverts back to what I'm used to as questions flood my mind—Who did this? Why were they here? Was that car involved that went racing out of here as we pulled up? It looked like Jennifer's Mercedes. These questions and hundreds more mingle through my mind, messing up my thoughts and plans for how this day was going to go.

"I want to get you as far away from this scene as possible until the ambulance gets here Nancy. Are you okay if we put you on the ground on the other side of my Jeep?" I ask. She doesn't say anything. She nods as I see the pain dance across her face.

"I know both of you are hurting in more ways than one right now. I…I," I pause, wanting to speak the words that will bring comfort to both Nancy and Taylor, but unable to find them. "We will get you two to the hospital and then take care of those that were here today. I know your husband was in the CIA Nancy."

The quick glance Nancy gives me upon hearing those words lasts only a second. The pain on her face is visible as she turns towards Taylor.

"It's okay Mom. I already knew. Deacon told me yesterday and don't w-w-worry," Taylor's voice trails off. She seems to be battling her own emotions. She looks into my eyes and seems to find a new reservoir of strength there. "I understand why you guys never told me," she concludes more confidently now.

Nancy's eyes are once again full of tears. I see so much of Taylor in her. I see where Taylor gets her compassion and her determination. I see where she gets her tenderness and her strength. We set Nancy down gently. Taylor kneels down at her side to embrace her mother. I gaze at Taylor in awe and respect. There is sadness and devastation all around her. But amid it all, she continues to be my angel dressed in armor—the sun glistens off her golden hair and her blue eyes are filled with love and compassion.

Not sure how long until the ambulance will be here, I ask Scott to keep watch while I go search for ID or anything that will lead me to those that are still alive. If he does have ID I hope he shows up on my disc, which will connect him to the bigger picture.

As I walk toward the house, my phone rings. I glance down and see UNKNOWN blazing across the otherwise blank screen.

"This is Deacon," I answer flatly.

"Deacon, it's Jennifer," I hear a panicked voice whisper hoarsely into the phone.

"Jen…," I start coldly, before being interrupted abruptly.

"I need your help and I need it now. I'm being held hostage by Tom. Dean told me to go to you if I ever was in trouble."

"Trouble doesn't begin to describe what you're in. We are way past trouble. You and Tom were clearly in a relationship. Add the blood on your skirt. And the fact that Tom really wants the disc. It sounds like the recipe for the perfect setup to me. Plus I just saw your Mercedes flying out of here."

"Deacon, I don't have time to explain. You have to believe me. I'm in a house just off La…."

With a scratchy scuffle, the line goes silent.

"Jennifer?" I say loudly. "Jennifer, can you hear me?"

I pull the phone away from my ear and glance at its face—call ended.

My mind starts analyzing the situation. I have three un-knowns—Jennifer is missing, or allegedly being held hostage, Tom must be dealt with, and I have to find out who killed Taylor's father and put Nancy in her current condition.

As far as Taylor's parents, I know Nancy is the best lead I have right now. However, the thought of questioning her in this condition just doesn't seem right. After I've collected all I can here, I hope I can put something together with the intel I got from Dean's office. Then I'll have her fill in any holes later tonight after she feels a little better—or at least safely lying in the hospital. I know I'll feel better with Taylor at her mom's side.

Just as I reach the body on the front steps I see the ambulance round the corner into the cul-de-sac, with lights going but no siren. "I'll be back for you," I say, hardly able to contain my desire to start putting the puzzle together.

The driver pulls in and does a one-eighty before pulling just past my Jeep next to Nancy. As I approach the crowd, the paramedic from the passenger's side gets to Nancy first.

"Sorry it has taken longer than usual. As you can imagine, things are kind of crazy in the city right now. Do we know what happened?" he asks, taking in the whole scene.

Scott, having the best understanding of her medical condition and probably being the least attached emotionally to the current situation answers, "Nancy here has a GSW in her upper left thigh. It appears to be a through and through missing anything major. She also has a GSW on her lower right arm. Again I think it missed everything major. You can take off my rudimentary bandages once you've got her loaded up and you're headed to the hospital. You can see the bruising on her face. Besides that, she can't move her extremities very easily and I think her back is broken. We've stabilized her as best we can. I only wish I could tell you how it all happened."

With that last sentence, the paramedic that was driving says, "How do you not know?"

Not wanting to rehash everything in front of Taylor or Nancy, I pull him aside while his partner works to prepare a real stretcher.

"Tim," I say, seeing his name embroidered on his shirt, "I'm going to make this as short as I can so you can get Nancy and Taylor to the hospital as quickly as possible. I'm Deacon and the girl kneeling at Nancy's side is her daughter Taylor. We were coming over to have dinner with her parents. Her father has passed away inside and the guy on the steps is an unknown, but he's dead as well. You might be wondering why we are all carrying weapons. I was in the Navy for some time and Scott over there was British SAS. As you probably understand, given the current situation, we don't go anywhere without some firepower."

"Say no more," he interrupts. "I understand completely. Let's get Nancy wrapped up and headed for the hospital. I'll let you take care of this scene."

With Taylor and Melissa doing all they can to help Nancy, I pull Scott to the side. "Do you think you could convince Melissa to go with Taylor in the ambulance? I don't know what comes next, but I'd feel much more comfortable if we didn't have her tagging along right now."

"I think I can," Scott says with encouragement. "What time do you think we will go by the hospital to pick them up?"

"I would like to have Taylor and Melissa back at my place tonight, but who knows what will happen next. Tell her we'll pick her up before the day is over."

While Tim and his partner work on Nancy, both Scott and I motion to the women to come over. "Scott and I need to tie up some loose ends here and feel it would be best if you two went with Nancy to the hospital in the ambulance."

As the words come out of my mouth, the expression on Melissa's face tells me Scott has his work cut out for him. Scott pulls her

314

over by the planters leading up the front walkway in order to convince her. I knew Taylor wouldn't even put up a fight.

"You know I'm going," she says after Melissa and Scott walk away.

"I knew you would. I only have one question for you. How long would you like to stay at the hospital with her? I'm good with whatever you want to do. I'll feel much better with you at the hospital as opposed to running around town with me trying to catch a predator—or more likely a whole herd of them."

"I know you w-will," Taylor starts with emotion riding so near the surface. "Do me one favor please, before you go busting down any doors."

"Anything babe."

"Get a couple more guys before you do anything too crazy. I'd feel a lot better should you find yourself in trouble with just Scott."

There is definitely wisdom in her words. "Okay. I'll do it. Patrick has some great guys, some ex-military as well. They will jump at the chance to be kicking in doors again."

"We are heading to the hospital now. Do any of you want to ride with us on the way?" Tim asks. Nancy is loaded in the ambulance and one door is already closed.

As Taylor embraces me, eyes flowing, she simply says, "I love you babe. Be safe," before turning and climbing into the back of the ambulance.

I see Melissa hugging Scott as well and saying her good byes before heading to the ambulance. With both women and Tim's partner inside, he closes the second door.

315

"You guys be safe," Tim calls out as he slides into the driver's seat.

"Thank you," Scott says.

"Thank you Tim. Keep that cargo safe for us," I add.

"Will do Deacon. Will do."

As the ambulance pulls out of the cul-de-sac, Scott and I look at each other with relief. "How'd you convince her to go?" I ask in dismay. I certainly had my doubts that he would be able to get her out of here after seeing that face she pulled as I brought it up.

"You didn't see, but I pointed out the dead guy on the front porch. I made it clear that would not be me and it most certainly would not be her because she would be as far away as possible from wherever the day takes us."

"Whatever works right? Taylor knew she was going with her mom, so my job was pretty easy."

"Well, what do you want to do next?" Scott asks, as we both stare at the trail of blood that has slowly trickled down the steps and is about to reach the road.

So many thoughts are running through my head. I need to get a picture of the dead man on the porch. Hopefully I can link him up to someone on the disc back at my place. We need to get Dennis to a mortuary so his body doesn't just sit here. Then we can head back to start digging.

"Can you get a mortuary headed this way?" I ask Scott. "To be honest, I'm surprised the cops haven't come yet. When Melissa called for the ambulance, having described the scene, I thought for sure the police would have come by now. If I'm not mistaken, they will want to investigate this and then they'll have the mortuary come."

As the words leave my mouth, what has to be an unmarked police vehicle rounds the corner into the cul-de-sac. With our weapons still visible, but slung, he approaches cautiously. Seeing that we still haven't made any attempt to go for our weapons, he puts his car in park about twenty feet from us and opens his door.

"The ambulance just left sir," I say in hopes of letting him know he's in the right place—as well as we are friend and not foe.

"And who are you guys," he yells, still standing behind his door with his hands concealed.

"We're the ones that called it in," Scott responds back.

"I'm the boyfriend of the daughter whose parents live here. We were coming over for dinner when we happened upon this scene. We've already cleared the house and sent the mother to the hospital. The father passed away from his injuries and the guy you see up there's an unknown. We're friendlies, I promise."

"Why the heavy firepower then?" he questions, seeing we both have ARs slung and side arms holstered.

"I know you'll understand this best, but with the given state of affairs the city finds itself in, we wouldn't go anywhere without them," I call back. "I'm Deacon and this is Scott. I promise, we're on your side."

With those words he pushes away from his car to shut the door to reveal he too was holding an AR. As he shuts the door, he slings his rifle and walks towards us.

"I'm Detective Bergquist. I'm part of the Las Vegas Metro Homicide Division."

"It's good to meet you," Scott and I both say.

317

Scott reaches out to shake his hand first. Detective Bergquist is about our same size, perhaps a little taller, wearing khaki pants with a leg holster. He's also wearing a collared shirt with his badge embroidered on the right side and his name on the left. As I reach in to shake his hand I see the glitter of a silver insignia on his collar that tells me this will go better than expected.

TWENTY THREE
BUDS Through & Through

"I have to ask you, why are you wearing that Trident," I say, pointing at the pendant on his right collar.

"I was a SEAL for eight years," Detective Bergquist responds as if it should be obvious.

"Bloody hell," Scott interjects rolling his eyes and turning like he's about to walk away, "a couple of bottom dwellers reminiscing about the good old days. Here we go."

"What team were you on? I was a sniper on SEAL team three —up until about a year ago."

"I was on SEAL team one and three from O-four to ten. I bet we know some of the same people."

"Yeah, yeah, yeah," Scott interrupts. "I hate to bring you two back from water world, but we've got a dead guy on the porch and a dead father in the house—not to mention Jennifer is…well…who knows where."

"Okay, okay," I jump in. "Scott here was British SAS. He gets a little upset when we talk Navy. He's got a point though. We'll talk while you start your investigation. Are you okay if I get a picture of this guy so I can compare him against a database I have back at my place?"

"Yeah, no problem. By the way, my name's Jared," Detective Bergquist adds before continuing. "Let's head up toward the house. Also, if you don't mind me asking, what kind of mission are you guys on?"

"It's a long story, but I'm the head of security at City Center. The head honcho, Dean Steele—you may know him, he too was a SEAL back in the day—was killed by some members of the Zeta Cartel. His secretary disappeared a few days ago to top it off."

"I've heard that name, but never met him."

"So anyway, we came here so I could meet my future in-laws and this is what we stumbled upon."

"Now we have to find out who did this and help them...," Scott pauses not sure he should continue his thought, "Um—figure out the error in their ways."

"You can say it," Jared adds abruptly. "When you find them they will fight and you will kill them. We live in the Wild Wild West now. Every town USA has become Fallujah or Kandahar or pick any hotspot you've been to. I understand completely and so do most officers on the force."

We continue to talk as I get my picture and Jared looks over the body. He doesn't recognize the deceased and I didn't expect him to. The amount of blood smattered across his face would make Mickey Mouse unrecognizable. After getting a few photographs he rolls him on his side so he can check for a wallet in hopes for some identification. I'm glad he does because if I can get a name it will help me so much more once I get back to my place.

As Jared opens the wallet I see his driver's license through the plastic sleeve. "Stanley Slack," he reads after pulling the license out. He then hands me the license so I can get a better look at the picture.

"Oh—I meant to ask—what's this database you have back at your place?" Jared questions as I look over the license.

"Dean had a disc labeled top secret in a hidden room in his office. We're pretty sure that's what Tom..." my voice trails off. When I say the name a light goes off in my head. "That's it...Tom Slack."

I'm sure Jared is wondering why I stopped mid-sentence. "Is that Thomas Slack? The one that has a body count growing by the minute?" Jared asks as he stands with a look of amazement. "Do you think this could be his son?"

"One and the same. The thought of him having a son has never crossed my mind. He wasn't listed in any of Tom's files when I looked it over just this morning and he certainly never mentioned him. I have a lot of Tom's known addresses. Rest assured he will be dealt with before the week is over," I say with assurance.

My mind begins racing as I begin sorting everything out. I try to remember all the names that I had read on the enemies list. Tom is a little older so it could be his son. I'm shocked I hadn't heard this before. Plus, Stanley's picture does have some resemblance to Tom. If it is his son then cleaning up this mess will be that much easier.

"Several guys from homicide are working cases all over the city involving him. In fact, they've been watching a couple places. They're pretty sure they'll pick him up within a couple weeks."

"Pick him up? That won't do," I say a little surprised.

"Well, I say pick up, but the hope is always that the tango will start shooting and the only thing 'picking him up' will be the hearse. If he comes quietly they won't kill him though."

"Oh, he won't come quietly!" I exclaim with assurance.

"Yeah, from what they've seen and read about him they're pretty sure it will be a shoot out. Normally it's something SWAT would go in on, but since the city has descended to its current state and continues falling fast, every unit has kind of become their own SWAT team. I mean, we all have rifles and shotguns. Just give us a couple flash bangs and a boomer and we're in."

"Makes sense," Scott agrees.

"Speaking of police work, do the military road blocks give you any hassle when you need to get through? Scott and I were wondering what they would do when we head back to my place loaded to bear as we are," I ask, hoping to hear some good news.

"Yeah that won't be good. The military have been ordered to seize all weapons on the streets. That's their main purpose of putting up the road blocks." Jared stops to ponder before continuing, "I think I might have a couple things to help you out with that. When you're ready to leave, I'll grab them."

Unsure what the detective could possible give me that would help, we continue to talk as he does his thing. When we move inside Scott tells him how we've searched everywhere and the only blood we could find was in the entry leading downstairs to where Dennis lies, and a little upstairs leading into the master. We explain how Dennis was in the CIA and had an expertise in nuclear weapons from his Navy days.

With all Jared's focus on the scene in front of him, Scott quietly gets my attention, taps on his watch, and mouths the words, "We need to go."

"Okay Jared," I say, breaking the silence.

He looks up.

"We need to get going. Is there anything else you need from us before we take off?"

"Not that I can think of now. Let me get your numbers on our way out so if I have any questions or if I get a lead then I can get back with you."

"Sounds good," Scott says.

"You're going to take care of Dennis, correct?"

"Oh yeah. I'll have a mortuary come by and pick up his body. Do you know who his wife would want to pick up the body? Any funeral home in particular I mean."

"I'm not sure."

"No problem. There's a rotation so they'll just send the next one. It could be some time though. I'm going to call the feds too. I'm sure they'll want to come look at the scene as well. I haven't called them yet because I didn't want them in the way of my own investigation. You know how those federal types can be," Jared says with a smile, knowing we both thought we were above everyone for a time.

When we get to his car, he opens the trunk and pulls out a light bar. "I had this for my personal car just in case I needed to use it. I haven't installed it yet, but this will be your first step to getting past the road blocks. When you pull up to one, flash the lights for a few seconds and then turn it off. Step two is in my glovebox."

As he opens the passenger door, he reaches in and opens the box. When his hand comes back out he's holding two shiny silver police badges. One detective badge and one officer badge.

"This will get you past the guard. When he has you roll down your window for ID just show him your badge. It will work every time with the military. Just don't use it with other officers. They won't understand why I've done it.

"Are you serious?" Scott asks, a little flabbergasted that we are being handed police badges and told to impersonate officers.

"I know you won't abuse them, and to be honest, you'll probably do more good with these two badges than half the department combined. Don't get me wrong, I love my fellow officers, but they don't have half the training you and I have."

I can't argue with his logic. Scott and I, with a mission and a motive, sure could do some cleaning up in this city.

"One other thing. If you have access to a different car that looks more like an undercover police car it would serve you well. Maybe just to better sell the little lie you'll have to tell to get through."

"Thanks. I'm sure we can find something else. Although, I do love my Jeep. What's the most common undercover car you guys use?" I ask.

"A Charger or Explorer. I would go with the Explorer though, if you can. More room for toys and people."

"I think we can manage that. Thank you so much for all your help. Before we take off, can I get your number?" I ask, knowing it will come in handy in the future.

"Of course. Just shoot me a text so I have your numbers as well.

Jared rattles off his number and I program it into my phone. Finishing, I see a missed call and message from my mom. She must have called while we were clearing the house. I'll call her later. She didn't want to know about the dangerous missions I took part of in the military, why scare her now?

As Scott and I walk to the car after saying our goodbyes, I turn back to Jared and say, "If you get a text from me in a few days with an address you might want to send some people over there to clean up the scene. They might find good old Thomas Slack ready for pick up."

Jared smiles from ear to ear before speaking, "Will do."

Scott and I jump in the Jeep and I start the engine, ready to head back to my place.

"What are the chances," Scott starts in. "Seriously, what are the chances. Of all the detectives in this great big city, the one that comes to us happens to be a SEAL from your former team? I'm not a big believer in God, but if I didn't know any better, I'd have to say He's definitely on your side."

"There's more to that statement than you know," I say with a slight grin as I glance in Scott's direction. "Stick with me and you're bound to see more. Mark my words Scott, you haven't seen anything yet."

"You think it's going to get a lot worse?" Scott questions, his forehead furrowed.

"Trust me when I tell you this," I pause, trying to frame the thought just right in my head so that Scott will understand, but won't dig deeper. "You know that talk on the radio of eminent earthquakes and natural disasters the likes not seen since who knows how long ago? Well, they are coming quicker than you think. Add to that the breakdown in society that already exists. Not to mention the talk of taking out the power grid like you told me. We are in for pandemonium. If I had to guess, like we have never seen anywhere. Not oversees, not the last few weeks, nothing you or I could imagine."

Scott mulls over my words without responding. I know he's seen the chaos and confusion in person and on the news, but I don't think he believed it would continue and get worse.

"I'll call Melissa," his says, breaking the silence and interrupting his own thoughts. The thought of worsening conditions reminds him of the one he loves most. "I'll see how the three of them are doing while we head back."

"Perfect."

When he gets Melissa on the phone we learn that Nancy just went into surgery to fix the damage in her back. It's nothing critical, but Taylor of course worries she'll lose her mother too. Everyone is safe though, which is most important. Melissa managed to make it to the cafeteria while Taylor stayed by her mother. I guess Taylor's appetite just wasn't there. I don't blame her. If my dad was just killed and my mother couldn't move, I don't think I'd be clamoring for a meal either.

When Scott finishes his conversation I have him help me install the light and make sure we know how to flip it on and off. We can't look like rookies as we pull up to the road block we're bound to encounter at Sunset and the Boulevard.

"So, what's the plan? How are we going to tackle these two issues?" Scott asks after mastering the light bar.

"Well, we've got to get some intel first, but I want you to start thinking about who we can trust."

"Who can we trust?" Scott interrupts, somewhat confused.

"Yeah. Taylor made me promise we would take a couple more guys with us should we go kicking in any doors. Which reminds me, send Detective Bergquist a text. See if he'll tip us off on the locations they know for sure Tom's been hanging his hat at night. I'd like to have Tom ready for pick up as soon as possible. Plus, I have this nagging feeling that Jennifer won't be too far from Tom."

"You're probably right. What about the ones that just killed Dennis and put Nancy in the hospital?"

"As for them, I'm hoping Stanley, our gracious doorstop back there, is Tom's son or at least part of his gang. If that's the case we can kill two birds with one stone. If not, I'll guess we'll find out more once we get back to my place," I say, hoping for the first scenario.

As we pull up to the road block Scott flips the lights on for a few seconds and then turns them off. As I begin to roll down my window I see the guard already opening the gate they've set up. As it lifts to its full height he waves us through.

Scott and I both give a wave as we pass.

"That was easier than I thought," I say, as we both breathe a sigh of relief.

"Let's just hope the mission we are about to embark on is that easy," Scott says as we turn right and make our way back to Veer Tower.

"I just sent Jared a text," Scott says.

"Thanks. Hopefully he responds back before the sun goes down so we can plan for the night."

"You said something back there to Jared I found pretty interesting," Scott continues with a wry smile without looking my way.

"Oh yeah. What was that?"

"You said you were at the Sanders' house to meet—and I quote—the 'in-laws,'" he says with his hands in the air as he turns to see the expression I make.

"You know we spend every free moment we have together and I would do anything for her. Then there's the dream I had the day I met her. I don't know what else to tell you, but I'm one-hundred percent positive she's the one."

"Not that I want you to doubt yourself, but seems so quick to forget about Christen."

"Now that you mention her, I had totally forgotten about her. She was great, but I never felt for Christen what I feel for Taylor. I would say more, but I don't have the words to explain it."

He doesn't respond and my thoughts wander back to my dad. I do have the words to explain it, but I know I can't tell Scott about it now. Everything my dad told me makes my mind so clear as to what I have to do. I know Taylor is part of my path moving forward.

"We've talked about marriage a little. To be completely honest with you, I was thinking about asking her to marry me up at Zion's. I didn't tell anyone."

"No you weren't," Scott shoots back with disbelief.

"Look in the glovebox under all the papers if you don't believe me."

Scott flings open the glovebox as he says, "Are you serious?"

"As a heart attack."

He rifles through the box and finds the little turquoise bag. "Tiffany huh?" The words come out with utter amazement.

"Only the finest for my girl. I know she doesn't care about name brands or even diamonds for that matter, but I know how women get over their rings even if they don't say it."

"Had you talked to her dad about this?"

"I hadn't. Looks like I won't be doing it here in this life either. I'll have to talk to her mom once we've tied up all the loose ends we have now."

When Scott pulls the ring out of the bag his mouth falls open and I'm pretty sure I hear an audible gasp. "That rock is enormous!" he exclaims. "You know I have to ask, how much did you pay for this sucker? It looks like one of those blue ring pops I used to trouble my mom for when I was a kid."

"Well, I'm guessing it cost a little more than a ring pop. I know you'll bug me until I tell you, so it cost just over ten grand." I know the cost exactly—twenty-five thousand five-hundred and nine dollars. I'm hoping just over ten grand will suffice even though it cost a bit more than ten grand. There is something about telling even your best friend about a purchase so high for something so tiny.

"TEN GRAND!" the words come out like I must have been out of my mind.

"I figure it's a once in a lifetime purchase and she's worth a lot more than that."

"How big is the diamond?" he asks with a little more composure.

"A carat and a half. I didn't want it too big. I didn't realize you were so interested in rings. This sounds like a conversation a couple of women would have."

"Well my friend, you know you've ruined me."

"Ruined you?" I say, wondering how that could possibly be.

"Yeah. You've ruined me. You know Melissa and I are planning to get married. I just haven't popped the question yet."

I start to laugh as I realize what Scott will have to do now.

"Oh, you're having a laugh are you? This isn't a laughing matter. When Melissa sees that ring she'll expect something about the same size. They'll compare rings and if they aren't about the same she might not say it, but I know she'll be thinking it—*why did he get me such a small diamond.*" He mimics Melissa's voice in the most endearing way possible.

I continue to laugh without saying a word. He's going to be in for a surprise when he goes shopping and finds out how much a ring that big really costs. Plus, I bought a near flawless blue diamond for my sparkling blue eyes, which makes it even more rare.

"Well, if things fall apart as I see them happening, you could always just pick one up for free after society has collapsed completely. I wouldn't feel too bad about doing that so you shouldn't have any problem with it. Isn't the motto of the SAS, 'First in, first to loot the treasure?'"

"'Who dares, wins' mate. Don't forget it, but you do have a point. Come on collapse," he says with excitement.

"You're too funny," I say with a snicker. "Just a day ago you were hoping and saying things will get better. Now it's let it fall like the Pharaohs of old."

"Hey, everything has to have its end. Right now is as good as any for the good old US of A. You Yanks had a great run right? Over two hundred years isn't too bad."

"We made it further than most other countries I guess," I add to the light-hearted banter.

"Who's going to be next? If you really do fall from the top, who's going to fill the void you Yanks leave?" Scott asks.

"I'm not sure," I simply respond. I have some ideas, but that's not what I want to think about right now.

"Well, I'm sure it won't be good for the world."

"You're probably right," I simply answer.

Arriving back at the tower, Patrick has the garage open and we pull inside. Las Vegas Boulevard has become the militarized zone. I remember doing a training exercise in South Korea a few years ago. A couple of us took a tour up to the border to see the demilitarized zone. They call it the demilitarized zone but, it looks much like this, tanks and towers, wires and weapons. The only difference here on the Boulevard is the troops patrol the middle, trying to keep the looters and less than reputable citizens out of both sides. It can't last much longer. If the city loses power like I saw, that will be the end of what little civility remains.

I park the Jeep in my usual spot. Catching me a little by surprise, Patrick opens my door. "How was it?" he questions with a hint of suspicion.

"It was interesting. Taylor's father was killed moments before we arrived at his place and her mother was holding strong. Melissa, Taylor, and her mom are all at the hospital now."

"I'm so sorry to hear that," the genuine care in his voice lets me know he really means it. "Is there anything you need me to do?" Patrick says, getting right back to business. "I just heard from all the properties. Things are looking really good around here."

"Actually there is something. You know our patrol cars, the Explorers, not the little cars?"

"Yeah, we have a bunch of them. You need one?"

"We do. Can you have one of the guys strip it of any mark-ings. We need to do some undercover work and I don't want anyone to recognize my Jeep while we're out in the night. Have them install this light bar too."

"I'll have someone get right on it. Anything else before you head upstairs?" Patrick asks, seeming a little underworked and eager to do something to break up the monotony.

"There's one other thing," Scott jumps in. "We need a couple guys who are willing to kick in some doors and possibly get shot at within the next few days."

"If you want to come Patrick, you can be one of the two," I say knowing he'll probably jump at the opportunity. "Make sure the other one is ex-military as well. It will make things run a lot smoother I'm sure."

"Count me in," he says, unable to keep the excitement from showing. "I've got one other man in mind. I know he's itching to see some action."

"Perfect. We won't be going tonight, but make sure you and he are on standby starting first thing tomorrow morning."

"Will do," Patrick says as he steps off the elevator to the main lobby.

"Thanks for everything Patrick. I couldn't do all this without you."

"You're welcome Deacon."

When the door closes I turn to Scott, "Let's go get some intel and then pick up the women, that is if they want to come back for the night."

"Sounds like a plan. I know Melissa won't want to sleep on a chair in the hospital tonight."

TWENTY FOUR

Recovery

Walking through the elevator door I realize Bobbi waits inside my place for news about Blake. Unfortunately, all we have is that he's not there and his roommate hasn't heard from him since the day this whole thing went south. I know it's not what she'll want to hear, but maybe the news of Taylor's loss will help her to realize she's not the only one suffering here.

"I just got a text from Blake!" Bobbi exclaims as Scott and I walk through the door. "He said he's sorry he hasn't been able to call, but he's okay, and he'll come for me as soon as he can. I guess he had to go to California and couldn't get to his phone until now." The excitement clearly painted across her face was sorely missed around here.

"That's great Bobbi! I'm glad you've heard from him." I want to say more about his place, but something doesn't quite seem right with his absence and break in. I don't want to scare her or take away any excitement she now feels.

"How did your trip go? Where are the girls?" Savanah asks realizing the women didn't come in with us.

"Well, about that," Scott starts in. "When we got to Taylor's parent's place someone had just been there and had killed her dad and left her mom with a couple of gunshot wounds and a broken back."

"That's awful!" Savanah gasps with her hand over her mouth. She doesn't ask another question, not sure how to take the news. She stands in disbelief.

334

"Taylor and Melissa are at the hospital with Nancy. At least they are safe and her mom will be fine after a surgery or two," I add to help bring a little assurance.

"That's good," Bobbi manages to mutter, fighting back the emotions that have plagued her for a month now. It's literally like a rollercoaster ride for her—for all of us for that matter.

"We just came back to get some info and then we're heading over to the hospital if you'd like to get out of here. I know a hospital isn't the ideal location, but a change of scenery might be good for you," Scott explains.

"Yeah, some fresh air might do you some good and I'm sure the women would love to see you," I add.

They ponder the thought for a moment before Savanah responds. "That sounds like a good idea."

Bobbi on the other hand wants to stay.

"We'll probably leave in about thirty to forty-five minutes," I say seeing she's still in Taylor's pink pajamas. I know she'll want to change before we head out.

"Okay. I'll go get ready then," Savanah says as she turns and heads for the room.

"Well, that's at least a little bit of good news for Bobbi," Scott sighs, seeing Bobbi turn her attention back to the television.

"We'll see," I say with a bit of hesitation. "Doesn't it seem strange to you that Blake would disappear and his things go missing. Then out of nowhere, the day we go by his place, of all days, he sends her a text? There's something fishy going on that doesn't pass the sniff test."

"At least she has somewhat snapped out of the stupor she's been in for almost a month," Scott asserts quietly.

"Yeah. That is good. Let's do this then."

Scott and I pull up a chair and dive into the disc. We slowly read through Tom's file looking for any connection to Mr. Stanley Slack, who met his end at the hands of Dennis Sanders. In the organizational link chart that accompanies Tom's file, he's got quite the band of misfits under his control. If Stanley is his son, he's got to be here somewhere.

We click in and out of file after file, delving as deep as we can, digging for the name Stanley. After thirty minutes of searching, we haven't been able to find one mention of a Stanley or see a picture that even closely resembles our corpse. With hope somewhat fading that we'll find anything that will lead us to Dennis's killers, a call from Taylor gives me the distraction I need.

"How are things going babe? Is your mom doing better?"

"She's just coming out of surgery. The doctor said she should make a full recovery," I can hear the relief in her voice.

"That's great babe. I'm glad she's doing well. Scott, Savanah, and I are about to head over to the hospital. What hospi…."

"Savanah is coming with you?" she questions.

"Yep. She wants to see you. Bobbi would come, but she got a text from Blake just before we got back to my place and her mood has made a hundred and eighty degree turn. I think she just wants some alone time. I think she is hoping he'll call or text her again."

"That's awesome!" she proclaims. "Tell her I'm so happy for her."

"Will do. What hospital did they end up taking you to?" I ask, so I know where we're going.

"Believe it or not, they ended up taking us clear over to Sunrise so we're not too far from you."

"That's great. We'll head that way then in another thirty minutes or so. We need to scour the intel disc a little more looking for anything that can help us," I stop, not wanting to mention her dad.

She senses my hesitation and says, "It's okay Deacon. It's hard, but with time the hurt will go. Did you get everything taken care of at the house? Did a mortuary come pick up my dad?"

"Actually, everything turned out better than I could have hoped. I'll tell you about it when I get there. Fair enough?"

"Fair enough," she echoes back. "Thank you so much Deacon. I can't tell you how much I love you and need you right now. I'll see you in a few. They're wheeling my mom to the recovery room right now so I've got to go. I love you babe."

"I love you too. See you in less than an hour."

As we hang up I turn to talk to Scott, but see him sitting on the couch talking to Melissa. I leave him to his conversation and dive back into the intel.

After about five minutes, Scott breaks my concentration, "When do you want to head over there?"

"Like thirty minutes," I respond.

"Okay," he says before telling Melissa the same.

I turn back to the computer. I've got to find something, anything that will get me closer to the answers I seek. I also scribble down some of Tom's known hangouts just in case we don't get anything back from Detective Bergquist. Tom has several known locations, but there is one in particular that seems to be mentioned throughout.

Perusing the packed files, I don't find anything that links Stanley to Tom. My gut still tells me there's a connection, but unfortunately it appears I'll be finding it on my own. Plus there's the diamond white Mercedes that looked suspiciously like Jennifer's leaving the scene in a hurry.

"You ready to go?" Scott asks pulling me out of the endless scanning.

"Yeah. Let me finish this last file and then I'll be ready." Of course nothing. "Looks like we'll have to find our own leads for little Stanley Slack."

"We'll figure it out. I don't know about you, but we always got our man. Maybe the SEALs are different though. Seems the bad guy is always slipping through your fingers huh?"

"I'm glad you haven't lost that sense of humor mate. For the record, no one slips through anything when we get involved. They may run and hide, but we always get our man. I don't know if you remember, it was a little before our time, but does the name Bin Laden mean anything to you? Yeah, that was the SEALs."

"Well, I guess we'll see won't we," Scott responds, jumping off the couch.

"Oh we will."

"Are you ready to go Savanah?" I call out from her door.

She appears in the doorway literally two seconds later. "Ready," she says with a forced smile not sure what to expect.

The elevator takes us straight to the parking garage and we load up the Jeep. I'm sure Patrick already has the incognito car ready, but we only plan on using that tonight. When we pull up to the exit, the door opens and we quickly make our way off the strip and over to the hospital. It might be day, but in Vegas the crazies are out twenty-four seven, three-hundred-sixty-five days a year.

We arrive in no time, without even a hiccup in route. "Did Melissa say which floor they were on?" I ask Scott, realizing Taylor and I didn't get into specifics.

"Melissa said recovery was on the fifth floor in the main building. She wasn't sure of the room."

"That's okay," I reason back, "I'm sure we won't be able to just walk in. We'll ask the front desk."

The kind lady wearing blue hospital scrubs with dark bags under her eyes from a lack of sleep greets us warmly, "How may I help you three?" I know she feels safe flanked by two large military police officers loaded to the hilt.

"We are here to see Nancy Sanders. She was brought in a few hours ago, and as we understand it, she just came out of surgery and was wheeled to recovery."

"May I ask your relation to Nancy?" she questions most kindly.

I can only assume security has been tightened and if I tell them she's a friend they won't let me in, so I tell the littlest of white lies. "She's my mother-in-law," I begin. "We found her clinging to life just a few hours ago. Her daughter, my wife, waits up there with her now."

"My wife also rode in with them and waits up there as well. Her name's Melissa."

"Well," she pauses still looking at her computer. I glance at Savanah who holds the perfect poker face to the lies she just heard.

"Looks like Nancy's in five-o-five. Jump on the elevator just down the hall, then get off on five, and head right. You can't miss it."

"Thank you so much," I begin, "have a great day."

"You do the same," she says with a smile as we part.

After walking a few steps out of ear shot from the receptionist, Savanah says smiling from ear to ear, "So boys, married already huh?"

"You know it's bound to happen, so I figured I'd make life easier now," I respond.

"What about those dark circles around her eyes? She looked like the walking dead with a huge grin," Scott adds.

"Yeah she was," I reply back. "She got one look at you and her lights certainly came on. Did you see the way she kept looking your way even though I was talking to her?"

"Just goes to show—the ladies fancy me more," Scott suggests with a smile.

"Fancy," I say with confusion. "Maybe they can't figure you out, but fancy isn't the word I'd use."

"I know. It's more of an infatuation isn't it?"

Getting on the elevator, Savanah jokes, "Now, now, boys— your wives are waiting. No need to fight over the dead."

We all laugh as the doors open to the elevator. When they open again to the fifth floor, we turn right and halfway down the hall we see Melissa leaning against the wall with her hands on her head. She never looks up as we walk down the hall. When Scott grabs her by the

340

waist she quickly looks up, frightened. She doesn't say a word, nor does Scott. With the unpredictable events of the day I know Melissa feels better to have Scott at her side again.

With the two of them lost in the moment, I see the door directly across from Melissa is five-o-five. Making my way in, past the little bathroom to the left, I see Taylor sitting at her mom's side, leaned over lying on a pillow. It appears Nancy is fast asleep. Savanah waits for me before she does anything.

Not wanting to wake her mom, I gently whisper, "Taylor," as I approach her side and put my hand on her exposed back. Knowing no one else would touch her that way here, she slowly turns with a pleasant smile.

"How's she doing?"

"She's resting. With what they did to her..." she trails off, the emotion still too close to the surface to finish her thought.

I embrace her as she stands and neither one of us say a word for several minutes. We hold each other like never before. Seeing Savanah at my side Taylor pulls her in as well. Tragedy has the ability to bring people closer or pull them further apart. From my experience, I know this will only bring us closer. Taylor breathes deep and long as I feel her chest against mine.

I become mesmerized by the feel and sound of her breathing until a hand grabs mine from behind. Taylor feels my slight jump and we both turn to see Nancy holding my hand with tears streaming down her face. Her blue eyes, as pretty as Taylor's but with an aged look of experience about them, move from mine to her daughter's.

"I-It's okay mom. You're safe. You just got out of surgery. Everything went perfect," Taylor assures her as she sits at her side to give her a kiss on the cheek.

I continue to hold her hand. Her eyes turn back to mine and she mouths the words, "Thank you."

"You're welcome," I say grabbing her hand with both hands now. "I only wish..." I stop, not wanting to remind her that her husband was dead by saying I only wish I would have got there sooner. "I hope you get better soon," I finish quickly.

"She will," Taylor exclaims.

As Nancy attempts to talk, Taylor puts her finger to her mouth and whispers, "You need to rest mom. The more you rest, the quicker you'll recover."

"Can I just say one thing? I know Deacon will want to hear it."

"Okay, then you'll rest," Taylor says assuredly.

"There were two men at the house. The older one was definitely in charge. He also kept referring to the younger one as son or boy. I don't know if that helps, but I had to tell you what I knew. I'm bad at descriptions, but they had dark hair."

"Thank you," I start, happy she has offered the information. I certainly wasn't going to ask in her current condition. "That helps more than you know. One of them was dead on the front steps when we arrived and we've already identified him. With what you've just told me, I'm pretty sure I know who the older one was. Now I want you to listen to your daughter and get some rest. You've been through hell today."

"Ok. I need to say one more thing," Nancy says, as she looks from me to her daughter. Taylor nods her head. "I was hoping our first meeting would have been under different circumstances, but I must say I am so happy my daughter has someone like you to keep her safe. You don't know how at ease that makes me feel in times like these."

"Thank you Nancy. I will definitely do everything I can to keep her at my side and safe. I'm sure she's told you how much she means to me, but I want you to hear it from me as well. She means everything to me. I love her more than life itself."

With those words, the tears in Nancy's eyes that had all but stopped begin again. I look over at Taylor and her eyes are glistening with emotion. With this scene unfolding, I feel the emotions coming to the surface as well. Taylor grabs my hands and the three of us hold each other, wishing this feeling of peace would never leave.

"Okay mom, time for you to close your eyes and get some rest," Taylor exhorts, breaking up our bonding moment.

"Okay. I love you sweetie. It's good to see you here too Savanah."

"Thank you Nancy. I'm glad you're okay. Get some rest," Savanah says holding her other hand.

"Be safe," Nancy simply says before closing her eyes and resting her hands at her side.

"Scott and I need to get back to my place. What do you want to do?" I ask, fairly confident that she'll choose to spend the night with her mom.

"Let's talk in the hall," Taylor whispers, before turning to tell her mom she'll be right back. She also grabs Savanah on the way out and thanks her for coming.

Out in the hall I fill Taylor in on what we learned about the possible perpetrators and how Detective Bergquist helped us out. She of course, says she is staying at the hospital. I go over our plans for the night and tell her if things are pretty quiet I'll probably come by and see her really late before heading back to my place to crash. She likes that idea and understands completely.

"I'll only stay the one night. I know I won't get any sleep here, but I want to be here for her first night so she's not alone."

"I understand completely. I'll bring your charger when I come back. It will probably be after midnight before I show up."

"Come whenever," she assures me with a big hug. "I love you so much Deacon. I hope you know that."

"I do blue eyes, but it sure feels good to hear it. I love you too babe. Get some rest and I'll see you tonight."

Taylor and Savanah head back in to be with Nancy. Savanah volunteered to stay with Taylor all night or maybe just until I come back. So Scott, Melissa, and I get on the elevator to head back to the car.

On the ride down Scott asks, "How's Mrs. Sanders doing?"

"She's doing well. I can only imagine the thoughts going through her head as well as the pain that must be penetrating her body."

"At least she's hooked up to machines now and being fed pain killers," Melissa points out.

"True," Scott agrees.

"I just hope she recovers quickly. Who knows what will happen to this place if things get worse."

The thought of conditions worsening dampers the mood. We walk out to the car in silence. I hope Scott has also already broken the news to Melissa that we're going out tonight. Tonight should be relatively easy since we're not planning on much more than recon work. The fun will come tomorrow night hopefully. It will also be much more difficult to convince Melissa that I need him. I'm hoping the fact that Patrick and one other guy are coming will help to ease her mind.

When we arrive back at Veer Tower, I see a white Explorer parked by the main elevator as we pull in along side it. Scott notices it as well and says, "Boy, that Patrick sure is excited to go out isn't he."

"I think he's bored. I wonder who he's enlisted to come with us."

Wanting to get some rest before we head out for the night, we bypass the lobby and head straight for my floor.

"What time do you want to go out tonight?" Scott asks as we approach our floor.

"A couple hours after dark. Has Detective Bergquist got back to you yet?"

"Yeah, he has. I was going to tell you at the hospital, but you were kind of busy. I think the address he sent me is one of the ones on that disc."

"Perfect. We'll start there and if we don't see anything we'll try another one."

"Soooounds good," Scott yawns as the elevator doors open.

"I'm feeling about the same. If you guys want to rest you can take Taylor's room for the night. I'm sure Bobbi won't mind for one night."

At that thought, Scott turns and gives Melissa a sly smile and winks. "I know what you're thinking," Melissa says in return, the smile growing on her face.

"I know you two have been crammed on the couch for the last month, but please do us a favor and whatever you need to do, do it in the shower."

Neither one says a word. When we get inside Bobbi is sitting on the couch watching a movie without a care in the world. When Bobbi doesn't say a word, I assume she hasn't heard anything else from Blake.

"I'll set my alarm for eleven," I say to Scott, grabbing some food from the kitchen.

"Alright. I'll get up then too," he responds as Melissa drags him down the hall to their room.

"How is Taylor's mom?" Bobbi asks.

"She's doing well. Lots of rest. Savanah and Taylor are going to stay the night with her so it should be pretty quiet here. Scott needs to get some rest so they are going to take Taylor's room for the night okay?"

"I'll just sleep on the couch tonight then," Bobbi responds without a care.

My room calls me as I sit lost in thought in the kitchen peeling an orange. It's just before seven now, so I resolve to take a quick shower before hitting the hay, hoping that will help to ease the tension that has been building as the day has progressed.

When the warm water hits my tired body, I instantly feel better. I know I've said it before, but there's nothing like a hot shower to take all your cares away. After ten minutes I step out, dry off, and jump in bed with just a pair of underwear on. Second to a hot shower, cool sheets and a big bed are the best.

TWENTY FIVE
Black Ops

Feeling as if I had just passed out, my alarm rings and I see it's eleven o'clock. I quickly turn it off and hear Scott's alarm still blazing in Taylor's room. It rings for five more seconds before either he or Melissa turns it off.

In the bathroom, I look my midsection over. It has only been a day since I rolled out of death's bed, but my wounds are already looking better. It doesn't hurt nearly as much as when I jumped that fence this morning either.

Hoping Scott is dressed and ready to go I hear his alarm again. He hit snooze the first time and now he is nine minutes behind.

I dress in black from head to toe. I even grab a black beanie just in case we decide to go anywhere on foot. When I step into the hall, Scott opens his door and comes out still in his underwear.

"That's what I thought," Scott says, seeing I'm dressed all in black. "Do you have any more black clothing?"

"Yeah, go on in and see what you can find. I've got plenty."

With Scott getting changed, I grab some pogey bate from the kitchen. We will most likely be sitting the whole night so some snacks are definitely in order. With my bag just about full, Scott comes into the kitchen.

"Ready?" he asks, all dressed in black now.

"Yeah. Let's get out of here."

"Do you have your contacts?" Scott asks pointing to his own eyes.

"No. I completely forgot about them. Let me put mine in really fast," I say, dashing through my door to find them still in the nightstand where Scott left them. I quickly wet them before putting them in and heading back to the hall.

On the ride down to the garage I realize I never got the keys for the undercover car. Almost to the lobby, I quickly hit the L so we can stop. I'm sure Patrick isn't here, but I'm positive he's left instructions for one of my guys. When the doors open, Scott stays holding the door as I head for the front desk.

Lenny waits at the front desk looking half asleep. "Did Patrick leave something for me?" I ask, almost causing him to fall out of his seat.

"Um," Lenny starts, rubbing his eyes as he jumps to his feet. "Yes he did sir. They're right here," he says in a rush as he opens the drawer and hands me a set of keys. "Do you need anything else sir?"

"I'm good Lenny," I say as I start to walk away. Looking over my shoulder I counsel, "I know it's rough Lenny, but remember, all the people living here are counting on you."

"I've got it sir," he says with a somewhat embarrassed grin, turning his head down.

Scott and I make our way to the garage and load up the car. Even though this will just be recon work tonight, you can never be over prepared. Scott carries two ARs. The one he carried earlier today and Melissa's. Of course the side arm rests firmly in place on his right hip. I've got Dean's AR and I've brought my CheyTac M300. It's not the same one I had on the team, but I had it custom made after I got out to be exactly like the issued rifle I had. I even put a thirty-five power scope on top so seeing things at a distance should be no problem.

When Dean put me in charge of security, I will admit, some of my team days came rushing back. I picked up a few toys I wish I had in the civilian world, but knew I would never buy on my own. Now carrying the thermal scope out to the car sure makes me feel like I made the right decision.

"So where are we heading?"

"The address Jared sent me is 3000 Island View Court," Scott says hesitantly.

"Why the hesitancy? Do you think there's something wrong with that address?" I question back. "You're not going to tell me it's on an island, are you?" I chuckle in jest.

"I take it you haven't googled the address then?"

"Nope. I remember it from the file. I believe it's his main house, right?" I say with a little less confidence.

Scott doesn't say anything and instead fiddles with his phone. I look over and see he is entering the address into Google Maps.

When the map loads, Scott hands me his phone without saying a word. Still sitting in the parking garage, I grab the phone and take a deep breath before turning my attention to the screen.

At first glance the picture shining at me in the dark doesn't look too bad. He has the map so far zoomed in all I see is the house with a nice pool in the backyard. It's a massive house. If I had to guess, the house is around four thousand square feet. When I pinch to zoom out and get a better overall picture of the area, the predicament placed before us jumps into view.

Tom's house sits in just about the dead center of Lake Sahara, at the end of a peninsula. I've never been inside that area, but I know it's a gated community. That will make our entrance even that much more difficult. Not to mention the line of sight to his house will be almost impossible without driving right up on the driveway.

"Well," I say with a sigh. "It is what it is. Maybe we can get a decent view from Waterside Circle over here," I say pointing out the different vantage points possible from the street to the east across the lake.

"Yeah it's possible. I'm going to send Detective Bergquist another text to see if he knows of anything else we should watch out for or possible areas to get the best view."

"Good idea. I'll start heading that way and hopefully we hear something. Otherwise we'll just drive around until we find a decent view."

The Lakes sit just south of Sahara which connects through Las Vegas Boulevard. We don't want to travel down the Boulevard for fear of running into the military. So, driving out the parking garage and then south to Tropicana, we head west to get away from the strip as quickly as possible. The roads are abandoned as we drive west. We decide to make our way north on Durango.

"How are we going to get past the guards?" Scott asks, as we continue to drive north.

"We have these badges, and I'm pretty sure a security guard won't question us if we want to get in. I bet he doesn't even ask us why we're going in."

"You're probably right. Do you feel awkward at all using the badges?"

"I did at first, but I see it as serving the greater good, so I've come to peace with it. You?"

"I've been good from the get go. I just thought you might be having an issue with it."

"Nope. I'm good now."

As we approach the east side of the lake, we see two communities—Lakeview and The Landing. Each community around the lake has its own guard station. Rounding the corner, the little guard shack that sits in our path has its light on. When we pull up to the shack, a man in his mid-seventies, if I had to guess, opens the window.

"How may I help you boys? A little late for a house call, isn't it?"

The way his cheeks jiggle as he speaks almost makes me laugh out loud. "This is when we do our best work though sir," I say with a smile. "We're police officers with Las Vegas Metro Homicide Division. I'm Detective Smith and this is Detective Anderson."

The old man's face quickly changes from business to excitement, as his gigantic grey eyebrow turns up. "What are you guys up to? A big case going on? I wouldn't put anything past these rich yuppies out here," he says as if he never sees any excitement around here.

"Yeah, we are working a murder case that just happened today actually. Do you mind if we head in?"

"Not at all. In fact, let me give you a code just in case I'm not here and one of the young punks is on the job. You can't trust these kids for anything."

"Thank you so much," I say turning to Scott with a huge grin on my face. "If you don't mind me asking, what does it take to get into the other communities around the lake? I see they all have guard stations."

"They do. This code I'm giving you will work for all the gates in each of the different communities. You can drive right past the guard and punch in the code. We, the guards that is, are all employed by the association. Just so you know, I think the whole lot is corrupt."

"Why do you say that," Scott questions, leaning over to get a better look at the old man.

"Well, I think there's a lot of cartel money floating around this lake if you know what I mean. But, you didn't hear that from me. I would have left years ago, but the pay is so great I'd be stupid to tuck tail and run," he says as he hands me a piece of paper with a six digit code written on it.

"I understand completely. Thank you for the info and the number," I say holding up the piece of paper. "We'll be sure to keep our heads down. Have a great night, sir, and take care of yourself. Things I fear, will only get worse from here on out," I say pulling the car out of park.

"I agree. Take care you young whippersnappers."

Driving off, Scott says somewhat confused, "Whippersnappers? What the hell's a whippersnapper?"

"You haven't heard that one before?"

"No," he says with a furrowed brow full of confusion. "You have?"

"My mom would say it to me and my friends. I always just thought of it as little trouble makers. I guess in his position looking down from the years he has we're all whippersnappers."

"I'm going to have to look that one up," Scott says in a matter of fact sort of way.

"Okay, Mr. Dictionary, but can we please go to the map first and figure out where we want to be now that were inside?"

Scott opens up his Google Maps while we pull over just inside the gate. "Okay, go right. Follow it around one bend and then at the next bend just about six or seven houses down pull over. Tom's house should be off to the left through the houses there. We'll have to find the perfect spot. If we want a better unobstructed view, we'll have to sneak into their backyards so we can get a view of the entire house."

I pull around the bend, cut the lights, and stop just in front of 3033 Waterside Circle. Even in the dark, the houses in this community really are something. To the casual observer, rows of driveways leading to double and triple garages is all that you can see from the street. However, each house is individual. A single tree or a small cluster of bushes seem to mark the property lines in between the tightly positioned stuccoed mansions. In the day, the occasional, but pristinely manicured front lawn is complimented by the warm glow of the terra-cotta colored tiled roofs.

Looking between the houses, I can see Tom's house across the lake. It's probably a couple hundred to three hundred feet across. We'll have to pull out some optics if we're going to see anything. I can see a light on inside Tom's house, but it's impossible to make anything out.

The scopes we brought along, coupled with the contacts we are already wearing, will certainly help tonight. Scott pulls his out first and puts it up to his eye to see if he can make anything out. "Back up like five or six feet," he whispers.

I slowly creep back, wishing I could turn off my rear lights.

"Right there," he says. I quickly put it into park. "This isn't a bad view, but sitting on their back dock right on the lake would be even better."

I roll down my window and pull my rifle out to get a look through my Nightforce scope. The view isn't bad, but Scott is right, we're going to have to do a little trespassing. The house we've parked in front of seems to be quiet with only the porch light and address lit up.

"Let's do it then," I start. "We'll head over that fence and slowly make our way through their backyard. I'm guessing with the lake they haven't fenced that in as well."

"What do you want to take?" Scott asks. "I'm thinking my scope, your sniper rifle, and the thermal scope should do it. Maybe the binos as well. If we do this right, we shouldn't run into anyone."

"I agree. We have enough to carry already and we want to be able to move quickly. I would bring your AR, though. You've got the suppressor on it should we have to shoot something."

"Will do," Scott answers.

We quietly gather all our things after making sure no light will turn on when we open the doors. Opening and then closing our doors ever so cautiously, we quickly make our way up to the fence on the west end of the house. The massive palm trees and perfectly manicured plants and bushes tell me someone truly cares about their yard. Hopefully they don't care too much. We certainly don't want motion sensors turning on lights as we move from the front yard into the back. Fortunately, we reach the fence without a flicker of light giving us away. Scott peeks over and gives the all clear.

"I sure hope they don't have dogs," Scott says.

"I sure hope so too."

Scott makes his way over the block fence, setting his rifle on the top before hopping over with no problem. Standing right here, I couldn't even hear him hit the ground. When he grabs his rifle I hand over mine and leap over as well. The landing was much gentler this time, since I'm trying to be as quiet as a mouse. We hug the fence that separates the house to the west and the one we are silently trespassing on. With eyes on the windows and outside lights, we slowly move south towards the lake. Cresting the rear of the house, the coast looks clear so Scott moves out while giving me a signal. Two fingers to his eyes then to the back of the house—watch his six and nine.

We continue to move towards the lake without the hint of humans doing anything in the area. We only move another twenty feet or so before hunkering down behind a boat docked in the backyard on the lake. I continue to watch the rear of the house for any signs we've disturbed the owner. After thirty seconds I still see no motion or lights come on and resolve we've accomplished the first mission.

Turning to get the full grasp of the view we now have Scott whispers, "Now we can do some surveillance."

With a clear view of the home across the lake, I slowly take in the dark water that bears the reflection of the full moon as the water gently ripples ever so slightly from a gentle breeze.

The temperature has been warming up now that spring has arrived and we couldn't have asked for a better night to do some recon work. The breeze, while nice when working, still brings a slight chill to the cold night air. Surveying Tom's home across the lake, I notice we can only see the east side and back, but not the entire west-side rear of the home.

"We should move just a little further northwest along the lake so we can see the entire backyard," I say, wanting to get the best view possible.

"Yeah, maybe just a couple houses down should do it. Just around the bend."

The house where we just settled in and the one just west have boat docks that basically connect. Moving ever so slightly, so as to not trip any motion sensors, we make our way further west. Coming to the end of the dock, they have an infinity pool that overlooks the lake with a narrow concrete edge just on the lake. We move even slower as we reach the twelve inch ledge that separates the lower portion of the pool and the lake. Scott keeps his eyes fixed on our twelve while I watch the house for any signs of movement.

After passing the pool, we have a couple of trees and a grassy area to cross before we arrive at the dock that we hope will offer the best view of Tom's lair. As we pass through the grassy area, almost ready to head onto the dock, Scott stops suddenly, giving the freeze signal with his closed fist without turning around.

Waiting with silent apprehension, Scott finally turns around to face me after thirty seconds. He then lays down on the grass turned toward the rear of the home we were about to cross onto. With another hand signal to join him, I also lay down facing the lake so I can see the house we're still most likely trespassing on.

"What do you have?" I whisper.

After another thirty seconds, he turns my direction and whispers back, "Light was on. Naked women getting food in the kitchen. Gone now. We can proceed."

"What would Melissa say about you checking out naked women while we're supposed to be doing recon work?"

"Nothing. It's all part of the job. I'm just glad I was lead. You probably would have fallen in the lake if you saw her. She was pretty good looking. Let's move out. No worry of ruining your virgin eyes now. I did it as a favor for you. You should thank me," Scott concludes as he slowly slides to his knees.

"Thank you. You're too kind," I say, slowly getting to my knees as well.

Before we even move an inch Scott gives me the freeze signal again and goes back to his knees.

"What, did the naked lady come back? We might be here all night."

"No. I just looked out on the dock and there's nothing to hide us out there. We're better off right here under the protection of the trees that block the windows from both houses," Scott says as he faces the lake without a care as to the home behind him or the naked woman that could come back at any minute.

"Aren't you afraid you might miss your new lady friend?" I say jokingly.

"Nay. She's probably gone for the night. Let's get to work now that the show is over."

"I'm glad you've decided to join me."

"Well, you know that's why you brought me along—to keep you safe and watch your back. Just doing my job," Scott adds.

"I couldn't ask for anything more," I whisper as I get into position behind a tree on the luscious green grass.

We watch for over an hour, intent on keeping quiet. One un-professional outburst could blow our operation. We need to hear if anyone is approaching from this side of the lake. Tom's house sits motionless, without a light going off or on. The one lit light hasn't changed. You can see his entire backyard, plus the entirety of the back of the house.

"I just got a text from Jared," Scott whispers.

"What did he say?"

Scott doesn't say a word and then I hear a slight rustle and a small thud on my side.

"What was that?"

"My phone. Read it."

I search without turning my head with my right hand and find the phone right where it hit. I pull it to my face and start to read:

I hear you guys are out there on the east side across the lake. That's good. I didn't realize until my team said they saw you head in that you'd be there tonight. For the future, don't go into the gate that leads to his street. He's got the guards paid off. I didn't know until tonight so I'm glad you didn't go in that way. If you want, I'll have my team follow you out and fill you in once you leave. Just let me know. They'll be there most of the night. Be safe.

"Tell him we'd love to hear what they know or what they've seen," I say after seeing his message. I slide the phone back to Scott so he can send the message.

It's already after one. If we don't see something soon, I fear this will be a colossal waste of time.

Another hour passes. Jared said his team will follow us out so we just need to find a quiet place to meet after we get out of the area.

Still keeping a close eye on the rear of the house, another thirty minutes passes and then a light flickers on in the kitchen on the main floor. Unable to see who flipped it on, I lift my sniper scope to my right eye and peer into the kitchen.

Hoping that I catch a glimpse of Tom, my mouth falls open as I see both Tom and Jennifer walk into the kitchen.

Tom puts his arms around Jennifer and pulls her into him in a strong embrace.

"I guess she really is working with him," Scott whispers.

"I guess so," I simply say back, not sure what to think at this exact moment.

I pan all around the lighted area and see another man I'm not familiar with holding an assault rifle, fully suppressed.

I pan back to Jennifer.

"Hang on Scott. Take a good look at Jennifer."

Even though I'm just seeing the left side of her face, I can tell her eye is slightly swollen and she's been beat across the face more than once.

"Is she really being held hostage?" I say between clenched teeth.

I can't focus. I pull away for only a brief second and then again I focus my rifle not on Jennifer this time, but on the man that has brought so much fear and death to this city—Tom.

I know for sure he's involved in Dean's and Dennis's deaths. Detective Bergquist informed me he's involved in much more murder as well. When I have him in my sight the urge to put my finger to the trigger and send one sailing across this lake surges in me. From this distance it would be so easy. If it wasn't for Jennifer, my bullet would

360

have already found its target. I can't kill him quite yet. Tom will most likely make it one last night. Tomorrow night, he won't be so lucky. Nor will all those that find comfort in the confines of his home.

We watch for ten minutes as Tom gives Jennifer some food to eat without saying a word. When the two of them finish I see Jennifer's mouth move. I quickly turn my rifle to Tom who gives a nod as he looks toward the man holding the rifle. Without missing anything, I turn my rifle next to the man who now walks to the back door and opens it. Jennifer walks out the back door and Tom follows right behind her after flipping off the light so they can't been seen as easily.

I watch, wishing we had a listening device, but I wouldn't have thought for a minute there would be someone outside this late at night. Jennifer must have wanted to go outside.

With my scope at full magnification, it's easy to see Jennifer sob ever so slightly. They only stay for a few minutes before Tom motions for Jennifer to get back in the house.

Why is she sobbing? None of this makes any sense.

With all three gone and the lights still off we only stay another ten minutes. Scott follows behind me this time and we quickly make our way back the same way we came. Not a light flickers as we quickly jump the fence and climb back into the car.

With all the equipment loaded and Scott and I sitting in the front seats I say with a slight smile, "Do you realize what Detective Bergquist's text means?"

"We're going to meet up with some detectives right now," Scott says matter of factly.

"Yes. We are going to meet up with them, but do you realize what else it means?"

"You, Patrick, and one other man are going to swim across the lake tomorrow night while I stand watch on this side," Scott says this time with confident uncertainty.

"You're right, except the part where you get to stay dry. We get to do a little frogman work tomorrow night. Put me right back into my element. I just hope whoever Patrick has can swim and isn't afraid to get a little wet."

"You see Deacon, I don't think it's sinking in. I was SAS. We don't get wet. There's a reason I chose SAS. If I wanted to get wet, I would have joined the Royal Navy. But I didn't. I joined the SAS. That water has to be about fifty degrees still."

"I know. It will be great. It will be a hot bath compared to the pacific. Plus, it's roughly only three hundred feet across. With gear and four guys we'll be across in no time."

"What about Jennifer?" Scott questions. "How are you going to get her back?"

"Who says she's even coming back. Hopefully we won't have to swim back across. Once everyone is either dead or captured we'll walk right out the front gate. We'll station a car on that side as well."

"Well, you've thought of just about everything, haven't you?" Scott says, still not kosher with the idea of swimming across the lake.

When we pull past the guard tower we give our new best friend a wave. His enthusiastic smile makes me happy and he returns the gesture. When we turn left to make our way out of the area I see head lights flip on behind us.

"Must be Jared's guys," Scott says.

"Must be. Let's take a different way back this time."

I head left on Durango and make our way over to Sahara. Just through the parking lot on the east I see a taco joint.

"Feeling a little hungry Scott?"

"You know me. I'm sure it will be pretty quiet in there if they want to follow us in."

"I just hope it's open. With the military curfew I bet it's closed."

We pull in and park. Jared's guys park just behind us across the driveway. As Scott pulls open the door we look back and the two officers open their doors to come in.

"Bet they were waiting to see if we looked like wankers," Scott says.

"Probably. Let's just hope they have some good intel."

"Excuse me!" a man behind the counter says apprehensively. "We're closed. Someone must have left the door unlocked."

Thinking quick, with Detective Bergquist's men still outside, I pull out my new police badge and say, "Sorry, we're just looking for a quiet place to sit down with our partners and grab a quick bite. We're all detectives with Las Vegas Metro. Would you mind?" I barely get the words out before I hear the door open behind me.

"Oh, no problem at all," he hesitantly quips back. "What can I get for you? This one will be on the house today. Everything is locked up anyways," he says more assuredly.

Scott and I order and so do Jared's guys. When they reach for their wallets I quickly add, "It's on the house guys, don't worry."

The man behind the counter gives an affirming nod and says, "I'll bring it out to you when it's ready."

363

We all make our way to the back corner of the restaurant and take our seats.

"I'm Deacon."

"I'm Scott."

"I'm Detective Johnson," the first one says. His dark brown eyes staring back and forth between the both of us, unsure of what Detective Bergquist has got them into.

"I'm Detective Dunbar," his partner says second, with the same apprehension as the first. He too looks a little unsure.

"I know this must be a little strange for you, but I promise we're on the same team." Normally I wouldn't say I was a SEAL, but I think it will definitely help in this instance. "Scott here was British SAS for the last eight years and I was a Navy SEAL during the same time."

The tension on their faces relaxes ever so slightly at hearing our background.

"We also run the security for all of City Center downtown as well as the Bellagio…which brings us to why we're here," I quickly get out, as our gracious host sets two trays full of food in front of us.

"Can I get you guys anything else?" he asks again, beaming from ear to ear.

"No, we're good. Thank you," Detective Johnson says.

"Yes. Thank you," I add as well as he turns and heads back behind the counter.

"So, as I was saying, Thomas Slack, the man you guys have been watching across the lake, he killed Dean, the manager of the Bellagio about a month ago when things went south. We are also pretty sure he killed my girlfriend's dad just yesterday and put her mom in the hospital."

"Sounds about right," Detective Johnson says pointedly. "He's also responsible for about half a dozen other murders in the city in the last month as well," he continues, feeling much more comfortable.

"Let me ask you a question then," Detective Dunbar says, "Who's that girl they bring out back just about every night at gun point? She's the only thing that hasn't made sense to us. We've seen them kiss and hug, but something is off for sure. It seems forced. Like she's not into it."

I had calmed down from seeing Jennifer earlier, but now the thought of her bruised body brings an inkling of anger to the surface. "That's Dean's personal secretary. Her name's Jennifer. Hearing she comes outside just about every night is music to our ears. We're still not sure if she's working for Tom or playing along until she can get free. They were dating when things went south, so who knows."

"Sooooo," Detective Johnson pauses, not quite sure what to say, "What can we help you with? Detective Bergquist seems to place every confidence in the world in you guys and we've been…asked… to give you whatever you need."

"What I'd like to know more than anything is how many men Tom has held up in his place? Have you seen more than what we saw tonight?" I question, hoping the numbers are low.

"Obviously we can't know for sure, but we figure he has the girl, himself, and at least four to five other men. They all have assault rifles when they come outside and who knows what they have inside," Detective Johnson says.

The two Detectives continue to talk, telling us all they've seen over the last two weeks of doing surveillance on Tom's residence. They haven't seen any other women who appear to be residents of the home, so that should make the task a little less worrisome. They also warn us about driving into the area that leads to Tom's place.

After ten minutes of talking and finishing up the food, we all stand to head out. "One last thought or maybe favor. I don't know what Jared told you guys, but if you could not be watching the house tomorrow night it will probably work out for the best for you and for us."

"Yeah, he mentioned something about that," Detective Johnson says with that same ear to ear smile the manager was giving us.

"Desperate times like these call for drastic measures, if you know what I mean," I say at seeing his smile. I know he knows what we'll do, it's just better if they don't have eye witness account of what happens."

"You know," Detective Johnson says, "I always wanted to join the Navy and be a SEAL. I think I would have made a great one."

"How old are you, if you don't mind me asking?"

"I'm twenty eight," he says hesitantly.

"Well, what are you waiting for? They need good men now more than ever. Your age and size would make you the perfect candidate as long as you're not afraid of drowning, and you can swim like a seal."

"The drowning yeah, but the swimming no problem."

"Well get going then."

"I just might," Detective Johnson adds, as we say our good-byes to the manager.

"You guys have a good night," Detective Johnson says as we each walk to our cars.

"You guys as well, and thanks again for the info."

"No problem. Anytime."

Scott and I jump in the car and head back to my place.

"It's been a pretty good night, hasn't it?" Scott questions after about five minutes of silence.

"It certainly has. I just hope Tom and Jennifer come out into the backyard tomorrow night because we'll be waiting there ready to put one right through his head. It would make our task a cinch."

"It certainly would."

When we pull up to the tower Scott jumps out and says, "Be safe and we'll see you in the morning."

"I will. I should be back in about an hour."

"See you."

I jump back onto the Boulevard and head toward the hospital, lost in thought. I can't help but think how things have gone so smoothly and how every piece of the puzzle has fallen into place. I also can't help thinking how great it will be to see my beautiful blue eyes.

TWENTY SIX
Left Field

The sweet smell of bacon wakes me. Light streams through my windows. I barely remember getting in bed, but the smell of bacon wakes me instantly as the aroma enters the room. I glance at my phone for the time and I'm surprised to see it's only eight in the morning.

After dropping by the hospital last night, Taylor, Savanah, and I came back. She wanted to stay, but her mother insisted she go home and get a good night sleep, "Don't worry about me," Nancy kept saying, "I'll be fine." After thirty minutes of her insistence, Taylor finally relented and we came home.

Nancy looked much better than when we found her yesterday afternoon. The doctors said she's making great progress and Taylor is hoping she can leave within a week. I told her the longer she can stay in the hospital the better, but I'm sure she's just worried about her being there.

Jumping out of bed, I throw on a t-shirt and head for the kitchen in hopes to find Taylor behind the counter. When I get there my hopes are dashed. "Oh, it's just you," I say, seeing Scott standing behind the counter shirtless, with Taylor's Kiss the Cook apron on.

"What's that supposed to mean," he fires back without skipping a beat.

"It's just that I don't see you in here too often, and I was hoping to see Taylor."

"Well," Scott says, "I was able to scrounge up some bacon and fresh eggs from the Aria last night after you dropped me off. I figured we ought to have a good meal before we take off today. I also snatched some lettuce, tomato, and bread for BLTs later."

"Well, I'm certainly not complaining. As long as I don't have to kiss the cook. The hotels must be getting in a few supplies these days now that the military has restored a little order."

Scott doesn't say anything to my last comment as Melissa pokes her head over the couch cushion and in a half asleep raspy voice says, "I can take care of that part."

I turn to see her twisted hair as if she'd been rolling around on the sofa all night. I give her a smile and she nods and falls back on the couch. She must have come out here with Scott because I swear they slept in Taylor's room last night. Bobbi still lies unconscious on the other portion of the couch.

"I'll take it," Scott says in a cheery tone as he continues to fry the bacon.

I can see the eggs are whipped, the bacon is almost fried, and the bread is ready to be toasted. With everything as good as can be expected, my mind turns to the events of the day. The planning that proceeds every mission from my Navy days takes over as my mind races over every detail of the dangerous mission that will be upon us before we know it.

The thought of wetsuits comes to mind since we'll be crossing the lake, but who knows if I can scrounge them up today. I've got mine, but I know Scott doesn't have one. Maybe the maintenance crews have some for cleaning the pools in the winter. I'll have to check on that this morning. We'll have all the weapons we need as long as we can get them across the lake. Handcuffs could also come in handy. We'll have our night vision contacts on from the start so seeing shouldn't be a problem. Once we reach the house, everything is pretty much up in the air. Anything goes at that point. Flash bangs will help should we need to use them.

Now, just the thought of letting Tom live or shooting him weighs on my mind. To be honest, I'm hoping Tom doesn't even give me the opportunity to turn him in. The thought of him pacing a jail cell turns my stomach. Dean deserves better. In fact, all those that have fallen prey to his ruthless reign deserve better. Who knows, Nancy and Dennis could fall into that group as well. Honestly, that's the big question mark of the night. Time will tell, as they say.

"Bon appétit," Scott announces, sliding a plate full of my favorite food across the counter. "What are you thinking buddy?"

"Oh, just about tonight."

"I have been too. What's the plan?"

"I'm thinking, or better yet, I'm hoping Jennifer comes out again with Tom and with one man in tow so we'll have an easy go at it. I don't worry about you or me, but if anything happens to Patrick or one of my guys…," I trail off not wanting to finish my thought.

"Just remember," Scott starts, "they volunteered. We're not holding a gun to their heads and making them come."

"I know, but still."

"Remember," a sweet soft voice whispers from behind me, as smooth cool hands caress me, "focus on the positive and it will all work out."

As I turn, Taylor's face comes into view as she leans in. I hold the kiss for only a few seconds before I grab her and pull her onto my lap, all the while still locked on her lips.

"The smell of bacon woke me up. You must have snuck out while I was in the bathroom. I didn't wake you?" Taylor adds.

"No. I thought you were out here beautiful, making the bacon."

Her eyes light up. Just when I thought her eyes couldn't be more exquisite, the sparkle and brilliant blue of her eyes pull me in.

"Thank you," she says, and then slides onto the stool next to me.

"Here you go babe," I say, sliding my plate over to her. "Go ahead and eat first."

She thanks me again and begins to eat after giving me another kiss. Scott continues to cook while trying to find out about Taylor's mom. She talks of how the doctors have been overly optimistic about her recovery, but the worry I mentioned earlier still shows in the way she approaches the subject. Her haltingly, maybe more hesitant way of talking, makes it obvious she's afraid of the unknown.

As I sit and listen to her talk, I can't help but think it would have been easier on Taylor in the long run, if both her parents had died. Not because I'm heartless, but then she wouldn't worry about either one of them. With the coming continued chaos, she could focus on herself without giving them a second thought.

With the thought of her mother clinging to life, my mother comes to mind with an ominous feeling. I know she called me just yesterday, and I wasn't able to answer it.

With my phone still sitting on the nightstand I say, "I'll be right back. I need to call my mom. She called yesterday while…," I quickly stop not wanting to uncover fresh wounds, "…when I couldn't answer. I just want to make sure she's alright."

I quickly peck Taylor on the cheek before heading to my room. When it comes on I see a voice mail from her as well. I raise the phone and start to listen:

"I don't know how long I have son," the frightened feeling as I hear her speak has my mind moving like a star burning across the sky, *"but listen to me very carefully. I love you more than you know. Your father loved you even though he might not have said it as often as he should. Please don't come for me. I know things will be too dangerous here as society falls further and further from where God wants it to be, but know this is all part of His plan."* The tears are fully flowing now as my mind screams. *"Remember what I told you son, this is the beginning of the end, but follow Christ and you will find peace. Oh no! I love you, Dea..."*

The phone only stays connected for five more seconds before it cuts out. If I didn't know any better, I would say I heard male voices speaking in a foreign language just before it cut out.

Without giving it a second thought, I quickly touch my mom's picture to dial her number. The phone rings and rings and rings and then finally goes to voicemail. After the tone I simply say, "Call me Mom. I love you," unsure of who could possibly be listening.

I dial again with the hope she was just in the shower, or just didn't hear it the first time. I push the fear I heard in her voice as the message ended from my head, not wanting to believe my mother was in trouble.

When she doesn't answer again my mind sets off on a roller coaster ride that I hadn't anticipated this morning. Racing beyond control, I realize I can track her phone. When my father died I set her phone up to allow me to track it so should the time ever come I could find her as long as she had her phone with her. When the app opens, I see the wheel turning as I wait for what seems like forever, which in reality was probably only five seconds. When it stops turning, the map opens to show both my location and my mom's location in California. I zoom in quickly, pulling my fingers apart on the screen faster than I ever have. When I get all the way zoomed in, I see her phone still sits at her house with full power.

I'm in shock. A tidal wave of emotions swirl around me again and again pulling me under. I feel like I'm drowning in doubt and uncertainty. There was so much fear in my mom's voice. I feel paralyzed. In my mind, I can see her hazel eyes. In spite of the fear that was so audible in her voice, her eyes burn with determination and love.

I find myself slowly making my way back to the kitchen, unconsciously looking for comfort, everything still foggy from hearing my mom's voicemail.

I look up and see Taylor. The light from her eyes pulls me out of the tidal wave and the fog dissipates.

When she hears me coming she turns and instantly sees that my whole demeanor has changed in the mere moments I've been in the bedroom. The fact I've been crying shines evident in my eyes as I approach Taylor.

"What's wrong?" she says, as she jumps to her feet and comes to my comfort.

"M-my m-mom...," and with those two little words I can't continue and surrender to her open arms. I've never really been one to let the water works flow, but with everything that has happened, and now this, I don't even try to stop them.

Scott looks concerned as I catch a glimpse of his face. I know that he has a lot of questions for me. I wish I had all the answers. I am looking for answers that I know won't come until I talk to my mom. I have to go as soon as possible. But I can't go. I have too many loose ends to tie up here. I've got Jennifer to figure out, Tom to take care of, and then there's Dennis's killer to find. All these ideas swim through my head like a raging river about to spill over its bank as Taylor holds me without saying another word.

"Can I help Deacon?" I hear Scott say slowly.

Knowing I still can't say anything with the internal struggle raging strong, I simply hand him my phone—the voicemail still open. He must get the idea because he doesn't say anything as he starts the message and puts it on speaker for the two of them to hear.

I listen again—holding onto Taylor in hopes that this time the comfort of her arms will make what I'm about to hear more bearable. The message plays and everyone sits frozen. I can't see Taylor's face, but I can feel the shutter run through her body at the same time Scott's mouth falls half open in disbelief. The message ends.

The silence in the room feels heavy and uncomfortable. Scott turns back to the stove top to quickly get the eggs off the pan before they burn. Melissa sits at the counter now, her face heavy with worry. Taylor grabs me tighter as if her holding me close will take away the thoughts racing through my head.

"I don't have words to help hold back what you must be feeling," Scott says, serving the eggs up to the four plates laid out on the counter, "but what I can say without any doubt is this—I will be there with you for whatever you decide to do."

A shutter shakes through my body with Scott's words. Taylor holds me even tighter as I know she feels it too.

"What do you need babe?" Taylor whispers in my ear so only I hear.

I don't say anything for another minute, still holding her tight. When I finally manage to mutter something, the only thing that leaves my mouth comes out soft and slow, "Foood." I need food. I need something to take my mind off the out-of-left-field fastball I've been hit with.

"Okay," her sweet voice whispers back. "Let's sit down and eat. We'll figure this all out."

We all sit down and begin to eat. Everyone remains silent—I think everyone is waiting for me to speak. I slowly eat, pondering the options I have and replaying the message over and over in my head. '*I don't know how long I have son.*' There must have been someone breaking into the house. It's the only thing that makes sense, as much as I don't want to think it. That, with what I heard at the end, pretty much makes the scenario clear in my mind.

She told me not to come and get her because things would be too much in commotion as society falls further and further. She had to have known I would come for her though, if I knew she was in trouble. She knows my background. She shouldn't have called if she didn't want me to come. With that I know what I have to do. The plans start forming in my head.

"I have to go to California," I say emphatically as I continue to eat.

"I know babe," Taylor starts.

"I wouldn't expect anything less. I would do the same thing if it were my mother on the other end," Scott says. "Count on me to be right there with you."

"Me too," Taylor adds.

The thought of Taylor tagging along sends another shiver through my body as my mind recalls the horrific detail of the destruction that awaits everyone. The only question that remains is when will it start? I guess whether it starts now or while were down there I'll feel safest with Taylor at my side. Not knowing what's going on with her four hundred miles away would make my next mission almost unbearable.

"We've got to wrap things up here before we leave though," I say in a rush.

"Sounds good," Scott says before continuing. "We'll follow the plan for tonight, hopefully kill two birds with one stone, if you catch my drift."

"Oh I do. I hope so more than you know."

The remainder of the day goes off without a hitch. I had my wetsuit hanging in the closet and Scott was able to round up three more from maintenance. They may not be as nice as they would like, but at least they'll keep them warm in the frigid lake tonight.

While Scott was running around rounding up gear, I was able to talk to Patrick about the mission tonight. Looks like he's found an Army Ranger from 1st Bat ready to roll out tonight. I've always had respect for the Rangers. Don't get me wrong, SEAL training is second to none in suck factor, but the training Rangers run through is no joke either. The missions they are thrown into in the real world are second only to the SEALs and Delta Force.

With all our gear loaded in the car just before five, Patrick and Ethan take off to get some rest before meeting back here at midnight. Scott and I do the same after filling our stomachs with the most mouth-watering BLTs I can remember. When you don't have something for such a long time—okay, maybe a month isn't that long—it's still amazing how much better it tastes. I swear a BLT never tasted as good as the ones Taylor made today.

While Taylor and I clean up the kitchen, Scott takes the spare room to get some shut eye.

"I'm just going to go tuck my boy in," Melissa says with a sly smile on her face as she follows Scott down the hallway toward the spare room.

"Is that what you call it?" Taylor says in a whisper looking back at me.

"That's what I was going to say," as we both begin to laugh lightly so they don't hear our humor.

"One day Deacon," Taylor begins, "one day when we're married we'll be there. As for now, I'll tuck you in too, and even tickle your back if you'd like?"

"You're speaking music to my ears babe. I really do love you Taylor. Probably more than you know. If I have anything to do about it, we'll be married before you know it."

My words bring Taylor to her breaking point as one tear falls from her big beautiful blue eyes. She wraps her arms around me and returns the expression of love she has for me, "I love you so much Deacon. I can't wait to be your wife."

We stand there lost in our moment until another warm hug embraces us both. Savanah, crying as well, captured our moment and couldn't hold back anymore, "I love you guys," she says through her own tears. "You give me so much hope in this otherwise dreary world."

"We love you too," Taylor says, reaching one hand out and around her best friend in the whole world. "There's hope sweetie. Don't you give up."

"I won't."

We stand for only a few more seconds before Taylor says, "I better get Deacon to bed."

"True. I need to be fully rested for tonight. I probably won't see you two tonight," I say to Savanah and Bobbi who still sits on the couch watching our little moment, "so have a good night and we'll see you tomorrow."

"Be careful tonight Deacon," Bobbi pleads.

"We will. Just another walk in the park."

"Okay, go put that boy to sleep," Savanah says, pushing the two of us towards the bedroom.

When I get into the room, I quickly rip my clothes from my tired body and jump into bed, making sure to leave my back exposed.

"I haven't seen you undress too many times, but that's got to be the fastest I've seen," Taylor says in a somewhat playful manner.

"What can I say? My hot momma wants to tickle my back and she's talking about marriage with me—two things that definitely turn me on."

"Let's keep you face down for sure then. We don't want you too turned on. I have to keep you respectable until the deal's done."

"Oh, the deal's done. I'll tell you about it in a few days."

"What's that supposed to mean?" Taylor asks, completely confused.

"I'll tell you about it in a couple days, I promise."

She doesn't say anything as she grabs my face to turn my eyes towards hers. I'm guessing she wants to try and read my expression.

"A few days. I promise," I say staring into her diamond blue eyes.

"Okay. I will wait, but you better believe I'll be asking in a few days if I haven't heard anything that makes that statement make more sense in my mind," she says, returning to run her cool hand across my back.

What Taylor doesn't know yet and it couldn't have worked out any better if I planned it, is that at the hospital early this morning I found Taylor, Savanah, and Nancy talking. When Nancy needed a cold drink and had a question for the nurse, Taylor insisted she go for her mother. Savanah decided to tag along with Taylor. That left me alone to talk to Nancy. While they were gone I told Nancy—and this was hard, but I had to do it—I told her I was going to ask her husband for Taylor's hand in marriage. I know it's old fashioned, but what can I say, I'm old fashioned when in comes to courting.

If Taylor could have seen the immense joy visible on her mother's face the moment I mentioned marriage, she would have followed suit for sure. Seeing her expression made the answer pretty obvious, but I still asked her if she would allow me to have Taylor's hand in marriage. She just nodded and reached for a hug. I'm pretty sure she stayed quiet because if she had opened her mouth to answer she would have let out a wail of happiness for the whole hospital to hear.

When Taylor and Savanah returned, Taylor could see something had changed inside her mother. Nancy played it off very well saying she just had a shooting pain, but it had gone now. We left right after at Nancy's insistence that Taylor get a good night's sleep. Actually, she spent most the day over there while Scott and I ran around planning and preparing for the night.

Taylor slowly slides her smooth fingers over my back while humming a tune I'm not familiar with. Normally I would ask, but the sense my body has for sleep right now keeps my mouth from asking. I feel her hands go up and down in patterns for several minutes until I feel nothing.

TWENTY SEVEN

Operation Kill Birds

𝄞

You wake up late for school man you don't wanna go.
You ask your mom, "Please?" but she still says, "No!"
You missed two classes and no homework,
But your teacher preaches class like you're some kind of jerk.
You've gotta fight for your right to party.

𝄞

Only Taylor could have done that after I fell asleep. I wake to the song we would always play before my team would go on a mission. I remember telling her about it once. Just to hear the song now puts me in the mood to do some house crashing. I love that woman. Always there to lift me up at the right time.

I listen through the first verse and chorus before it repeats. Turning it off, I jump out of bed and head to the closet. No sooner had I entered the closet do I feel hands slide around my waist.

"Did you have a nice rest?" Taylor asks, while bending around to kiss me on the cheek.

"Very nice. I don't remember falling asleep, I don't remember dreaming, and I did wake up to the best song before heading out."

"I thought you'd like that. I'd never heard that song before, but I remember you telling me you guys would listen to it. So I set it as your alarm and then went out to the front room and listened to it. Just one question—Why that song of all the fight songs out there?" Taylor asks puzzled.

"Well," I pause, putting my thoughts in place, "we just figured it fit so well. As you know we did a lot of partying in the military. We definitely had to fight for that right. What can I say, it put us in the mood. It became almost like a ritual. The most you would see anyone doing was bobbing their heads. It would get us focused."

"Fair enough. You go and fight tonight and I promise you we'll have a party when you get back."

The way the words roll off her tongue catch me a little by surprise. When I turn, face somewhat confused, she sees the slight smile as well and instantly realizes what I was thinking.

"Now, now, Deacon," she begins, "don't go getting the wrong idea. I know that sounded like more than it was, but we'll have our own party on the roof."

I start to speak, but before I can Taylor adds one more bit of information to make the point crystal clear, "With our clothes on, or at least some swimwear on."

"It's a date, my dear. I know what you meant. I was just messing with you. I wouldn't dare do anything, even though you can't blame me for the thought crossing my mind."

"I appreciate that. Now get ready. Scott came out of the room ready about ten minutes ago," she says before planting one more on me and heading out of the room.

With my bag packed and dressed from head to toe in jet black clothing, I leave my room for the kitchen. Scott, already sitting at the counter, has begun to eat something. I pull up a chair alongside him and sit down without saying a word.

"You ready for this?" Scott asks.

"Born ready. You?"

"Yep," he says nonchalantly.

I see he's eating a peanut butter and jelly sandwich and some chips. There's another plate slid in front of me with the same open-faced sandwich and chips.

"Thanks babe," I say. Taylor just smiles back and joins me, sitting on my lap.

"Where's Melissa?" I ask Scott, not seeing her at his side nor in the living room.

"She's sleeping. I couldn't bring myself to wake her. I think it will be best if she's not awake when we leave. She's having a hard time with this one. Probably more than any of the others I've been on since we were forced into this mess. How are you doing Taylor?" Scott asks.

When she doesn't speak, I turn to look her in the eyes and can tell she's having a hard time as well. Just before I'm about to open my mouth she says, "It's hard…but I know you guys will be back before sunrise. Then Deacon and I can have our own little party on the roof in the moonlight."

"That's my girl. Keep that positive attitude and all will work out."

We quickly finish our food and make our way for the door. We are going to be down at the car about ten minutes early, but I'm sure Patrick and Ethan will already be there waiting, the anticipation keeping them awake.

"Be safe out there," Taylor says as she holds me tighter than she ever has.

I hold her and whisper, "You know I will. Just another walk in the park. We'll be relaxing on the roof before you know it."

"I love you Deacon," she whispers back, pulling away enough to kiss me with her sweet lips.

"I love you too."

When I turn to open the door, Scott is standing across the hall, leaning against the open elevator door, arms crossed in front of himself, with a look that says, *'That's enough, let's get going.'* I'm just glad he didn't say it. Taylor might have given him an ear full. As I close the door, I blow a kiss to Taylor. I see her return the favor just as the door closes.

Loaded on the elevator and lowering to the parking garage, Scott and I run through all the gear we're bringing—knives, rifles with scopes, handguns, night vision contacts for the group, binoculars, wetsuits—already in the car—and extra mags. With everything covered, when the elevator doors open to the parking garage, we make our way to the car. Neither Patrick nor Ethan are in sight, which seems a little surprising. I thought for sure they'd be here.

We quickly load our gear in the back and jump in the front seats. Just as our doors close, Patrick and Ethan emerge from the highly lit elevator. As they walk towards us, I can't help but think it was wrong to have them come. I just hope they make it through this thing unscathed.

I quickly start the car in order to roll down the window and yell, "You guys ready for this," as they make their way to the car.

"Like you wouldn't believe," Ethan calls back enthusiastically.

"Well then…let's do this."

As we drive west, we methodically cover the plan down to every possibility we can think of—from crossing the lake to kicking in doors. We decide Scott or I should be in lead most of the time. I thought Patrick and Ethan would give me flack for it. I glance back at them in the rearview mirror and I can sense that the reality of the situation is sinking in. The "this-is-about-to-get-real" look so common to even the best prepared soldiers going into combat is plastered across their faces now. Scott hands each one a pair of night vision contacts and explains how they work. After several failed attempts, they finally manage to put them in their eyes.

"These things are amazing!" Patrick says after blinking rapidly several times to charge them.

"Unbelievable! Boy, you guys always got the good stuff." Ethan asserts.

"What can I say? We actually just started field testing those my last year in. Never had one problem so I'm sure they are being pushed out to the Ranger Bats by now."

"I know this may be a little preemptive, but..." Ethan trails off, not sure he should ask his question. "Never mind," he quickly sputters.

"What? Come on, you can ask. What's up?" I ask, wondering what he was about to say.

"Okay. Would it be possible...or can I keep a pair of these after this is over?" Ethan asks sheepishly.

I mull it over for a second before responding. "I'll tell you what, you two make it through this thing alive and you can both keep them. We've only got one extra pair though, so don't go losing them. When they handed us these boxes on orientation day the rep said each box was worth about a hundred grand. Figure the math on that one."

"Twenty grand a piece!" Patrick chokes out.

"You've got to be kidding me!" Ethan exclaims.

"Wait 'til you try them out," Scott says. "I've only used them a few times since we found the box, but trust me, they are worth the twenty grand without a doubt."

"When else have you used them?" I ask. I only remember him using them the night we found them and recon night.

"I used them those nights I went out looking for meds for you. Of course you don't remember. You were knocking on deaths door, remember?" Scott says.

"True. You've got me there. I don't remember much."

When we arrive at the gate, the same old gray-haired security guard stands ready inside his post. I quickly tell the guys that he thinks we're cops just so they know. As soon as we pull up to his window he greets me with the same jovial hello as before, cheeks flapping just like last time.

"I see you young whippersnappers have brought some more team members back. What'll be tonight?" he asks, with the gate already opening for us.

"Oh—same old same old. Could be a little more exciting though. We'll see. Have a good night and remember to keep your head down. These people are crazy out here."

"Oh I will. Take care and be safe," he says as we pull forward flipping the lights off as we enter the complex.

It's just after midnight as we pull into our parking spot. I quickly throw in my contacts and get out of the car. With every light off and the area relatively dark, the contacts bring the scene laid before me into full focus. As I look between the houses, across the lake, the house sits silent, pitch black, and foreboding.

We all quickly change into our wetsuits. I told them we probably didn't really need to wear them, but they all insisted. I get the feeling that they are trying to get the full SEAL experience. I tried to explain that we only wore them on really long swims in the frigid ocean, but there was no dissuading them. I guess it could help should we have to stay in the water longer. Plus they are skin tight and black which should make us more stealthy, or at least that's my hope.

With gear gathered and the game plan covered, I pause remembering my dad's words, "Pray son." I quickly close my eyes and utter a pray for the first time since I was a kid.

"God. I sure hope you hear me now. Please help us get through this one to fight another day. I know there will be many more. Amen."

"What are you doing mate?" Scott quips inquisitively.

"I said a little prayer for us."

"Not a bad idea mate," Scott says as he quickly does the same.

"What did you say buddy," I ask knowing he's not the praying type either.

"Please help us not to die."

"That works," Ethan says having finished his own prayer.

We head over the same fence as before. Quietly, we make our way down the side of the house. No one makes a noise and we don't hear any from either house as we slowly move down to the dock. The moon sits full, only a few clouds dot the night sky, giving us the perfect loom to make the contacts even more effective, but also lighting the dark a little too much. They work pretty well without moonlight, but the moon makes them that much better.

"Will water mess these contact up?" Patrick says as he prepares to enter the water. Scott too looks at me not sure of the answer.

"No. What good would they be to a SEAL if they couldn't get wet? Which reminds me—open your eyes under water while you're swimming—another feature I forgot about."

What I don't tell them is that these little beauties act as goggles under water. It will be like icing on the cake for them. The goggle feature lets you see perfectly as long as you have visibility. There probably won't be much to see, but at least it will be clear.

Pulling my binoculars out of my bag before getting in the lake, I scan the shore line on the other side and the entire back of the house. Without a light or sign of movement, I quickly put them away and slide into the lake without making a noise. The others follow suit and the mission begins.

We slowly make our way across the lake without too much noise. The moon reflects brilliantly on the water as we swim, increasing the likelihood of our position being revealed. However, no one is out and most lights are off, so I'm not too worried about it.

Swimming through the water, I realize the other benefit of wearing this suit, besides the warmth—I'm not being dragged down by boots and clothing. I got used to it in the Navy, but boy it's nice to be free of that weight especially when also carrying all this gear. It's probably a lifesaver for the others as well, since they're probably not used to swimming in full combat gear like I was.

I'm carrying my bag, a handgun on my right thigh, and my new assault rifle. I was going to bring the sniper rifle, but I figured close combat calls for something more personal. Plus, I wanted to have a suppressor for tonight's activities in hopes of keeping the altercation as discreet as possible.

Scott too has a bag, his rifle, and a handgun strapped to his thigh. The other two both carry the same, but instead of flash bangs and binoculars, they have medical gear and water.

As we near land, Patrick and I head left as Scott heads right with Ethan. We reach a short stone wall that separates Tom's house from the lake. I grab hold, pulling up just enough to check to see if the coast looks clear. There are bushes and trees to the left and right of the pool, exactly where we've pulled up to conceal us as we set up for the wait.

I slowly pull up out of the water without making a noise, as I've done so many times in the past. Patrick follows suit, only making a slight noise as he hits against the wall. Glancing across the pool, I see Scott and Ethan getting into position. Keeping a low profile, we low crawl into the best position across the grass to put a bullet through someone's head should they come outside tonight. Scott and Ethan do the same.

In position for the long hall, I quietly pull out my radio and earpiece and put them on. Slowly switching the radio on, I call Scott in a whisper. He doesn't answer. I can still see him across the way, or at least a portion of him. His radio must not be ready yet.

"Scott?" I whisper again, a little more loudly.

"In position," Scott whispers into the radio, which comes through crystal clear on my end.

"Us too. Now we wait. You know what to do," I respond back in a whisper as well.

As we discussed already, Scott will take the one closest to him and I will take the one closest to me. The only thing we can't cover is the scream Jennifer is bound to make when she sees the two men drop at her side and the very real possibility that their blood will splatter all over her face. Hopefully they're not too close and our angle will prevent any blood from hitting her in the head.

I glance up at the moon. It has easily been an hour. Still no sign of movement. The anticipation is building. Last night they came out just after two thirty. We agreed that if they held to the pattern, we would take the easy shot outside and keep Jennifer safe. Otherwise, we would wait until three thirty before we entered the house by force.

We wait another hour. Still no movement. The clock creeps past two and the moon sinks even lower. I can only hope things happen quickly because the adrenaline is wearing off now with all this waiting.

Another half hour ticks by. If everything goes as anticipated, the time has come for Tom and Jennifer to make their entrance. Just like clockwork, a light flickers on in the dark house and three figures appear. The first comes into view. I instantly recognize him as Tom's sidekick from last night. Jennifer comes into view next, accompanied by what I hope will be Tom. An unexpected twist. It's not Tom. It appears to be another hired hand, armed with a hefty assault rifle.

"Where's Tom?" I hear Scott whisper over the radio in my right ear.

"No idea. Let's hope he shows up. If not we'll have to go in and find him. Be alert. Scan the windows for any sign of movement," I finish telling Scott as I turn to Patrick and give him the two fingers to the eyes and then pointing at the windows all along our side of the house. Just to be sure I add, "Watch for movement." Now is not the time for miscommunication.

We all watch in anticipation as Jennifer eats. I can't help but think this may be her only meal each day. She was already as thin as a toothpick. It shouldn't surprise me, but I still catch myself thinking about the filth that fills this world. The complete lack of human decency baffles my mind. It's not just the third world countries that face these problems. I guess it's just sad to see it in my own back yard.

After ten minutes, Jennifer finishes her food and signals to go outside.

Holding down the radio button, I quickly whisper, "Game time." Scott doesn't respond with anything more than a click.

As Jennifer walks to the door I see the same thug from last night shake his head left and right, letting her know she's not going out tonight. The tears almost instantly begin to fall from her eyes. She turns back into the house, but doesn't move away from the door. I can tell she's talking, but it's impossible to hear her. I can only hope she's pleading with them to let her go out.

"If she moves away from that door without coming out, right now might be the safest time to free her if she is indeed being held," I tell the others.

"I've got a bead on the guy in the kitchen. I can't see the other one from last night," Scott whispers.

"I've got the other," I whisper, my heart now thumping like it did back in the day.

We wait breathless, for about a minute as the scene unfolds in front of us. I was really hoping for some safety when we rescued Jennifer, but things aren't looking too good right now.

Another thirty seconds passes without Jennifer moving away from the door and then she turns again and opens the door. Just as the door opens I hear her captor callously call out, "One minute, no more."

When Jennifer exits, she moves out onto the grass just past the balcony that shades the back deck during the day. Her two guards quickly move out on both sides of her, but giving her a little space.

With the moonlight beaming down on her face, I can see she looks even worse for the wear. She's got a nice gash over her left eye and her right eye appears to be swollen. It's not from the crying either, although that isn't helping her right now. The beatings, though not good, give me a little hope she's still on my team.

I slowly squeeze my radio with my left hand to signal Scott, "Three—two—one."

PFTT!

We must have pulled our triggers at exactly the same time because I only hear the slight crack of my AR as it goes off. I see both men slump to the ground, letting me know that Scott fired as well.

Jennifer stands frozen without making a sound as she quickly looks left and then right. Without skipping a beat she heads for the water telling me she doesn't want to be there.

"Jennifer. It's Deacon. Over here," I call out, catching her completely by surprise.

At the sound of my voice she breaks free from what I'm sure was pure panic and quickly scampers over to the sound of my voice.

When she gets within five feet I say, "Right over here," which causes her to jump just a little.

She quickly lies down behind us and the tears flow more freely now.

"You're safe now Jennifer. We might not have much time so I need you to listen carefully. You can either stay right out here while we go inside and finish what we've started, or you can head back across the lake to a white Explorer parked in the street," I say, pointing diagonally directly across the lake. "If you're up for it, swimming across the lake would probably be safest since we don't know what we'll find in here."

Jennifer takes a few deep breaths to compose herself before answering. "I can swim back, but just so you know…," she trails off attempting to calm herself before saying anything else. "There's at least five to seven more men in there. Tom didn't get me up tonight so I'm sure he's sleeping."

"Is there anything else you can tell us that will help?" I quickly ask as the seconds tick on and the unknown awaits.

"No. I wish I knew more. If you've been watching I come from a room in the basement just down the hall from the kitchen. That's the extent of my knowledge. I'm sorry."

"You've got nothing to be sorry about. I just wish you didn't have to go through this. Here are the keys and my phone. They'll be fine inside this bag. As soon as you've slipped into the water and are making your way back we'll go inside. There are some towels and food in the car. Make yourself at home. Call your family and let them know you're okay. I'm not sure how long this will take, but we hope not long."

"Thank you," she says, grabbing the bag.

I can see in her eyes the reality of what is transpiring is finally sinking in. The tears well up again. When she opens her mouth to talk, I quickly put a finger to her lips, "You're alright Jennifer. Take a nice swim and we'll talk when this is all over."

With her eyes sparkling in the moonlight, she slowly slides over the wall and into the frigid water. She quickly, but quietly glides across the water with a grace that only comes from someone who has done quite a bit of swimming. We won't need to worry about her. She'll also be able to drive the car around to pick us up when this ends. Scott will be thrilled about that for sure.

"Jennifer's making the swim across now. You guys ready?" I ask.

"Let the party begin," he answers simply.

TWENTY EIGHT
Party Time

With no sign of movement from inside the house, we quickly converge on our first two unfortunate victims and pull their bodies into the bushes. No reason to give anything away if we don't have to.

Scott moves to the back door and slowly opens it to let the three of us in, as he falls in behind. I know it's a feeble attempt at keeping Patrick and Ethan safe, but with me taking point and Scott pulling up the rear, I feel it gives them the best chance at making it out of here unscathed. I seriously considered sending one of them back with Jennifer, but if asked, I knew neither one of them would volunteer.

We pause just inside the door listening for any sound that would alert us to movement in the house. With utter silence, we methodically make our way through the kitchen. I quickly creek open a door in the kitchen to see it stocked with food—pantry—I knew it. Moving to the next opening just off the kitchen, I motion to Scott to wait there to keep an eye on the unknown foyer, hall, and stairs in the entry.

We quietly open two doors to find a half bath and a laundry room, which means the other door most likely leads to the garage on the west side of the house. Opening the door I see two black SUVs just like the one James was driving before we brought his life to its much needed conclusion. Maybe we'll borrow one of these when we head out of here.

After quickly covering the garage to make sure there wasn't anyone hiding out in there, we head back to Scott and Ethan.

Moving beyond Scott, we enter into the open great room with a massive stone fireplace on the east wall. Just off to the right from this room there is a foyer. The ten foot front door makes it obvious the entrance lies through there. There's another opening that leads to the master bedroom, if I had to guess as well. If Tom were anywhere, I would say that's the place.

Before making an entrance, we quickly check the front entry and the stairs to find an office just off the entrance. With no noise and no one in sight an ominous feeling feels my gut. What if no one's here? At least we've tied up one loose end before I head to California.

"PUT YOUR HANDS UP!" I hear Scott call out from the great hall, and then a shot splits the wall where Scott was watching. "Deacon, Tom's just gone back into his room. I may have got his left arm as he turned tail and rushed back into his room!"

My mind begins to race, but mission mode quickly kicks in. "Ethan, watch the stairs coming up and down here. Anything moves up or down, shoot it. Patrick, I want you outside on the east end of this house so he can't high tail it out of here. I need you to keep an eye on the front. Make sure he's not calling for backup."

Both give nods and start moving into position. I'm glad I've got them with us now because this much unknown with just Scott and I wouldn't turn out too well.

Scott, already having position, moves over to the door to check the unseen entry. Turning he says, "Small hall, door on the left."

Confident that Tom has already armed himself, we wait just outside in the great room not wanting to commit suicide by moving into the fatal funnel leading into his room. We wait for what must be almost a minute before I yell in at him.

P-TAFT!

The un-silenced sound of Ethan's AR brings this situation abruptly to the it's-gotten-real reality I had moments before. "One down," Ethan calls out as I hear the body thud down the stairs. No need for silence now.

"Tom. It's Deacon," I call out. "Jennifer's miles from here by now, safe and sound. I suggest if you want this to end well for you, you walk out here with your hands up."

"Deacon, my good buddy. What have you been up to?" he calls out in an almost playful manner.

There's good and bad to speaking in situations like this. You don't want to give your position away for one thing, but at least you know where they are as well. It's definitely a two-edged sword.

"He's at the front of the house," Scott whispers as we wait.

"I'll tell you what I'll do for you Deacon," he starts up in that same playful tone, "I'll let you leave right now before the gang gets here. That way you at least live to fight another day. Another five minutes and I can't promise anything."

P-TAFT!

"Two down," Ethan yells. This time the thud seems more distant. He must have been coming up from the basement.

"Tom. I don't know how many guys you have here now, but four are already dead. You can't have too many more. Do you want to end up like them?" I ask, turning to Scott to have him pull out the white smoke grenade in my pack.

"You're the only one leaving this place in a body bag buddy. It doesn't have to be that way though. You still have time," Tom says with more uncertainty in his tone.

397

"He's still up front. Whether he's bluffing or not, the neighbors have certainly called the cops by now. We need this to be over now," Scott whispers worriedly.

"I'm going to throw this in there. It should fill every square inch in less than a minute. Then we'll go in and finish this thing when we hear his rifle run empty."

"Let's do it then," Scott mutters.

"Tom," I call out once more to get his location.

"Have you made up your mind then?" Tom calls back. "You want to walk out of here as opposed to being carried out?"

As he posses the questions, I pull the pin and quickly move up to his still open master door. With a quick glance, a little more risky than Taylor would have liked, I see his bedroom in and to the left with a wall just inside the door leading to a master bathroom door that's closed.

Not seeing him, and realizing the smoke will not fill his space, leaving us exposed, I quickly motion for Scott to move forward.

Waiting at his door so as to not lose ground, I call Patrick on the radio, "If you see a window open on the east side shoot at anyone coming through."

"Will do," Patrick calls back. "I have a good view of the front so I'll let you know if anyone makes it in here."

"Thanks," I quickly call back before turning to Scott. "That door opens in. I'm going to kick it in and drop the smoke. In less than thirty seconds he won't be able to see a thing, which means he'll be firing blindly. What I wouldn't give for some concussion grenades right now."

"Hell, I'd settle for a frag grenade," Scott says with a grin.

I give him a quick smile before turning my attention back to Tom. "Tom, it's only a matter of time before we take you."

"I doubt it," he quickly calls back. "Maybe only a minute now buddy."

"He's still up front," Scott whispers as we slowly move down the wall and stop about five feet from the bathroom door.

P-TAFT!

"Another one down," Ethan calls out a second later.

With five down and Tom cornered in the bathroom, there can't be many more. Jennifer said she thought there were five to seven and with Tom that makes six.

"There's no one left to save you Tom. We just took care of your last hired hand. They're not too bright either. My Ranger out there has been plucking them off like flies."

He doesn't say anything at first. Maybe some sense has sunk into him as he contemplates his fate, should he choose not take my advice.

"What are you thinking about Tom? Come to your senses yet?"

I wish we were already headed out of here, but blind corners and tight spaces in an American home are suicide without knowing what is around the corner.

"How about you come through that door. Then we'll see who has come to their senses," Tom taunts.

I don't respond, but instead turn to Scott and whisper, "You think you could kick that door clean off it's hinges?"

With a smile, Scott simply replies, "With pleasure."

As he moves in front he gives me the silent signal with his left hand—three, two, one. When he hits the door on the left side in the center, it flies off and crashes into the counter across the bathroom. I release the smoke grenade into the bathroom.

BRATATAT, BRATATAT, BRATATAT!

Tom's machine gun goes off—striking the walls and breaking porcelain. He must be hitting his toilet at the rear of his home. The smoke fills the tiny space and begins billowing out into the master. I wait ten seconds then move forward and throw a flash bang towards him, counting it off so it hopefully explodes right in his face.

MOOB! BRATATAT, BRATATAT, BRATATAT!

His gun explodes again as the grenade goes off, further destroying his toilet and striking the walls. The glass shower wall shatters and crashes to the floor.

Another ten seconds passes. As soon as he stops firing I launch another grenade in his direction.

MOOB! BRATATAT, BRATA, CLICK.

As I hear his slide lock to the rear, I round the corner, dropping to my stomach. Tom is dropping his magazine with another one ready to load.

"DON'T DO IT," I yell, so he knows I'm right in front of him.

It's too late. As he locks the new magazine in, he begins to turn the assault rifle my direction to fire blindly through the smoke. I shoot one round right to the center of his chest.

PFTT!

It hits center mass and Tom drops the rifle. I quickly move forward keeping my suppressor pointed right at his head. When I reach him, I kick the assault rifle and the hand gun he had at his side

400

further into the closet. He's still breathing, but not for long. We all knew he was never leaving here in handcuffs.

"Your mo…" he trails off in a death cough as blood spills from his lips.

"What did you say?" I quickly fire back, thinking he was about to mention my mother.

"We have…," he stops dead without finishing his sentence.

I drop to the ground grabbing him by the shirt, "WHAT DID YOU SAY!" I scream, this time hoping to get anything out of him.

His eyes are open, but empty. He's gone.

As I stare into his lifeless eyes, Patrick comes over on the radio, "Two large SUVs are pulling up to the house."

Having completed everything we set out to do tonight, I accept that searching this house won't be an option now.

"Everyone head for the lake. Looks like another swim," I say, grabbing Tom's cell phone that sits at his right side. If he was going to tell me they have my mother, at least I'll have some leads on his phone—names, numbers, and, I pray, some addresses.

Ethan, Scott, and I make our way out the back door. Patrick sits at the water's edge ready to slip in. The four of us quickly slide into the water as chaos fills the house. Scott, Patrick, and Ethan quickly move out in front as I hold up the rear. The last thing we need now is Tom's henchmen firing at us across the lake.

I slowly swim backwards, keeping an eye on the back door. Finally, after moving about fifty feet from land, I see one man come out the back and start searching franticly through the back yard.

"That's right. There's nothing out here," I say to myself as he makes his way back to the door.

After opening the door, he stops and turns to look out over the lake. He starts walking to the corner to get a better view. When he rounds the pool and comes to the corner I know he'll see us. Raising my rifle, without giving it a second thought, I fire one round.

PFTT!

The sound cracks as the bullet carries across the lake and finds its target. When he falls face first into the lake, I assume that surely the noise will bring others out of the house. Almost halfway across the lake, I continue to swim backwards, waiting for more men to turn up, but they don't. When I turn back around to see how far ahead the guys have made it, I see they've already reached the other side.

"Come on, I've got you covered now," Scott says, proned out looking through his scope.

Without having to watch my back, I make quick time to the shore. Climbing out of the water, I look at my watch for the first time and realize we were only in the house for fifteen minutes. I guess Tom was right about his men, they were Johnny on the spot.

"You guys ready to go home?" I ask as everyone stands.

"Yep," they all say in unison.

With the mission complete, we quickly climb the fence and hurry back to the car. When I see Jennifer sitting in the front seat, I feel relieved. Even though she seemed confident, I still wasn't certain about letting her swim alone after going through what she has. Nor were my fears of her completely tamed.

When I open the driver's door, she asks open-eyed and hoping, "Did you get him?"

"We got him, and six of his buddies found a similar fate."

Jennifer sits pondering for a few second before adding, "That's good. That's really good."

We quickly strip off our wetsuits and throw our clothes back on before mounting up. With the car loaded, we head down the road and out the gate. My old friend sitting in his shack smiles as we roll by, giving us a goodbye wave. I return the gesture as we pass him. Should be the last time I see that jiggle.

"Well," I begin, "sorry you didn't see much action Patrick."

"No biggie. I shot up James that one day. I'm just glad you guys all made it out okay."

"Yeah me too," Jennifer says, sandwiched in between Ethan and Patrick.

"Then you've got Buffalo Bill here picking 'em off like flies as they came up or down the stairs," Scott says, turning to look at Ethan.

"I know right," Ethan says proudly. "I couldn't believe how idiotic they were."

"Oh, come on now. You know tangos and turds are only running on half a brain cell. You've had to have seen some pretty stupid things in the Ranger Bat," I say.

"True, true. I guess I just thought here they would have a little more sense than the ones still living in mud huts."

No one says much after that. I think the silence has caused the night's events to sink in deep. I for one, feel blessed to have walked out, or better, swum out of this alive. I drop Jennifer off at the Bellagio with Ethan and Patrick so he can update security there on procedures for keeping her safe. I won't have another incident like that if I can help it. Plus, I've got to let everyone know Patrick will be in charge for some time until I get back from California.

Pointing at his eyes as he walks away, Ethan smiles and says, "Thanks Deacon. Have a good night." I'm sure he's still thinking about the contacts he's wearing. They are pretty amazing.

Keeping the conversation light, Scott questions inquisitively, "Is there anything else these contacts can do? I mean—let's think about this—night vision, underwater vision, I'm surprised I can't see through walls now."

"Now you're just being ridiculous."

"I'm serious. I know technology has come a long ways, but these things are amazing!" Scott exclaims.

"Well, we've only got one extra pair so don't lose the ones you've got. They might yet come in…"

"Oh!" he blurts out as if I wasn't just talking. "I know you didn't see it because you would have already said something, but did you happen to catch the pictures hanging on the walls inside Tom's room?"

"No. I was a little preoccupied to be checking out his family photos," I say.

"Well then, I'm glad I saw them 'cause this will make you and Taylor happy. There were pictures of Tom and his son all over. I would have mentioned it at the time, but you were kind of focused and I didn't want to break that."

"So, what you're telling me Scott, if I'm hearing what you're saying, is that within forty-eight hours the little Slack family has been taken care of by Mr. Sanders and us?"

"That's it. I'm betting Tom and, what was his son's name?"

404

"Stanley," I quickly say.

"Yeah. So I bet the both of them were there at Taylor's house and Tom left his dying son on the front porch. What a father."

"Well then it's settled. With only my mom in question, I should be able to head west without any worries here."

We drive silently to the tower after that. Lost in thought for what the future now holds, and I'm sure Scott has thoughts of his own future. I can't shake the thought of my mother tied up in a dingy cell in a basement somewhere or even worse, dead in her own home.

We arrive at the tower in no time and park the car. It's too early now and the quiet ride back hasn't helped with the lack of sleep settling in. We head upstairs to find my place quiet and everyone sleeping except Taylor. When I walk through the door Taylor throws her arms around me. The sun dress and swimming suit I can see underneath says she's ready for a soak on the roof.

She doesn't say a word, the relief in her eyes tells me everything.

"Let me throw on some shorts and we'll head up there. I'll tell you all about it, or at least what you want to know."

"One thing," she says as I wipe the tears that have slowly started falling from her eyes, "Is Jennifer safe?"

"She's safe," I respond back. "Patrick and Ethan are taking her up to Dean's penthouse now. She's definitely on our side."

"That's the best news I've heard all night," Taylor adds.

"Wait 'til we head upstairs then. I've got more news for you."

As Scott heads into Taylor's room to find Melissa I quickly whisper, "Send Jared a text. Let him know the laundry is ready for pickup and Tom's house. Tip him off though. You know the guys that

405

might be there still." He doesn't say a word, the smile that forms on his face before he closes the door let's me know he knows just what to say.

When we arrive on the roof I see the jets are turned on and steam is rising from the water. "You've been up here already haven't you?" I say with a smile.

"Maybe," she says back. "We couldn't get into a cold hot tub could we?"

"True. I hadn't even thought about this tub being cold."

Taylor slips her sundress off and I can't help thinking just how lucky I am. What did I do to deserve this well-rounded girl? She has her head on straighter than any girl I've ever met and she's all mine. I'm going to ask her to marry me tonight. I can't wait much longer.

"Before I forget, and before we head to California, I want to go back to that spot you took me to on our first date. Let's go tonight, as in after the sun comes up and then goes down again. That tonight."

"I haven't been up there since that day. Sounds like the perfect place to go before we leave," Taylor says, settling in to my arms as we find our place in the water.

We talk for some time. I tell Taylor all about the night's events and how we rescued Jennifer. She couldn't believe she would swim back by herself after going through her ordeal. I told her about Tom and the others Ethan single-handedly took care of with ease. How the dead guy on her parents' porch was Tom's son and that we figured it was Tom and Stanley that killed her dad and seriously injured her mother. Knowing that her father's killer was no longer living or maybe just mentioning her father, brought the tears back.

We talked for about an hour before finally heading to bed. With all the rooms filled and the couch taken, Taylor changes in my room and says she's sleeping with me.

"Since you'll be asleep before your head hits the pillow I'll be safe," she says slightly grinning.

"Only you babe, could make me smile at a time like this. Oh how I love you."

"I love you too Deacon," she says as we climb into bed.

TWENTY NINE
Christen

When I finally wake the next morning it's to the touch of Taylor tickling my arm.

"Whaaaaaa time is it?" I manage through my massive yawn.

"Just after twelve," Taylor says, sliding over to give me a good afternoon kiss. "You've been asleep for eight hours." Her lips bring me right to and I grab her around the waist to pull her close. "I like that," she adds, as I return the kiss like we hadn't locked lips in ages.

"I do too," I say slowly sliding my hand down her back.

"Now, now, Deacon," she says, grabbing my hand and sliding it back up her back. "You know the rules. Signed, sealed, and I'll deliver," she says smiling, so her bright blue eyes sparkle as she gazes into mine.

"I know. You are my rock."

"Not that I'm one for diamonds, but that rock will get you closer," she says grinning from ear to ear.

"You think you're so clever don't you?" If she only knew what was coming tonight.

"Someone may have mentioned it at some point," she retorts. "What do you want for breakfast babe? We still have some eggs and bacon. Scott must have taken every last egg in the kitchen. I've already showered. Jump in and I'll whip you up some."

"Will do, but I need one more thing before you leave," I say grinning from ear to ear. I wait for the questioning look to flash across her face. When she turns her head slightly right and narrows her eyes,

I pull her in quickly, planting one more kiss on her soft lips before letting her go. As I pull away I simple say, "Just a kiss," with the same smile as before.

Taylor slides out of bed, and heading out the door, gives me the *I-love-you-so-much-look* before disappearing into the hall without saying a word.

I too slide out of bed and make my way into the bathroom. Dropping my drawers, I turn on the shower and wait as the water slowly gets warmer. As I'm about to step into the warm water, the thought of my mother flashes through my mind. Grabbing my phone, I quickly dial her number in hopes she will answer this time. After ringing multiple times it goes to her voicemail. I check the location to find it still fully charged and sitting inside her home.

"Dear God. Please let me find her alive," I plead, with my eyes cast upward.

When the words come out of my mouth I'm somewhat surprised, even more so because I said them aloud. Funny thing about saying those words—it felt good. That's two prayers in less than twenty four hours. I can't explain it, but it felt good. Maybe I need to do that more often. My dad did say my mother always had it right, and she talked to God all the time.

With those thoughts heavy on my mind, I slip into the shower. The hot water courses over my body, slowly washing my worries away. The past month has been one thing after another. What I really want now is nothing more than just that, nothing. I know what I have to do before we start this unknown journey to San Diego or where ever the clues lead me, and nothing right now seems to be just what I need.

I let my mind go blank, something they taught us before going to survival school. The pure simplicity of clearing your mind has helped me a ton over the years. The technique was taught in order to help us focus on the task at hand, but it sure works well when you just want to relax.

When my phone rings just outside the shower, a small glimmer of hopes tells me it's my mother. When I look through the glass onto the counter, the picture puzzles me. It's Christen. I haven't thought about her for months. When I see her picture flash across the screen, I can't help but think of the time we had together.

Leaving the water running, I step out just enough to grab my phone. "Christen," I say so she understands I'm confused at her calling.

"Deacon. I'm glad you're alive. I just left your place. I take it you don't live over here anymore?" she says sounding relieved.

"No. I moved in January when Dean promoted me."

"Promoted you?" Christen questions, not knowing all that has happened since she left.

"Yeah, I'm head of security now. I live in a suite at Veer Tower. We've been held up here since the chaos started. Um...how are you doing? I take it you're back in Vegas?" I ask, still confused from this call out of nowhere and wondering what issues this will cause with Taylor.

"I just flew in this morning," Christen starts. "Europe has fallen apart faster than the US. I barely made it out. The military is getting US citizens home as best as they can. Wait, who has been held up there with you?" she asks probingly.

"My girlfriend Taylor, Scott, Melissa, and some other friends," I say, leaving out Savanah and Bobbi. She doesn't know them anyways.

"Can you meet me today?" she asks.

"Deacon," Scott yells from my bedroom door, "It's time to eat."

"Who was that?" Christen questions.

"Scott. He says breakfast is ready. It's a long story, but I just got up. Can I…call you back in a little bit? You're okay right?"

"Yeah, I'm fine. I just really want to see you and talk face to face, if you can," Christen proposes before adding, "if you want to."

"I'd love to talk to you, but I have to get some things figured out. I'll call you back as soon as I can, okay?"

"Okay," she responds half-heartedly. "I'll wait for your call."

"Talk to you soon Christen. Bye."

"Bye," she says before hanging up the phone.

Why is this happening to me now of all times. I can't give her what she wants now, I know it. I love Taylor and nothing will change that. I'm getting engaged tonight.

"What are you doing to me God?" I say out loud, turning off the shower.

"What was that Deacon?" Taylor asks, just outside my bathroom door.

The thought of telling Taylor that my ex-girlfriend has come back to town and wants to see me doesn't sit well in my stomach, especially on the afternoon before I've planned to propose to her.

411

"Give me a sec," I say grabbing my towel and wrapping it around my still soaking body. I've got to talk to her about it and right now's as good a time as any. "Okay, come on in."

Taylor cracks open the door to make sure I'm covered, keeping her eyes focused on mine.

"I'm covered babe. I need to tell you something," I say as she pushes the door fully open and steps into the bathroom.

"What's up? Did I just hear you say something to God?" she asks perplexed.

"I said, 'What are you doing to me God.'"

"Okay," she says waiting to hear the explanation.

"So," I say slowly and drawn out as my mind races, trying to think of the right words to say.

Just tell her the truth enters my mind as clear as if someone was standing right next to me.

With renewed courage I begin, "Christen just called me while I was showering." I pause waiting for a word or sign that she understands that Christen was my girlfriend.

"Christen, your ex-girlfriend Christen," she says, folding her arms in slight disdain.

"Yes. She just got back into town and wants to see me."

"See you huh?" Taylor sighs. "Now I see why you were talking to God."

"Look, if you only feel comfortable with me talking on the phone…" Taylor cuts me off mid-sentence.

"Does she know we're together?" Taylor questions, with her flaming blue eyes penetrating every inch of me.

"Yes she does, but the conversation didn't last too long. She just said she was back from Europe and hoped to see me. There's nothing in this world that will separate me from you." When she doesn't say anything I quickly add, "I love you more than anything. You know that right?"

"I know you do Deacon. I love you too, but I hope you can see how this is strange for me," she says grabbing me tight.

"I can. Now you can see why I was questioning God. After we eat I'll just call her and tell her we can't meet. It will be fine."

"No. I trust you Deacon. You can go see her. I'm not worried," Taylor says, not sounding so sure of the words leaving her lips.

"It's really not that important Taylor. I can just call her."

"No really, you're fine. Just don't spend too much time with her. Exes don't call out of the blue just to be friends."

"I know. I'll meet her in one of the lobbies as I make my way through all the hotels today so I'm not alone with her. I think it's best she doesn't come here."

"That sounds good Deacon. Now put some clothes on and come and eat, that is if Scott hasn't eaten it all already," she says turning to leave the room.

I quickly dress and make my way out to the kitchen. The meal Taylor has made tastes just as good as the one yesterday. Without the impending mission hanging over my head, I enjoy this one much more.

The four of us sit and eat. I explain my plans for the day— how I need to fill in Patrick on what to do in my absence, how I've got to go see each hotel security manager, and how I want to go see Jennifer before we leave. Since I haven't really talked to her about what happened while Tom held her captive, I want to see if anything she can tell me will help find my mother. I've got his cell phone, but any eye-witness accounts could help.

We also talk about our trip to California. Scott and Melissa want to come with us. Melissa's family live back east so she really has no one here but Scott. Scott is an only child and both of his parents have passed away so I know he's coming along to keep me safe. I couldn't ask for a better best friend. He knows this morning's mission won't be our last and wouldn't dare let me have all the fun.

When we finish, I head back to my room to finish getting ready. Taylor follows me into the closet. Based on the expression on her face, I think doubts are still racing through her head.

"I promise you babe, you have nothing to worry about," I say sensing her apprehension. "If I could tell you more I would, but believe me when I tell you you'll understand better tonight."

"Okay. I do trust you. You know that right?"

"I do."

"It's just hard when I've got a million thoughts racing through my head and it's impossible to keep out the bad ones. I trust you."

"That's good. While I'm running around the hotels, making sure the ship is running smoothly, do you want me to drop you off so you can see your mother one last time before we leave? I can't promise when or if we'll make it back here any time soon." I know getting Taylor talking to her mom will help ease her mind.

"That's a good idea. I'll go get ready," she says leaving me alone in the closet.

With everyone either gone or getting ready to leave, Taylor and I say our goodbyes and head for the elevator. Scott and Melissa have volunteered to stock the Explorer with food, gas, guns, ammo, and anything else that might come in handy on our next journey. Bobbi, feeling safe enough to venture out, left before I woke up. They said she was going to see family. Savanah has family in town. However, with the four of us vacating my place for who knows how long, she's trying to secure a safe place to stay. Taylor told her she could stay here, but she said she'd feel better with family around.

With everyone busy or taken care of, Taylor and I set off to the hospital. Arriving at the entrance, I pull up to the curb and park the car.

"Hold on babe," I say opening my door and stepping out. I quickly move around to her side and open her door.

Reaching one hand in to take hers she says, "Thank you," and steps out of the car. "When do you think you'll be back?" Taylor asks.

"I can be back whenever you're ready. It will take me a few hours to get all the resorts covered, but you say the word and I'll come and get you."

"Okay," Taylor says leaning in close to give me a hug, much like the one she gave me this morning when I came through the door. "I love you Deacon."

"I love you too Taylor. Just remember tonight."

"Oh, I'm thinking about it. Trust me. I've got no idea, but I'm trusting you."

"Love you," I say, giving her a kiss.

"Love you too. Be good and watch for my call," she adds, heading for the door.

Once she disappeared inside the hospital, I jump in the Jeep and head back to the hotels. Not wanting to call Christen with Taylor in the car and make things even more awkward than they already are, I dial her number en route to the Bellagio. The phone rings only once before she picks up, like she was holding it in her hand just waiting for me to call. This isn't going to be easy. I tell her we can meet in the Bellagio lobby in thirty minutes if she wants. She of course agrees and that was the extent of our conversation. I've got to keep things professional so she understands there's no chance of us getting back together.

I first head for Veer to pick up Patrick. He needs to be with me as we meet all the managers. I know some won't want Patrick running things, but he's really the only option. I can trust him and he's literally the best man for the job. After seeing Ethan perform this morning I'm putting him in charge of Veer Towers as well. He doesn't know it yet, but I'm sure he'll be excited. He was already second in command anyway so it really shouldn't be a surprise.

Patrick and I make our way to the Bellagio on foot. It's amazing how much more relaxed and calm things are here now. The last time I walked through Crystals and over to the Bellagio the scene unfolding before me was enough to send most people running for the hills. Now the serenity that has set back in seems even more tranquil than before—if you can look past my men fully loaded and ready for war.

It's the middle of the day, so most people are inside with the temperature rising every day. When we arrive at the Bellagio, the broken entrance windows have been replaced and this entrance looks like it always has. I take Patrick inside to meet the security manager. Patrick knows them all, but it's good for everyone to hear it directly from me that Patrick is running the show now.

416

I leave Patrick and the new Bellagio manager to chat as the butterflies build in my stomach. I'm sure Christen has arrived by now, so I head out to the lobby. Rounding the corner, I see Christen sitting under the beautifully blown glass in the lobby. Memories of the last time we met here comes racing to my mind. She's even sitting in the same chair.

My old feelings for her hadn't completely come back after talking to her on the phone, but seeing her in person again, I can feel them building inside me. Her long blonde hair has grown three inches and she looks to be even more beautiful than the last time I saw her. She too has big blue eyes, but they still pale in comparison to Taylor's large blue diamonds. She's wearing short cut jean shorts and a t-shirt. She stands when she sees me coming.

"Hello Deacon," she says, reaching for a hug. "I've missed you so much."

I try not to hold the hug too long, but I can tell she's not letting go any time soon. "It's good to see you too."

With those words not being the ones she wanted to hear, she lets go. With slight confusion on her face I know all too well, I ask, "You want to sit down?"

"Sure," she says sitting in the same chair she just stood up from.

"I don't know any other way to say this then to just straight up," I start out.

"Okay," Christen says more confused than before.

"I got the feeling you were hoping I was still single and you want to get back together. Does that sound about right?" I ask, keeping a close eye on Christen.

417

"Um…well…yep, that's basically it, although I wasn't planning on this conversation starting right there."

"I know. I just don't want any false expectation to build as we catch up on the last several months that we've been apart." At hearing false expectation, her countenance changes.

"So you have a girlfriend then?" she questions, already knowing the answer.

"I told you that on the phone. In January I met a girl. Her name's Taylor. We've been dating ever since then. In fact I'm going to ask her to marry me tonight."

"Well," Christen says standing and gathering her things. She is certainly more feisty than Taylor. Thinking about it now, I probably shouldn't have mentioned marriage. We dated for twice the time Taylor and I have and I hadn't even thought of purchasing a ring for Christen.

"Don't go Christen. I had to make it clear. I didn't want your hopes to build just to be crushed later on."

"Why didn't you just tell me on the phone?" she fires back, raising her voice a notch.

"I did, but I think you didn't want to hear it. Your phone call caught me off guard. I had just woken up, I was in the shower, and hearing your voice threw me for a loop. Can we please just sit back down and talk as friends? I'd like to hear how things went in Spain."

With a little reluctance, Christen finally sits back down without saying a word. She softens a little and we begin to talk. A little strained at first, but after some time she makes it back to the mellow Christen I knew all too well.

She tells me about school and the chaos that erupted through-out Europe. She tells a pretty good tale of how she managed to hop a flight out of Barcelona after the airport in Madrid was completely destroyed by protesting people. I tell her about my promotion and restoring order in the hotels the night things went south here. I leave out the gun shot wound and laying comatose for almost month. I figure she doesn't need to feel any sympathy for me. She's going to have enough on her plate now that she's back and plan A hasn't panned out for her.

She asks about Taylor. I'm sure she wants to get a glimpse of the woman who has replaced her. I show her a picture on my phone and she can't believe how beautiful Taylor looks. I agree and in a lapse of judgement I almost mention it could have been her if she wasn't so ambitious, but luckily I catch myself, realizing I don't want to open that can that was closed the day I dropped her off at the airport.

"Are you ready to head over to the Vdara?" Patrick says, clearing his throat to get my attention. I glance at my watch to see that we've been catching up for forty-five minutes.

"Yeah, let me just say goodbye and then we'll head over there."

"Well," Christen begins, "it's been great catching up with you. I'll be around while I try to figure out how to get to Southern California, so don't forget about me."

"I won't. Give me a hug," I say, pulling her in for one last embrace. "Take care of yourself."

"I will."

"If you need anything, don't be afraid to call. If I can help, I will okay?" I say, hoping she realizes there's a place still for her in my heart. It's just not the same place it used to be, and when it comes down to it, it never will be what I have with Taylor.

"Okay Deacon. You take care as well and tell Taylor she's a lucky girl."

As she pulls away, I can see her eyes glistening. She was always good at holding her emotions at bay—but the moment—and the harsh reality of it all have gotten the best of her now. She quickly turns towards the front entrance without saying another word.

"Something tells me that's not the last time you'll see her," Patrick says standing right behind me.

"Unfortunately, I think you're right."

"Old girlfriend?" Patrick questions as I turn.

"Yep. Just last year. I probably would have married her if she didn't run off to Europe for school."

"You ready to get going then?" Patrick says.

"Not quite. I want to go up and see Jennifer before we leave here so I don't have to make my way back here later. I want you to come too."

When Jennifer opens the door, she embraces me instantly. "Thank you so much Deacon."

"Don't just thank me. Patrick here was there too."

With that news she grabs him as well so the two of us are locked up in her arms.

After a few seconds I say, "This is awkward."

Jennifer laughs through her tears, but lets us go and invites us inside. She doesn't have anything that will help me down the road, but the story she tells makes everything I've thought and seen fall into place.

Apparently Dean put Jennifer up to dating Tom to find out if he was working for someone else. She reluctantly agreed and started her double agent gig. It wasn't hard with Tom hitting on her every chance he had. When Tom got fired, Dean and Jennifer became targets for Tom and so when he couldn't find Jennifer that day he came back knowing she had to be here somewhere.

We talk for ten minutes before telling her Patrick will make sure she's safe since I'm headed to California to find my mom. She wishes me luck and thanks us again for saving her before letting us leave. After one more awkward hug at the door, we head for Vdara.

With Bellagio taking the most time, and I knew it would with Jennifer and Christen there, we quickly cover the other hotels in line. This time was much more pleasant though, since no one wanted to kill us. Brett wasn't at work, so I left that situation to him to deal with quickly.

At Veer Tower, I pull Ethan into Patrick's office and simply say, "This is your office now." In complete disbelief he could hardly speak. Patrick was with me when I told Ethan and he kept looking from me to Patrick. We just nodded and he kept looking back and forth with his mouth wide open. I know he'll do a fabulous job. I've already said it, but Rangers are top notch and I would go into battle with them any day. Handling two buildings should be a walk in the park for him.

THIRTY

Choices

With night falling fast and the day going off without a hitch, Taylor and I drive to Sunrise Mountain.

Wanting to set Taylor's mind free of anything she might be thinking happened today with Christen I say, "Let me get this out now 'cause I don't want to bring it up later."

"What's that?" Taylor says absentmindedly, as she stares out the window.

"So, I talked to Christen for about forty-five minutes today in the lobby of the Bellagio," Taylor instantly snaps to, turning her attention on me. "First thing I told her as we sat down there among the patrons was I had you and there was nothing that would change that."

"What did she say to that?" Taylor quickly questions back, fully engaged in the conversion now.

"She wasn't too happy. I told her I felt as if she wanted to get back together, but how that would be impossible. She got up, ready to storm out of there, and I told her to sit back down and we could talk. She mellowed out after that."

"Did she try and kiss you?" Taylor asks grabbing my free hand.

"No. She did want a hug though."

"That's to be expected, I guess," Taylor adds, sounding much more relaxed than when I started this conversation. "So it went well?"

"Yeah. She'll be fine. A lot of her extended family lives here and she has tons of friends around Vegas as well. She did mention she wanted to go to Southern California, but I didn't say anything about our plans. When we parted she told me to tell you you're a lucky girl."

"Oh, that's sweet. Enough about her though. What do you have planned tonight babe?" she asks playfully.

"Wouldn't you like to know, blue eyes? All in good time babe. All in good time. We're almost there."

We pull into our spot. No one else is parked in the area. Exactly what I wanted. We've only been here once together. I remembered her saying she just stays in the car when she comes. I hope she's okay getting out.

"Stay right there babe. In fact, will you put this blindfold on for about two minutes? I need to prepare some things."

The simper that proceeds her words tells me she's clueless to the events I have planned for the night. "Okay," she says slowly.

"Don't worry," I start, tying a blue bandana around her head. "You'll like what I've got planned. I promise."

"I trust you Deacon. I just thought I was going to have to wait two or three days before I found out. Now that it's here, the suspense is killing me."

I quickly jump out of the car and grab the blanket and basket out of the back. Melissa and Scott were instrumental in helping me prepare this portion.

With the blanket laid out in the small grassy area, I quickly set out the food I had them prepare. When I pull the food out, a sneaky suspicion that room service prepared this creeps over me. I don't care. It looks really nice and it will make the night even better.

With everything in place just how I imagined it, I open Taylor's door and grab her right hand, "Come with me beautiful."

At the touch of my hand and hearing my words she lets out a sigh. I quickly close the door and escort her to the blanket. "I've never got out of my car here," she says apprehensively.

"That's what I thought. This wouldn't be the same if we stayed in my car, so I hope you don't mind."

"Can I take the blindfold off now?" she asks reaching for the knot tied at the back.

"I'll take care of that," I say, quickly kneeling down behind her to slip the blindfold off over her beautiful blond hair. "What do you think?" I add, sitting down at her side.

As she surveys her surroundings, she notices the food so personally prepared, the glasses filled with bubbling soda, and the basket—which she stares at too long for my comfort. The ring waits inside the basket for dessert. She also looks out over the city, commenting about how peaceful things are up here.

"You ready to eat?" I ask, taking her hand.

"Let's eat."

We eat slowly, savoring each bite, but more each other's company. We talk of our time together and how things have progressed faster than either of us thought possible. Marriage could have come up several times, but I think we're both avoiding the topic. I'm steering clear because I know what I'm about to do. I can't help thinking she's keeping clear because she knows what's coming now that I've got this spread all laid out.

When we finish the food, I lay back, looking up at the stars. Taylor lies down on my shoulder so she can cuddle right up to my face, kissing me on the cheek as she does. We continue to talk about the future and the uncertainty that going to California brings. Taylor doesn't seem the least bit worried as we both exchange ideas about what we could face.

We talk, looking up at the night sky, for another five minutes. The time seems perfect to have dessert. "Would you like to have dessert now?" I ask, hoping she says yes.

"That depends on what you have," Taylor says coyly.

"Depends on what you want?" I respond, keeping the game going.

"Okay," she says, resolved to catch me, "I'll take a piece of strawberry cheesecake."

"One piece of strawberry cheesecake coming up," I say, reaching over to open the basket. She couldn't have played into my hand more perfectly.

"No you don't," she quickly retorts, not believing for a second I have some.

When I pull out a plate, uncover the contents, her mouth falls open. Before her eyes lies two pieces of strawberry cheesecake on a single plate, with fresh strawberries to top it off. Perfectly placed between the two slices sits a silver strawberry. I sent Scott all over kingdom come to locate one today.

"That looks like Cheesecake Factory cheesecake?" Taylor questions, not noticing the silver strawberry.

"As a matter of fact, it is," I say, pleased at the reaction thus far from Taylor.

"What's that silver thing in the middle?" Taylor asks, as she grabs the fork to get her first bite.

"You've never seen one of those before at work?" I ask, with an overly exaggerated raise of my eyebrow, as if it's common practice at the Cheesecake Factory.

"Out of the two of us," she rebuttals playfully, "I think I would know if we had silver strawberries to put on patrons' plates when they order cheesecake."

"That's what you'd think, isn't it," I say, pushing myself up to one knee and setting the plate down in front of her.

I watch her eyes eagerly follow the silver strawberry as I pick it up. I chuckle to myself, amused by her endearing innocence.

"Taylor. You know I love you more than anything humanly possible right?"

"Yes," she answers back in eager anticipation, her blue eyes shining so brightly.

I begin, as she sits up to be eye level with me. I open the strawberry and the words I've wanted, no, longed to say, flow out so effortlessly that I know instantly I've made the right choice. "Taylor Sanders, will you marry me?"

Her glistening eyes, filled almost to the breaking point, glance at the sparkling solitaire blue diamond placed perfectly in the silver strawberry.

It only takes a split second before she turns her blue eyes on me, "Yes Deacon. Yes, I will marry you."

With the sweetest words uttered from her lips I've ever heard, I slip the rock onto her finger. "Like a glove."

"It's perfect Deacon," she whispers, slipping past the breaking point. "I couldn't have asked for a better night."

"I can't even begin to tell you how I've longed for this moment Taylor."

"I feel the same way Deacon. I feel the same way."

Neither of us say a word as we embrace. As I move in for our first kiss as an engaged couple, I brush a strand of hair behind her ear and kiss her in the most magical moment of my lifetime. The stars that reflect so powerfully from her blue eyes give me a glimpse of eternity and tell me everything will be alright.

With my mind going into overdrive, I pull back, not wanting to ruin this once-in-a-lifetime moment. "Do you want to lay down?"

"Sounds good," she answers back.

As I lay on my back, Taylor assumes the same position as before, except she's holding her left hand in the air so she can see the diamond on her finger.

"You know how I feel about diamonds, but this one, this one, I didn't even know existed. Is it a diamond?" she ask innocently. She really doesn't know.

"Yep. The blue ones are even more rare than the clear ones— just like you, my precious, blue diamond. Having never shopped for diamonds before, I didn't even know blue ones existed."

"Shopped?" Taylor says perplexed. "When did you buy this Deacon?"

"I told you I knew I would marry you from the moment we met. I bought it to propose when we went to Zion's. That plan obviously fell through, so this has been the first real chance I've had to do it. It's been killing me having to wait these last few days."

"Well," she begins with a smile, "it was certainly worth the wait. I love you so much. I can't wait to be your wife," she says sliding up on top of me. When she leans in to kiss me, I feel her features fit so comfortably against mine. I realize the position I've put myself in to keep my hormones in check was probably not the most wise. It feels like she is in possession of the key to a door, that once opened, won't be easily closed.

I don't attempt to change our position at first, savoring the moment I've thought about way too much. With thoughts racing through my mind so powerful I don't think I can stop myself, one comes through as if the wind was whispering to me—

The deal is almost sealed, don't ruin it now.

The words come with such force. I stop instantly, slowly rolling Taylor onto my side.

"I know the deal is pretty much sealed Taylor, but let's not ruin it now."

"Look who's the rock now," Taylor says, obviously filled with passion.

"Don't get me wrong," I continue, "You know I'd love nothing more than to finish what we've started here, but we both know the ring is just the ticket. The concert hasn't begun yet."

As she slowly sits up, I can see the fire in her eyes. "I know. I don't know what came over me. It's probably the passion that's been building in me since January. Then you pop this gigantic blue diamond on me. Sitting up here having a picnic with everything that has happened over the last month and the feelings inside me just wanted to come out."

"Trust me. You've stopped me several times so I know exactly what you mean. It's a good thing one of us has been holding strong at all times."

"It sure is. I know I would have enjoyed it more than anything I've ever done, but I would have been mad at myself after for not being strong enough to wait until we were married. Thanks for being my anchor Deacon," she says, cuddling up to me as we both stare out over the city so full of light.

With all the lights on in the city, we can barely make out the stars above us. Also, as I look into the dark sky above, I can't help but think of my dad. Does he know we're engaged? Does he know what we've been through over the last few days? The questions continue to come when the answer hits me squarely between the eyes—of course he does. He's probably the one who told me to restrain myself minutes ago.

Lost in thought, the large boom I hear echo over the city wakes me from my wondering. As we both look out over the city, we see explosion after explosion as vast sections of the city go dark. With perfect precession, the explosion do what I feared more than anything. In a matter of minutes the once glowing city goes dark. Only head lights from cars frozen on the major freeways can been seen now.

"We've got to get back to my place right now!" I say, jumping to my feet and pulling Taylor up with me.

We quickly gather everything up and throw it in the back of the Jeep before I open Taylor's door and help her in.

"Buckle up," I say, knowing it's going to be a rough ride home —if we can make it all.

I jump into the front seat about to start the car when an image, like déjà vu, flashes through my mind.

"What is it Deacon?" Taylor asks, seeing me lost in thought as she grabs my hand.

"The dream Taylor. The dream I told you about the first night we came up here. This is exactly what I saw."

"It's okay. We're both fine Deacon. We need to get my mother out of the hospital and back to your place. She won't be safe there now."

"We need to do more than that Taylor. We need to get out of this city all together. How about this, we'll go by and see how the hospital looks. If everything looks fine we'll go back to my place and hunker down for the night. Then tomorrow during the day, we'll go over and see if she wants to leave. She can stay at my place if she'd feel safer. There'll be plenty of security there and people to take care of her."

"Okay," Taylor says timidly. "What if she won't come?"

"We'll have to leave her then. She's a grown woman. We have to accept what she thinks is best. Who knows, the hospital might be a safe zone through all this. They'll have back-up power to keep machines running so she'll probably be best if she stays put. Plus, the injured will still have to be attended to so I'm sure that place will be locked up before the night's over."

My words make sense and Taylor agrees to bypass the hospital for the night so we can get back to the safety of the tower. We quickly head west through the not-so-nice part of Vegas. As we pass house after house, I can see people from all backgrounds coming out of their homes looking for trouble. Vegas has truly become the devil's playground. The further west we go, the more trouble I start to see. The gun shots ringing out all around us don't make the mood any lighter.

When we arrive at Lamb Boulevard, I see two men standing in the road, blocking a car from moving forward. When the taller of the two hits the window, sending glass all over the man inside, he quickly flings open the door to throw the man out.

I quickly grab my handgun, handing it to Taylor and say, "Shoot, don't ask questions, if anyone but me tries to get in the car."

Taylor doesn't say a word as I exit the vehicle. I know she's in shock, but desperate times call for desperate measures. When I round the front of the Jeep, I start running full bore, hitting the man standing on the driver's side completely unaware. He slams into the side of the car, knocking the wind right out of him. Without thinking twice, I slam him backwards into the ground with his head leading the way. When it hits, the thud sounds life threatening. I pull back, ever so slightly, to see he's out cold. He might be dead or he might be knocked out. I know I don't have time to check, nor do I care.

When the man trying to break in the passenger side finally realizes what just happened, he comes around the front of the car, pipe in hand, ready for a fight. I move forward as the man raises the pipe to strike. It's not even a challenge. The untrained criminal can't keep a pipe in his hand any easier than a baby can keep candy away from his brother.

With the pipe banging across the street, the man sees his buddy for the first time, and turns tail and runs at full speed across Lamb. What he didn't see coming was another car traveling north—with no intention of stopping. The car clips the man sending him up and over the roof in an instant. The car doesn't stop, hardly affected, as the man crumples to the ground with a thud even more deadly sounding than the last.

Turning my attention to Taylor, I notice she's still safe, but her hand covers her mouth as she certainly just saw the man get hit.

I quickly run over to the car to make sure they are alright. As I get my first glimpse of the occupants I see clear as day the family I was supposed to help and in turn would help Taylor and me.

Realizing we can't stay here in the middle of the road, I quickly say, "Follow me please. We need to talk. You don't know it, but you are supposed to help me, and I am supposed to help you."

"Okay. We'll follow you, but we only have minutes," the man utters in broken English.

"What's your name?" I ask, testing to see if they'll proffer their names. "My name's Deacon Wright and my fiancée in the car is Taylor."

"This is my wife Julia and our two daughters, Isabela and Veronica. My name is Jose Luis," he says with his thick Hispanic accent evident in every syllable he utters.

"Thank you so much for saving us," Julia says, still in shock.

"You're welcome. I'm going to jump in my Jeep. Please follow me. We'll head somewhere safe close by to talk really quick. We're too exposed here in the middle of the road."

"Okay. We'll follow you," Jose says.

I quickly run to the car and get in as Taylor unlocks the door.

"W-w-what are you going to do with the two guys you left lying in the street?" Taylor asks, not sure what else to say.

"In any other circumstance, I would help them, but we don't have time, and I need to get information from this family," I say, knowing she won't have a clue what I'm talking about.

"This family?" she answers back, dumbfounded that I could possibly get anything of value from them.

"It's a long story, but I'll tell you when we meet up with them just up the road." I know the answer won't satisfy her curiosity, but we have no other choice. We have to get out of here.

I quickly drive up the road to the Subway just off to the right. With all the lights out and no cars in the parking lot, we should be safe to talk for a few minutes.

I watch my rear view mirror the whole time making sure Jose doesn't back out on me. When he pulls into the parking lot right behind me, I quickly pull into the furthest spot possible from the road. Jose does the same, pulling up right next to me.

Taylor and I quickly get out of the car. Normally, I would ask Taylor to stay in the car, but I know she wants to hear what's about to transpire.

"Quédense en el coche hijas," Jose commands in Spanish, peeling himself out of the car. Having made that command many times fighting the drug cartels, I know he just told his daughters to stay in the car. It's certainly for the best.

"Jose and Julia, thanks for trusting us. I know you don't have much time. We don't have time either, so I'm going to make this short. I can't tell you how or why, but I'm supposed to go with you wherever you're headed, but I have a problem. I've got to go to California to find my mother before I can meet back up with you."

Neither of them say a word. A feeling reminiscent of those I felt in paradise fills my being. Then, with the same undeniable feeling as before, a voice says—Go with them son.

"We are heading north—to Daybreak. It's just outside Salt Lake City. We have family there. They've been begging us to come since this madness started a month ago. You can come with us if you want, but we can't wait for you to go to California. We are leaving now."

"Deacon," Julia begins, sounding like an angel in this fallen city, "You've been touched by something greater, I can feel it. Do you want to know where that feeling comes from?"

"I'm pretty sure I already know," I say back, the burning feeling consuming my entire body.

"We can teach you more, but you cannot stay here. This place will fall into utter disorder in a matter of days. It will not be safe for people like us or you. You have the light, Deacon. I can see it your eyes too Taylor," Julia says, turning to look Taylor right in the eyes.

As Taylor puts her hand on my forearm she says, "Deacon, I feel we need to go with them, but I'm torn. My mom and your mom could be lost forever."

"My sentiments exactly." Those thoughts and my mother's last words ring through my head causing a confusion I lack the ability to sort out at this moment.

Torn between safety and sure hell, I turn to Taylor at a crossroad. For the first time in my life, I don't know which road to take.

Dear Reader,

I want to thank you for taking the time to read my first novel. Putting your hard earned dollars into an unknown humbles me more than you know.

This book is the first of five novels detailing Deacon's journey through a time I believe will shortly transpire here upon the earth. Please, if you feel so inclined, leave me a rating if you enjoyed this book. I and many others, to many to name, have poured through this book for errors. If you find something we have missed please don't hesitate to reach out to me.

My email is j.c.jensen@troncoink.com. I look forward to your questions and comments. I truly enjoy writing and look forward to your four and five star reviews.

Be looking for the next novel in this series, *Deacon Wright: The War Within*. I don't have a timeline for this book, but you can go to www.troncoink.com for more information when it becomes available.

Again, my heartfelt thanks to those that support my work. I look forward to many years providing you with inspiring stories.

Thank you,

J.C.Jensen

Made in the USA
Columbia, SC
06 January 2020

86152337R00241